HENRY JAMES

THE AMERICAN

ESSAYS

HENRY JAMES

THE AMERICAN ESSAYS

EDITED WITH AN INTRODUCTION
AND NEW FOREWORD

BY LEON EDEL

PRINCETON UNIVERSITY PRESS
PRINCETON, NEW JERSEY

Published by Princeton University Press, 41 William Street,
Princeton, New Jersey 08450

Library of Congress Cataloging-in-Publication Data
James, Henry, 1843–1916.
The American essays / Henry James; edited with an introduction
and new foreword by Leon Edel.
p.   cm.
Reprint. Originally published: New York: Vintage Books, 1956.
1. American literature—History and criticism.   I. Edel, Leon,
1907–   . II. Title.
PS121.J3   1989
810.9—dc20   89-10684

ISBN 0-691-06822-4
ISBN 0-691-01471-X, pbk.
First Princeton University Press printing, 1989

This book was originally published in the United States by Vintage
Books, Inc., and in Canada by McClelland and Stewart Limited. It is
reprinted by arrangement with Leon Edel. The illustration on the paperback cover is a portrait of Henry James by Philip Burne-Jones,
from Lamb House, Rye, and is reproduced here by permission of the
National Trust Photographic Library

Princeton University Press books are printed on acid-free paper, and
meet the guidelines for permanence and durability of the Committee
on Production Guidelines for Book Longevity of the Council on Library Resources

10   9   8   7   6   5   4   3   2   1
10   9   8   7   6   5   4   3   2   1, pbk.

Printed in the United States of America by Princeton University
Press, Princeton, New Jersey

CONTENTS

PART THREE: AMERICAN LETTERS 1898

PART FOUR: AMERICAN MEMORIES

FOREWORD

by Leon Edel

THIS VOLUME of Henry James's fugitive essays on American writers, together with some of his early and late notes and reviews, was assembled by me for Alfred Knopf's then new Vintage paperback series in the early 1950s. The American novelist's involvement in his native literature was understandably large, but scattered, particularly since his writings on Europe had prime place in his work. I valued most at the time, as I believe most critics did, the place Hawthorne occupied in his writings, and there were certain other capital essays, like the one devoted to Emerson, which I found and still regard as masterly. There were also certain lively notes on minor writers contributed to an early weekly literary publication in London that ultimately turned into the *Times Literary Supplement*. Even if heterogeneous, the volume had the unity of James's penetrating mind and style; and then there were the additional pieces on Whitman, which showed the extent of his recantation of his assault long before on *Drum Taps*. The volume gave readers glimpses of early Jamesian appreciations and his tender feeling for the problems faced by his immediate predecessors as well as his contemporaries.

By the 1950s our national criticism had begun to overcome its lagging distrust of James as someone outside the "mainstream" of American writing, and the superficial and distinctly unsubtle distinction that Philip Rahv resolved into a difference between "palefaces and redskins"—James being the paleface, inevitably, and Whitman the redskin. The failure of criticism at that time resided in a fantasy that James was a paleface because he lived too much abroad. How fashions change may be seen when we remind ourselves that in our time T. S. Eliot and Ernest Hemingway also lived abroad. But we need not waste words on these vagaries of a criticism in which the dividing line between journalism and literature has never been sufficiently defined.

A so-called James "revival" occurred during the 1940s, at the time of the novelist's centenary, and resulted in the discovery by publishers that much of James was out of print. A new generation of readers, in tune with James's modernist role and the extent of his critical perceptions, soon rectified the literary-cultural lag and helped substitute the pre-Proustian James for the top-hat socialite.

Knopf published my gathering-in of the American essays with a strange cover that included a cut-out of the Alice Boughton photo of James in his top-hat. The hat confirmed the view of those who dismissed James as a stuffed shirt of letters. Beside the black and white cut-out, the cover designer placed the same figure in striped technicolor, in strips of blue and red—a sort of waving of the stripes without the stars, given the word "American" in the title.

The collection was well received in the then burgeoning American studies that swept the country in the same sudden way of women's studies in a later decade. I was not prepared however for a letter of praise I received from Edmund Wilson. He found things in it I had tended to take for granted, since I had been reared in Canada and was deficient in the finer points of American history. I had paid more attention to the literary contents. Edmund, announcing the volume to be "fascinating," said I had "really done a service in collecting this stuff." "What is particularly valuable to me," he said, "—with my interest in the American writing of the latter part of the [nineteenth] century—is the series of letters written in 1895 and giving a kind of cross-section of current publications. It is wonderful to have James on Grant, John Jay Chapman, Whitman, and all the rest. And Robert W. Chambers! There is one key passage in the discussion of [Theodore] Roosevelt which I am going to use when I get around to doing a full length study of T. R.—in which he [James] quotes and takes exception to Roosevelt's statement that 'an educated man must not go into politics as such . . . or he will be upset by some other American with no education at all.' "

Wilson went on to say that from the point of view of a political career, Teddy Roosevelt was right. Roosevelt's great strength had been that as a young man he "didn't adopt the attitude of what was then called the silk-stocking reformer, but plunged into the political bearpit and dealt with them on their own terms." He also said he delighted in a brief allusion to Harriet Beecher Stowe. He had always had difficulty in imagining what she looked like and "James has undoubtedly hit her off in these few words—which confirm my impression of her: vague but very observant."

I might as well add his comment about the cover. It "enchants me," he said. "I assume you did not design it. I can't make out whether James has been bandaged or turned into a barber-pole or whether there is supposed to be some reference to the Stars and Stripes."

I quote Wilson's letter mainly because it suggested to me at the time that there were a great many nuggets of critical interpretation and observation in these scattered writings to be appreciated today by historians and "Americanists" who sometimes see James only through a haze of aestheticism. He was not detached from his time. No one, among American writers, was more contemporary or had a more powerful grasp of American history and American myth.

INTRODUCTION

IN THIS VOLUME I have collected all of Henry James's essays on American letters together with certain of his miscellaneous writings and reviews on American subjects. The material was widely scattered, and almost half of it appears here for the first time in book form. The earliest paper is of 1865, when James was twenty-two; the last was written in 1915, a few months before his death. These writings therefore span James's half-century of creation.

In our present era of saturated American studies, the gaps in the collection will be all too apparent. No essay on Poe; only the most casual—and to some persons heretical—mention of Thoreau; no estimate of Cooper or Irving; no full-length essay on Whitman and, above all, nothing on Melville. The list of absences is long, and there seems to be a redundancy of those present: two papers on Lowell; three pieces on Hawthorne, complementary to the book James wrote about him; two essays on Emerson; and then scattered pieces on minor, long-forgotten writers who happen to have attracted James's attention. If these may seem to us as rather slim pickings in the great mass of James's work, we must nevertheless recognize their intrinsic worth. Read in their totality, they constitute a vivid store of American observations, impressions, and memories. They are the work of a writer who was always aware of his country's claim upon him and upon his art. And now, assembled, these writings can be placed securely on the Jamesian shelf beside the two volumes on American subjects published early and late by James himself—his critical study of Hawthorne of 1879 and *The American*

Scene of 1907. This collection may also be regarded as a companion volume to *The American Novels and Stories of Henry James*, which F. O. Matthiessen assembled and Alfred A. Knopf published in 1947.

The essays are informal, and this is perhaps their greatest charm. When James is writing about the French novelists, he is formal and "learned": he is dealing with matters close to the art he so consistently and assiduously practiced; but when he comes to Emerson, to the people of Brook Farm he used to see in his father's library when he was a boy, to the distant memories of Margaret Fuller's time, and to the Salem and Concord of Hawthorne, he is essentially relaxed, and his pen is being dipped into the inkwell of recollection as well as the inkwell of criticism. The best essays are the occasional pieces—the occasion being invariably commemorative and elegiac. We owe the American essays to no special desire on James's part to create a systematic body of literary portraits in the manner of Sainte-Beuve, as he attempted in his writings on the French poets and novelists, but to the accidents of publishing, the death of a friend, or the appearance of a given book—such as the Emerson-Carlyle correspondence —which evoked his interest and brought him to his writing-desk.

In surveying the American essays, we must at the same time recognize that editors themselves, in that distant time, tended to encourage James to write, not about his American contemporaries, but about Balzac and Zola and George Sand. No one seems to have suggested to him that he should sketch Longfellow, whom he knew, and with whom he spent certain evenings discussing Turgenev in the 1870's, or Oliver Wendell Holmes, or some of the other figures he lightly touches in the essay on Mr. and Mrs. Fields. Cultivated Americans were likely to want to know what was going on in foreign pastures; they were only too well aware of what was going on in their own. And American magazine editors had in James a writer ideally qualified to report on the state of letters abroad. The result is that when James finally was asked to write about the state of letters in America, it was by an English magazine, and it resulted in those casual "American letters" here reprinted for the first time. Indeed, we owe James's study of Hawthorne—one of the mellowest and most beautiful of his critical works—to the initiative of an English editor and an English publisher. In the end, Henry James was in the anomalous position of writing about Europe for America and about America for Europe.

We are made particularly conscious of the gaps resulting from this anomaly when we come upon brief allusions, in certain of his other writings, to the American writers James did not treat of. He speaks of Poe in his essay on Baudelaire, saying just enough to make us want more—to want, indeed, a long and explicative essay. Poe was, says James, "vastly the greater charlatan" by comparison with Baudelaire, but also "the greater genius." Readers of the essay on Emerson will find a passage on Thoreau which seems to cry for amplification—that in which James describes the author of *Walden* as preoccupied with "things not of the essence." The things are "the non-payment of taxes, the non-wearing of a necktie, the preparation of one's food one's self, the practice of a rude sincerity." The best we can do with James on Walt Whitman is to reprint his youthful review of *Drum-Taps*, which he later recanted, and which hardly represents his mature feelings about the great gray poet; some inkling of these is given us in the again sketchy, but tantalizing, paragraphs on *Calamus* and *The Wound-Dresser*.

Above all, we experience a deep sense of frustration when we come upon the solitary mention of Herman Melville, a mere name thrown into an enumeration that includes Ik Marvel, in which the novelist recalls his boyhood readings in *Putnam's Magazine*. It is here that we inevitably experience the deepest regret: for our literature would cherish a Henry James essay on the author of *Moby-Dick*. But this is to lean upon the hindsight of our time, and of our own rediscovery of Melville. We can only, from our position of vantage, recognize the fact that in spite of their dissimilarity, James and Melville alone, among the writers of their day, had glimpsed faraway places and distant horizons and had understood that there were things that could not be measured by an American yardstick. Melville was a cosmopolitan of the spirit; James, more fortunate in his career, was a cosmopolitan of fact. Melville discovered among the Polynesians certain fundamental truths that James discovered among the Europeans. It was inevitable that they would not be understood by their contemporaries, to whom the Atlantic and Pacific seaboards were boundaries enough for a continent just being opened up. Only in our time have they been able to receive the recognition they long ago deserved.

II

But I have said enough about the things that are not in this volume. What of the subjects James *did* treat —the Americans he chose to commemorate, sometimes in more than one essay? He knew personally most of the figures he dealt with, save Hawthorne, who died when James had barely reached his twenty-second year. And of those he knew, he wrote with a sympathy quickened by friendship and an objectivity that friendship, happily, did not blur. Sometimes the truth may be cushioned by James's soft words; but it is always within sight; it never strays from fundamentals. I find it difficult to agree with T. S. Eliot that "even in handling men whom he could, one supposes, have carved joint from joint—Emerson or Norton—his touch is uncertain; there is a desire to be generous, a political motive, an admission (in dealing with American writers) that under the circumstances this was the best possible, or that it has

fine qualities." Henry James, however, was not the kind
of critic who carves other writers joint from joint; and
if Mr. Eliot is trying to suggest that the novelist is "pulling
his punches" in his "desire to be generous," the answer
is quite simply that James *wanted* to be generous and
knew how to be without sacrificing the truth. Criticism
is often a matter of tone; and much can be said without
dismembering the object criticized. And when the tone
is gentle and ironic and deeply affectionate, it need not
necessarily denote an "uncertain touch."

> Emerson's personal history is condensed into the single
> word Concord, and all the condensation in the world
> will not make it look rich. It presents a most con-
> tinuous surface . . . fifty years of residence in the
> home of one's forefathers, pervaded by walking in the
> woods and the daily addition of sentence to sentence.
> . . . On three occasions later—three journeys to Europe
> —he was introduced to a more complicated world; but
> his spirit, his moral taste, as it were, abode always
> within the undecorated walls of his youth. There he
> could dwell with that ripe unconsciousness of evil
> which is one of the most beautiful signs by which we
> know him.

The touch is more subtle, but certainly no less uncertain, in the picture of Norton:

> . . . how a son of the Puritans the most intellectually
> transmuted, the most liberally emancipated and initiated
> possible, could still plead most for substance when pro-
> posing to plead for style, could still try to lose himself
> in the labyrinth of delight while keeping tight hold of
> the clue of duty, tangled even a little at his feet; could
> still address himself all consistently to the moral con-
> science while speaking as by his office for our imagina-
> tion and our free curiosity.

There is something of the gentle ironic and certainly of the generous in James's way of telling us that Norton often managed to tangle his Puritan sense of duty with his judgment of art and style: and the criticism strikes me as no less forceful because it is cushioned in urbanity. So too can we discover this type of criticism—by what might be called the *overtone* of language—in James's discussion of Emerson and Brook Farm:

> He said the best for his friends of the Dial, of Fruitlands and Brook Farm, in saying that they were fastidious and critical; but he was conscious in the next breath that what there was around them to be criticized was mainly a negative. Nothing is more perceptible today than that their criticism produced no fruit—that it was little else than a very decent and innocent recreation—a kind of Puritan carnival. The New England world was for much the most part very busy, but the Dial and Fruitlands and Brook Farm were the amusement of the leisure class. Extremes meet, and as in older societies that class is known principally by its connection with castles and carriages, so at Concord it came, with Thoreau and Mr. W. H. Channing, out of the cabin and the wood-lot. . . .

Mr. Eliot might have put James to a much sterner test by taking the case of Howells. In writing about Emerson and Norton, the novelist was praising—and appraising—the dead. Howells, however, was alive, and a personal friend. Here indeed one might suspect a "political motive." And yet there is critical neatness in the way in which James states a truth validated by time:

> He adores the real, the natural, the colloquial, the moderate, the optimistic, the domestic, and the democratic; looking askance at exceptions and perversities and superiorities, at surprising and incongruous phenomena in general.

No critic today could offer us a more accurate one-sentence summary of the essence of William Dean Howells. Thus James judged his friends in kindness and in truth, without experiencing a need to tear them limb from limb—yet still capable of placing them in their proper critical frame for our inspection at this later time.

III

Henry James's American essays—those dealing with literary subjects—belong inevitably beside *The American Scene*, that late, restless, impressionistic travel volume in which the novelist painted his native land as he re-discovered it in 1905: the changed modern America that had replaced the more provincial and tight little Atlantic seaboard society he had known in the 1880's before he settled abroad. *The American Scene* is a long and ruminative poem, a brilliant reverie over persons and places, the tone of old things, the sense of James's American past; and there also exists as fruit of the same journey certain essays peripheral to this book which deal with the speech and manners of American women.* The America Henry James had known when he began to write was still reaching for remote frontiers and just beginning to break the prairie's soil. It was an America too busy with daily tasks to have much time for culture or for the deeper questions of civilization with which Henry James was concerned. The boardwalked town with its rough meetinghouse and church, or the Western hamlet, since celebrated as all saloon and pistol-shooting, knew little of judgments and standards; it measured everything by its own local and limited yardstick. Boston, with its spacious and leisurely Common, and New York, in its huddled state near the Battery, were the principal

* See Henry James's address to the students of Bryn Mawr, "The Question of Our Speech" (Boston, 1905), and his essays on "The Speech and Manners of American Women," published in *Harper's Bazaar*, November–July, 1907–8.

repositories of culture and America's as yet meager stock of historical memory. Henry James knew both these cities, and it was upon them that he focused his artist's eye, for he had no experience of gold rushes or pioneering or railroad-building. Taking the geography of his native city as example, he later imaged the American mores as divided between *uptown* and *downtown*. In *downtown* the husbands were busy with their measureless ticker-tape; *uptown* was the world in which their wives and children, with servants and music-masters, tutors and governesses, lived upon the proceeds of *downtown*. In James's fiction, as in these essays, we can discover his growing fear that this kind of society, composed of absentee husbands and wives at loose ends, would become wholly feminized and lack masculine responsibility both in the rearing of the children and in the growth and development of cultural and civilizing forces. As late as 1898 we find him contemplating the American business man as a figure for fiction in a similar light.

. . . the typical American figure is above all that "business man" whom the novelist and the dramatist have scarce yet seriously touched, whose song has still to be sung and his picture still to be painted. He is often an obscure, but not less often an epic hero, seamed all over with the wounds of the market and the dangers of the field, launched into action and passion by the immensity and complexity of the general struggle, a boundless ferocity of battle—driven above all by the extraordinary, the unique relation in which he, for the most part, stands to the life of his lawful, his immitigable womankind, the wives and daughters who float, who splash on the surface and ride the waves, his terrific link with civilization, his social substitutes and representatives, while, like a diver for shipwrecked treasure, he gasps in the depths and breathes through an air-tube. . . .

Cowperwood and Babbitt, Dodsworth and Jason, and even Wick Cutter, not to speak of tycoons like James's own Adam Verver, were to come after he wrote this, but the breathless sentence, with its extravagant final flourish, suggests a picture of American life—one essential aspect of it—more penetrating than most that were to be painted by James's successors. In the remark about the "unique relation," in which the American woman ultimately becomes the social substitute and cultural representative of her money-preoccupied husband, we can discern the future empire-builders, the ambassadress wives.

IV

Those who conceive of criticism only as a kind of law-giving may be led to observe that in the section to which I have here given the title "Other Voices" certain of the voices have been long silent and long forgotten, and they may hold this to be a kind of critical laxity on James's part. Every writer, sooner or later in his time, deals with certain of his minor contemporaries, the law of life being that greatness need not deal only with greatness and that the commerce of literature is fed by sources small as well as great. James was well aware of Henry Harland's superficiality and Miss Woolson's limitations; when he mourned Wolcott Balestier, it was not so much the unformed writer as the active youth who had died too soon. The case of Henry Harland interested him, for Harland was a "story-teller at large," like himself, a man who dealt in international subjects and painted pictures far from home. "Who shall say, at the rate things are going, what is going to be 'near' home in the future and what is to be far from it?" James asked. London, in the time of Fenimore Cooper, he observed, was "fearfully—or perhaps only fortunately—far from Chicago, and Paris stood to London in a real relation almost equally awkward

for an Easter run. . . . The globe is fast shrinking, for
the imagination, to the size of an orange."

This was also in 1898 and we can measure the distance
it has shrunk since then by invoking neither an orange,
nor even a golf ball, but perhaps an atom. James's curiosity, however, not only extended to the wider dimension,
the world at large, but could also focus on the narrower,
the regional, as his essay on Constance Fenimore Woolson,
the grand-niece of Fenimore Cooper, shows. James liked
her tales of Mackinac and of the South of the reconstruction period and her stories of Italy (though these have
dated considerably for us). He liked their sensitivity and
the acuteness of the feminine observation, and his tribute
to Miss Woolson partakes not only of gallantry—as it
might seem to us—but also of a certain measure of critical
appraisal which was distinctly valid in its time.

Alert as James was in the criticism of fiction, he seems to
have had as I have observed, no acute appreciation of
poetry, and this seems strange in one who was himself
in the end an image-weaver and a builder of metaphor.
His early piece on Whitman and his overvaluation of
Lowell's poetry, while recognizing its derivativeness,
might be ascribed to the emotion of the moment rather
than to critical judgment. Certainly we would not invoke
Lycidas today in discussing Lowell's verses on the death
of Agassiz; and it is difficult to read Lowell's Ode in
commemoration of the Civil War dead almost a century
after it was written with quite those intensities of feeling
James describes. It seems more likely that James was re-
covering his own feelings about the war than that he
was reading the poem as poem.

V

The image of Henry James as a figure uprooted and
forlorn—disconnected from his homeland and adrift between countries—has given way slowly to the upright
figure we now know, the citizen of the world, who

nevertheless remained distinctively American. An entire generation in the United States sought to disown him as artist because he became a British subject in 1915, six months before his death. What his critics on this side of the water overlooked—and he was violently criticized —was that when James yielded his American citizenship, he had kept it loyally and faithfully during a forty-year residence abroad. He became British during a world's upheaval in defense of "this decent and dauntless people," as he termed the English among whom he had lived and worked so long.

Today, I suspect, such a gesture would not provoke as much acute discussion. T. S. Eliot gave up his American citizenship long ago without ceasing to be considered an American poet, and England has reaffirmed its belief in W. H. Auden as a British poet, though he has embraced American citizenship. We have come to recognize the difference between the technical ties of citizenship and the deeper roots of the creative spirit and to understand, with James, what he observes in his essay on the "story-teller at large": that we must look more closely "into the old notion that, to have a quality of his own, a writer must needs draw his sap from the soil of his origin." What is patently clear, however, is that James none the less did draw his original sap from that soil: and that his whole artistic life was devoted to the very question that in our century has become America's primary concern.

This question is quite simply the relation between America and the world, the figure the American cuts when he moves out into the older society from which, by a process of immigration and transatlantic change, he has become detached; or the relations between the American and the primitive—as exemplified in Melville and Cooper—which is another side of the problem. Not all novelists, dedicated to their craft, could, when James started to write, harness their cart of fiction to the

pioneer and the railway. James's own life had been such
that he had to make a choice between Europe and America. "One can't do both—one must choose," he wrote in
his notebooks in 1881. "No European writer is called upon
to assume that terrible burden, and it seems hard that
I should be. The burden is necessarily greater for an
American—for he *must* deal, more or less, even if only by
implication, with Europe; whereas no European is obliged
to deal in the least with America. No one dreams of
calling him less complete for not doing so. (I speak of
course of people who do the sort of work that I do; not
of economists, of social science people.)" And then he
added these prophetic words: "The painter of manners
who neglects America is not thereby incomplete as yet;
but a hundred years hence—fifty years hence perhaps—
he will doubtless be accounted so."

It is not difficult to relate such generalizations to the
core of James's fiction. He was to chronicle for us the
outraged innocence of the American discovering a
Europe he could measure only by his own inflexible
standards and in an unawareness of any others. By the
same token the European, shut up in his citadel of culture
and civilization, was foredoomed by his rigidities to mis-
understand the American. The fate of Daisy Miller derives
from her being simply unprepared for the idea that
what occurred in Schenectady did not necessarily correspond with what might go on in Vevey or in Rome;
and the fate of Christopher Newman was determined
by things "too deep" for the open, trusting, hardfisted
Californian. The work of Henry James is a record of
innocence either wholly untouched by Europe or cor-
rupted by it. Otherwise expressed, it becomes the tragedy
of unwareness. It expresses to the full the novelist's brood-
ing sense of what it meant to be an American, creator of
a New World that in the fulness of time would have
to meet and face the Old.

It is this understanding of the destiny of America, its

future role as a nation among nations, which gives
Henry James's writings about his own country and its
people a singular relevance today. His own generation
thought him too Europeanized to understand his simpler
compatriots—too Europeanized and too critical. What we
can discern now is that when he criticized, it was out
of love; and that when he appraised, it was in the measured truth of the artist rather than in the platitude of the
jingo. What lends dignity and breadth to the American
essays above their directness and simplicity, their grace
of style and utterance, is the exploratory reach of James's
mind—and this mind, and the pen it guided, were ever
concerned with the American consciousness and the
American character.

LEON EDEL

PART ONE

The New England Voice

*

J

*

HAWTHORNE'S FRENCH AND
ITALIAN JOURNALS [1]

MR. HAWTHORNE is having a posthumous productivity almost as active as that of his lifetime. Six volumes have been compounded from his private journals, an unfinished romance is doing duty as a "serial," and a number of his letters, with other personal memorials, have been given to the world. These liberal excisions from the privacy of so reserved and shade-seeking a genius suggest forcibly the general question of the proper limits of curiosity as to that passive personality of an artist of which the elements are scattered in portfolios and table-drawers. It is becoming very plain, however, that whatever the proper limits may be, the actual limits will be fixed only by a total exhaustion of matter. There is much that is very worthy and signally serviceable to art itself in this curiosity, as well as much that is idle and grossly defiant of the artist's presumptive desire to limit and define the ground of his appeal to fame. The question is really brought to an open dispute between this instinct of self-conservatism and the general fondness for squeezing an orange dry. Artists, of course, as time goes on, will be likely to take the alarm, empty their table-drawers, and level the approaches to their privacy. The critics, psychologists, and gossip-mongers may then glean amid the stubble.

Our remarks are not provoked by any visible detriment conferred on Mr. Hawthorne's fame by these recent pub-

[1] Passages from the French and Italian Note-Books of Nathaniel Hawthorne (Boston: J. P. Osgood & Co.; 1872). This review appeared, unsigned, in the *Nation*, March 14, 1872.

lications. He has very fairly withstood the ordeal; which, indeed, is as little as possible an ordeal in his case, owing to the superficial character of the documents. His journals throw but little light on his personal feelings, and even less on his genius *per se*. Their general effect is difficult to express. They deepen our sense of that genius, while they singularly diminish our impression of his general intellectual power. There can be no better proof of his genius than that these common daily scribblings should unite so irresistible a charm with so little distinctive force. They represent him, judged with any real critical rigor, as superficial, uninformed, incurious, inappreciative; but from beginning to end they cast no faintest shadow upon the purity of his peculiar gift. Our own sole complaint has been not that they should have been published, but that there are not a dozen volumes more. The truth is that Mr. Hawthorne belonged to the race of magicians, and that his genius took its nutriment as insensibly—to our vision—as the flowers take the dew. He was the last man to have attempted to explain himself, and these pages offer no adequate explanation of him. They show us one of the gentlest, lightest, and most leisurely of observers, strolling at his ease among foreign sights in blessed intellectual irresponsibility, and weaving his chance impressions into a tissue as smooth as fireside gossip. Mr. Hawthorne had what belongs to genius—a style individual and delightful; he seems to have written as well for himself as he did for others—to have written from the impulse to keep up a sort of literary tradition in a career singularly devoid of the air of professional authorship; but, as regards substance, his narrative flows along in a current as fitfully diffuse and shallow as a regular correspondence with a distant friend—a friend familiar but not intimate—sensitive but not exacting. With all allowance for suppressions, his entries are never confidential; the author seems to have been reserved even with himself. They are a record of things slight and usual. Some of the facts noted are incredibly minute; they imply a peculiar *leisure* of attention. How little his journal was the receptacle of Mr. Hawthorne's deeper feelings is indicated by the fact that during a long and dangerous illness of his daughter in Rome, which he speaks of later as "a trouble that pierced into his very vitals," he never touched his pen.

These volumes of Italian notes, charming as they are, are on the whole less rich and substantial than those on England. The theme, in this case, is evidently less congenial. "As I walked by the hedges yesterday," he writes at Siena, "I could have fancied that the olive trunks were those of apple-trees, and that I were in one or other of the two lands that I love better than Italy." There are in these volumes few sentences so deeply sympathetic as that in which he declares that "of all the lovely closes that I ever beheld, that of Peterborough Cathedral is to me the most delightful; so quiet is it, so solemnly and nobly cheerful, so verdant, so sweetly shadowed, and so presided over by the stately minster and surrounded by the ancient and comely habitations of Christian men." The book is full, nevertheless, of the same spirit of serene, detached contemplation; equally full of refined and gently suggestive description. Excessively detached Mr. Hawthorne remains, from the first, from Continental life, touching it throughout mistrustfully, shrinkingly, and at the rare points at which he had, for the time, unlearned his nationality. The few pages describing his arrival in France betray the irreconcilable foreignness of his instincts with a frank simplicity which provokes a smile. "Nothing really thrives here," he says of Paris; "man and vegetables have but an artificial life, like flowers stuck in a little mould, but never taking root." The great city had said but little to him; he was deaf to the Parisian harmonies. Just so it is under protest, as it were, that he looks at things in Italy. The strangeness, the remoteness, the Italianism of manners and objects, seem to oppress and confound him. He walks about bending a puzzled, ineffective gaze at things, full of a mild, genial desire to apprehend and penetrate, but with the light wings of his fancy just touching the surface of the massive consistency of fact about him, and with an air of good-humored confession that he is too simply an idle Yankee *flâneur* to conclude on such matters. The main impression produced by his observations is that of his simplicity. They spring not only from an unsophisticated, but from an excessively natural mind. Never, surely, was a man of literary genius less a man of letters. He looks at things as little as possible in that composite historic light which forms the atmosphere of many imaginations. There is something extremely pleasing in this simplicity, within which the character of the man rounds itself so completely and so firmly. His judgments abound in common sense; touched as they often are by fancy, they are never distorted by it. His errors and illusions never impugn his fundamental wisdom; even when (as is almost the case in his appreciation of works of art) they provoke a respectful smile, they contain some saving particle of sagacity. Fantastic romancer as he was, he here refutes conclusively the common charge that he was either a melancholy or a morbid genius. He had a native relish for the picturesque grays and browns of life; but these pages betray a childlike evenness and clearness of intellectual temper. Melancholy lies deeper than the line on which his fancy moved. Toward the end of his life, we believe, his cheerfulness gave way; but was not this in some degree owing to a final sense of the inability of his fancy to grope with fact?—fact having then grown rather portentous and overshadowing.

It was in midwinter of 1858 that Mr. Hawthorne journeyed from England to Italy. He went by sea from Marseilles to Civita Vecchia, and arrived at Rome weary, homeless, dejected, and benumbed. "Ah! that was a dismal time!" he says with a shudder, alluding to it among the happier circumstances of his second visit. His imagination dampened and stiffened by that Roman cold of which he declares himself unable to express the malignity, seems to have been slow to perceive its opportunities. He spent his first fortnight shivering over his fire, venturing out by snatches, and longing for an abode in the tepid, stagnant, constant climate—as one may call it—of St. Peter's. There seems from the first to have been nothing inflammable in his perception of things; there was a comfortable want of *eagerness* in his mind. Little by little, however, we see him thaw and relent, and in his desultory strolls project a ray of his gentle fancy, like a gleam of autumnal American sunshine, over the churches, statues, and ruins. From the first he is admirably honest. He never pretends to be interested unless he has been really touched; and he never attempts to work himself into a worshipful glow because it is expected of a man of fancy. He has the tone of expecting very little of himself in this line, and when by chance he is pleased and excited, he records it with modest surprise. He confesses to indifference, to ignorance and weariness, with a sturdy candor which has far more dignity, to our sense, than the merely mechanical heat of less sincere spirits. Mr. Hawthorne would assent to nothing that he could not understand; his understanding on the general æsthetic line was not comprehensive; and the attitude in which he figures to the mind's eye throughout the book is that of turning away from some dusky altar-piece with a good-humored shrug, which is not in the least a condemnation of the work, but simply an admission of personal incompetency. The pictures and statues of Italy were a heavy burden upon his conscience; though indeed, in a manner, his conscience bore them lightly—it being only at the end of three months of his Roman residence that he paid his respects to the *Transfiguration,* and a month later that he repaired to the Sistine Chapel. He was not, we take it, without taste; but his taste was not robust. He is "willing to accept Raphael's violin-player as a good picture"; but he prefers "Mr. Brown," the American landscapist, to

Claude. He comes to the singular conclusion that "the most delicate, if not the highest, charm of a picture is evanescent, and that we continue to admire pictures prescriptively and by tradition, after the qualities that first won them their fame have vanished." The "most delicate charm" to Mr. Hawthorne was apparently simply the primal freshness and brightness of paint and varnish, and —not to put too fine a point upon it—the new gilding of the frame. "Mr. Thompson," too, shares his admiration with Mr. Brown: "I do not think there is a better painter . . . living—among Americans at least; not one so earnest, faithful, and religious in his worship of art. I had rather look at his pictures than at any, except the very old masters; and taking into consideration only the comparative pleasure to be derived, I would not except more than one or two of those." From the statues, as a general thing, he derives little profit. Every now and then he utters a word which seems to explain his indifference by the Cis-Atlantic remoteness of his point of view. He remains unreconciled to the nudity of the marbles. "I do not altogether see the necessity of our sculpturing another nakedness. Man is no longer a naked animal; his clothes are as natural to him as his skin, and we have no more right to undress him than to flay him." This is the sentiment of a man to whom sculpture was a sealed book; though, indeed, in a momentary "burst of confidence," as Mr. Dickens says, he pronounces the Pompey of the Spada Palace "worth the whole sculpture gallery of the Vatican"; and when he gets to Florence, gallantly loses his heart to the Venus de' Medici and pays generous tribute to Michelangelo's Medicean sepulchers. He has indeed, throughout, that mark of the man of genius that he may at any moment surprise you by some extremely happy "hit," as when he detects at a glance, apparently, the want of force in Andrea del Sarto, or declares in the Florentine cathedral that "any little Norman church in England would impress me as much and more. There is something,

I do not know what, but it is in the region of the heart, rather than in the intellect, that Italian architecture, of whatever age or style, never seems to reach." It is in his occasional sketches of the persons—often notabilities— whom he meets that his perception seems finest and firmest. We lack space to quote, in especial, a notice of Miss Bremer and of a little tea-party of her giving, in a modest Roman chamber overhanging the Tarpeian Rock, in which in a few kindly touches the Swedish romancer is herself suffused with the atmosphere of romance, and relegated to quaint and shadowy sisterhood with the inmates of *The House of the Seven Gables.*

Mr. Hawthorne left Rome late in the spring, and traveled slowly up to Florence in the blessed fashion of the days when, seen through the open front of a crawling *vettura*, with her clamorous beggars, her black-walled mountain-towns, the unfolding romance of her landscape, Italy was seen as she really needs and deserves to be seen. Mr. Hawthorne's minute and vivid record of this journey is the most delightful portion of these volumes, and, indeed, makes well-nigh as charming a story as that of the enchanted progress of the two friends in *The Marble Faun* from Monte Beni to Perugia. He spent the summer in Florence—first in town, where he records many talks with Mr. Powers, the sculptor, whom he invests, as he is apt to do the persons who impress him, with a sort of mellow vividness of portraiture which deepens what is gracious in his observations, and gains absolution for what is shrewd; and afterwards at a castellated surburban villa—the original of the dwelling of his Donatello. This last fact, by the way, is a little of a disenchantment, as we had fancied that gentle hero living signorial-wise in some deeper Tuscan rurality. Mr. Hawthorne took Florence quietly and soberly—as became the summer weather; and bids it farewell in the gravity of this sweet-sounding passage, which we quote as one of many:

"This evening I have been on the tower-top star-
gazing and looking at the comet which waves along the
sky like an immense feather of flame. Over Florence
there was an illuminated atmosphere, caused by the
lights of the city gleaming upward into the mists which
sleep and dream above that portion of the valley as well
of the rest of it. I saw dimly, or fancied I saw, the Hill
of Fiesole, on the other side of Florence, and remembered how ghostly lights were seen passing thence to
the Duomo on the night when Lorenzo the Magnificent
died. From time to time the sweet bells of Florence
rang out, and I was loath to come down into the lower
world, knowing that I shall never again look heaven-
ward from an old tower-top, in such a soft calm
evening as this."

Mr. Hawthorne returned to Rome in the autumn,
spending some time in Siena on his way. His pictures of
the strange, dark little mountain-cities of Radicofani and
Bolsena, on his downward journey, are masterpieces of
literary etching. It is impossible to render better that
impression as of a mild nightmare which such places make
upon the American traveler. "Rome certainly draws itself
into my heart," he writes on his return, "as I think even
London, or even Concord itself, or even old sleepy Salem
never did and never will." The result of this increased
familiarity was the mature conception of the romance of
his *Marble Faun*. He journalizes again, but at rarer intervals, though his entries retain to the last a certain appealing charm which we find it hard to define. It lies
partly perhaps in what we hinted at above—in the fascination of seeing so potent a sovereign in his own fair
kingdom of fantasy so busily writing himself simple,
during such a succession of months, as to the dense realities of the world. Mr. Hawthorne's, however, was a rich
simplicity. These pages give a strong impression of moral
integrity and elevation. And, more than in other ways,

they are interesting from their strong national flavor. Exposed late in life to European influences, Mr. Hawthorne was but superficially affected by them—far less so than would be the case with a mind of the same temper growing up among us today. We seem to see him strolling through churches and galleries as the last pure American—attesting by his shy responses to dark canvas and cold marble his loyalty to a simpler and less encumbered civilization. This image deepens that tender personal regard which it is the constant effect of these volumes to produce.

NATHANIEL HAWTHORNE

(1804–1864)[1]

It is perhaps an advantage in writing of Nathaniel Hawthorne's work that his life offers little opporunity to the biographer. The record of it makes so few exactions that in a critical account of him—even as brief as this—the work may easily take most of the place. He was one of those happy men of letters in whose course the great

[1] This essay first appeared in vol. XII of an anthology, *Library of the World's Best Literature*, edited by Charles Dudley Warner (New York, 1879), and was never reprinted by James.

milestones are simply those of his ideas that found successful form. Born at Salem, Massachusetts, on July 4, 1804,
of established local Puritan—and in a conspicious degree,
sturdy seafaring—stock, he was educated at his birthplace
and at Bowdoin College, Maine, where H. W. Longfellow
was one of his fellow students. Another was Franklin
Pierce, who was to be elected President of the United
States in 1852, and with whom Hawthorne formed relations that became an influence in his life. On leaving
college in 1825 he returned to Salem to live, and in 1828
published in Boston a short romance called *Fanshawe*, of
which the scene, in spite of its being a "love-story," is
laid, but for a change of name, at Bowdoin, with professors and undergraduates for its male characters. The experiment was inevitably faint, but the author's beautiful
touch had begun to feel its way. In 1837, after a dozen
years spent in special solitude, as he later testified, at
Salem, he collected as the first series of *Twice-Told Tales*
various more or less unremunerated contributions to the
magazines and annuals of the day. In 1845 appeared the
second series, and in 1851 the two volumes were, with a
preface peculiarly graceful and touching, reissued together; he is in general never more graceful than when
prefatory. In 1851 and 1854 respectively came to light
The Snow Image and *Mosses from an Old Manse*, which
form, with the previous double sheaf, his three main
gatherings-in of the shorter fiction. I neglect, for brevity
and as addressed to children, *Grandfather's Chair* and *The
Wonder Book* (1851), as well as *Tanglewood Tales*
(1852). Of the other groups, some preceded, some followed, the appearance in 1850 of his second novel, *The
Scarlet Letter*.

These things—the experiments in the shorter fiction—
had sounded, with their rare felicity, from the very first
the note that was to be Hawthorne's distinguished mark—
that feeling for the latent romance of New England,
which in summary form is the most final name to be

given, I think, to his inspiration. This element, which is what at its best his genius most expresses, was far from obvious—it had to be looked for; and Hawthorne found it, as he wandered and mused, in the secret play of the Puritan faith: the secret, I say particularly, because the direct and ostensible, face to face with common tasks and small conditions (as I may call them without prejudice to their general grimness), arrived at forms of which the tender imagination could make little. It could make a great deal, on the other hand, of the spiritual contortions, the darkened outlook, of the ingrained sense of sin, of evil, and of responsibility. There had been other complications in the history of the community surrounding him—savages from behind, soldiers from before, a cruel climate from every quarter, and a pecuniary remittance from none. But the great complication was the pressing moral anxiety, the restless individual conscience. These things were developed at the cost of so many others that there were almost no others left to help them to make a picture for the artist. The artist's imagination had to deck out the subject, to work it up, as we nowadays say; and Hawthorne's was—on intensely chastened lines, indeed—equal to the task. In that manner it came into exercise from the first, through the necessity of taking for granted, on the part of the society about him, a life of the spirit more complex than anything that met the mere eye of sense. It was a question of looking behind and beneath for the suggestive idea, the artistic motive; the effect of all of which was an invaluable training for the faculty that evokes and enhances. This ingenuity grew alert and irrepressible as it maneuvered for the back view and turned up the under side of common aspects—the laws secretly broken, the impulses secretly felt, the hidden passions, the double lives, the dark corners, the closed rooms, the skeletons in the cupboard and at the feast. It made, in short, and cherished, for fancy's sake, a mystery and a glamour where there were otherwise none very ready to its hand; so that it

ended by living in a world of things symbolic and al-
legoric, a presentation of objects casting, in every case,
far behind them a shadow more curious and more amusing
than the apparent figure. Any figure therefore easily became with him an emblem, any story a parable, any appearance a cover: things with which his concern is—
gently, indulgently, skillfully, with the lightest hand in
the world—to pivot them round and show the odd little
stamp or sign that gives them their value for the collector.

The specimens he collected, as we may call them, are
divisible into groups, but with the mark in common that
they are all early products of the dry New England air.
Some are myths and mysteries of old Massachusetts—
charming ghostly passages of colonial history. Such are
"The Grey Champion," "The Maypole of Merry Mount,"
the four beautiful "Legends of the Province House."
Others, like "Roger Malvin's Burial," "Rappaccini's
Daughter," "Young Goodman Brown," are "moralities"
without the moral, as it were; small cold apologues, frosty
and exquisite, occasionally gathered from beyond the sea.
Then there are the chapters of the fanciful all for fancy's
sake, of the pure whimsical, and of observation merely
amused and beguiled; pages, many of them, of friendly
humorous reflections on what, in Salem or in Boston, a
dreamer might meet in his walks. What Hawthorne encountered he instinctively embroidered, working it over
with a fine, slow needle, and with flowers pale, rosy, or
dusky, as the case might suggest. We have a handful of
these in "The Great Carbuncle" and "The Great Stone
Face," "The Seven Vagabonds," "The Threefold Destiny,"
"The Village Uncle," "The Toll Gatherer's Day," "A
Rill from the Town Pump," and "Chippings with a
Chisel." The inequalities in his work are not, to my sense,
great; and in specifying, we take and leave with hesitation.

The Scarlet Letter, in 1850, brought him immediate
distinction, and has probably kept its place not only as the
most original of his novels, but as the most distinguished

piece of prose fiction that was to spring from American soil. He had received in 1839 an appointment to a small place in the Boston custom-house, where his labors were sordid and sterile, and he had given it up in permissible weariness. He had spent in 1841 near Roxbury, Massachusetts, a few months in the co-operative community of Brook Farm, a short-lived socialistic experiment. He had married in the following year and gone to live at the old Manse at Concord, where he remained till 1846, when, with a fresh fiscal engagement, he returned to his native town. It was in the intervals of his occupation at the Salem custom-house that *The Scarlet Letter* was written. The book has achieved the fortune of the small supreme group of novels: it has hung an ineffaceable image in the portrait gallery, the reserved inner cabinet, of literature. Hester Prynne is not one of those characters of fiction whom we use as a term of comparison for a character of fact: she is almost more than that—she decorates the museum in a way that seems to forbid us such a freedom. Hawthorne availed himself, for her history, of the most striking anecdote the early Puritan chronicle could give him—give him in the manner set forth by the long, lazy Prologue or Introduction, an exquisite commemoration of the happy dullness of his term of service at the custom-house, where it is his fancy to pretend to have discovered in a box of old papers the faded relic and the musty documents which suggested to him his title and his theme.

It is the story as old as the custom of marriage—the story of the husband, the wife, and the lover; but bathed in a misty, moonshiny light, and completely neglecting the usual sources of emotion. The wife, with the charming child of her guilt, had stood under the stern inquisitorial law in the public pillory of the adulteress; while the lover, a saintly young minister, undetected and unbetrayed, has in an anguish of pusillanimity suffered her to pay the whole fine. The husband, an ancient scholar, a man of abstruse and profane learning, finds his revenge years after

the wrong, in making himself insidiously the intimate of
the young minister, and feeding secretly on the remorse,
the inward torments, which he does everything to quicken
but pretends to have no ground for suspecting. The march
of the drama lies almost wholly in the malignant pressure
exercised in this manner by Chillingworth upon Dimmes-
dale; an influence that at last reaches its climax in the
extraordinary penance of the subject, who in the darkness, in the sleeping town, mounts, himself, upon the
scaffold on which, years before, the partner of his guilt
has undergone irrevocable anguish. In this situation he
calls to him Hester Prynne and her child, who, belated in
the course of the merciful ministrations to which Hester
has now given herelf up, pass, among the shadows, within
sight of him; and they in response to his appeal ascend for
a second time to the place of atonement, and stand there
with him under cover of night. The scene is not complete,
of course, till Chillingworth arrives to enjoy the spectacle
and his triumph. It has inevitably gained great praise, and
no page of Hawthorne's shows more intensity of imagination; yet the main achievement of the book is not what
is principally its subject—the picture of the relation of
the two men. They are too faintly—the husband in particular—though so fancifully figured. *The Scarlet Letter*
lives, in spite of too many cold *concetti*—Hawthorne's
general danger—by something noble and truthful in the
image of the branded mother and the beautiful child.
Strangely· enough, this pair are almost wholly outside the
action; yet they preserve and vivify the work.

The House of the Seven Gables, written during a residence of two years at Lenox, Massachusetts, was published in 1851. If there are probably no four books of any
author among which, for a favorite, readers hesitate longer
than between Hawthorne's four longest stories, there are
at any rate many for whom this remains distinctly his
largest and fullest production. Suffused as it is with a
pleasant autumnal haze, it yet brushes more closely than

its companions the surface of American life, comes a
trifle nearer to being a novel of manners. The manners
it shows us indeed are all interfused with the author's
special tone, seen in a slanting afternoon light; but detail
and illustration are sufficiently copious; and I am tempted
for my own part to pronounce the book, taking subject
and treatment together, and in spite of the position as a
more concentrated classic enjoyed by *The Scarlet Letter*,
the closest approach we are likely to have to the great
work of fiction, so often called for, that is to do us na-
tionally most honor and most good. The subject reduced
to its essence, indeed, accounts not quite altogether for all
that there is in the picture. What there is besides is an
extraordinary charm of expression, of sensibility, of humor, of touch. The question is that of the mortal shrink-
age of a family once uplifted, the last spasm of their
starved gentility and flicker of their slow extinction. In the
haunted world of Hawthorne's imagination the old Pyncheon house, under its elm in the Salem by-street, is the
place where the ghosts are most at home. Ghostly even
are its actual tenants, the ancient virgin Hepzibah, with
her turban, her scowl, her creaking joints, and her map of
the great territory to the eastward belonging to her family
—reduced, in these dignities, to selling profitless penny-
worths over a counter; and the bewildered bachelor
Clifford, released, like some blinking and noble *déterré* of
the old Bastile, from twenty years of wrongful imprison-
ment. We meet at every turn, with Hawthorne, his favorite fancy of communicated sorrows and inevitable
atonements. Life is an experience in which we expiate the
sins of others in the intervals of expiating our own. The
heaviest visitation of the blighted Pyncheons is the responsibility they have incurred through the misdeeds of a
hard-hearted witch-burning ancestor. This ancestor has an
effective return to life in the person of the one actually
robust and successful representative of the race—a bland,
hard, showy, shallow "ornament of the bench," a massive

hypocrite and sensualist, who at last, though indeed too late, pays the penalty and removes the curse. The idea of the story is at once perhaps a trifle thin and a trifle obvious—the idea that races and individuals may die of mere dignity and heredity, and that they need for refreshment and cleansing to be, from without, breathed upon like dull mirrors. But the art of the thing is exquisite, its charm irresistible, its distinction complete. *The House of the Seven Gables,* I may add, contains in the rich portrait of Judge Pyncheon a character more solidly suggested than —with the possible exception of the Zenobia of *The Blithedale Romance*—any other figure in the author's list.

Weary of Lenox, Hawthorne spent several months of 1852 at West Newton near Boston, where *The Blithedale Romance* was brought forth. He made the most, for the food of fancy, of what came under his hand—happy in an appetite that could often find a feast in meager materials. The third of his novels is an echo, delightfully poetized, of his residence at Brook Farm. "Transcendentalism" was in those days in New England much in the air; and the most comprehensive account of the partakers of this quaint experiment appears to have been held to be that they were Transcendentalists. More simply stated, they were young, candid radicals, reformers, philanthropists. The fact that it sprang—all irresponsibly indeed—from the observation of a known episode, gives *The Blithedale Romance* also a certain value as a picture of manners; the place portrayed, however, opens quickly enough into the pleasantest and idlest dream-world. Hawthorne, we gather, dreamed there more than he worked; he has traced his attitude delightfully in that of the fitful and ironical Coverdale, as to whom we wonder why he chose to rub shoulders quite so much. We think of him as drowsing on a hillside with his hat pulled over his eyes, and the neighboring hum of reform turning in his ears, to a refrain as vague as an old song. One thing is certain: that if he failed his companions as a laborer in the field, it was only that he might associate them with another sort of success.

We feel, however, that he lets them off easily, when we think of some of the queer figures and queer nostrums then abroad in the land, and which his mild satire—incuring none the less some mild reproach—fails to grind in its mill. The idea that he most tangibly presents is that of the unconscious way in which the search for the common good may cover a hundred interested impulses and personal motives; the suggestion that such a company could only be bound together more by its delusions, its mutual suspicions and frictions, than by any successful surrender of self. The book contains two images of large and admirable intention: that of Hollingsworth, the heavy-handed radical, selfish and sincere, with no sense for jokes, for forms, or for shades; and that of Zenobia, the woman of "sympathies," the passionate patroness of "causes," who plays as it were with revolution, and only encounters embarrassment. Zenobia is the most graceful of all portraits of the strong-minded of her sex; borrowing something of her grace, moreover, from the fate that was not to allow her to grow old and shrill, and not least touching from the air we attribute to her of looking, with her fine imagination, for adventures that were hardly, under the circumstances, to be met. We fill out the figure, perhaps, and even lend to the vision something more than Hawthorne intended. Zenobia was, like Coverdale himself, a subject of dreams that were not to find form at Roxbury; but Coverdale had other resources, while she had none but her final failure. Hawthorne indicates no more interesting aspect of the matter than her baffled effort to make a hero of Hollingsworth, who proves, to her misfortune, so much too inelastic for the part. All this, as we read it today, has a soft, shy glamour, a touch of the poetry of far-off things. Nothing of the author's is a happier expression of what I have called his sense of the romance of New England.

In 1853 Franklin Pierce, then President, appointed him

consul at Liverpool, which was the beginning of a residence of some seven years in England and in Italy, the period to which we owe *The Marble Faun* and *Our Old Home*. The material for the latter of these was the first to be gathered; but the appearance of *The Marble Faun*, begun in Rome in 1858 and finished during a second stay in England, preceded that of its companion. This is his only long drama on a foreign stage. Drawn from his own air, however, are much of its inspiration and its character. Hawthorne took with him to Italy, as he had done to England, more of the old Puritan consciousness than he left behind. The book has been consecrated as a kind of manual of Roman sights and impressions, brought together indeed in the light of a sympathy always detached and often withheld; and its value is not diminished by its constant reference to an order of things of which, at present, the yearning pilgrim—before a board for the most part swept bare—can only pick up the crumbs. The mystical, the mythical, are in *The Marble Faun* more than ever at hide-and-seek with the real. The author's fancy for freakish correspondences has its way, with Donatello's points of resemblance to the delightful statue in the Capitol. What he offers us is the history of a character blissfully immature, awakening to manhood through the accidental, the almost unconscious, commission of a crime. For the happy youth before his act—the first complete act of his life—there have been no unanswered questions; but after it he finds himself confronted with all the weary questions of the world. This act consists of his ridding of an obscure tormentor—the obscurity is rather a mistake— a woman whom he loves, and who is older, cleverer, and more acquainted with life than himself. The humanizing, the moralizing of the faun is again an ingenious conceit; but it has had for result to have made the subject of the process—and the case is unique in Hawthorne's work— one of those creations of the story-teller who give us a name for a type. There is a kind of young man whom we

have now only to call a Donatello, to feel that we sufficiently classify him. It is a part of the scheme of the
story to extend to still another nature than his the same
sad initiation. A young woman from across the Atlantic,
a gentle copyist in Roman galleries of still gentler Guidos
and Guercinos, happens to have caught a glimpse, at the
critical moment, of the dismal secret that unites Donatello
and Miriam. This, for her, is the tree of bitter knowledge,
the taste of which sickens and saddens her. The burden is
more than she can bear, and one of the most charming
passages in the book describes how at last, at a summer's
end, in sultry solitude, she stops at St. Peter's before a
confessional, and Protestant and Puritan as she is, yields
to the necessity of kneeling there and ridding herself of
her obsession. Hawthorne's young women are exquisite;
Hilda is a happy sister to the Phœbe of *The House of the
Seven Gables* and the Priscilla of *The Blithedale Romance.*

The drama in *The Marble Faun* none the less, I think,
is of an effect less complete than that of the almost larger
element that I can only call the landscape and the spirit.
Nothing is more striking than the awkward grace with
which the author utters, without consenting to it—for he
is full of half-amiable, half-angry protest and prejudice—
the message, the mystery of the medium in which his
actors move. Miriam and her muffled bandit have faded
away, and we have our doubts and even our fears about
Kenyon and his American statuary; but the breath of old
Rome, the sense of old Italy, still meet us as we turn the
page, and the book will long, on the great sentimental
journey, continue to peep out of most pockets.

He returned to America in 1860, settled once more at
Concord, and died at Plymouth, New Hampshire, in the
arms of Franklin Pierce, in 1864. At home, with the aid
of many memories and of the copious diaries ultimately
published by his wife and children, he brought forth, one
by one, the chapters eventually collected under the title of
Our Old Home. The American *Note Books,* the English,

and the French and Italian, were given to the world after his death—in 1868, 1870, and 1871 respectively; and if I add to these the small "campaign" *Life of Franklin Pierce* (1852), two posthumous fragments, *Septimius Felton* and *The Dolliver Romance*, and those scraps and shreds of which his table drawers were still more exhaustively emptied, his literary catalogue—none of the longest—becomes complete.

The important item in this remainder is the close, ripe cluster, the series presented by himself, of his impressions of England. These admirable papers, with much of the same fascination, have something of the same uncomforted note with which he had surrendered himself to the charm of Italy: the mixture of sensibility and reluctance, of response and dissent, the strife between his sense of beauty and his sense of banishment. He came to the Old World late in life—though after dabbling for years, indeed, in the fancied phenomena of time, and with inevitable reserves, mistrusts, and antagonisms. The striking thing to my sense, however, is not what he missed but what he so ingeniously and vividly made out. If he had been, imaginatively, rather old in his youth, he was youthful in his age; and when all is said, we owe him, as a contribution to the immemorial process of lively repartee between the motherland and the daughter, the only pages of the business that can be said to belong to pure literature. He was capable of writing *The Marble Faun*, and yet of declaring, in a letter from Rome, that he bitterly detested the place and should rejoice to bid it farewell forever. Just so he was capable of drawing from English aspects a delight that they had yielded not even to Washington Irving, and yet of insisting, with a perversity that both smiled and frowned, that they rubbed him mainly all the wrong way. At home he had fingered the musty, but abroad he seemed to pine for freshness. In truth, for many persons his great, his most touching sign will have been his aloofness wherever he is. He is outside of everything, and an alien everywhere. He is an æsthetic solitary. His beautiful, light imagination is the wing that on the autumn evening just brushes the dusky window. It was a faculty that gave him much more a terrible sense of human abysses than a desire rashly to sound them and rise to the surface with his report. On the surface—the surface of the soul and the edge of the tragedy—he preferred to remain. He lingered, to weave his web, in the thin exterior air. This is a partial expression of his characteristic habit of dipping, of diving just for sport, into the moral world without being in the least a moralist. He had none of the heat nor of the dogmatism of that character; none of the impertinence, as we feel he would almost have held it, of an intermeddling. He never intermeddled; he was divertedly and discreetly contemplative, pausing oftenest wherever, amid prosaic aspects, there seemed most of an appeal to a sense for subtleties. But of all cynics he was the brightest and kindest, and the subtleties he spun are mere silken threads for stringing polished beads. His collection of moral mysteries is the cabinet of a dilettante.

THE HAWTHORNE CENTENARY

LETTER FROM HENRY JAMES
TO THE HON. ROBERT S. RANTOUL[1]

Rye, Sussex, England
June 10, 1904

Dear Sir:

I much regret my being able to participate only in that spirit of sympathy that makes light of distance—that defies difference of latitude and hemisphere—in the honors you are paying, at his birthplace, to the beautiful genius to whom Salem owes the most precious gift perhaps that an honest city may receive from one of her sons—the gift of a literary association high enough in character to emerge thus brilliantly from the test of Time. How happily it has lasted for you, and *why* it has lasted—this flower of romantic art, never to become a mere desiccated specimen, that Hawthorne interwove with your sturdy annals—I shall attempt, by your leave, briefly to say; but

---

[1] The letter was written for the observances of the Hawthorne centenary held June 23, 1904 at Salem, Massachusetts, and was published in the *Proceedings* by the Essex Institute at Salem during that year.

your civic pride is at any rate fortunate in being able to found your claim to have contributed to the things of the mind on a case and a career so eminent and so interesting. The spirit of such occasions is always, on the spot, communicative and irresistible; full of the amenity of each man's—and I suppose still more of each woman's—scarce distinguishing, in the general friendliness, between the *loan* of enthusiasm and the gift, between the sound that starts the echo and the echo that comes back from the sound. But being present by projection of the mind, present afar off and under another sky, *that* has its advantages too—for other distinctiors, for lucidity of vision and a sense of the reasons of things. The career commemorated may perhaps so be looked at, over a firm rest, as through the telescope that fixes it, even to intensity, and helps it to become, as we say, objective—and objective not strictly to cold criticism, but to admiration and wonder themselves, and even, in a degree, to a certain tenderness of envy. The earlier scene, now smothered in flowers and eloquence and music, possibly hangs before one rather more, under this perspective, in *all* its parts— with its relation, unconscious at the time, to the rare mind that had been planted in it as in a parent soil, and with the relation of that mind to its own preoccupied state, to the scene itself as enveloping and suggesting medium: a relation, this latter, to come to consciousness always so much sooner, so much more nervously, so much more expressively, than the other! By which I mean that there is, unfortunately for the prospective celebrity, no short cut possible, on the part of his fellow townsmen, to the expensive holiday they are keeping in reserve for his name. It is there, all the while—somewhere in the air at least, even while he lives; but they cannot get *at* it till the Fates have forced, one by one, all the locks of all the doors and crooked passages that shut it off; and the celebrity meantime, by good luck, can have little idea what is missing.

I at all events almost venture to say that, save for the

pleasure of your company, save for that community of demonstration which is certainly a joy in itself, I could not wish to be better placed than at this distance for a vision of the lonely young man that Hawthorne then was, and that he was in fact pretty well always to remain, dreaming his dreams, nursing his imagination, feeling his way, leading his life, intellectual, personal, economic, in the place that Salem then was, and becoming, unwittingly and unsuspectedly, with an absence of calculation fairly precious for the final effect, the pretext for the kind of recognition you greet him with today. It is the addition of all the limitations and depressions and difficulties of genius that makes always—with the factor of Time thrown in—the sum total of posthumous glory. We see, at the end of the backward vista, the restless unclassified artist pursue the *immediate*, the pressing need of the hour, the question he is not to come home to his possibly un-inspiring hearthstone without having met—we see him chase it, none too confidently, through quite familiar, *too* familiar streets, round wellworn corners that don't trip it up for him, or into dull doorways that fail to catch and hold it; and then we see, at the other end of the century, these same streets and corners and doorways, these quiet familiarities, the stones he trod, the objects he touched, the air he breathed, positively and all impatiently *waiting* to bestow their reward, to measure him out success, in the great, in the almost superfluous, abundance of the eventual! This general quest that Hawthorne comes back to us out of the old sunny and shady Salem, the blissfully homogeneous community of the forties and fifties, as urged to by his particular, and very individual, sense of life, is that of man's relation to his environment seen on the side that we call, for our best convenience, the romantic side: a term that we half the time, nowadays, comfortably escape the challenge to define precisely be-cause *The Scarlet Letter* and *The House of the Seven Gables* have made that possible to us under cover of mere triumphant reference to them. That is why, to my sense, our author's Salem years and Salem impressions are so interesting a part of his development. It was while they lasted, it was to all appearance under their suggestion, that the romantic spirit in him learned to expand with that right and beautiful felicity that was to make him one of its rarest representatives. Salem had the good fortune to assist him, betimes, to this charming discrimination—that of looking for romance near at hand, and where it grows thick and true, rather than on the other side of the globe and in the Dictionary of Dates. We see it, nowadays, more and more, inquired and bargained for in places and times that are strange and indigestible to us; and for the most part, I think, we see those who deal in it on these terms come back from their harvest with their hands smelling, under their brave leather gauntlets, or royal rings, or whatever, of the plain domestic blackberry, the homeliest growth of our actual dusty waysides. These adventurers bring home, in general, simply what they have taken with them, the mechanical, at best the pedantic, view of the list of romantic properties. The country of romance has been for them but a particular spot on the map, colored blue or red or yellow—they have to *take* it from the map; or has been this, that, or the other particular set of complications, machinations, coincidences, or escapes, this, that, or the other fashion of firearm or cutlass, cock of hat, frizzle of wig, violence of scuffle, or sound of expletive: mere accidents and outward patches, all, of the engaging mystery—no more of its essence than the brass band at a restaurant is of the essence of the dinner. What was admirable and instinctive in Hawthorne was that he saw the quaintness or the weirdness, the interest *behind* the interest, of things, as continuous with the very life we are leading, or that we were leading—you, at Salem, certainly were leading—round about him and under his eyes; saw it as something deeply within us, not as something infinitely disconnected from us; saw it in short in the very application of the spectator's, the poet's mood, in the kind of reflection the things we know best and see oftenest may make in our minds. So it is that such things as *The Seven Gables, The Blithedale Romance, The Marble Faun*, are singularly fruitful examples of the real as distinguished from the the artificial romantic note. Here "the light that never was on land or sea" keeps all the intimacy and yet adds all the wonder. In the first two of the books I have named, especially, the author has read the romantic effect into the most usual and contemporary things—arriving by it at a success that, in *The Seven Gables* perhaps supremely, is a marvel of the free-playing, yet ever unerring, never falsifying instinct. We have an ancient gentlewoman reduced to keep a shop; a young photographer modestly invoking fortune; a full-fed, wine-flushed "prominent citizen" asleep in his chair; a weak-minded bachelor spending his life under the shadow of an early fault that has not been in the least heroic; a fresh New England girl of the happy complexion of thousands of others—we have, thrown together, but these gently persuasive challenges to mystification, yet with the result that they transport us to a world in which, as in that of Tennyson's Lotus-Eaters, it seems always afternoon. And somehow this very freedom of the spell remains all the while truth to the objects observed—truth to the very Salem in which the vision was born. *Blithedale* is scarcely less fine a case of distinction conferred, the curiosity and anxiety dear to the reader purchased, not by a shower of counterfeit notes, simulating munificence, but by that artistic economy which understands *values* and uses them. The book takes up the parti-colored, angular, audible, traceable Real, the New England earnest, aspiring, reforming Real, scattered in a few frame houses over a few stony fields, and so invests and colors it, makes it rich and strange—and simply by finding a felicitous *tone* for it—that its characters and images remain for us curious winged creatures preserved in the purest amber of the imagination.

All of which leads me back to what I said, to begin with, about our romancer's having borne the test of Time. I mentioned that there is a reason, in particular, why he has borne it so well, and I think you will recognize with me, in the light of what I have tried to say, that he has done so by very simply, quietly, slowly, and steadily becoming for us a Classic. If we look at the real meaning of our celebration today, ask ourselves what is at the back of our heads or in the bottom of our hearts about it, we become conscious of that interesting process and eloquent plea of the years on Hawthorne's behalf—of that great benefit, that effect of benevolence, for him, from so many of the things the years have brought. We are in the presence thus of one of the happiest opportunities to see how a Classic comes into being, how three such things as the *Scarlet Letter*, the *Gables*, and *Blithedale*—to choose only a few names where I might choose many—acquire their final value. They acquire it, in a large measure, by the manner in which later developments have worked in respect to them—and, it is scarce too much to say, acquire it in spite of themselves and by the action of better machinery than their authors could have set in motion, stronger (as well as longer!) wires than their authors could have pulled. Later developments, I think, have worked in respect to them by *contrast*—that is the point—so much more either than by a generous emulation or by a still more generous originality. They have operated to make the beauty—the other beauty—delicate and noble, to throw the distinction into relief. The scene has changed and everything with it—the pitch, and the tone, and the quantity, and the quality, above all; reverberations are gained, but proportions are lost; the distracted Muse herself stops her ears and shuts her eyes: the brazen trumpet has so done its best to deafen us to the fiddle-string. But to the fiddle-string we nevertheless return; it sounds, for our sense, with the slightest lull of the general noise—such a lull as, for reflection, for taste, a little even for criticism, and much, certainly, for a legitimate complacency, our present occasion beneficently makes. Then it is that such a mystery as that of the genius we commemorate may appear a perfect example of the truth that the state of being a classic is a *comparative* state—considerably, generously, even when blindly, brought about, for the author on whom the crown alights, by the generations, the multitudes worshipping other gods, that have followed him. He must obviously have been in himself exquisite and right, but it is not to that only, to being in himself exquisite and right, that any man ever was so fortunate as to owe the supreme distinction. He owes it more or less, at the best, to the *relief* in which some happy, some charming combination of accidents has placed his intrinsic value. This combination, in our own time, has been the contagion of the form that we may, for convenience, and perhaps, as regards much of it, even for compliment, call the journalistic—so pervasive, so ubiquitous, so unprecedentedly prosperous, so wonderful for outward agility, but so unfavorable, even so fatal, to development from within. Hawthorne saw it—and it saw him—but in its infancy, before these days of huge and easy and immediate success, before the universal, the overwhelming triumph of the monster. He *had* developed from within—as to feeling, as to form, as to sincerity and character. So it is, as I say, that he enjoys his relief, and that we are thrown back, by the sense of difference, on his free possession of himself. He lent himself, of course, to his dignity—by the way the serious, in him, flowered into the grace of art; but our need of him, almost quite alone as he stands, in one tray of the scales of Justice, would add, if this were necessary, to the earnestness of our wish to see that he be undisturbed there. Vigilance, in the matter, however, assuredly, is happily not necessary! The grand sign of being a classic is that when you have "passed," as they say at examinations, you have passed; you have become one once for all; you have taken your degree and may be left to the light and the ages.

HENRY JAMES

Hon. Robert S. Rantoul

THE CORRESPONDENCE OF CARLYLE AND EMERSON

IN THE DELUGE of "new books," in which so many of us at present are occupied in swimming for our lives, it is not often that there floats toward us a pair of volumes so well deserving to be arrested in their passage as this substantial record [1] of a beautiful and distinguished friendship. The book has a high interest, and we have found it even more absorbing than we expected. It is only superficially, indeed, that it may be spoken of as new; for the persons and things it commemorates have already receded —so fast we move today—into a kind of historical perspective. The last letter that passed between the correspondents is of the date only of 1872; Carlyle died nine

[1] *The Correspondence of Thomas Carlyle and Ralph Waldo Emerson. 1834–1872.* In two volumes. (Boston: J. R. Osgood & Co.; 1883.) This essay review appeared in the *Century Magazine,* June 1883, and was never reprinted by James.

and Emerson ten years later. But we seem to see them
from a distance; the united pair presents itself in something of the uplifted relief of a group on canvas or in
marble. They have become, as I say, historical: so many
of their emotions, their discussions, their interests, their
allusions belong to a past which is already remote. It
was, in fact, in the current of an earlier world that
the Correspondence began. The first letter, which is from
Emerson as the last is from Carlyle, is of the date of 1834.
Emerson was the voice of New England in those days,
and New England has changed not a little. There is something peculiarly young and tender in the social scene in
which we see him engaged; for, in the interval that
separates us from the period included in the whole of
the first of these volumes and in the greater part of the
second, a great many things have come and gone. The
questions of those years are not the questions of these.
There were more questions then, perhaps; at least, they
made more show. It may seem to the reader of Emerson's
early letters that at that time there was nothing in New
England but questions. There were very few things, and
even few persons. Emerson's personal references are rare.
Bronson Alcott, W. E. Channing, Margaret Fuller, Thoreau, an occasional American about to go to Europe,
carrying a letter or a book to Carlyle, constitute in this
direction the chief objects of mention. Transcendentalism
has come and gone, and the abolition of slavery, and the
novelty of the Unitarian creed, and the revelation of
Goethe, and the doctrine of a vegetable diet, and a great
many other reforms then deemed urgent. Carlyle's extraordinary personality has, moreover, thanks to recent
publications, revealed itself with unlooked-for vividness.
Of few distinguished men has the public come into such
complete possession so soon after death has unlocked the
cabinets. The deeply interesting volumes given to the
world so promptly by Mr. Froude have transmuted the
great Scotch humorist from a remote and mysterious

personage—however portentous, disclosing himself in dusky, smoky ejaculations and rumblings—into a definite and measurable, an almost familiar figure, with every feature marked and every peculiarity demonstrated. We know Carlyle, in short; we may look at him at our ease, and the advantage, though we have enjoyed it but for a year or two, has become part of our modern illumination. When we receive new contributions accordingly, we know what to do with them, and where, as the phrase is, to fit them in; they find us prepared. I should add that if we know Carlyle, we know him in a great measure because he was so rich, so original a letter-writer. The letters in Mr. Froude's volumes constituted the highest value of those memorials and led us to look for entertainment as great in the Correspondence which Mr. Charles Eliot Norton had had for some time in his keeping, and which, though his name does not appear on the title-page, he has now edited with all needful judgment and care. Carlyle takes his place among the first of English, among the very first of all letter-writers. All his great merits come out in this form of expression; and his defects are not felt as defects, but only as striking characteristics and as tones in the picture. Originality, nature, humor, imagination, freedom, the disposition to talk, the play of mood, the touch of confidence—these qualities, of which the letters are full, will, with the aid of an inimitable use of language—a style which glances at nothing that it does not render grotesque—preserve their life for readers even further removed from the occasion than ourselves, and for whom possibly the vogue of Carlyle's published writings in his day will be to a certain degree a subject of wonder. The light thrown upon his character by the mass of evidence edited by Mr. Froude had not embellished the image nor made the reader's sympathy advance at the same pace as his curiosity. But the volumes that lie before us seemed to promise a more genial sort of testimony, and the promise has been partly kept. Carlyle is here in intercourse with a friend for whom, almost alone among the persons with whom he had dealings, he appears to have entertained a sentiment of respect—a constancy of affection untinged by that humorous contempt in which (in most cases) he indulges when he wishes to be kind, and which was the best refuge open to him from his other alternative of absolutely savage mockery. Of the character, the sincerity, the genius, the many good offices of his American correspondent, he appears to have had an appreciation which, even in his most invidious hours, never belied itself. It is singular, indeed, that throughout his intercourse with Emerson he never appears to have known the satiric fury which he directed at so many other objects—accepting his friend *en bloc*, once for all, with reservations and protests so light that, as addressed to Emerson's own character, they are only a finer form of consideration. Emerson, on the other hand, who was so much more kindly a judge, so much more luminous a nature, holds off, as the phrase is, comparatively, and expresses, at times, at least, the disapprobation of silence. Carlyle was the more constant writer of the two, especially toward the end of their correspondence; he constantly expresses the desire to hear from Emerson oftener. The latter had not an abundant epistolary impulse; the form and style of his letters, charming as they are, is in itself a proof of that. But there were evidently certain directions in which he could not go with his friend, who has likewise sundry tricks of style which act at times even upon the placid nerves of the inventor of Transcendentalism. He thinks, for instance, that Carlyle's satire of the "gigmania" has been overdone; and this, although Emerson himself was as little as possible of a gigmaniac. I must add that it would be wrong to suppose that the element of reserve, or of calculated silence, plays in the least a striking part in the letters of either. There is nothing more striking, and nothing finer, than their confident frankness. Altogether the charm of the book is that as one reads it one is in excellent company. Two men of rare and beautiful genius converse with each other, and the conversation is a kind of exhibition.

There was something almost dramatic in the beginning of their friendship. Emerson, a young Bostonian, then unknown, went to Europe for the first time in 1833. He had read Carlyle's contributions to the *Edinburgh Review*, and on his return from Italy, spending the summer in England, had no greater care than to become acquainted with the author. Carlyle, hardly better known then than Emerson—poor, struggling, lonely, discouraged, but pregnant with all his future eloquence—was spending at the farm of Craigenputtock, in the south of Scotland, those melancholy, those almost savage years of which we have so rich a report in the letters and journals published by Mr. Froude. "I found the house amid desolate, heathery hills, where the lonely scholar nourished his mighty heart." So writes Emerson in the first chapter of the *English Traits*. The two spent a day of early autumn together, walking over the moors, and when they separated it was with a presentiment of the future and a conviction on the part of each that he had made a rare acquisition. Carlyle has commemorated in several places the apparition of the generous young American—"one of the most lovable creatures in himself that we had ever looked upon," he wrote to his mother; and toward the end of his life, in one of these letters, he glances back at it in the tenderest manner, across the years. "I shall never forget the visitor," at a later date, too, Mrs. Carlyle wrote, "who years ago, in the desert, descended on us out of the clouds, as it were, and made one day there look like enchantment for us, and left me weeping that it was only one day." Emerson went back to America, and the first letter in this collection is of the date of nine months later—May 1834. This letter contains, by the way, an allusion to Carlyle's situation at that time,

which, in the light thrown upon his state of mind and
circumstances at Craigenputtock by the "lonely scholar's"
own letters, journals, and reminiscences, may provoke a
smile. "I remembered with joy the favored condition of
my lonely philosopher, his happiest wedlock, his fortunate
temper, his steadfast simplicity, his all means of happiness
—not," Emerson indeed adds, "that I had the remotest
hope that he should so far depart from his theories as to
expect happiness." Carlyle's fortunate temper and steadfast simplicity sound today like bold touches of satire.
It is true that his idiosyncrasies were as yet more or less
undeveloped. The Correspondence speedily became brisk,
the more so that, in the winter of 1834–5, Carlyle had
settled himself in London, that life and work had opened
to him with a somewhat better promise, and that the
transmission to his American disciple of his new compositions offered repeated occasion for letters.

They pass with frequency for the following fifteen
years, when there is an interruption of a twelvemonth.
They begin again in 1850, and continue at the rate of
two or three a year, till 1856. After this they are less
frequent, though the mutual regard of the writers evidently knew no diminution. In 1872, Emerson went abroad
again (he had visited England for a second time in
1847); and after his return the letters cease. Many of
the early ones are occupied with the question of the
republication of Carlyle's writings in America. Emerson
took upon himself to present *Sartor Resartus* and some of
its successors to the American public, and he constantly
reports to the author upon the progress of this enterprise.
He transmits a great many booksellers' accounts as well
as a considerable number of bills of exchange, and among
the American publishers is a most faithful and zealous
representative of his friend. Some of these details, which
are very numerous, are tedious; but they are interesting
at the same time, and Mr. Norton has done well to

print them all. In the light of the present relations of British authors to the American public, they are curious reading. There appears to have been a fortunate moment (it was not of long duration) when it was possible for the British author to reap something of a harvest here. It would appear that, between 1838 and 1847, Emerson sent Carlyle some five hundred and thirty pounds, the proceeds of the sale of several of his works in this country. The sum is not large, but it must be measured by the profit that he had up to that time derived in England. It was in Boston that *Sartor Resartus*, with which the English publishers would have so little to do, first made its way into the light, after a precarious and abbreviated transit through *Fraser's Magazine*. "It will be a very brave day," Carlyle wrote in 1838, after Emerson had made arrangements for the issue of the *French Revolution* in Boston, "it will be a very brave day when cash actually reaches me, no matter what the *number* of the coins, whether seven or seven hundred, out of Yankee-land; and strange enough, what is not unlikely, if it be the *first* cash I realize for that piece of work— Angle-land continuing still *in*solvent to me." Six years later, in 1844, he writes, on the occasion of a remittance from Emerson of thirty-six pounds, "America, I think, is like an amiable family tea-pot; you think it is all out long since, and lo, the valuable implement yields you another cup, and another!" Encouragement had come to him from America as well as money; and there is something touching in the care with which Emerson assures him of the growth of his public on this side of the ocean, and of there being many ingenuous young persons of both sexes to whom his writings are as meat and drink. We had learned from Mr. Froude's publications that his beginnings were difficult; but this Correspondence throws a new light upon those grim years—I mean in exposing more definitely the fact that he was for some

time on the point of coming to seek his fortune in this
country. Both his own and Emerson's early letters are
full of allusions to this possible voyage: for Emerson, in
particular, the idea appears to have a fascination; he
returns to it again and again, keeps it constantly before
his correspondent, never ceases to express his desire that
Carlyle should embark for Boston. There was a plan of
his giving lectures in the United States, and Emerson, at
Carlyle's request, collects all possible information as to the
expenses and the rewards of such an attempt. It would
appear that the rewards of the lecturer's art, fifty years
ago, were extremely slender in comparison of what they
have since become; though it must be added that Emerson
gives a truly touching description of the cost of living.
One might have entertainment at the best hotels for the
sum of eight dollars a week. It is true that he gives us
no reassurance as to what the best hotels in America,
fifty years ago, may have been. Emerson offers his friend
the most generous hospitality; on his return from Europe,
he had married and settled himself at Concord. To Concord he entreats Mr. and Mrs. Carlyle to take their way;
their room is ready and their fire is made. The reader
at this point of the correspondence feels a certain suspense: he knows that Carlyle never did come to America,
but like a good novel the letters produce an illusion. He
holds his breath, for the terrible Scotchman may after all
have embarked, and there is something really almost
heart-shaking in the thought of his transporting that
tremendous imagination and those vessels of wrath and
sarcasm to an innocent New England village. The situation becomes dramatic, like the other incident I have
mentioned, in the presence of Emerson's serene good faith,
his eagerness for the arrival of such a cloud-compelling
host. The catastrophe never came off, however, and the
air of Concord was disturbed by no fumes more irritating
than the tonic emanations of Emerson's own genius. It
is impossible to imagine what the historian of the French

Revolution, of the iron-fisted Cromwell, and the Voltairean Frederick, would have made of that sensitive spot, or what Concord would have made of Carlyle.

Emerson, indeed, throughout had no hesitations on this score, and talked of the New England culture to his lurid correspondent without the least fear that his delicate specimens would be scorched. He sends him Mr. Alcott, he sends him Margaret Fuller, and others besides, who have a varying fortune at the little house in Cheyne Walk. It is true that Carlyle gave him constantly the encouragement of a high and eloquent esteem for his own utterances. He was evidently a great and genuine admirer of the genius, the spirit of his American friend, and he expresses this feeling on a dozen occasions.

"My friend! you know not what you have done for me there [in the oration of *The American Scholar*]. It was long decades of years that I had heard nothing but the infinite jangling and jabbering, and inarticulate twittering and screeching, and my soul had sunk down sorrowful and said there is no articulate speaking then any more, and thou art solitary among stranger-creatures; and lo, out of the West comes a clear utterance, clearly recognizable as a *man's* voice, and I *have* a kinsman and brother: God be thanked for it! I could have *wept* to read that speech; the clear high melody of it went tingling through my heart; I said to my wife, 'There, woman!' . . . My brave Emerson! And all this has been lying silent, quite tranquil in him, these seven years, and the 'vociferous platitude' dinning his ears on all sides, and he quietly answering no word; and a whole world of thought has silently built itself in these calm depths, and, the day having come, says quite softly, as if it were a common thing, 'Yes, *I am* here, too.' Miss Martineau tells me, 'Some say it is inspired; some say it is mad.' Exactly so; no *say* could be suitabler."

That is from a letter of 1837, and though at a later date (in 1850) he speaks of seeing "well enough what a great deep cleft divides us in our ways of practically looking at this world"; though, too (in 1842), he had already uttered a warning against Emerson's danger (with his fellow transcendentalists) of "soaring away . . . into perilous altitudes, beyond the curve of perpetual frost . . . and seeing nothing under one but the everlasting snows of Himmalayah"—the danger of "inanity and mere injuring of the lungs!"—though, as I say, he threw out his reflections upon certain inevitable disparities, his attitude toward the Concord philosopher remained (I have already noted it) an eminently hospitable one. "The rock-strata, miles deep, unite again; and the two poor souls are at one," he adds in the letter written in 1850, from which I have just quoted. When *English Traits* came out, Carlyle wrote: "Not for seven years and more have I got hold of such a Book;—Book by a real *man*, with eyes in his head; nobleness, wisdom, humor, and many other things in the heart of him. Such Books do not turn up often in the decade, in the century." He adds, indeed, rather unexpectedly: "In fact, I believe it to be worth all the Books ever written by New England upon Old." Carlyle speaks as if there had been an appreciable literature of that kind. It is faint praise to say that *English Traits* was the authority on the subject. He declares in another letter that "My Friend Emerson, alone of all voices out of America, has sphere-music in him for me." These words, written in 1843, are part of a paragraph in which Carlyle expresses his feelings with regard to the American "reforming" class at large. The high esteem in which he held his correspondent did not impel him to take an enthusiastic view of certain persons with whom, apparently, he supposed his correspondent to be in some degree associated. "Another Channing, whom I once saw here, sends me a 'Progress-of-the-Species' Periodical from New York. *Ach Gott!* These people and their affairs

seem all 'melting' rapidly enough into thaw-slush, or
one knows not what. Considerable madness is visible in
them . . . I am terribly sick of all that;—and wish it
would stay at home at Fruitland, or where there is good
pasture for it . . . [a] bottomless hubbub, which is not
all cheering." Several of the wanderers from "Fruitland"
knocked at his door, and he speaks of them to Emerson
with a humorous irreverence that contrasts character-
istically with Emerson's own tone of consideration (that
beautiful courtesy which he never lost) for the same
persons. One of them, "all bent on saving the world by a
return to acorns and the golden age," he desires to be
suffered to love him as he can, "and live on vegetables
in peace; as I, living *partly* on vegetables, will continue
to love him!" But he warns Emerson against the "English
Tail" of the same visitor, who, arrived in London, apparently had given away his confidence on terms too
easy. "Bottomless imbeciles ought not to be seen in company with Ralph Waldo Emerson, who has already
men listening to him on this side of the water." Of
Margaret Fuller, however—one of those who had attempted "the flight of the unwinged," as he calls it—
Carlyle speaks in the most affectionate though the most
discriminating manner:

> "Poor Margaret, that is a strange tragedy that history
> of hers, and has many traits of the Heroic in it,
> though it is wild as the prophecy of a Sybil. Such a
> predetermination to *eat* this big Universe as her oyster
> or her egg, and to be absolute empress of all height
> and glory in it that her heart could conceive, I have
> not before seen in any human soul. Her 'mountain
> *me*' indeed:—but her courage too is high and clear,
> her chivalrous nobleness indeed is great; her veracity,
> in its deepest sense, *à toute épreuve*."

It is difficult to resist quoting, where so much is quot-
able; but the better way is to urge the reader to go

straight to the book. Then he will find himself interested, even more than in the happy passages of characterization in which it abounds, in the reflection it offers of two contrasted characters of men of genius. With several qualities in common, Carlyle and Emerson diverged, in their total expression, with a completeness which is full of suggestion as to their differences of circumstance, race, association, temper. Both were men of the poetic quality, men of imagination; both were Puritans; both of them looked, instinctively, at the world, at life, as a great total, full of far-reaching relations; both of them set above everything else the importance of conduct— of what Carlyle called veracity and Emerson called harmony with the universe. Both of them had the desire, the passion, for something better—the reforming spirit, an interest in the destiny of mankind. But their variations of feeling were of the widest, and the temperament of the one was absolutely opposed to the temperament of the other. Both were men of the greatest purity and, in the usual sense, simplicity of life; each had a high ideal, each kept himself unspotted from the world. Their Correspondence is to an extraordinary degree the record, on either side, of a career with which nothing base, nothing interested, no worldly avidity, no vulgar vanity or personal error, was ever mingled—a career of public distinction and private honor. But with these things what disparities of tone, of manner, of inspiration! "Yet I think I shall never be killed by my ambition," Emerson writes in a letter of the date of 1841. "I behold my failures and shortcomings there in writing, wherein it would give me much joy to thrive, with an equanimity which my worst enemy might be glad to see. . . . My whole philosophy—which is very real—teaches acquiescence and optimism. Only when I see how much work is to be done, what room for a poet—for any spiritualist—in this great, intelligent, sensual, and avaricious America, I lament my fumbling fingers and stammering tongue." Emerson speaks the word in that passage; he was an optimist, and this in spite of the fact that he was the inspiration of the considerable body of persons who at that time, in New England, were seeking a better way. Carlyle, on the other hand, was a pessimist —a pessimist of pessimists—and this great difference between them includes many of the others. The American public has little more to learn in regard to the extreme amenity of Emerson, his eminently gentle spirit, his almost touching tolerance, his deference toward every sort of human manifestation; but many of his letters remind us afresh of his singular modesty of attitude and of his extreme consideration for that blundering human family whom he believed to be in want of light. His optimism makes us wonder at times where he discovered the errors that it would seem well to set right, and what there was in his view of the world on which the spirit of criticism could feed. He had a high and noble conception of good, without having, as it would appear, a definite conception of evil. The few words I have just quoted in regard to the America of 1841, "intelligent, sensual, and avaricious," have as sharp an ironical ring in them as any that I remember to have noticed in his part of the Correspondence. He has not a grain of current contempt; one feels, at times, that he has not enough. This salt is wanting in his taste of things. Carlyle, on the other hand, who has fearfully little amenity (save in his direct relation to Emerson, where he is admirable), has a vivid conception of evil without a corresponding conception of good. Curiously narrow and special, at least, were the forms in which he saw this latter spirit embodied. "For my heart is sick and sore on behalf of my own poor generation," he writes in 1842. "Nay, I feel withal as if the one hope of help for it consisted in the possibility of new Cromwells and new Puritans." Eleven years later, returning from a visit to Germany, he writes that "truly and really the Prussian soldiers, with their intelligent *silence*, with the touches of effective Spartanism I saw or fancied in them, were the class of people that pleased me best." There could be nothing more characteristic of Carlyle than this confession that such an impression as that was the most agreeable that he had brought back from a Continental tour. Emerson, by tradition and temperament, was as deeply rooted a Puritan as Carlyle; but he was a Puritan refined and sublimated, and a certain delicacy, a certain good taste would have prevented him from desiring (for the amelioration of mankind) so crude an occurrence as a return of the regiments of Oliver. Full of a local quality, with a narrow social horizon, he yet never would have ventured to plead so undisguisedly (in pretending to speak for the world at large) the cause of his own parish. Of that "current contempt" of which I just now spoke, Carlyle had more than enough. If it is humorous and half-compassionate in his moments of comparative tolerance, it is savage in his melancholy ones; and, in either case, it is full of the entertainment which comes from great expression. "Man, all men, seem radically dumb, jabbering mere jargons and noises from the teeth outward; the inner meaning of them—of them and of me, poor devils—remaining shut, buried forever. . . . Certainly could one generation of men be forced to live without rhetoric, babblement, hearsay, in short with the tongue well cut out of them altogether, their fortunate successors would find a most improved world to start upon!" Carlyle's pessimism was not only deep, but loud; not of the serene, but of the irritable sort. It is one of the strangest of things to find such an appreciation of silence in a mind that in itself was, before all things, expressive. Carlyle's expression was never more rich than when he declared that things were immeasurable, unutterable, not to be formulated. "The gospel of silence, in thirty volumes," that was a happy epigram of one of his critics; but it does not prevent us from believing that, after all, he really loved, as it were, the inarticulate. And we believe it for this reason, that the working of his own genius must have been accompanied with an extraordinary internal uproar, sensible to himself, and from which, in a kind of agony, he was forced to appeal. With the spectacle of human things resounding and reverberating in his head, awaking extraordinary echoes, it is no wonder that he had an ideal of the speechless. But his irritation communed happily for fifty years with Emerson's serenity; and the fact is very honorable to both.

"I have sometimes fancied I was to catch sympathetic activity from contact with noble persons," Emerson writes in a letter from which I have already quoted; "that you would come and see me; that I should form stricter habits of love and conversation with some men and women here who are already dear to me." That is the tone in which he speaks, for the most part, of his own life; and that was the tone which doubtless used to be natural in Concord. His letters are especially interesting for the impression they give us of what we may call the thinness of the New England atmosphere in those days—the thinness, and, it must be added, the purity. An almost touching lightness, sparseness transparency marked the social scenery in those days; and this impression, in Emerson's pages, is the greater by contrast with the echoes of the dense, warm life of London that are transmitted by his correspondent. One is reminded, as we remember being reminded in the perusal of Hawthorne's *American Notebooks,* of the importance of the individual in that simple social economy—of almost any individual who was not simply engaged in buying and selling. It must be remembered, of course, that the importance of the individual was Emerson's great doctrine; everyone had a kingdom within himself—was potential sovereign, by divine right, over a multitude of inspirations and virtues. No one maintained a more hospitable attitude than his toward anything that anyone might have to say.

There was no presumption against even the humblest, and the ear of the universe was open to any articulate voice. In this respect the opposition to Carlyle was complete. The great Scotchman thought *all* talk a jabbering of apes; whereas Emerson, who was the perfection of a listener, stood always in a posture of hopeful expectancy and regarded each delivery of a personal view as a new fact, to be estimated on its merits. In a genuine democracy all things are democratic; and this spirit of general deference, on the part of a beautiful poet who might have availed himself of the poetic license to be fastidious, was the natural product of a society in which it was held that everyone was equal to everyone else. It was as natural on the other side that Carlyle's philosophy should have aristocratic premises, and that he should call aloud for that imperial master, of the necessity for whom the New England mind was so serenely unconscious. Nothing is more striking in Emerson's letters than the way in which people are measured exclusively by their moral standards, designated by moral terms, described according to their morality. There was nothing else to describe them by. "A man named Bronson Alcott is great, and one of the jewels we have to show you. . . . A man named Bronson Alcott is a majestic soul, with whom conversation is possible. He is capable of the truth, and gives one the same glad astonishment that he should exist which the world does. . . . The man Alcott bides his time. —— —— is a beautiful and noble youth, of a most subtle and magnetic nature. . . . I have a young poet in the village named Thoreau, who writes the truest verses. I pine to show you my treasures. . . . One reader and friend of yours dwells now in my house, Henry Thoreau, a poet whom you may one day be proud of, a noble manly youth, full of melodies and inventions." Carlyle, who held melodies and inventions so cheap, was probably not a little irritated (though, faithful to his constant consideration for Emerson, he shows it but mildly) by this enumeration of characters so vaguely constituted. "In fact, I do again desiderate some *concretion* of these beautiful *abstracta*." That remark which he makes in regard to one of Emerson's discourses, might have been applied to certain of his friends. "The *Dial*, too, it is all spirit-like, aëriform, aurora-borealis-like. Will no *Angel* body himself out of that; no stalwart Yankee *man*, with color in the cheeks of him and a coat on his back?" Emerson speaks of his friends too much as if they were disembodied spirits. One doesn't see the color in the cheeks of them and the coats on their back. The fine touch in his letters, as in his other writings, is always the spiritual touch. For the rest, felicitous as they are, for the most part they suffer a little by comparison with Carlyle's; they are less natural, more composed, have too studied a quaintness. It was his practice, apparently, to make two drafts of these communications. The violent color, the large, avalanche-movement of Carlyle's style— as if a mass of earth and rock and vegetation had detached itself and came bouncing and bumping forward—make the efforts of his correspondent appear a little pale and stiff. There is always something high and pure in Emerson's speech, however, and it has often a perfect propriety —seeming, in answer to Carlyle's extravagances, the note of reason and justice. "Faith and love are apt to be spasmodic in the best minds. Men live on the brink of mysteries and harmonies into which they never enter, and with their hand on the door-latch they die outside."

Emerson's views of the world were what the world at all times thought highly peculiar; he neither believed nor thought nor spoke in the most apprehensible manner. He says himself (in 1840) that he is "gently mad"— surrounded, too, by a number of persons in the same condition. "I am gently mad myself and am resolved to live cleanly. George Ripley is talking up a colony of agriculturists and scholars, with whom he threatens to take the field and the book. One man renounces the use of animal food; and another of coin; and another of domestic hired service; and another of the State; and on the whole, we have a commendable share of reason and hope." But Emerson's "madness" was as mild as moonlight, compared with the strange commixture of the nature of his friend. If the main interest of these letters is, as I have said, their illustration of the character of the writers, the effect of Carlyle's portion of them is to deepen our sense, already sufficiently lively, of his enormous incongruities. Considerably sad, as he would have said himself, is the picture they present of a man of genius. One must allow, of course, for his extraordinary gift of expression, which set a premium on every sort of exaggeration; but even when one has done so, darkness and horror reside in every line of them. He is like a man hovering on the edge of insanity—hanging over a black gulf and wearing the reflection of its bottomless deeps in his face. His physical digestion was of the worst; but it was nothing compared with his moral digestion. Truly, he was not genial, and he was not gracious; as how should he have been in such conditions? He was born out of humor with life; he came into the world with an insurmountable prejudice; and to be genial and gracious naturally seemed of small importance in the face of the eternal veracities—veracities of such a grim and implacable sort. The strangest thing, among so many that were strange, was that his magnificent humor —that saving grace which has eased off the troubles of life for so many people who have been blessed with it —did so little to lighten his burden. Of this humor these volumes contain some admirable specimens—as in the description of "the brave Gambardella," the Neapolitan artist who comes to him with an introduction from Emerson; of the fish-eating Rio, historian of Christian Art; of the "loquacious, scriblacious" Heraud; of the "buckramed and mummy-swathed" Miss Martineau, and many more besides. His humor was in truth not of comic but of tragic intention, and not so much a flame as an all-enveloping smoke. His treatment of all things is the humorous—unfortunately in too many cases the ill-humorous. He even hated his work—hated his subjects. These volumes are a sort of record of the long weariness and anguish (as one may indeed call it) with which he struggled through his *Cromwell*, his *French Revolution*, and the history of Frederick. He thought, after all, very little of Frederick, and he detested the age in which he lived, the "putrid eighteenth century—an ocean of sordid nothingness, shams, and scandalous hypocrisies." He achieved a noble quantity of work, but all the while he found no inspiration in it. "The reason that I tell you nothing about Cromwell is, alas, that there is nothing to be told. I am, day and night, these long months and years, very miserable about it—nigh broken-hearted often. . . . No history of it *can* be written to this wretched, fleering, sneering, canting, twaddling, God-forgetting generation. How can I explain men to Apes by the Dead Sea?" Other persons have enjoyed life as little as Carlyle; other men have been pessimists and cynics; but few men have rioted so in their disenchantments, or thumped so perpetually upon the hollowness of things with the view of making it resound. Pessimism, cynicism, usually imply a certain amount of indifference and resignation; but in Carlyle these forces were nothing if not querulous and vocal. It must be remembered that he had an imagination which made acquiescence difficult—an imagination haunted with theological and apocalyptic visions. We have no occasion here to attempt to estimate his position in literature, but we may be permitted to say that it is mainly to this splendid imagination that he owes it. Both the moral and the physical world were full of pictures for him, and it would seem to be by his great pictorial energy that he will live. To get an idea of the solidity and sincerity of this gift one must read his notes on a tour in Ireland in 1849; it is a revelation of his attention to external things and his perception of the internal states that they express. His doctrine, reduced to the fewest words, is that life is very serious and that everyone should do his work honestly. This is the gist of the matter; all the rest is magnificent vocalization. We call it magnificent, in spite of the fact that many people find him unreadable on account of his unprecedented form. His extemporized, empirical style, however, seems to us the very substance of his thought. If the merit of a style lies in complete correspondence with the feeling of the writer, Carlyle's is one of the best. It is not defensible, but it is victorious; and if it is neither homogeneous, nor, at times, coherent, it bristles with all manner of felicities. It is true, nevertheless, that he had invented a manner, and that his manner had swallowed him up. To look at realities and not at imitations is what he constantly and sternly enjoins; but all the while he gives us the sense that it is not at things themselves, but straight into this abysmal manner of his own that he is looking.

All this, of course, is a very incomplete account of him. So large a genius is full of interest of detail, and in the application in special cases of that doctrine of his which seems so simple there is often the greatest suggestiveness. When he does look *through* his own manner into the vivid spots of history, then he sees more in them than almost anyone else. We may add that no account of him would have even a slight completeness which should fail to cite him as a signal instance of the force of local influences, of the qualities of race and soil. Carlyle was intensely of the stock of which he sprang, and he remained so to the end. No man of equal genius was probably ever less of a man of the world at large—more exclusively a product of his locality, his clan, his family. Readers of his *Reminiscences* and of Mr. Froude's memoir will remember how the peasant-group in which he was born—his parents, his brothers and sisters—appeared to constitute one of the great facts of the universe for him;

and we mean not as a son and a brother simply, but as a student of human affairs. He was impressed, as it were, with the historical importance of his kinsfolk. And as one finds a little of everything in a man of genius, we find a great deal of tenderness even in the grimness of Carlyle; so that we may say, as the last word of all (for it qualifies our implication that he was narrow), that his tenderness was never greater than when, in spite of the local limitation, he stretched across the ocean, in gratitude for early sympathy, for early services, and held fast to the friendship of Emerson. His family was predominant for him, as we say, and he cleaved to his relations, to his brothers. But it was as a brother that he addressed Emerson.

EMERSON

MR. ELLIOT CABOT has made a very interesting contribution to a class of books of which our literature, more than any other, offers admirable examples: he has given us a biography[1] intelligently and carefully composed. These two

---

[1] *A Memoir of Ralph Waldo Emerson;* by James Elliot Cabot. (Two volumes; London, 1887.) First published in *Macmillan's Magazine*, December 1887, this essay was reprinted by James in *Partial Portraits* (1888).

volumes are a model of responsible editing—I use that
term because they consist largely of letters and extracts
from letters: nothing could resemble less the manner in
which the mere bookmaker strings together his frequently
questionable pearls and shovels the heap into the presence
of the public. Mr. Cabot has selected, compared, dis-
criminated, steered an even course between meagerness
and redundancy, and managed to be constantly and happily illustrative. And his work, moreover, strikes us as the
better done from the fact that it stands for one of the two
things that make an absorbing memoir a good deal more
than for the other. If these two things be the conscience
of the writer and the career of his hero, it is not difficult
to see on which side the biographer of Emerson has found
himself strongest. Ralph Waldo Emerson was a man of
genius, but he led for nearly eighty years a life in which
the sequence of events had little of the rapidity, or the
complexity, that a spectator loves. There is something we
miss very much as we turn these pages—something that
has a kind of accidental, inevitable presence in almost
any personal record—something that may be most definitely indicated under the name of color. We lay down
the book with a singular impression of paleness—an impression that comes partly from the tone of the biographer
and partly from the moral complexion of his subject, but
mainly from the vacancy of the page itself. That of
Emerson's personal history is condensed into the single
word Concord, and all the condensation in the world will
not make it look rich. It presents a most continuous surface. Mr. Matthew Arnold, in his *Discourses in America*,
contests Emerson's complete right to the title of a man
of letters; yet letters surely were the very texture of his
history. Passions, alternations, affairs, adventures had absolutely no part in it. It stretched itself out in enviable
quiet—a quiet in which we hear the jotting of the pencil
in the notebook. It is the very life for literature (I mean
for one's own, not that of another): fifty years of resi-

dence in the home of one's forefathers, pervaded by reading, by walking in the woods and the daily addition of sentence to sentence.

If the interest of Mr. Cabot's penciled portrait is incontestable and yet does not spring from variety, it owes nothing, either, to a source from which it might have borrowed much and which it is impossible not to regret a little that he has so completely neglected: I mean a greater reference to the social conditions in which Emerson moved, the company he lived in, the moral air he breathed. If his biographer had allowed himself a little more of the ironic touch, had put himself once in a way under the protection of Sainte-Beuve and had attempted something of a general picture, we should have felt that he only went with the occasion. I may overestimate the latent treasures of the field, but it seems to me there was distinctly an opportunity—an opportunity to make up moreover in some degree for the white tint of Emerson's career considered simply in itself. We know a man imperfectly until we know his society, and we but half know a society until we know its manners. This is especially true of a man of letters, for manners lie very close to literature. From those of the New England world in which Emerson's character formed itself Mr. Cabot almost averts his lantern, though we feel sure that there would have been delightful glimpses to be had and that he would have been in a position—that is, that he has all the knowledge that would enable him—to help us to them. It is as if he could not trust himself, knowing the subject only too well. This adds to the effect of extreme discretion that we find in his volumes, but it is the cause of our not finding certain things, certain figures and scenes, evoked. What is evoked is Emerson's pure spirit, by a copious, sifted series of citations and comments. But we must read as much as possible between the lines, and the picture of the transcendental time (to mention simply one corner) has yet to be painted—the lines have yet to be bitten in. Meanwhile we are held and charmed by the image of Emerson's mind and the extreme appeal which his physiognomy makes to our art of discrimination. It is so fair, so uniform and impersonal, that its features are simply fine shades, the gradations of tone of a surface whose proper quality was of the smoothest and on which nothing was reflected with violence. It is a pleasure of the critical sense to find, with Mr. Cabot's extremely intelligent help, a notation for such delicacies.

We seem to see the circumstances of our author's origin, immediate and remote, in a kind of high, vertical moral light, the brightness of a society at once very simple and very responsible. The rare singleness that was in his nature (so that he was *all* the warning moral voice, without distraction or counter-solicitation), was also in the stock he sprang from, clerical for generations, on both sides, and clerical in the Puritan sense. His ancestors had lived long (for nearly two centuries) in the same corner of New England, and during that period had preached and studied and prayed and practiced. It is impossible to imagine a spirit better prepared in advance to be exactly what it was—better educated for its office in its far-away unconscious beginnings. There is an inner satisfaction in seeing so straight, although so patient, a connection between the stem and the flower, and such a proof that when life wishes to produce something exquisite in quality she takes her measures many years in advance. A conscience like Emerson's could not have been turned off, as it were, from one generation to another: a succession of attempts, a long process of refining was required. His perfection, in his own line, comes largely from the non-interruption of the process.

As most of us are made up of ill-assorted pieces, his reader, and Mr. Cabot's, envies him this transmitted unity, in which there was no mutual hustling or crowding of elements. It must have been a kind of luxury to be—that is to feel—so homogeneous, and it helps to account for his serenity, his power of acceptance, and that absence of personal passion which makes his private correspondence read like a series of beautiful circulars or expanded cards *pour prendre congé*. He had the equanimity of a result; nature had taken care of him and he had only to speak. He accepted himself as he accepted others, accepted everything; and his absence of eagerness, or in other words his modesty, was that of a man with whom it is not a question of success, who has nothing invested or at stake. The investment, the stake, was that of the race, of all the past Emersons and Bulkeleys and Waldos. There is much that makes us smile, today, in the commotion produced by his secession from the mild Unitarian pulpit: we wonder at a condition of opinion in which any utterance of his should appear to be wanting in superior piety—in the essence of good instruction. All that is changed: the great difference has become the infinitely small, and we admire a state of society in which scandal and schism took on no darker hue; but there is even yet a sort of drollery in the spectacle of a body of people among whom the author of *The American Scholar* and of the Address of 1838 at the Harvard Divinity College passed for profane, and who failed to see that he only gave his plea for the spiritual life the advantage of a brilliant expression. They were so provincial as to think that brilliancy came ill-recommended, and they were shocked at his ceasing to care for the prayer and the sermon. They might have perceived that he *was* the prayer and the sermon: not in the least a secularizer, but in his own subtle insinuating way a sanctifier.

Of the three periods into which his life divides itself, the first was (as in the case of most men) that of movement, experiment, and selection—that of effort too and painful probation. Emerson had his message, but he was a good while looking for his form—the form which, as he himself would have said, he never completely found and of which it was rather characteristic of him that his later years (with their growing refusal to give him the *word*), wishing to attack him in his most vulnerable point, where his tenure was least complete, had in some degree the effect of despoiling him. It all sounds rather bare and stern, Mr. Cabot's account of his youth and early manhood, and we get an impression of a terrible paucity of alternatives. If he would be neither a farmer nor a trader he could "teach school"; that was the main resource and a part of the general educative process of the young New Englander who proposed to devote himself to the things of the mind. There was an advantage in the nudity, however, which was that, in Emerson's case at least, the things of the mind did get themselves admirably well considered. If it be his great distinction and his special sign that he had a more vivid conception of the moral life than anyone else, it is probably not fanciful to say that he owed it in part to the limited way in which he saw our capacity for living illustrated. The plain, God-fearing, practical society which surrounded him was not fertile in variations: it had great intelligence and energy, but it moved altogether in the straightforward direction. On three occasions later—three journeys to Europe—he was introduced to a more complicated world; but his spirit, his moral taste, as it were, abode always within the undecorated walls of his youth. There he could dwell with that ripe unconsciousness of evil which is one of the most beautiful signs by which we know him. His early writings are full of quaint animadversion upon the vices of the place and time, but there is something charmingly vague, light, and general in the arraignment. Almost the worst he can say is that these vices are negative and that his fellow-townsmen are not heroic. We feel that his first impressions were gathered in a community from which misery and extravagance, and either extreme, of any sort, were equally absent. What the life of New England fifty years ago offered to the observer was the common lot, in a kind of achromatic picture, without particular intensifications. It was from this table of the usual, the merely typical joys and sorrows that he proceeded to generalize—a fact that accounts in some degree for a certain inadequacy and thinness in his enumerations. But it helps to account also for his direct, intimate vision of the soul itself—not in its emotions, its contortions and perversions, but in its passive, exposed, yet healthy form. He knows the nature of man and the long tradition of its dangers; but we feel that whereas he can put his finger on the remedies, lying for the most part, as they do, in the deep recesses of virtue, of the spirit, he has only a kind of hearsay, uninformed acquaintance with the disorders. It would require some ingenuity, the reader may say too much, to trace closely this correspondence between his genius and the frugal, dutiful, happy but decidedly lean Boston of the past, where there was a great deal of will but very little fulcrum—like a ministry without an opposition.

The genius itself it seems to me impossible to contest—I mean the genius for seeing character as a real and supreme thing. Other writers have arrived at a more complete expression: Wordsworth and Goethe, for instance, give one a sense of having found their form, whereas with Emerson we never lose the sense that he is still seeking it. But no one has had so steady and constant, and above all so natural, a vision of what we require and what we are capable of in the way of aspiration and independence. With Emerson it is ever the special capacity for moral experience—always that and only that. We have the impression, somehow, that life had never bribed him to look at anything but the soul; and indeed in the world in which he grew up and lived the bribes and lures, the beguilements and prizes, were few. He was in an admirable position for showing, what he constantly endeavored to show, that the prize was within. Anyone who in New England at that time could do that was sure of success, of listeners and sympathy: most of all, of course, when it was a question of doing it with such a divine persuasiveness. Moreover, the way in which Emerson did it added to the charm—by word of mouth, face to face, with a rare, irresistible voice and a beautiful mild, modest authority. If Mr. Arnold is struck with the limited degree in which he was a man of letters, I suppose it is because he is more struck with his having been, as it were, a man of lectures. But the lecture surely was never more purged of its grossness—the quality in it that suggests a strong light and a big brush—than as it issued from Emerson's lips; so far from being a vulgarization, it was simply the esoteric made audible, and instead of treating the few as the many, after the usual fashion of gentlemen on platforms, he treated the many as the few. There was probably no other society at that time in which he would have got so many persons to understand that; for we think the better of his audience as we read him, and wonder where else people would have had so much moral attention to give. It is to be remembered however that during the winter of 1847–8, on the occasion of his second visit to England, he found many listeners in London and in provincial cities. Mr. Cabot's volumes are full of evidence of the satisfactions he offered, the delights and revelations he may be said to have promised, to a race which had to seek its entertainment, its rewards and consolations, almost exclusively in the moral world. But his own writings are fuller still; we find an instance almost wherever we open them.

"All these great and transcendent properties are ours. . . . Let us find room for this great guest in our small houses. . . . Where the heart is, there the muses, there the gods sojourn, and not in any geography of fame. Massachusetts, Connecticut River, and Boston Bay, you think paltry places, and the ear loves names of foreign and classic topography. But here we are, and if we will tarry a little we may come to

learn that here is best. . . . The Jerseys were hand-
some enough ground for Washington to tread, and
London streets for the feet of Milton. . . . That country is fairest which is inhabited by the noblest minds."

We feel, or suspect, that Milton is thrown in as a hint
that the London streets are no such great place, and it all
sounds like a sort of pleading consolation against bleak-
ness.

The beauty of a hundred passages of this kind in
Emerson's pages is that they are effective, that they do
come home, that they rest upon insight and not upon
ingenuity, and that if they are sometimes obscure it is
never with the obscurity of paradox. We seem to see the
people turning out into the snow after hearing them,
glowing with a finer glow than even the climate could
give and fortified for a struggle with overshoes and the
east wind.

"Look to it first and only, that fashion, custom, authority, pleasure, and money, are nothing to you, are
not as bandages over your eyes, that you cannot see;
but live with the privilege of the immeasurable mind.
Not too anxious to visit periodically all families and
each family in your parish connection, when you meet
one of these men or women be to them a divine man;
be to them thought and virtue; let their timid aspira-
tions find in you a friend; let their trampled instincts be
genially tempted out in your atmosphere; let their
doubts know that you have doubted, and their wonder
feel that you have wondered."

When we set against an exquisite passage like that, or like
the familiar sentences that open the essay on History
("He that is admitted to the right of reason is made free-
man of the whole estate. What Plato has thought, he may
think; what a saint has felt, he may feel; what at any time
has befallen any man, he can understand"); when we

compare the letters, cited by Mr. Cabot, to his wife from
Springfield, Illinois (January 1853), we feel that his spiritual tact needed to be very just, but that if it was so it
must have brought a blessing.

> "Here I am in the deep mud of the prairies, misled I
> fear into this bog, not by a will-of-the-wisp, such as
> shine in bogs, but by a young New Hampshire editor,
> who over-estimated the strength of both of us, and
> fancied I should glitter in the prairie and draw the
> prairie birds and waders. It rains and thaws incessantly,
> and if we step off the short street we go up to the
> shoulders, perhaps, in mud. My chamber is a cabin; my
> fellow-boarders are legislators. . . . Two or three gov-
> ernors or ex-governors live in the house. . . . I cannot
> command daylight and solitude for study or for more
> than a scrawl." . . .

And another extract:—

> "A cold, raw country this, and plenty of night-travel-
> ling and arriving at four in the morning to take the
> last and worst bed in the tavern. Advancing day brings
> mercy and favour to me, but not the sleep. . . . Mer-
> cury 15° below zero. . . . I find well-disposed, kindly
> people among these sinewy farmers of the North, but
> in all that is called cultivation they are only ten years
> old."

He says in another letter (in 1860): "I saw Michigan and
its forests and the Wolverines pretty thoroughly"; and
on another page Mr. Cabot shows him as speaking of his
engagements to lecture in the West as the obligation to
"wade, and freeze, and ride, and run, and suffer all manner
of indignities." This was not New England, but as regards
the country districts throughout, at that time, it was a
question of degree. Certainly never was the fine wine of
philosophy carried to remoter or queerer corners: never
was a more delicate diet offered to "two or three gover-

nors, or ex-governors," living in a cabin. It was Mercury, shivering in a mackintosh, bearing nectar and ambrosia to the gods whom he wished those who lived in cabins to endeavor to feel that they might be.

I have hinted that the will, in the old New England society, was a clue without a labyrinth; but it had its use, nevertheless, in helping the young talent to find its mold. There were few or none ready-made: tradition was certainly not so oppressive as might have been inferred from the fact that the air swarmed with reformers and improvers. Of the patient, philosophic manner in which Emerson groped and waited, through teaching the young and preaching to the adult, for his particular vocation, Mr. Cabot's first volume gives a full and orderly account. His passage from the Unitarian pulpit to the lecture-desk was a step which at this distance of time can hardly help appearing to us short, though he was long in making it, for even after ceasing to have a parish of his own he freely confounded the two, or willingly, at least, treated the pulpit as a platform. "The young people and the mature hint at odium and the aversion of faces, to be presently encountered in society," he writes in his journal in 1838; but in point of fact the quiet drama of his abdication was not to include the note of suffering. The Boston world might feel disapproval, but it was far too kindly to make this sentiment felt as a weight: every element of martyrdom was there but the important ones of the cause and the persecutors. Mr. Cabot marks the lightness of the penalties of dissent; if they were light in somewhat later years for the transcendentalists and fruit-eaters they could press but little on a man of Emerson's distinction, to whom, all his life, people went not to carry but to ask the right word. There was no consideration to give up, he could not have been one of the dingy if he had tried; but what he did renounce in 1838 was a material profession. He was "settled," and his indisposition to administer the communion unsettled him. He calls the whole business, in writing to Carlyle, "a tempest in our wash-bowl"; but it had the effect of forcing him to seek a new source of income. His wants were few and his view of life severe, and this came to him, little by little, as he was able to extend the field in which he read his discourses. In 1835, upon his second marriage, he took up his habitation at Concord, and his life fell into the shape it was, in a general way, to keep for the next half-century. It is here that we cannot help regretting that Mr. Cabot had not found it possible to treat his career a little more pictorially. Those fifty years of Concord—at least the earlier part of them—would have been a subject bringing into play many odd figures, many human incongruities: they would have abounded in illustrations of the primitive New England character, especially during the time of its queer search for something to expend itself upon. Objects and occupations have multiplied since then, and now there is no lack; but fifty years ago the expanse was wide and free, and we get the impression of a conscience gasping in the void, panting for sensations, with something of the movement of the gills of a landed fish. It would take a very fine point to sketch Emerson's benignant, patient, inscrutable countenance during the various phases of this democratic communion; but the picture, when complete, would be one of the portraits, half a revelation and half an enigma, that suggest and fascinate. Such a striking personage as old Miss Mary Emerson, our author's aunt, whose high intelligence and temper were much of an influence in his earlier years, has a kind of tormenting representative value: we want to see her from head to foot, with her frame and her background; having (for we happen to have it) an impression that she was a very remarkable specimen of the transatlantic Puritan stock, a spirit that would have dared the devil. We miss a more liberal handling, are tempted to add touches of our own, and end by convincing ourselves that Miss Mary Moody Emerson, grim intellectual virgin and daughter of a hundred

ministers, with her local traditions and her combined love
of empire and of speculation, would have been an inspiration for a novelist. Hardly less so the charming Mrs.
Ripley, Emerson's life-long friend and neighbor, most
delicate and accomplished of women, devoted to Greek
and to her house, studious, simple, and dainty—an admirable example of the old-fashioned New England lady.
It was a freak of Miss Emerson's somewhat sardonic humor to give her once a broomstick to carry across Boston
Common (under the pretext of a "moving"), a task accepted with docility but making of the victim the most
benignant witch ever equipped with that utensil.

These ladies, however, were very private persons and
not in the least of the reforming tribe: there are others
who would have peopled Mr. Cabot's page to whom he
gives no more than a mention. We must add that it is
open to him to say that their features have become faint
and indistinguishable today without more research than
the question is apt to be worth: they are embalmed—in a
collective way—the apprehensible part of them, in Mr.
Frothingham's clever *History of Transcendentalism in
New England*. This must be admitted to be true of even
so lively a "factor," as we say nowadays, as the imaginative, talkative, intelligent, and finally Italianized and
shipwrecked Margaret Fuller: she is now one of the dim,
one of Carlyle's "then-celebrated" at most. It seemed indeed as if Mr. Cabot rather grudged her a due place in the
record of the company that Emerson kept, until we came
across the delightful letter he quotes toward the end of
his first volume—a letter interesting both as a specimen
of inimitable, imperceptible edging away, and as an illustration of the curiously generalized way, as if with an
implicit protest against personalities, in which his intercourse, epistolary and other, with his friends was conducted. There is an extract from a letter to his aunt on the
occasion of the death of a deeply loved brother (his own)
which reads like a passage from some fine old chastened

essay on the vanity of earthly hopes: strangely unfamiliar, considering the circumstances. Courteous and humane to the furthest possible point, to the point of an almost profligate surrender of his attention, there was no familiarity in him, no personal evidity. Even his letters to his wife are courtesies, they are not familiarities. He had only one style, one manner, and he had it for everything—even for himself, in his notes, in his journals. But he had it in perfection for Miss Fuller; he retreats, smiling and flattering, on tiptoe, as if he were advancing. "She ever seems to crave," he says in his journal, "something which I have not, or have not for her." What he had was doubtless not what she craved, but the letter in question should be read to see how the modicum was administered. It is only between the lines of such a production that we read that a part of her effect upon him was to bore him; for his system was to practice a kind of universal passive hospitality—he aimed at nothing less. It was only because he was so deferential that he could be so detached; he had polished his aloofness till it reflected the image of his solicitor. And this was not because he was an "uncommunicating egotist," though he amuses himself with saying so to Miss Fuller: egotism is the strongest of passions, and he was altogether passionless. It was because he had no personal, just as he had almost no physical wants. "Yet I plead not guilty to the malice prepense. 'Tis imbecility, not contumacy, though perhaps somewhat more odious. It seems very just, the irony with which you ask whether you may not be trusted and promise such docility. Alas, we will all promise, but the prophet loiters." He would not say even to himself that she bored him; he had denied himself the luxury of such easy and obvious short cuts. There is a passage in the lecture (1844) called "Man the Reformer" in which he hovers round and round the idea that the practice of trade, in certain conditions likely to beget an underhand competition, does not draw for the nobler parts of character, till the reader is tempted to interrupt him with "Say at once that it is impossible for a gentleman!"

So he remained always, reading his lectures in the winter, writing them in the summer, and at all seasons taking wood-walks and looking for hints in old books.

"Delicious summer stroll through the pastures. . . . On the steep park of Conantum I have the old regret—is all this beauty to perish? Shall none re-make this sun and wind; the sky-blue river; the river-blue sky; the yellow meadow, spotted with sacks and sheets of cranberry-gatherers; the red bushes; the iron-gray house, just the colour of the granite rocks; the wild orchard?"

His observation of Nature was exquisite—always the direct, irresistible impression.

"The hawking of the wild geese flying by night; the thin note of the companionable titmouse in the winter day; the fall of swarms of flies in autumn, from combats high in the air, pattering down on the leaves like rain; the angry hiss of the wood-birds; the pine throwing out its pollen for the benefit of the next century." . . . (*Literary Ethics.*)

I have said their was no familiarity in him, but he was familiar with woodland creatures and sounds. Certainly, too, he was on terms of free association with his books, which were numerous and dear to him; though Mr. Cabot says, doubtless with justice, that his dependence on them was slight and that he was not "intimate" with his authors. They did not feed him but they stimulated; they were not his meat but his wine—he took them in sips. But he needed them and liked them; he had volumes of notes from his reading, and he could not have produced his lectures without them. He liked literature as a thing to refer to, liked the very names of which it is full, and used them, especially in his later writings, for purposes of ornament, to dress the dish, sometimes with an un-measured profusion. I open *The Conduct of Life* and find a dozen on the page. He mentions more authorities than is the fashion today. He can easily say, of course, that he follows a better one—that of his well-loved and irrepress-ibly allusive Montaigne. In his own bookishness there is a certain contradiction, just as there is a latent incomplete-ness in his whole literary side. Independence, the return to nature, the finding out and doing for one's self, was ever what he most highly recommended; and yet he is constantly reminding his readers of the conventional signs and consecrations—of what other men have done. This was partly because the independence that he had in his eye was an independence without ill nature, without rude-ness (though he likes that word), and full of gentle amiabilities, curiosities, and tolerances; and partly it is a simple matter of form, a literary expedient, confessing its character—on the part of one who had never really mastered the art of composition—of continuous expres-sion. Charming to many a reader, charming yet ever slightly droll, will remain Emerson's frequent invocation of the "scholar": there is such a friendly vagueness and convenience in it. It is of the scholar that he expects all the heroic and uncomfortable things, the concentrations and relinquishments, that make up the noble life. We fancy this personage looking up from his book and arm-chair a little ruefully and saying: "Ah, but why *me* always and only? Why so much of me, and is there no one else to share the responsibility?" "Neither years nor books have yet availed to extirpate a prejudice then rooted in me [when as a boy he first saw the graduates of his col-lege assembled at their anniversary], that a scholar is the favorite of heaven and earth, the excellency of his country, the happiest of men."

In truth, by this term he means simply the cultivated man, the man who has had a liberal education, and there is a voluntary plainness in his use of it—speaking of such

people as the rustic, or the vulgar, speak of those who
have a tincture of books. This is characteristic of his
humility—that humility which was nine tenths a plain
fact (for it is easy for persons who have at bottom a great
fund of indifference to be humble), and the remaining
tenth a literary habit. Moreover an American reader may
be excused for finding in it a pleasant sign of that prestige,
often so quaintly and indeed so extravagantly acknowledged, which a connection with literature carries with it
among the people of the United States. There is no
country in which it is more freely admitted to be a distinction—*the* distinction; or in which so many persons
have become eminent for showing it even in a slight degree. Gentlemen and ladies are celebrated there on this
ground who would not on the same ground, though they
might on another, be celebrated anywhere else. Emerson's
own tone is an echo of that, when he speaks of the scholar
—not of the banker, the great merchant, the legislator, the
artist—as the most distinguished figure in the society
about him. It is because he has most to give up that he is
appealed to for efforts and sacrifices. "Meantime I know
that a very different estimate of the scholar's profession
prevails in this country," he goes on to say in the address
from which I last quoted (the *Literary Ethics*), "and the
importunity with which society presses its claim upon
young men tends to pervert the views of the youth in respect to the culture of the intellect." The manner in which
that is said represents, surely, a serious mistake: with the
estimate of the scholar's profession which then prevailed in New England Emerson could have had no quarrel; the ground of his lamentation was another side of the
matter. It was not a question of estimate, but of accidental
practice. In 1838 there were still so many things of prime
material necessity to be done that reading was driven to
the wall; but the reader was still thought the cleverest,
for he found time as well as intelligence. Emerson's own
situation sufficiently indicates it. In what other country,

on sleety winter nights, would provincial and bucolic populations have gone forth in hundreds for the cold comfort of a literary discourse? The distillation anywhere else would certainly have appeared too thin, the appeal too special. But for many years the American people of the middle regions, outside of a few cities, had in the most rigorous seasons no other recreation. A gentleman, grave or gay, in a bare room, with a manuscript, before a desk, offered the reward of toil, the refreshment of pleasure, to the young, the middle-aged, and the old of both sexes. The hour was brightest, doubtless, when the gentleman was gay, like Doctor Oliver Wendell Holmes. But Emerson's gravity never sapped his career, any more than it chilled the regard in which he was held among those who were particularly his own people. It was impossible to be more honored and cherished, far and near, than he was during his long residence in Concord, or more looked upon as the principal gentleman in the place. This was conspicuous to the writer of these remarks on the occasion of the curious, sociable, cheerful public funeral made for him in 1883 by all the countryside, arriving, as for the last honors to the first citizen, in trains, in wagons, on foot, in multitudes. It was a popular manifestation, the most striking I have ever seen provoked by the death of a man of letters.

If a picture of that singular and very illustrative institution the old American lecture-system would have constituted a part of the filling-in of the ideal memoir of Emerson, I may further say, returning to the matter for a moment, that such a memoir would also have had a chapter for some of those Concord-haunting figures which are not so much interesting in themselves as interesting because for a season Emerson thought them so. And the pleasure of that would be partly that it would push us to inquire how interesting he did really think them. That is, it would bring up the question of his inner reserves and skepticisms, his secret ennuis and ironies, the way he sympathized for courtesy and then, with his delicacy and generosity, in a world after all given much to the literal, let his courtesy pass for adhesion—a question particularly attractive to those for whom he has, in general, a fascination. Many entertaining problems of that sort present themselves for such readers: there is something indefinable for them in the mixture of which he was made—his fidelity as an interpreter of the so-called transcendental spirit and his freedom from all wish for any personal share in the effect of his ideas. He drops them, sheds them, diffuses them, and we feel as if there would be a grossness in holding him to anything so temporal as a responsibility. He had the advantage, for many years, of having the question of application assumed for him by Thoreau, who took upon himself to be, in the concrete, the sort of person that Emerson's "scholar" was in the abstract, and who paid for it by having a shorter life than that fine adumbration. The application, with Thoreau, was violent and limited (it became a matter of prosaic detail, the non-payment of taxes, the non-wearing of a necktie, the preparation of one's food one's self, the practice of a rude sincerity—all things not of the essence), so that, though he wrote some beautiful pages, which read like a translation of Emerson into the sounds of the field and forest and which no one who has ever loved nature in New England, or indeed anywhere, can fail to love, he suffers something of the *amoindrissement* of eccentricity. His master escapes that reduction altogether. I call it an advantage to have had such a pupil as Thoreau; because for a mind so much made up of reflection as Emerson's everything comes under that head which prolongs and reanimates the process—produces the return, again and yet again, on one's impressions. Thoreau must have had this moderating and even chastening effect. It did not rest, moreover, with him alone; the advantage of which I speak was not confined to Thoreau's case. In 1837 Emerson (in his journal) pronounced Mr. Bronson Alcott the most extraordinary man and the highest genius of his time: the sequence of which was that for more than forty years after that he had the gentleman living but half a mile away. The opportunity for the return, as I have called it, was not wanting.

His detachment is shown in his whole attitude toward the transcendental movement—that remarkable outburst of Romanticism on Puritan ground, as Mr. Cabot very well names it. Nothing can be more ingenious, more sympathetic and charming, than Emerson's account and definition of the matter in his lecture (of 1842) called "The Transcendentalist"; and yet nothing is more apparent from his letters and journals than that he regarded any such label or banner as a mere tiresome flutter. He liked to taste but not to drink—least of all to become intoxicated. He liked to explain the transcendentalists but did not care at all to be explained by them: a doctrine "whereof you know I am wholly guiltless," he says to his wife in 1842, "and which is spoken of as a known and fixed element, like salt or meal. So that I have to begin with endless disclaimers and explanations: 'I am not the man you take me for.'" He was never the man anyone took him for, for the simple reason that no one could possibly take him for the elusive, irreducible, merely gustatory spirit for which he took himself.

"It is a sort of maxim with me never to harp on the omnipotence of limitations. Least of all do we need any suggestion of checks and measures; as if New England were anything else. . . . Of so many fine people it is true that being so much they ought to be a little more, and missing that are naught. It is a sort of King René period; there is no doing, but rare thrilling prophecy from bands of competing minstrels."

That is his private expression about a large part of a ferment in regard to which his public judgment was that

"That indeed constitutes a new feature in their portrait, that they are the most exacting and extortionate
critics. . . . These exacting children advertise us of our
wants. There is no compliment, no smooth speech with
them; they pay you only this one compliment of insatiable expectation; they aspire, they severely exact, and
if they only stand fast in this watch-tower, and stand
fast unto the end, and without end, then they are terrible friends, whereof poet and priest cannot but stand
in awe; and what if they eat clouds and drink wind,
they have not been without service to the race of man."

That was saying the best for them, as he always said
it for everything; but it was the sense of their being
"bands of competing minstrels" and their camp being only
a "measure and check," in a society too sparse for a synthesis, that kept him from wishing to don their uniform.
This was after all but a misfitting imitation of his natural
wear, and what he would have liked was to put that off—
he did not wish to button it tighter. He said the best for
his friends of the *Dial,* of Fruitlands and Brook Farm, in
saying that they were fastidious and critical; but he was
conscious in the next breath that what there was around
them to be criticized was mainly a negative. Nothing is
more perceptible today than that their criticism produced
no fruit—that it was little else than a very decent and
innocent recreation—a kind of Puritan carnival. The New
England world was for much the most part very busy,
but the *Dial* and Fruitlands and Brook Farm were the
amusement of the leisure-class. Extremes meet, and as in
older societies that class is known principally by its connection with castles and carriages, so at Concord it came,
with Thoreau and Mr. W. H. Channing, out of the cabin
and the wood-lot.

Emerson was not moved to believe in their fastidious-
ness as a productive principle even when they directed
it upon abuses which he abundantly recognized. Mr.

Cabot shows that he was by no means one of the professional abolitionists or philanthropists—never an enrolled
"humanitarian."

> "We talk frigidly of Reform until the walls mock us.
> It is that of which a man should never speak, but if he
> have cherished it in his bosom he should steal to it in
> darkness, as an Indian to his bride. . . . Does he not do
> more to abolish slavery who works all day steadily in
> his own garden, than he who goes to the abolition
> meeting and makes a speech? He who does his own
> work frees a slave."

I must add that even while I transcribe these words there
comes to me the recollection of the great meeting in the
Boston Music Hall, on the first day of 1863, to celebrate
the signing by Mr. Lincoln of the proclamation freeing
the Southern slaves—of the momentousness of the occasion, the vast excited multitude, the crowded platform,
and the tall, spare figure of Emerson, in the midst, reading
out the stanzas that were published under the name of the
Boston Hymn. They are not the happiest he produced for
an occasion—they do not compare with the verses on the
"embattled farmers," read at Concord in 1857, and there
is a certain awkwardness in some of them. But I well remember the immense effect with which his beautiful voice
pronounced the lines—

> "Pay ransom to the owner
>   And fill the bag to the brim.
>   Who is the owner? The slave is owner,
>   And ever was. Pay *him!*"

And Mr. Cabot chronicles the fact that the *gran' rifiuto*
—the great backsliding of Mr. Webster when he cast his
vote in Congress for the Fugitive Slave Law of 1850—
was the one thing that ever moved him to heated denun-
ciation. He felt Webster's apostasy as strongly as he had
admired his genius. "Who has not helped to praise him?

Simply he was the one American of our time whom we could produce as a finished work of nature." There is a passage in his journal (not a rough jotting, but, like most of the entries in it, a finished piece of writing), which is admirably descriptive of the wonderful orator and is moreover one of the very few portraits, or even personal sketches, yielded by Mr. Cabot's selections. It shows that he could observe the human figure and "render" it to good purpose.

"His splendid wrath, when his eyes become fire, is good to see, so intellectual it is—the wrath of the fact and the cause he espouses, and not at all personal to himself. . . . These village parties must be dish-water to him, yet he shows himself just good-natured, just nonchalant enough; and he has his own way, without offending any one or losing any ground. . . . His expensiveness seems necessary to him; were he too prudent a Yankee it would be a sad deduction from his magnificence. I only wish he would not truckle [to the slaveholders]. I do not care how much he spends."

I doubtless appear to have said more than enough, yet I have passed by many of the passages I had marked for transcription from Mr. Cabot's volumes. There is one, in the first, that makes us stare as we come upon it, to the effect that Emerson "could see nothing in Shelley, Aristophanes, Don Quixote, Miss Austen, Dickens." Mr. Cabot adds that he rarely read a novel, even the famous ones (he has a point of contact here as well as, strangely enough, on two or three other sides with that distinguished moralist M. Ernest Renan, who, like Emerson, was originally a dissident priest and cannot imagine why people should write works of fiction); and thought Dante "a man to put into a museum, but not into your house; another Zerah Colburn; a prodigy of imaginative function, executive rather than contemplative or wise." The confession of an insensibility ranging from Shelley to Dickens and

from Dante to Miss Austen and taking Don Quixote and
Aristophanes on the way, is a large allowance to have to
make for a man of letters, and may appear to confirm
but slightly any claim of intellectual hospitality and general curiosity put forth for him. The truth was that,
sparely constructed as he was and formed not wastefully,
not with material left over, as it were, for a special function, there were certain chords in Emerson that did not
vibrate at all. I well remember my impression of this on
walking with him in the autumn of 1872 through the galleries of the Louvre and, later that winter, through those
of the Vatican: his perception of the objects contained in
these collections was of the most general order. I was
struck with the anomaly of a man so refined and intelligent being so little spoken to by works of art. It would be
more exact to say that certain chords were wholly absent;
the tune was played, the tune of life and literature, altogether on those that remained. They had every wish to be
equal to their office, but one feels that the number was
short—that some notes could not be given. Mr. Cabot
makes use of a singular phrase when he says, in speaking
of Hawthorne, for several years our author's neighbor at
Concord and a little—a very little we gather—his companion, that Emerson was unable to read his novels—he
thought them "not worthy of him." This is a judgment
odd almost to fascination—we circle round it and turn it
over and over; it contains so elusive an ambiguity. How
highly he must have esteemed the man of whose genius
The House of the Seven Gables and *The Scarlet Letter*
gave imperfectly the measure, and how strange that he
should not have been eager to read almost anything that
such a gifted being might have let fall! It was a rare accident that made them live almost side by side so long in
the same small New England town, each a fruit of a long
Puritan stem, yet with such a difference of taste. Hawthorne's vision was all for the evil and sin of the world;
a side of life as to which Emerson's eyes were thickly

bandaged. There were points as to which the latter's conception of right could be violated, but he had no great
sense of wrong—a strangely limited one, indeed, for a
moralist—no sense of the dark, the foul, the base. There
were certain complications in life which he never suspected. One asks one's self whether that is why he did
not care for Dante and Shelley and Aristophanes and
Dickens, their works containing a considerable reflection
of human perversity. But that still leaves the indifference
to Cervantes and Miss Austen unaccounted for.

It has not, however, been the ambition of these remarks
to account for everything, and I have arrived at the end
without even pointing to the grounds on which Emerson
justifies the honors of biography, discussion, and illustration. I have assumed his importance and continuance, and
shall probably not be gainsaid by those who read him.
Those who do not will hardly rub him out. Such a book as
Mr. Cabot's subjects a reputation to a test—leads people to
look it over and hold it up to the light, to see whether
it is worth keeping in use or even putting away in a
cabinet. Such a revision of Emerson has no relegating
consequences. The result of it is once more the impression
that he serves and will not wear out, and that indeed we
cannot afford to drop him. His instrument makes him
precious. He did something better than anyone else; he
had a particular faculty, which has not been surpassed, for
speaking to the soul in a voice of direction and authority.
There have been many spiritual voices appealing, con-
soling, reassuring, exhorting, or even denouncing and ter-
rifying, but none has had just that firmness and just that
purity. It penetrates further, it seems to go back to the
roots of our feelings, to where conduct and manhood
begin; and moreover, to us today, there is something in it
that says that it is connected somehow with the virtue
of the world, has wrought and achieved, lived in thousands of minds, produced a mass of character and life.
And there is this further sign of Emerson's singular

power, that he is a striking exception to the general rule that writings live in the last resort by their form; that they owe a large part of their fortune to the art with which they have been composed. It is hardly too much, or too little, to say of Emerson's writings in general that they were not composed at all. Many and many things are beautifully said; he had felicities, inspirations, unforgettable phrases; he had frequently an exquisite eloquence.

> "O my friends, there are resources in us on which we have not yet drawn. There are men who rise refreshed on hearing a threat; men to whom a crisis which intimidates and paralyses the majority—demanding not the faculties of prudence and thrift, but comprehension, immovableness, the readiness of sacrifice, come graceful and beloved as a bride. . . . But these are heights that we can scarce look up to and remember without contrition and shame. Let us thank God that such things exist."

None the less we have the impression that that search for a fashion and a manner on which he was always engaged never really came to a conclusion; it draws itself out through his later writings—it drew itself out through his later lectures, like a sort of renunciation of success. It is not on these, however, but on their predecessors, that his reputation will rest. Of course the way he spoke was the way that was on the whole most convenient to him; but he differs from most men of letters of the same degree of credit in failing to strike us as having achieved a style. This achievement is, as I say, usually the bribe or toll-money on the journey to posterity; and if Emerson goes his way, as he clearly appears to be doing, on the strength of his message alone, the case will be rare, the exception striking, and the honor great.

1887

JAMES RUSSELL LOWELL[1]

AFTER a man's long work is over and the sound of his
voice is still, those in whose regard he has held a high
place find his image strangely simplified and summarized.
The hand of death, in passing over it, has smoothed the
folds, made it more typical and general. The figure retained by the memory is compressed and intensified; accidents have dropped away from it and shades have ceased
to count; it stands, sharply, for a few estimated and cherished things, rather than, nebulously, for a swarm of possibilities. We cut the silhouette, in a word, out of the confusion of life, we save and fix the outline, and it is with
his eye on this profiled distinction that the critic speaks.
It is his function to speak with assurance, when once his
impression has become final; and it is in noting this circumstance that I perceive how slenderly prompted I am
to deliver myself on such an occasion as a critic. It is not
that due conviction is absent; it is only that the function
is a cold one. It is not that the final impression is dim; it
is only that it is made on a softer part of the spirit than

---

[1] This essay was first published in the *Atlantic Monthly*,
January 1892, and was reprinted by James in *Essays in London*
(1893). Lowell had died in Cambridge on August 12, 1891.

the critical sense. The process is more mystical, the deposited image is insistently personal, the generalizing principle is that of loyalty. I can therefore not pretend to write of James Russell Lowell in the tone of detachment and classification; I can only offer a few anticipatory touches for a portrait that asks for a steadier hand.

It may be professional prejudice, but as the whole color of his life was literary, so it seems to me that we may see in his high and happy fortune the most substantial honor gathered by the practice of letters from a world preoccupied with other things. It was in looking at him as a man of letters that one drew closest to him, and some of his more fanatical friends are not to be deterred from regarding his career as in the last analysis a tribute to the dominion of style. This is the idea that his name most promptly evokes; and though it was not by any means the only idea he cherished, the unity of his career is surely to be found in it. He carried style—the style of literature—into regions in which we rarely look for it: into politics, of all places in the world, into diplomacy, into stammering civic dinners and ponderous anniversaries, into letters and notes and telegrams, into every turn of the hour—absolutely into conversation, where indeed it freely disguised itself as intensely colloquial wit. Any friendly estimate of him is foredoomed to savor potently of reminiscence, so that I may mention how vividly I recall the occasion on which he first struck me as completely representative.

The association could only grow, but the essence of it was all there, on the eve of his going as minister to Spain. It was late in the summer of 1877; he spent a few days in London on his way to Madrid, in the hushed gray August, and I remember dining with him at a dim little hotel in Park Street, which I had never entered before and have never entered since, but which, whenever I pass it, seems to look at me with the melancholy of those inanimate things that have participated. That particular evening remained, in my fancy, a kind of bridge between his old bookish and his new worldly life; which however had much more in common than they had in distinction. He turned the pages of the later experience with very much the same contemplative reader's sense with which, in his library, he had, for years, smoked the student's pipe over a thousand volumes: the only difference was that a good many of the leaves were still to cut. At any rate, he was enviably gay and amused, and this preliminary hour struck me, literally, as the reward of consistency. It was tinted with the promise of a singularly interesting future, but the saturated American time was all behind it, and what was to come seemed an ideal opportunity for the nourished mind. That the American years had been diluted with several visits to Europe was not a flaw in the harmony, for to recollect certain other foreign occasions—pleasant Parisian and delightful Italian strolls—was to remember that if these had been months of absence for him, they were for me, on the wings of his talk, hours of repatriation. This talk was humorously and racily fond, charged with a perfect drollery of reference to the *other* country (there were always two—the one we were in and the one we weren't), the details of my too sketchy conception of which, admitted for argument, he showed endless good nature in filling in. It was a joke polished by much use that I was dreadfully at sea about my native land; and it would have been pleasant indeed to know even less than I did, so that I might have learned the whole story from Mr. Lowell's lips.

His America was a country worth hearing about, a magnificent conception, an admirably consistent and lovable object of allegiance. If the sign that, in Europe, one knew him best by was his intense national consciousness, one felt that this consciousness could not sit lightly on a man in whom it was the strongest form of piety. Fortunately for him, and for his friends, he was one of the most whimsical, one of the wittiest of human beings, so

that he could play with his patriotism and make it various. All the same, one felt in it, in talk, the depth of
passion that hums through much of his finest verse—
almost the only passion that, to my sense, his poetry contains, the accent of chivalry, of the lover, the knight
ready to do battle for his mistress. Above all it was a
particular allegiance to New England—a quarter of the
earth in respect to which the hand of long habit, of that
affection which is usually half convenience, never let go
the prime idea, the standard. New England was heroic
to him, for he felt in his pulses the whole history of her
origines; it was impossible to know him without a sense
that he had a rare divination of the hard realities of her
past. *The Biglow Papers* show to what a tune he could
play with his patriotism—all literature contains, I think,
no finer sport; but he is serious enough when he speaks
of the

. . . "strange New World, that yit wast never young,
Whose youth, from thee, by gripin' need was wrung,
Brown foundlin' of the woods whose baby-bed
Was prowled round by the Injun's cracklin' tread,
And who grew'st strong thro' shifts and wants and pains,
Nussed by stern men with empires in their brains."

He was never at trouble to conceal his respect for such
an origin as that, and when he came to Europe in 1877 this
sentiment was, in his luggage, one of the articles on which
he could most easily put his hand.

One of the others was the extraordinary youthfulness
which could make a man considerably younger than himself (so that it was only with the lapse of years that the
relation of age settled upon the right note) constantly
forget that he had copious antecedents. In the times when
the difference counted for more—old Cambridge days
that seem far away now—I doubtless thought him more
professorial than he felt, but I am sure that in the sequel
I never thought him younger. The boy in him was never

more clamorous than during the last summer that he spent
in England, two years before his death. Since the recollection comes of itself, I may mention as my earliest impression of him the charm that certain of his Harvard
lectures—on English literature, on Old French—had for a
very immature person who was supposed to be pursuing,
in one of the schools, a very different branch of knowledge, but who on dusky winter afternoons escaped with
irresponsible zeal into the glow of Mr. Lowell's learned
lamplight, the particular incidence of which, in the small,
still lecture-room, and the illumination of his head and
hands, I recall with extreme vividness. He talked com-
municatively of style, and where else, in all the place, was
any such talk to be heard? It made a romance of the hour
—it made even a picture of the scene; it was an unforgettable initiation. If he was American enough in Europe, in
America he was abundantly European. He was so steeped
in history and literature that to some yearning young
persons he made the taste of knowledge almost sweeter
than it was ever to be again. He was redolent, intellectually speaking, of Italy and Spain; he had lived in long
intimacy with Dante and Cervantes and Calderón; he embodied, to envious aspirants, the happy intellectual fortune
—independent years in a full library, years of acquisition
without haste and without rest, a robust love of study
which went sociably arm in arm with a robust love of
life. This love of life was so strong in him that he could
lose himself in little diversions as well as in big books. He
was fond of everything human and natural, everything
that had color and character, and no gaiety, no sense of
comedy, was ever more easily kindled by contact. When
he was not surrounded by great pleasures he could find
his account in small ones, and no situation could be dull
for a man in whom all reflection, all reaction, was witty.

I waited some years really to know him, but it was to
find at once that he was delightful to walk with. He spent
the winter of 1872-3 in Paris, and if I had not already been

fond of the streets of that city, his example and companionship would have made me so. We both had the habit of long walks, and he knew his Paris as he knew all his subjects. The history of a thing was always what he first saw in it—he recognized the object as a link in an interminable chain. He led at this season the most home-keeping, book-buying life, and Old French texts made his evenings dear to him. He had dropped (and where he dropped he usually stayed) into an intensely local and extremely savory little hotel in the Faubourg Saint-Germain, unknown to tourists but patronized by deputies, where the *table d'hôte*, at which the host sat down with the guests and contradiction flourished, was a page of Balzac, full of illustration for the humorist. I used sometimes, of a Sunday evening, to dine there, and to this day, on rainy winter nights, I never cross the Seine amid the wet flare of the myriad lamps, never note the varnished rush of the river or the way the Louvre grows superb in the darkness, without a recurrent consciousness of the old sociable errand, the sense of dipping into a still denser Paris, with the *Temps* and M. Sarcey[2] in my pocket.

We both spent the following winter—he at least the larger part of it—in Florence, out of manifold memories of which certain hours in his company, certain charmed Italian afternoons in Boboli gardens, on San Miniato terraces, come back to me with a glow of their own. He had indeed memories of earlier Italian times, some of which he has admirably recorded—anecdotes, tormenting to a late comer, of the superseded, the missed. He himself, in his perpetual freshness, seemed to come so late that it was always a surprise to me that he had started so early. Almost any Italy, however, was good enough for him, and he kept criticism for great occasions, for the wise relapse, the study-chair and the vanquished

[2] Francisque Sarcey (1827–99) for many years wrote a weekly column on the Parisian theater which James greatly admired.

hesitation (not timid but overbrimming, like a vessel dangerous to move) of that large prose pen which was so firm when once set in motion. He liked the Italian people—he liked the people everywhere, and the warm street life and the exquisite idiom; the Tuscan tongue, indeed, so early ripe and yet still so perfectly alive, was one of the comforts of the world to him. He produced that winter a poem so ample and noble that it was worthy to come into being in classic air—the magnificent elegy on the death of Agassiz, which strikes me as a summary of all his vigors and felicities, his most genial achievement, and (after the Harvard Commemoration Ode) the truest expression of his poetic nature. It is hard to lend to a great old house, in Italy, even when it has become a modern inn, any associations as romantic as those it already wears; but what the high-windowed face of the Florentine Hôtel du Nord speaks to me of today, over its chattering cab-stand and across the statued pillar of the little square of the Holy Trinity, is neither its ancient honor nor its actual fall, but the sound, one December evening, by the fire the poet pronounces "starved," of

> "I cannot think he wished so soon to die
> With all his senses full of eager heat,
> And rosy years that stood expectant by
> To buckle the winged sandals on their feet,
> He that was friends with Earth, and all her sweet
> Took with both hands unsparingly."

Of Mr. Lowell's residence in Spain I know nothing but what I gathered from his talk, after he took possession, late in the spring of 1879, of the post in London rendered vacant by the retirement of Mr. John Welsh; much of it inevitably referring to the domestic sorrow—the prolonged illness of his admirable wife—which cast over these years a cloud that darkened further during the early part of his English period. I remember getting from him a sense that a diplomatic situation at Madrid was

not quite so refreshing a thing as might have been expected, and that for the American representative at least
there was not enough business to give a savor to duty.
This particular representative's solution of every personal
problem, however, was a page of philology in a cloud of
tobacco, and as he had seen the picture before through
his studies, so now he doubtless saw his studies through
the picture. The place was a part of it, where the ghost
of Charles V still walked and the princesses were what
is called in princesses literary. The diplomatic circle was
animated—if that be the word—by whist; what his own
share of the game was enlivened by may be left to the
imagination of those who remember the irrepressibility,
on his lips, of the comic idea. It might have been taken for
granted that he was well content to be transferred to
England; but I have no definite recollection of the degree
of his satisfaction beforehand. I think he was mainly conscious of the weight of the new responsibility, so that
the unalloyed pleasure was that of his friends and of the
most enlightened part of the public in the two countries,
to which the appointment appeared to have an unusual
felicity. It was made, as it were, for quality, and that
continued to be the sign of the function so long as
Mr. Lowell exercised it. The difficulty—if I may speak
of difficulty—was that all judgment of it was necessarily
a priori. It was impossible for him to know what a success, in vulgar parlance, he might make of a totally untried
character, and above all to foresee how this character
would adapt itself to his own disposition. During the
years of his residence in London on an official footing it
constantly struck me that it was the office that inclined,
at every turn, to him, rather than he who inclined to
the office.

I may appear to speak too much of this phase of his
life as the most memorable part of it—especially considering how short a time it occupied in regard to the whole;[3]

[3] Lowell was minister in London from 1879 to 1885.

but in addition to its being the only long phase of which
I can speak at all closely from personal observation, it is
just to remember that these were the years in which all
the other years were made most evident. "*We* knew him
and valued him ages before, and never stinted our appreciation, never waited to care for him till he had
become the fashion," his American readers and listeners,
his pupils and colleagues, might say; to which the answer
is that those who admired him most were just those who
might naturally rejoice in the multiplication of his opportunities. He came to London with only a vague notion,
evidently, of what these opportunities were to be, and
in fact there was no defining them in advance; what they
proved to be, on the spot, was anything and everything
that he might make them. I remember hearing him say,
a day or two after his arrival: "Oh, I've lost all my wit—
you mustn't look to me for good things *now*." The words
were uttered to a gentleman who had found one of his
"things" very good, and who, having a political speech
to make in a day or two, had thriftily asked his leave to
bring it in. There could have been no better example of
the experimental nature of his acceptance of the post;
for the very foundation of the distinction that he gave it
was his great reserve of wit. He had no idea how much
he had left till he tried it, and he had never before had
so much occasion to try it. This uncertainty might per-
vade the minds even of such of his friends as had a
near view of his start; but those friends would have
had singularly little imagination if they had failed to be
struck, in a general way, with the highly civilized character of his mission. There are circumstances in operation
(too numerous to recite) which combine to undermine
greatly the comfort of the representative of the United
States in a foreign country; it is, to speak summarily, in
many respects a singularly embarrassing honor. I cannot
express more strongly how happy Mr. Lowell's opportunity seemed to be than by saying that he struck

people at the moment as enviable. It was an inten-
sification of the impression given by the glimpse of
him on his way to Spain. The true reward of an
English style was to be sent to England, and if his career
in that country was, throughout, amusing, in the highest
sense of the term, this result was, for others at least, a part
of their gratified suspense as to the further possibilities
of the style.

From the friendly and intimate point of view it was
presumable from the first that there would be a kind of
drama, a spectacle; and if one had already lived a few
years in London one could have an interesting prevision
of some of its features. London is a great personage, and
with those with whom she establishes a relation she always
plays, as it were, her game. This game, throughout Mr.
Lowell's residence, but especially during the early part,
was exciting; so much so that I remember being positively
sorry, as if I were leaving the theater before the fall of
the curtain, when, at that time, more than once, I found
myself, by visits to the Continent, obliged to turn my
back upon it. The sight of his variety was a help to
know London better; and it was a question whether *he*
could ever know her so well as those who could freely
consider the pair together. He offered her from the first
a nut to crack, a morsel to roll under her tongue. She
is the great consumer of spices and sweets; if I were not
afraid of forcing the image, I should say that she is too
unwieldy to feed herself, and requires, in recurring seasons, as she sits prodigiously at her banquet, to be approached with the consecrated ladle. She placed this implement in Mr. Lowell's hands with a confidence so immediate as to be truly touching—a confidence that speaks
for the eventual amalgamation of the Anglo-Saxon race in
a way that, surely, no casual friction can obliterate. She
can confer conspicuity, at least for the hour, so well that
she is constantly under the temptation to do so; she holds
a court for those who speak to her, and she is perpetually

trying voices. She recognized Mr. Lowell's from the first and appointed him really her speaker-in-chief. She has a peculiar need, which when you know her well you understand, of being eased off with herself, and the American minister speedily appeared just the man to ease her. He played into her talk and her speeches, her commemorations and functions, her dinners and discussions, her editorials and anecdotes. She has immense wheels which are always going round, and the ponderous precision of which can be observed only on the spot. They naturally demand something to grind, and the machine holds out great iron hands and draws in reputations and talents, or sometimes only names and phrases.

Mr. Lowell immediately found himself, in England, whether to his surprise or no I am unable to say, the first of after-dinner speakers. It was perhaps somewhat to the surprise of his public there, for it was not to have been calculated in advance that he would have become so expert in his own country—a country sparing of feast-days and ceremonies. His practice had been great before he came to London, but his performance there would have been a strain upon any practice. It was a point of honor with him never to refuse a challenge, and this attitude, under the circumstances, was heroic, for he became a convenience that really tended to multiply occasions. It was exactly his high competence in these directions that constituted the practical good effect of his mission, the particular manner in which it made for civilization. It was the *revanche* of letters; that throughout was the particular note of the part he played. There would have been no *revanche* if he had played it inadequately; therefore it was a pleasure to feel that he was accomplished up to the hilt. Those who didn't like him pronounced him too accomplished, too omniscient; but, save in a sense that I will specify, I never saw him commit himself unadvisedly, and much is to be forgiven a love of precise knowledge which keeps a man out of mistakes.

He had a horror of them; no one was ever more in love with the idea of being right and of keeping others from being wrong. The famous Puritan conscience, which was a persistent part of his heredity, operated in him perhaps most strongly on the scholarly side. He enjoyed the detail of research and the discussion of differences, and he had an instinct for rectification which was unflinching. All this formed a part of the enviability I have noted— the serenity of that larger reputation which came to him late in life, which had been paid for in advance, and in regard to which his finished discharge of his diplomatic duties acted, if not certainly as a cause, at least as a stimulus. The reputation was not doubtless the happiest thing; the happiest thing was the inward opportunity, the chance to absorb into an intelligence extraordinarily prepared a pecularly full revelation.

He had studied English history for forty years in the texts, and at last he could study it in the pieces themselves, could handle and verify the relics. For the man who in such a position recognizes his advantages, England makes herself a museum of illustration. She is at home in the comfortable dust of her ages, where there is no need of excavation, as she has never been buried, and the explorer finds the ways as open to him as the corridors of an exhibition. It was an exhibition of which Mr. Lowell never grew tired, for it was infinitely various and living; it brought him back repeatedly after his public mission had expired, and it was perpetually suggestive to him while that mission lasted. If he played his part so well here—I allude now more particularly to the social and expressive side of it—it was because he was so open to suggestion. Old England spoke to him so much as a man of letters that it was inevitable he should answer her back. On the firmness and tact with which he acquitted himself of his strictly diplomatic work I shall not presume to touch; his success was promptly appreciated in quarters where the official record may be found, as well as in others less discoverable today, columns congruous with their vituperative "headings," where it must be looked for between the lines. These latter responsibilities, begotten mainly of the Irish complication, were heavy ones, but they were presumably the keenest interest of his term, and I include them essentially in the picture afforded by that term of the supremely symmetrical literary life— the life in which the contrasts have been effectively timed; in which the invading and acclaiming world has entered too late to interfere, to distract, but still in time to fertilize; in which contacts have multiplied and horizons widened gradually; in which, in short, the dessert has come after the dinner, the answer after the question, and the proof after the patience.

I may seem to exaggerate in Mr. Lowell's history the importance of the last dozen years of his life—especially if the reckoning be made of the amount of characteristic production that preceded them. He was the same admirable writer that he appears today before he touched diplomacy—he had already given to the world the volumes on which his reputation rests. I cannot attempt in this place and at this hour a critical estimate of his writings; the perspective is too short and our acquaintance too recent. Yet I have been reading him over in fragments, not to judge him, but to recall him, and it is as impossible to speak of him without the sense of his high place as it would be with the pretension to be final about it. He looms, in such a renewed impression, very large and ripe and sane, and if he was an admirable man of letters there should be no want of emphasis on the first term of the title. He was indeed in literature a man, essentially masculine, upright, downright. Presenting to us survivors that simplified face that I have spoken of, he almost already looks at us as the last accomplished representative of the joy of life. His robust and humorous optimism rounds itself more and more; he has even now something of the air of a classic, and if he really becomes one it will be in virtue of his having placed as fine an irony at the service of hope as certain masters of the other strain have placed at that of despair. Sturdy liberal as he was, and contemptuous of all timidities of advance and reservations of faith, one thinks of him today, at the point at which we leave him, as the last of the literary conservatives. He took his stand on the ancient cheerful wisdom, many of the ingenious modern emendations of which seemed to him simply droll.

Few things were really so droll as he could make them, and not a great many perhaps are so absolute. The solution of the problem of life lay for him in action, in conduct, in decency; his imagination lighted up to him but scantily the region of analysis and apology. Like all interesting literary figures, he is full of tacit as well as of uttered reference to the conditions that engendered him; he really testifies as much as Hawthorne to the New England spirit, though in a totally different tone. The two writers, as witnesses, weigh against each other, and the picture would be imperfect if both had not had a hand in it. If Hawthorne expressed the mysticism and the gloom of the transplanted Puritan, his passive and haunted side, Lowell saw him in the familiar daylight of practice and prosperity and good health. The author of *The Biglow Papers* was surely the healthiest of highly cultivated geniuses, just as he was the least flippant of jesters and the least hysterical of poets. If Hawthorne fairly cherished the idea of evil in man, Lowell's vision of "sin" was operative mainly for a single purpose—that of putting in motion the civic lash. *The Biglow Papers* are mainly an exposure of national injustice and political dishonesty; his satiric ardor was simply the other side of the medal of his patriotism. His poetry is not all satirical, but the highest and most sustained flights of it are patriotic, and in reading it over I am struck with the vivid virtue of this part of it—something strenuous and antique, the watchful citizen smiting the solemn lyre.

The look at life that it embodies is never merely curious, never irresponsible; it is only the author's humor that is whimsical, never his emotion nor his passion. His poetical performance might sometimes, no doubt, be more intensely lyrical, but it is hard to see how it could be more intensely moral—I mean of course in the widest sense of the term. His play is as good as a game in the open air; but when he is serious he is as serious as Words-worth, and much more compact. He is the poet of pluck and purpose and action, of the gaiety and liberty of virtue. He commemorates all manly pieties and affections, but rarely conceals his mistrust of overbrimming sensibility. If the ancients and the Elizabethans, he somewhere says, "had not discovered the picturesque, as we understand it, they found surprisingly fine scenery in man and his destiny, and would have seen something ludicrous, it may be suspected, in the spectacle of a grown man run-ning to hide his head in the apron of the Mighty Mother whenever he had an ache in his finger or got a bruise in the tussle for existence." It is visible that the poetic occasion that was most after his own heart was the storm and stress of the Civil War. He vibrated in this long tension more deeply than in any other experience. It was the time that kindled his steadiest fire, prompted his noblest verse, and gave him what he relished most, a ground for high assurance, a sense of being sturdily in the right and having something to stand up for. He never feared and never shirked the obligation to be positive. Firm and liberal critic as he was, and with nothing of party spirit in his utterance, save in the sense that his sincerity was his party, his mind had little affinity with superfine estimates and shades and tints of opinion; when he felt at all he felt altogether—was always on the same side as his likings and loyalties. He had no experimental sympathies, and no part of him was traitor to the rest.

This temper drove the principle of subtlety in his intelligence, which is a need for the last refinement, to take refuge in one particular and I must add very spacious corner, where indeed it was capable of the widest expansion. The thing he loved most in the world after his country was the English tongue, of which he was an infallible master, and his devotion to which was in fact a sort of agent in his patriotism. The two passions at any rate were closely connected, and I will not pretend to have determined whether the western republic was dear to him because he held that it was a magnificent field for the language, or whether the language was dear to him because it had felt the impact of Massachusetts. He himself was not unhappily responsible for a large part of the latter occurrence. His linguistic sense is perhaps the thing his reputation may best be trusted to rest upon—I mean, of course, in its large outcome of style. There is a high strain of originality in it, for it is difficult to recall a writer of our day in whom the handling of words has been at once such an art and such a science. Mr. Lowell's generous temperament seems to triumph in one quarter, while his educated patience triumphs in the other. When a man loves words singly, he is apt not to care for them in an order, just as a very great painter may be quite indifferent to the chemical composition of his colors. But Mr. Lowell was both chemist and artist; the only wonder was that with so many theories about language he should have had so much lucidity left for practice. He used it both as an antiquarian and as a lover of life, and was a capital instance of the possible harmony between imagination and knowledge—a living proof that the letter does not necessarily kill.

His work represents this reconciled opposition, referable as it is half to the critic and half to the poet. If either half suffers just a little it is perhaps, in places, his poetry, a part of which is I scarcely know what to say but too literary, more the result of an interest in the general form than of the stirred emotion. One feels at

moments that he speaks in verse mainly because he is
penetrated with what verse has achieved. But these moments are occasional, and when the stirred emotion does
give a hand to the interest in the general form the
product is always of the highest order. His poems written
during the war all glow with a splendid fusion—one
can think of nothing at once more personal and, in
the highest sense of the word, more professional. To me,
at any rate, there is something fascinating in the way
in which, in the Harvard Commemoration Ode for
instance, the air of the study mingles with the hot breath
of passion. The reader who is eternally bribed by form
may ask himself whether Mr. Lowell's prose or his poetry
has the better chance of a long life—the hesitation being
justified by the rare degree in which the prose has the
great qualities of style; but in the presence of some of
the splendid stanzas inspired by the war time (and among
them I include, of course, the second series of *The
Biglow Papers*) one feels that, whatever shall become
of the essays, the transmission from generation to
generation of such things as these may safely be left
to the national conscience. They translate with equal
exaltation and veracity the highest national mood,
and it is in them that all younger Americans, those now
and lately reaching manhood, may best feel the great
historic throb, the throb unknown to plodding peace.
No poet surely has ever placed the concrete idea of his
country in a more romantic light than Mr. Lowell; none,
certainly, speaking as an American to Americans, has
found on its behalf accents more eloquently tender, more
beguiling to the imagination.

"Dear land whom triflers now make bold to scorn,
  (Thee from whose forehead Earth awaits her morn.)

"Oh Beautiful! my Country! ours once more!
  Smoothing thy gold of war-dishevelled hair
  O'er such sweet brows as never other wore,

And letting thy set lips,
Freed from wrath's pale eclipse,
The rosy edges of their smile lay bare!"

Great poetry is made only by a great meaning, and the national bias, I know, never made anything better that was not good in itself; but each time I read over the Harvard Commemoration Ode, the more full and strong, the more august and pathetic, does it appear. This is only a proof that if the national sentiment preserves it the national sentiment will show excellent taste—which she has been known in some cases not to do.

If I were not afraid of falling into the tone of literary criticism, I should speak of several of the impressions—that is of the charmed absorption—accompanying an attentive reperusal of the four or five volumes of Mr. Lowell's poetry. The word I have already used comes back to me: it is all so masculine, so fine without being thin, so steadied by the temperament of the author. It is intensely literary and yet intensely warm, warm with the contact of friendly and domestic things, loved local sights and sounds, the color and odor of New England, and (here particularly warm without fever) with the sanest, lucidest intellectual life. There is something of seasonable nature in every verse—the freshness of the spirit sociable with earth and sky and stream. In the best things there is the incalculable magic note—all the more effective from the general ground-tone of reason. What could be more strangely sweet than the little poem of "Phœbe," in *Heartsease and Rue*—a reminiscence of the saddest of small bird-notes caught in the dimmest of wakeful dawns? What could be more largely vivid, more in the grand style of friendship and portraiture, than the masterly composition on the death of Agassiz, in which the very tenderness of regret flushes faintly with humor and ingenuity broadens at every turn into eloquence? Such a poem as this—immensely fortunate in reflecting an ex-

traordinary personality—takes its place with the few
great elegies in our language, gives a hand to *Lycidas* and
to *Thyrsis*.

I may not go into detail, or I should speak of twenty
other things, especially of the mellow, witty wisdom of
The Cathedral and of the infinite, intricate delicacy of
Endymion—more tremulous, more penetrating, than any
other of the author's poetic productions, I think, and
exceptionally fine in surface. As for *The Biglow Papers*,
they seem to me, in regard to their author, not so much
produced as productive—productive of a clear, delightful
image of the temper and nature of the man. One says
of them, not that they are *by* him, but that they are his
very self, so full of his opinions and perceptions, his
humor and his wit, his character, his experience, his talk,
and his intense consciousness of race. They testify to
many things, but most of all to the thing I have last
named; and it may seem to those whose observation of
the author was most complete during the concluding
years of his life that they could testify to nothing more
characteristic. If he was inveterately, in England and on
the Continent, the American abroad (though jealous
indeed of the liberty to be at home even there), so the
lucubrations of Parson Wilbur and his contributors are
an unsurpassably deliberate exhibition of the primitive
home-quality. I may seem to be going far when I say
that they constitute to my sense the author's most literary
production; they exemplify at any rate his inexhaustible
interest in the question of style and his extraordinary
acuteness in dealing with it. They are a wonderful study
of style—by which I mean of organized expression—and
nothing could be more significant than the fact that he
should have put his finest faculty for linguistics at the
service of the Yankee character.

He knew more, I think, about the rustic American
speech than all others together who have known anything
of it, so much more closely, justly, and sympathetically

had he noted it. He honored it with the strongest scientific interest, and indeed he may well have been on terms of reciprocity with a dialect that had enabled him to produce a masterpiece. The only drawback I can imagine to a just complacency in this transaction would have been the sense that the people are few, after all, who can measure the minute perfection of the success—a success not only of swift insight, but of patient observation. Mr. Lowell was as capable of patience in illustrating New England idiosyncrasies as he was capable of impatience. He never forgot, at any rate, that he stood there for all such things—stood for them particularly during the years he spent in England; and his attitude was made up of many curious and complicated and admirable elements. He was so proud—not for himself, but for his country—that he felt the need of a kind of official version of everything at home that in other quarters might be judged anomalous. Theoretically he cared little for the judgment of other quarters, and he was always amused— the good-natured British Lion in person could not have been more so—at "well-meaning" compliment or commendation; it required, it must be admitted, more tact than is usually current to incur the visitation of neither the sharper nor the sunnier form of his irony. But in fact the national consciousness was too acute in him for slumber at his post, and he paid in a certain restlessness the penalty of his imagination, of the fatal sense of perspective and the terrible faculty of comparison. It would have been intolerable to him moreover to be an empirical American, and he had organized his loyalty with a thoroughness of which his admirable wit was an efficient messenger. He never anticipated attack, though it would be a meager account of his attitude to say it was defensive; but he took appreciation for granted and eased the way for it with reasons that were cleverer in nothing than in appearing casual. These reasons were innumerable, but they were all the reasons of a lover. It was not simply that he loved his country—he was literally in love with it.

If there be two kinds of patriotism, the latent and the patent, his kind was essentially the latter. Some people for whom the world is various and universal, and who dread nothing so much as seeing it minimized, regard this particular sentiment as a purely practical one, a prescription of duty in a given case, like a knack with the coiled hose when the house is on fire or the plunge of the swimmer when a man is overboard. They grudge it a place in the foreground of the spirit—they consider that it shuts out the view. Others find it constantly comfortable and perpetually fresh—find, as it were, the case always given; for them the immediate view *is* the view and the very atmosphere of the mind, so that it is a question not only of performance, but of contemplation as well. Mr. Lowell's horizon was too wide to be curtained out, and his intellectual curiosity such as to have effectually prevented his shutting himself up in his birthchamber; but if the local idea never kept his intelligence at home, he solved the difficulty by at least never going forth without it. When he quitted the hearth it was with the household god in his hand, and as he delighted in Europe it was to Europe that he took it. Never had a household god such a magnificent outing, nor was made free of so many strange rites and climes; never in short had any patriotism such a liberal airing. If, however, Mr. Lowell was loath to admit that the American order could have an infirmity, I think it was because it would have cost him so much to acknowledge that it could have communicated one to an object that he cherished as he cherished the English tongue. *That* was the innermost atmosphere of his mind, and he never could have afforded on this general question any policy but a policy of annexation. He was capable of convictions in the light of which it was clear that the language he wrote so admirably had encountered in the United States not corruption but conservation. Any conviction of his on this subject was a contribution to science, and he was zealous to show that the speech of New England was most largely that of an England older and more vernacular than the England that today finds it queer. He was capable of writing perfect American to bring out this archaic element. He kept in general the two tongues apart, save in so far as his English style betrayed a connection by a certain American tact in the art of leaving out. He was perhaps sometimes slightly paradoxical in the contention that the language had incurred no peril in its western adventures; this is the sense in which I meant just now that he occasionally crossed the line. The difficulty was not that his vision of pure English could not fail in America sometimes to be clouded—the peril was for his vision of pure American. His standard was the highest, and the wish was often no doubt father to the thought. *The Biglow Papers* are delightful, but nothing could be less like *The Biglow Papers* than the style of the American newspaper. He lent his wit to his theories, but one or two of them lived on him like unthrifty sons.

None the less it was impossible to be witness of his general action during his residence in England without feeling that, not only by the particular things he did but by the general thing he was, he contributed to a large ideal of peace. We certainly owe to him (and by "we" I mean both countries—he made that plural elastic) a mitigation of danger. There is always danger between country and country, and danger in small and shameful forms as well as big and inspiring ones; but the danger is less and the dream of peace more rosy when they have been beguiled into a common admiration. A common aversion even will do—the essential thing is the disposition to share. The poet, the writer, the speaker, ministers to this community; he is Orpheus with his lute—the lute that pacifies the great stupid beasts of international prejudice; so that if a quarrel takes place over the piping form of the loved of Apollo it is as if he were rent again by the Mænads. It was a charm to the observant mind to see how Mr. Lowell kept the Mænads in their place—a work admirably continued by his successor in office, who had indeed under his roof an inestimable assistant in the process. Mr. Phelps[4] was not, as I may say, single-handed; which was his predecessor's case even for some time prior to an irreparable bereavement. The prying Furies at any rate, during these years, were effectually snubbed, and will, it is to be hoped, never again hold their snaky heads very high. The spell that worked upon them was simply the voice of civilization, and Mr. Lowell's advantage was that he happened to find himself in a supremely good place for producing it. He produced it both consciously and unconsciously, both officially and privately, from principle and from instinct, in the hundred spots, on the thousand occasions, which it is one of the happiest idiosyncrasies of English life to supply; and since I have spoken so distinctly of his patriotism, I must add that after all he exercised the virtue most in this particular way. His new friends liked him because he was at once so fresh and so ripe, and this was predominantly what he understood by being a good American. It was by being one in this sense that he broke the heart of the Furies.

The combination made a quality which pervaded his whole intellectual character; for the quality of his diplomatic action, of his public speeches, of his talk, of his influence, was simply the genius that we had always appreciated in his critical writings. The hours and places with which he had to deal were not equally inspiring; there was inevitably colorless company, there were dull dinners, influences prosaic and functions mechanical; but he was substantially always the messenger of the Muses

[4] Edward J. Phelps (1822–1900) succeeded Lowell as minister to England in 1885, a few months after the death of Mrs. Lowell.

and of that particular combination of them which had permitted him to include a tenth in their number—the infallible sister to whom humor is dear. I mean that the man and the author, in him, were singularly convertible: it was what made the author so vivid. It was also what made that voice of civilization to whose harmony I have alluded practically the same thing as the voice of literature. Mr. Lowell's style was an indefeasible part of him, as his correspondence, if it be ever published, will copiously show; it was in all relations his natural channel of communication. This is why, at the opening of this paper, I ventured to speak of his happy exercise of a great opportunity as at bottom the revenge of letters. This, at any rate, the literary observer was free to see in it; such an observer made a cross against the day, as an anniversary for form, and an anniversary the more memorable that form, when put to tests that might have been called severe, was so far from being found wanting in substance, met the occasion in fact so completely. I do not pretend that during Mr. Lowell's residence in England the public which he found constituted there spent most of its time in reading his essays; I only mean that the faculty it relished in him most was the faculty most preserved for us in his volumes of criticism.

It is not an accident that I do not linger over the contents of these volumes—this has not been a part of my undertaking. They will not go out of fashion, they will keep their place and hold their own; for they are full of broad-based judgment, and of those stamped sentences of which we are as naturally retentive as of gold and silver coin. Reading them lately in large portions, I was struck not only with the particular "good things" that abound in them, but with the soundness and fullness of their inspiration. It is intensely the air of letters, but it is like that of some temperate and restorative clime. I judge them perhaps with extravagant fondness, for I am attached to the class to which they belong; I like such an atmosphere, I like the aromatic odor of the bookroom. In turning over Mr. Lowell's critical pages, I seem to hear the door close softly behind me and to find in the shaded lamplight the conditions most in harmony with the sentient soul of man. I see an apartment brown and book-lined, which is the place in the world most convertible into other places. The turning of the leaves, the crackling of the fire are the only things that break its stillness—the stillness in which mild miracles are wrought. These are the miracles of evocation, of resurrection, of transmission, of insight, of history, of poetry. It may be a little room but it is a great space; it may be a deep solitude, but it is a mighty company. In this critical chamber of Mr. Lowell's there is a charm, to my sense, in knowing what is outside of the closed door—it intensifies both the isolation and the experience. The big new western order is outside, and yet within all seems as immemorial as Persia. It is like a little lighted cabin, full of the ingenuities of home, in the gray of a great ocean. Such ingenuities of home are what represent in Mr. Lowell's case the conservatism of the author. His home was the past that dipped below the verge—it was there that his taste was at ease. From what quarter his disciples in the United States will draw their sustenance it is too soon to say; the question will be better answered when we have the disciples more clearly in our eye. We seem already however to distinguish the quarter from which they will *not* draw it. Few of them as yet appear to have in their hand, or rather in their head, any such treasure of knowledge.

It was when his lifetime was longest that the fruit of culture was finest in him and that his wit was most profuse. In the admirable address on Democracy that he pronounced at Birmingham in 1884, in the beautiful speech on the Harvard anniversary of 1886, things are so supremely well said that we feel ourselves reading some consecrated masterpiece; they represent, great literary art in its final phase of great naturalness. There are places where he seems in a sort of mystical communication with the richest sources of English prose. "But this imputed and vicarious longevity, though it may be obscurely operative in our lives and fortunes, is no valid offset for the shortness of our days, nor widens by a hair's-breadth the horizon of our memories." He sounds like a younger brother of Bacon and of Milton, either of whom, for instance, could not have uttered a statelier word on the subject of the relinquishment of the required study of Greek than that "oblivion looks in the face of the Grecian Muse only to forget her errand." On the other hand, in the address delivered in 1884 before the English Wordsworth Society, he sounds like no one but his inveterately felicitous self. In certain cases, Wordsworth, like Elias the prophet, " 'stands up as fire and his word burns like a lamp.' But too often, when left to his own resources and to the conscientious performance of the duty laid upon him to be a great poet *quand même*, he seems diligently intent on producing fire by the primitive method of rubbing the dry sticks of his blank verse one against the other, while we stand in shivering expectation of the flame that never comes." It would be difficult to express better the curious evening chill of the author of *The Excursion,* which is so like the conscious mistake of camping out in autumn.

It was an extreme satisfaction to the very many persons in England who valued Mr. Lowell's society that the termination of his official mission there proved not the termination of the episode. He came back for his friends —he would have done anything for his friends. He also, I surmise, came back somewhat for himself, inasmuch as he entertained an affection for London which he had no reason for concealing. For several successive years he reappeared there with the brightening months, and I am not sure that this irresponsible and less rigorously sociable period did not give him his justest impressions. It surrendered him, at any rate, more completely to his friends and to several close and particularly valued ties. He felt that he had earned the right to a few frank predilections. English life is a big pictured story-book, and he could dip into the volume where he liked. It was altogether delightful to turn some of the pages with him, and especially to pause—for the marginal commentary in finer type, some of it the model of the illuminating footnote —over the massive chapter of London.

It is very possible not to feel the charm of London at all; the foreigner who feels it must be tolerably sophisticated. It marks the comparative community of the two big branches of the English race that of all aliens under this heavy pressure, Americans are the most submissive. They are capable of loving the capital of their race almost with passion, which for the most part is the way it is loved when it is not hated. The sentiment was strong in Mr. Lowell; one of the branches of his tree of knowledge had planted itself and taken root here and at the end he came back every year to sit in the shade of it. He gave himself English summers, and if some people should say that the gift was scarcely liberal, others who met him on this ground will reply that such seasons drew from him in the circle of friendship a radiance not inherent in their complexion. This association became a feature of the London May and June—it held its own even in the rank confusion of July. It pervaded the quarter he repeatedly inhabited, where a commonplace little house, in the neighborhood of the Paddington station, will long wear in its narrow front, to the inner sense of many passers, a mystical gold-lettered tablet. Here he came and went, during several months, for such and such a succession of years; here one could find him at home in the late afternoon, in his lengthened chair, with his cherished pipe and his table piled high with books. Here he practiced little jesting hospitalities, for he was irrepressibly and amusingly hospitable. Whatever he was in his latest time, it was, even in muffled miseries of gout, with a mastery of laughter and forgetfulness. Nothing amused him more than for people to dine with him, and few things, certainly, amused *them* as much. His youth came back to him not once for all, but twenty times for every occasion. He was certainly the most boyish of learned doctors.

This was always particularly striking during the several weeks of August and September that he had formed the habit of spending at Whitby, on the Yorkshire coast. It was here, I think, that he was most naturally at his ease, most humorously evaded the hard bargain of Time. The place is admirable—an old red-roofed fishing-town in one of the indentations of a high, brave coast, with the ruins of a great abbey just above it, an expanse of purple moor behind, and a convenient extension in the way of an informal little modern watering-place. The mingled breath of the sea and the heather makes a medium that it is a joy to inhale, and all the land is picturesque and noble, a happy hunting-ground for the good walker and the lover of grand lines and fine detail. Mr. Lowell was wonderful in both of these characters, and it was in the active exercise of them that I saw him last. He was in such conditions a delightful host and a prime initiator. Two of these happy summer days, on the occasion of his last visit to Whitby, are marked possessions of my memory: one of them a ramble on the warm wide moors, after a rough lunch at a little stony upland inn, in company charming and intimate, the thought of which today is a reference to a double loss; the other an excursion, made partly by a longish piece of railway, in his society alone, to Rievaulx Abbey, most fragmentary but most graceful of ruins. The day at Rievaulx was as exquisite as I could have wished it if I had known that it denoted a limit, and in the happy absence of any such revelation altogether given up to adventure and success.

I remember the great curving green terrace in Lord Feversham's park—prodigious and surely unique; it hangs over the abbey like a theatrical curtain—and the temples of concord, or whatever they are, at either end of it, and the lovable view, and the dear little dowdy inn parlor at Helmsley, where there is moreover a massive fragment of profaner ruin, a bit of battered old castle, in the grassy *préau* of which (it was a perfect English picture) a company of well-grown young Yorkshire folk of both sexes were making lawn-tennis balls fly in and out of the past. I recall with vividness the very waits and changes of the return and our pleased acceptance of everything. We parted on the morrow, but I met Mr. Lowell a little later in Devonshire—O clustered charms of Ottery!—and spent three days in his company. I traveled back to London with him, and saw him for the last time at Paddington. He was to sail immediately for America. I went to take leave of him, but I missed him, and a day or two later he was gone.

I note these particulars, as may easily be imagined, wholly for their reference to himself—for the emphasized occasion they give to remembrance and regret. Yet even remembrance and regret, in such a case, have a certain free relief, for our final thought of James Russell Lowell is that what he consistently lived for remains of him. There is nothing ineffectual in his name and fame—they stand for delightful things. He is one of the happy figures of literature. He had his trammels and his sorrows, but he drank deep of the tonic draught, and he will long count as an erect fighting figure on the side of optimism and beauty. He was strong without narrowness; he was wise without bitterness and glad without fatuity. That appears for the most part the temper of those who speak from the quiet English heart, the steady pulses of which were the sufficient rhythm of his eloquence. This source of influence will surely not forfeit its long credit in the world so long as we continue occasionally to know it by what is so rich in performance and so stainless in character.

JAMES RUSSELL LOWELL

(1819–1891)[1]

THE FORMULA would not be hard to find which would best, at the outset, introduce to readers the author of the following extracts and specimens. With a certain close propriety that seems to give him, among Americans of his time, the supreme right, James Russell Lowell wears the title of a man of letters. He was a master of verse and a political disputant; he was to some extent a journalist, and in a high degree an orator; he administered learning in a great university; he was concerned, in his later years, with public affairs, and represented in two foreign countries the interests of the United States. Yet there is only one term to which, in an appreciation, we can without a sense of injustice give precedence over the others. He

---

[1] This essay first appeared in Vol. XVI of an anthology, *Library of the World's Best Literature,* edited by Charles Dudley Warner (New York, 1897) and was never reprinted by James.

was the American of his time most saturated with literature and most directed to criticism; the American also
whose character and endowment were such as to give this
saturation and this direction—this intellectual experience,
in short—most value. He added to the love of learning the
love of expression; and his attachment to these things—
to poetry, to history, to language, form, and style—was
such as to make him, the greater part of his life, more
than anything a man of study: but his temperament was
proof against the dryness of the air of knowledge, and he
remained to the end the least pale, the least passionless of
scholars.

He was born at Cambridge, Massachusetts, on February
22, 1819, and died in the same house on August 12, 1891.
His inheritance of every kind contributed to the easy
play of his gifts and the rich uniformity of his life. He
was of the best and oldest New England—of partly
clerical—stock; a stock robust and supple, and which
has given to its name many a fruit-bearing branch. We
read him but dimly in not reading into him, as it were,
everything that was present, around him, in race and
place; and perhaps also in not seeing him in relation to
some of the things that were absent. He is one more
instance of the way in which the poet's message is almost
always, as to what it contains or omits, a testimony to
personal circumstance, a communication of the savor of
the mother soil. He figures to us thus—more handsomely
than any competitor—as New England conscious of its
powers and its standards, New England accomplished
and articulate. He grew up in clerical and collegiate air,
at half an hour's walk from the cluster of homely halls
that are lost today in the architectural parade of the
modernized Harvard. He spent fifty years of his life in the
shade, or the sunshine, of Alma Mater; a connection
which was to give his spirit just enough of the unrest of
responsibility, and his style just too much perhaps of the
authority of the pedagogue. His early years unfolded

with a security and a simplicity that the middle ones en-
riched without disturbing; and the long presence of
which, with its implications of leisure, of quietude, of
reflection and concentration, supplies in all his work an
element of agreeable relish not lessened by the suggestion
of a certain meagerness of personal experience. He took
his degree in 1838; he married young, in 1844, then again
in 1857; he inherited, on the death of his father in 1861,
the commodious old house of Elmwood (in those days
more embowered and more remote), in which his life
was virtually to be spent. With a small family—a single
daughter—but also a small patrimony, and a deep indifference—his abiding characteristic—to any question
of profit or fortune, the material condition he had from
an early time to meet was the rather blank face turned to
the young American who in that age, and in the consecrated phrase, embraced literature as a profession. The
embrace, on Lowell's part as on that of most such aspirants, was at first more tender than coercive; and he was
no exception to the immemorial rule of propitiating the
idol with verse. This verse took in 1841 the form of his
first book; a collection of poems elsewhere printed and
unprinted, but not afterwards republished.

His history from this time, at least for many years,
would be difficult to write save as a record of stages,
phases, dates too particular for a summary. The general
complexion of the period is best presented in the simple
statement that he was able to surrender on the spot to
his talent and his taste. There is something that fairly
charms, as we look at his life, in the almost complete
elimination of interference or deviation: it makes a picture
exempt from all shadow of the usual image of genius
hindered or inclination blighted. Drama and disaster could
spring as little from within as from without; and no one
in the country probably led a life—certainly for so long a
time—of intellectual amenity so great in proportion to
its intensity. There was more intensity perhaps for such a

spirit as Emerson's: but there was, if only by that fact, more of moral ravage and upheaval; there was less of applied knowledge and successful form, less of the peace of art. Emerson's utterance, his opinions, seem today to give us a series, equally full of beauty and void of order, of noble experiments and fragments. Washington Irving and Longfellow, on the other hand, if they show us the amenity, show us also, in their greater abundance and diffusion, a looseness, an exposure; they sit as it were with open doors, more or less in the social draft. Hawthorne had further to wander and longer to wait; and if he too, in the workshop of art, kept tapping his silver hammer, it was never exactly the nail of thought that he strove to hit on the head. What is true of Hawthorne is truer still of Poe; who, if he had the peace of art, had little of any other. Lowell's evolution was all in what I have called his saturation, in the generous scale on which he was able to gather in and to store up impressions. The three terms of his life for most of the middle time were a quiet fireside, a quiet library, a singularly quiet community. The personal stillness of the world in which for the most part he lived, seems to abide in the delightful paper—originally included in *Fireside Travels*—on "Cambridge Thirty Years Ago." It gives the impression of conditions in which literature might well become an alternate world, and old books, old authors, old names, old stories, constitute in daily commerce the better half of one's company. Complications and distractions were not, even so far as they occurred, appreciably his own portion; except indeed for their being—some of them, in their degree—of the general essence of the life of letters. If books have their destinies, they have also their antecedents; and in the face of the difficulty of trying for perfection with a rough instrument, it cannot of course be said that even concentration shuts the door upon pain. If Lowell had all the joys of the scholar and the poet, he was also, and in just that degree, not a stranger to the pangs and the weariness that accompany the sense of exactitude, of proportion, and of beauty; that feeling for intrinsic success, which in the long run becomes a grievous burdon for shoulders that have in the rash confidence of youth accepted it, becomes indeed in the artist's breast the incurable, intolerable ache.

But such drama as could not mainly, after all, be played out within the walls of his library, came to him, on the whole, during half a century, only in two or three other forms. I mention first the subordinate—which were all, as well, in the day's work: the long grind of teaching the promiscuous and preoccupied young, and those initiations of periodical editorship which, either as worries or as triumphs, may never perhaps be said to strike very deep. In 1855 he entered, at Harvard College, upon the chair just quitted by Longfellow: a comprehensive professorship in literature, that of France and that of Spain in particular. He conducted on its foundation, for four years, the *Atlantic Monthly;* and carried on from 1862, in conjunction with Mr. Charles Eliot Norton, the *North American Review,* in which his best critical essays appeared. There were published the admirable article on Lessing, that on "Rousseau and the Sentimentalists," that on Carlyle's *Frederick the Great,* the rich, replete paper on "Witchcraft," the beautiful studies (1872–5) of Dante, Spenser, and Wordsworth; and the brilliant *jeux d'esprit,* as their overflow of critical wit warrants our calling them, on such subjects as (1866) sundry infirmities of the poetical temper of Swinburne, or such occasions as were offered (1865) by the collected writings of Thoreau, or (1867) by the *Life and Letters* of James Gates Percival— occasions mainly to run to earth a certain shade of the provincial spirit. Of his career from early manhood to the date of his going in 1877 as minister to Spain, the two volumes of his correspondence published in 1893 by Mr. Norton give a picture reducible to a presentment of study in happy conditions, and of opinions on "moral" questions; an image subsequently thrown somewhat into the shade, but still keeping distinctness and dignity for those who at the time had something of a near view of it. Lowell's great good fortune was to believe for so long that opinions and study sufficed him. There came in time a day when he lent himself to more satisfactions than he literally desired; but it is difficult to imagine a case in which the literary life should have been a preparation for the life of the world. There was so much in him of the man and the citizen, as well as of the poet and the professor, that with the full reach of curiosities and sympathies, his imagination found even in narrow walls windows of long range. It was during these years, at any rate, that his poetical and critical spirit were formed; and I speak of him as our prime man of letters precisely on account of the unhurried and unhindered process of the formation. Literature was enough, without being too much, his trade: it made of his life a reservoir never condemned, by too much tapping, to show low water. We have had critics much more frequent, but none more abundant; we have had poets more abundant, but none more acquainted with poetry. This acquaintance with poetry bore fruits of a quality to which I shall presently allude; his critical activity, meantime, was the result of the impulse given by the responsibilities of instructorship to the innermost turn of his mind. His studies could deepen and widen at their ease. The university air soothed, but never smothered; Europe was near enough to touch, but not tormentingly to overlap; the intimate friends were more excellent than numerous, the college feasts just recurrent enough to keep wit in exercise, and the country walks not so blank as to be unsweetened by a close poetic notation of every aspect and secret of nature. He absorbed and lectured and wrote, talked and edited and published; and had, the while, struck early in the day the note from which, for a long time, his main public identity was to spring.

This note, the first of *The Biglow Papers*, was sounded in the summer of 1846, the moment of the outbreak of the Mexican War. It presented not quite as yet so much an "American humorist" the more as the very possibility or fact of the largest expressiveness in American humor. If he was the first of the dialectic and colloquial group in the order of time, so he was to remain, on this ground, the master and the real authority. *The Biglow Papers* were an accident, begun without plan or forecast: but by the accident the author was, in a sense, determined and prompted; he himself caught from them and from their success a fuller idea of the "Yankee" character, lighted up by every advantage that wit and erudition could lend it. Lowell found himself, on the spot, committed to giving it such aid to literary existence as it could never have had without him. His conception of all the fine things of the mind—of intelligence, honesty, judgment, knowledge— was placed straight at the service of the kind of American spirit that he was conscious of in himself, and that he sought in his three or four typical figures to make ironic and racy.

The Biglow Papers are in this relation an extraordinary performance and a rare work of art: in what case, on the part of an artist, has the national consciousness, passionately acute, arrived at a form more independent, more objective? If they were a disclosure of this particular artist's humor, and of the kind of passion that could most possess him, they represent as well the element that for years gave his life its main enlargement, and as may be said its main agitation—the element that preserved him from dryness, from the danger of the dilettante. This safeguard was his care for public things and national questions; those to which, even in his classrooms and his polishings of verse, all others were subordinate. He was politically an ardent liberal and had from the first engaged with all the force of his imagination on the side that has figured at all historical moments as the cause of reform. Reform, in his younger time, meant, above all, resistance to the extension of slavery; then it came to mean—and

by so doing, to give occasion during the Civil War to a
fresh and still finer *Biglow* series—resistance to the pretension of the Southern States to set up a rival republic.
The two great impulses he received from without were
given him by the outbreak of the war, and—after these
full years and wild waves had gradually ebbed—by his
being appointed minister to Spain. The latter event began
a wholly new period, though serving as a channel for
much, for even more perhaps, of the old current; meanwhile, at all events, no account of his most productive
phases at least can afford not to touch on the large part,
the supreme part, played in his life by the intensity, and
perhaps I may go so far as to say the simplicity, of his
patriotism. Patriotism had been the keynote of an infinite
quantity of more or less felicitous behavior; but perhaps
it had never been so much as in Lowell the keynote of
reflection and of the moral tone, of imagination and conversation. Action, in this case, could mainly be but to *feel*
as American as possible—with an inevitable overflow of
course into whatever was the expression of the moment.
It might often have seemed to those who often—or even
to those who occasionally—saw him, that his case was
almost unique, and that the national consciousness had
never elsewhere been so cultivated save under the stress of
national frustration or servitude. It was in fact, in a manner, as if he had been aware of certain forces that made
for oppression; of some league of the nations and the arts,
some concensus of tradition and patronage, to treat as
still in tutelage or on its trial the particular connection of
which he happened most to be proud.

The secret of the situation was that he could only,
could actively, "cultivate" as a retort to cultivation. There
were American phenomena that, as he gathered about the
world, cultivation in general deemed vulgar; and on this
all his genius rose within him to show what *his* cultivation
could make of them. It enabled him to make so much that
all the positive passion in his work is for the direct benefit

of patriotism. That, beyond any other irritation of the lyric temperament, is what makes him ardent. In nothing, moreover, is he more interesting than in the very nature of his vision of this humorous "Yankeeism" of type. He meant something it was at that time comparatively easy, as well as perhaps a trifle more directly inspiring, to mean; for his life opened out backward into Puritan solidities and dignities. However this be, at any rate, his main care for the New England—or, as may almost be said, for the Cambridge—consciousness, as he embodied it, was that it could be fed from as many sources as any other in the world, and assimilate them with an ingenuity all its own: literature, life, poetry, art, wit, all the growing experience of human intercourse. His great honor is that in this direction he led it to high success; and if *The Biglow Papers* express supremely his range of imagination about it, they render the American tone the service of placing it in the best literary company—that of all his other affinities and echoes, his love of the older English and the older French, of all classics and romantics and originals, of Dante and Goethe, of Cervantes and the Elizabethans; his love, in particular, of the history of language and of the complex questions of poetic form. If they had no other distinction, they would have that of one of the acutest of all studies in linguistics. They are more literary, in short, than they at first appear; which is at once the strength and the weakness of his poetry in general, literary indeed as most of it is at sight. The chords of his lyre were of the precious metal, but not perhaps always of the last lyric tenuity. He struck them with a hand not idle enough for mere moods, and yet not impulsive enough for the great reverberations. He was sometimes too ingenious, as well as too reasonable and responsible; this leaves him, on occasion, too much in the grasp of a certain morally conservative humor—a side on which he touches the authors of "society" verse—or else mixes with his emotion an intellectual substance, a something alien, that tends to·

stiffen and retard it. Perhaps I only mean indeed that he
had always something to say, and his sturdiness as well as
his "cleverness" about the way it should be said. It is congruous, no doubt, with his poetic solidity that his highest
point in verse is reached by his "Harvard Commemoration
Ode," a poem for an occasion at once public and intimate;
a sustained lament for young lives, in the most vividly
sacrificed of which he could divide with the academic
mother something of the sentiment of proud ownership.
It is unfair to speak of lines so splendid as these as not
warmed by the noble thought with which they are
charged—even if it be of the very nature of the English
ode to show us always, at its best, something of the chill of
the poetic Exercise.

I may refer, however, as little to the detail of his verse
as to that of the robust body of his prose. The latter
consists of richly accomplished literary criticism, and of
a small group of public addresses; and would obviously be
much more abundant were we in possession of all the
wrought material of Harvard lectures and professorial
talks. If we are not, it is because Lowell recognized no
material as wrought till it had passed often through the
mill. He embarked on no *magnum opus*, historical, bio-
graphical, critical; he contented himself with uttering
thought that had great works in its blood. It was for the
great works and the great figures he cared; he was a critic
of a pattern mainly among ourselves superseded—superseded so completely that he seems already to have receded
into time, and to belong to an age of vulgarity less
blatant. If he was in educated appreciation the most distinct voice that the United States had produced, this is
partly, no doubt, because the chatter of the day and the
triumph of the trivial could even then still permit him to
be audible, permit him to show his office as supported on
knowledge and on a view of the subject. He represented
so well the use of a view of the subject that he may be
said to have represented best what at present strikes us

as most urgent; the circumstance, namely, that so far from being a chamber surrendering itself from the threshold to the ignorant young of either sex, criticism is positively and miraculously *not* the simplest and most immediate, but the most postponed and complicated of the arts, the last qualified for and arrived at, the one requiring behind it most maturity, most power to understand and compare.

One is disposed to say of him, in spite of his limited production, that he belonged to the massive race, and even has for the present the air of one of the last of it. The two volumes of his *Letters* help, in default of a biography, the rest of his work in testifying to this; and would do so still more if the collection had comprised more letters of the time of his last period in Europe. His diplomatic years—he was appointed in 1880 minister to England—form a chapter by themselves; they gave a new turn to his career, and made a different thing of what was to remain of it. They checked, save here and there for an irrepressible poem, his literary production; but they opened a new field—in the motherland of "occasional" oratory—for his beautiful command of the spoken word. He spoke often from this moment, and always with his admirable mixture of breadth and wit; with so happy a surrender indeed to this gift that his two finest addresses, that on *Democracy* (Birmingham, 1884) and that on the Harvard Anniversary of 1886, connect themselves with the reconsecration, late in life, of his eloquence. It was a singular fortune, and possible for an American alone, that such a want of peculiarly professional, of technical training, should have been consistent with a degree of success that appeared to reduce training to unimportance. Nothing was more striking, in fact, than that what Lowell had most in England to show was simply all the air and all the effect of preparedness. If I have alluded to the best name we can give him and the best niche we can make for him, let this be partly because letters exactly met in

him a more distinguished recognition than usually falls
to their lot. It was they that had prepared him really; prepared him—such is the subtlety of their operation—even
for the things from which they are most divorced. He
reached thus the phase in which he took from them as
much as he had given; represented them in a new, insidious way. It was of course in his various speeches that
his preparedness came out most; most enjoyed the super-
lative chance of becoming, by the very fact of its exercise,
one of the safeguards of an international relation that he
would have blushed not to have done his utmost to keep
inviolable. He had the immense advantage that the very
voice in which he could speak—so much at once that of
his masculine, pugnacious intellect, and that of the best
side of the race—was a plea for everything the millions
of English stock have in common. This voice, as I may
call it, that sounds equally in every form of his utterance,
was his great gift to his time. In poetry, in satire, in prose,
and on his lips, it was from beginning to end the manliest,
the most ringing, to be heard. He was essentially a fighter;
he could always begin the attack; could always, in criticism as in talk, sound the charge and open the fire. The
old Puritan conscience was deep in him, with its strong
and simple vision, even in æsthetic things, of evil and of
good, of wrong and of right; and his magnificent wit
was all at its special service. He armed it, for vindication
and persuasion, with all the amenities, the "humanities"
—with weapons as sharp and bright as it has ever carried.

AN AMERICAN ART-SCHOLAR
CHARLES ELIOT NORTON[1]

I GLADLY embrace the occasion to devote a few words to the honored memory of my distinguished friend the late Charles Eliot Norton, who, dying at Cambridge, Massachusetts, on the 21st of October last, after having reached his eightieth year, had long occupied—and with an originality of spirit and a beneficence of effect all his own—the chair of the History of the Fine Arts at Harvard University, as well as, in the view of the American world surrounding that seat of influence, the position of one of the most accomplished of scholars and most efficient of citizens. This commemorative page may not disclaim the personal tone, for I can speak of Charles Norton but in the light of an affection which began long years ago, even though my part in our relation had to be, for some time, markedly that of a junior; of which tie I was to remain ever after, despite long stretches of material separation, a conscious and grateful beneficiary. I can speak of him therefore as I happened myself to see and know him—with interest and sympathy acting, for

[1] This essay first appeared in the *Burlington Magazine*, January 1909, and was reprinted in *Notes on Novelists* (1914). From NOTES ON NOVELISTS by Henry James; copyright 1914 by Charles Scribner's Sons, 1942 by Henry James. Reprinted by permission of the publishers.

considerable periods together, across distances and superficial differences, yet with the sense of his extremely individual character and career suffering no abatement, and
indeed with my impression of the fine consistency and
exemplary value of these things clear as never before.

I find this impression go back for its origin very far—
to one autumn day when, an extremely immature as-
pirant to the rare laurel of the critic, I went out from
Boston to Cambridge to offer him a contribution to the
old, if I should not rather say the then middle-aged,
North American Review, of which he had recently undertaken the editorship. I already knew him a little, enough
to have met casual kindness at his hands; but my vision
of his active presence and function, in the community
that had happily produced and that was long to enjoy
him, found itself, I think, completely constituted at that
hour, with scarce an essential touch to be afterwards
added. He largely developed and expanded as time went
on; certain more or less local reserves and conservatisms
fell away from him; but his temper and attitude, all his
own from the first, were to give a singular unity to his
life. This intensity of perception on his young visitor's
part may perhaps have sprung a little from the fact that
he accepted on the spot, as the visitor still romantically
remembers, a certain very first awkward essay in criticism,[2] and was to publish it in his forthcoming number;
but I little doubt whether even had he refused it the
grace of the whole occasion would have lost anything to
my excited view, and feel sure that the interest in particular would have gained had he charmingly put before me
(as he would have been sure to do) the ground of his
discrimination. For his eminent character as a "repre-

[2] Henry James telescopes matters somewhat. Extant correspondence at Harvard shows that he addressed his first
article to Norton by post July 1864 and did not call on him
at Shady Hill until the early months of 1865. (See Leon Edel:
Henry James: The Untried Years (1953), pp. 206–9.)

sentative of culture" announced itself exactly in proportion as one's general sense of the medium in which it was to be exerted was strong; and I seem verily to recall that even in the comparative tenderness of that season I had grasped the idea of the precious, the quite far-reaching part such an exemplar might play. Charles Norton's distinction and value—this was still some years before his professorate had taken form—showed early and above all the note and the advantage that they were to be virtues of American application, and were to draw their life from the signal American opportunity; to that degree that the detailed record of his influence would be really one of the most interesting of American social documents, and that his good work is best lighted by a due acquaintance with the conditions of the life about him, indispensable for a founded recognition of it. It is not too much to say that the representative of culture—always in the high and special sense in which he practiced that faith—had before him in the United States of those days a great and arduous mission, requiring plentiful courage as well as plentiful knowledge, endless good humor as well as assured taste.

What comes back to me then from the early day I have glanced at is exactly that prompt sense of the clustered evidence of my friend's perfect adaptation to the civilizing mission, and not least to the needfully dauntless and unperturbed side of it. His so pleasant old hereditary home, with its ample acres and numerous spoils—at a time when acres merely marginal and, so to speak, atmospheric, as well as spoils at all felicitously gathered, were rare in the United States—seemed to minister to the general assurance, constituting as they did such a picture of life as one vaguely supposed recognizable, right and left, in an old society, or, otherwise expressed, in that "Europe" which was always, roundabout one, the fond alternative of the cultivated imagination, but of which the possible American copy ever seemed far to seek. To put it in a nutshell, the pilgrimage to the Shady Hill of those years had, among the "spoils," among pictures and books, drawings and medals, memories and relics and anecdotes, things of a remote but charming reference, very much the effect of a sudden rise into a finer and clearer air and of a stopgap against one's own coveted renewal of the more direct experience. If I allude to a particular, to a personal yearning appreciation of those matters, it is with the justified conviction—this justification having been, all along, abundantly perceptible—that appreciation of the general sort only waited to be called for, though to be called for with due authority. It was the sign of our host, on the attaching spot, and almost the principal one, that he spoke, all round and with the highest emphasis, as under the warrant of authority, and that at a time when, as to the main matter of his claim and his discourse, scarce anyone pretended to it, he carried himself valiantly under that banner. The main matter of his discourse offered itself just simply as the matter of *civilization*—the particular civilization that a young roaring and money-getting democracy, inevitably but almost exclusively occupied with "business success," most needed to have brought home to it. The New England air in especial was no natural conductor of any appeal to an æsthetic aim, but the interest of Professor Norton's general work, to say nothing of the interest of his character for a closer view, is exactly that the whole fruitful enterprise was to prove, intimately, a New England adventure; illustrating thus at the same time and once more the innate capacity of New England for leavening the great American mass on the finer issues.   .

To have grown up as the accomplished man at large was in itself at that time to have felt, and even in some degree to have suffered, this hand of differentiation; the only accomplished men of the exhibited New England Society had been the ministers, the heads of the congregations—whom, however, one docks of little of their credit in saying that their accomplishments and their earnestness had been almost wholly in the moral order. The advantage of that connection was indeed what Norton was fundamentally to have enjoyed in his descent, both on his father's and his mother's side (pre-eminently on the latter, the historic stock of the Eliots) from a long line of those stalwart pastoral worthies who had notably formed the aristocracy of Massachusetts. It was largely, no doubt, to this heritage of character and conscience that he owed the strong and special strain of confidence with which he addressed himself to the business of perfect candor toward his fellow citizens—his pupils in particular; they, to whom this candor was to become in the long run the rarest and raciest and most endearing of "treats," being but his fellow citizens in the making. This view of an urgent duty would have been a comparatively slight thing, moreover, without the special preoccupations, without the love of the high humanities and curiosities and urbanities in themselves, without the conception of science and the ingrained studious cast of mind, which had been also an affair of heredity with him and had opened his eyes betimes to educative values and standards other than most of those he saw flourish near at hand. He would defer to dilettantism as little as to vulgarity, and if he ultimately embraced the fine ideal of taking up the work that lay close to him at home, and of irrigating the immediate arid tracts and desert spaces, it was not from ignorance of the temptation to wander and linger where the streams already flowed and the soil had already borne an abiding fruit.

He had come to Italy and to England early in life; he had repeated his visits to these countries with infinite relish and as often as possible—though never, as a good New Englander, without certain firm and, where they had to be, invidious discriminations; he was attached to them by a hundred intellectual and social ties; but he had been from the first incapable of doubting that the best activity and the liveliest interest lay where it always, given certain conditions, lies in America—in a measure of response to intellectual and æsthetic "missionary" labor more traceable and appreciable, more distinguishably attested and registered, more directly and artlessly grateful, in a word, than in the thicker elemental mixture of Europe. On the whole side of taste and association his choice was thus betimes for conscious exile and for a considerably, though doubtless not altogether irremediably, deprived state; but it was at the same time for a freedom of exhortation and a play of ironic comment less restricted, after all, in the clear American air, than on ground more pretentiously enclosed—less restricted, that is, from the moment personal conviction might be absolute and indifference to every form of provincial bewilderment equally patient and complete. The incontestable *crânerie* of his attitude—a thing that one felt to be a high form of sincerity—always at last won success; the respect and affection that more and more surrounded him and that finally made his situation sole of its kind and pre-eminently happy, attest together the interesting truth that unqualified confidence in one's errand, the serenest acceptance of a responsibility and the exercise of a critical authority never too apt to return critically upon itself, only require for beneficent action that they be attended at once with a fund of illustration and a fund of good humor.

Professor Norton's pre-eminent work in the interpretation of Dante—by which I mean his translation, text and notes, of the *Divine Comedy* and the *New Life,* an achievement of infinite piety, patience, and resource; his admirable volume on *Church-Building in the Middle Ages* (to say nothing of his charming earlier one, *Study and Travel in Italy,* largely devoted to the cathedral of Orvieto); his long and intimate friendship with Ruskin, commemorated by his publication, as joint-executor to

Ruskin's will, of the best fruits of the latter's sustained correspondence with him; his numerous English friendships, in especial—to say nothing of his native—all with persons of a highly representative character: these things give in part the measure of his finest curiosities and of his appetite, in all directions, for the best sources and examples and the best company. But it is probable that if his Harvard lectures are in form for publication, and if his general correspondence, and above all his own easily handsomest show in it, comes to be published, as most emphatically it should be, they will testify not in the least to any unredeemed contraction of life, but to the largest and happiest and most rewarded energy. An exhilarated invocation of close responsibility, an absolute ease of mind about one's point of view, a thorough and never-failing intellectual wholeness, are so far from weakening the appeal to young allegiances that, once they succeed at all, they succeed the better for going all their length. So it was that, with admirable urbanity of form and uncompromising straightness of attack, the Professor of the History of the Fine Arts at Harvard for a quarter of a century let himself go; thinking no trouble wasted and no flutter and no scandal other than auspicious if only he might, to the receptive and aspiring undergraduate mind, brand the ugly and the vulgar and the inferior wherever he found them, tracking them through plausible disguises and into trumpery strongholds; if only he might convert young products of the unmitigated American order into material for men of the world in the finer sense of that term; if only, in short, he might render more supple their view, liable to obfuscation from sights and sounds about them, of the true meaning of a liberal education and of the civilized character and spirit in the civilized State.

What it came to thus was that he availed himself to the utmost of his free hand for sowing and planting ideals—ideals that, though they might after all be vague and

general things, lacking sometimes a little the clearer connections with practice, were yet a new and inspiring note
to most of his hearers, who could be trusted, just so far as
they were intelligent and loyal, not to be heavily embar-
rassed by them, not to want for fields of application. It
was given him, quite unprecedentedly, to be popular, to
be altogether loved and cherished, even while "rubbing it
into" whomever it might concern that such unfortunates
were mainly given over to mediocrity and vulgarity, and
that half the crude and ugly objects and aspects, half the
low standards and loose ends surrounding them and which
they might take for granted with a facility and a complacency alike deplorable, represented a platitude of imagination that dishonored the citizen on whom a university worthy of the name should have left its stamp.
Happy, it would thus in fact seem, beyond any other
occasion for educative influence, the immense and delightful opportunity he enjoyed, the clear field and long
reach attached to preaching an æsthetic crusade, to pleading for the higher amenities in general, in a new and
superficially tutored, yet also but superficially prejudiced,
country, where a consequently felt and noted rise of the
tide of manners may be held to have come home to him,
or certainly to have visited his dreams. His effect on the
community at large, with allowances of time, was ever
indubitable—even though such workers have everywhere
to take much on trust and to remember that bushels of
doctrine, and even tons of example, make at the most
ounces and grains of responsive life. It can only be the
very general and hopeful view that sustains and rewards—
with here and there, at wide intervals, the prized individual instance of the sown seed actively emerging and
flowering.

If not all ingenious disciples could give independent
proof, however, all could rally and feel the spirit; all could
crowd to a course of instruction which, largely elective

and optional, yet united more listeners than many others put together, and in which the subject itself, the illustration of European artistic endeavor at large, or, in other words, the record of man's most comprehensive sacrifice to organized beauty, tended so to take up, on familiar ground, the question of manners, character, conscience, tone, to bristle with questions addressed to the actual and possible American scene. That, I hasten to add, was of course but one side of the matter; there were wells of special science for those who chose to draw from them, and an inner circle of pupils whose whole fruitful relation to their philosopher and friend—the happy and easy privilege of Shady Hill in general, where other charming personal influences helped, not counting as least in this— can scarce have failed to prepare much practical evidence for observation still to come. The ivory tower of study would ever, by his natural bent, I think, have most solicited Charles Norton; but he liked, as I say, he accepted without a reserve, the function of presiding over young destinies; he believed in the personal and the social communication of light, and had a gift for the generous and personal relation that perhaps found its best issue, as I have already hinted, in his admirable letters. These were not of this hustled and hustling age, but of a cooler and steadier sphere and rhythm, and of a charming mannerly, substantial type to which he will have been, I think, among correspondents truly animated by the social spirit and a due cosmopolite ideal, one of the last systematically to sacrifice. With the lapse of years I ceased to be, I admit, a near spectator of his situation; but my sense of his activity—with more intimate renewals, besides, occasionally taking place—was to be, all along, so constantly fed by echo and anecdote and all manner of indirect glimpses, that I find myself speak quite with the confidence, and with all the attachment, of a continuous "assistant."

        •   •   •

With which, if I reflect on this, I see how interesting a *case*, above all, my distinguished friend was ever to remain to me—a case, I mean, of such a mixture of the elements as would have seemed in advance, critically speaking, quite anomalous, or at least highly incalculable. His interest was predominantly in Art, as the most beneficial of human products; his ostensible plea was for the æsthetic law, under the wide wing of which we really move, it may seem to many of us, in an air of strange and treacherous appearances, of much bewilderment and not a little mystification, of terribly fine and complicated issues in short, such as call for the highest interpretative wisdom. But if nothing was of a more delightful example than Professor Norton's large and nourished serenity in all these connections, a serenity seasoned and tempered, as it were, by infinite interest in his "subject," by a steadying faith in exact and extensive knowledge, so to a fond and incorrigible student of character the case, as I have called it, and the long and genial career, may seem to shine in the light of quite other importances, quite other references, than the presumed and the nominal. Nothing in fact *can* be more interesting to a haunter of other intellectual climes and a worshipper at the æsthetic shrine *quand même* than to note once more how race and implanted quality and association always in the end come by their own; how, for example, a son of the Puritans the most intellectually transmuted, the most liberally emancipated and initiated possible, could still plead most for substance when proposing to plead for style, could still try to lose himself in the labyrinth of delight while keeping tight hold of the clue of duty, tangled even a little in his feet; could still address himself all consistently to the moral conscience while speaking as by his office for our imagination and our free curiosity. All of which vision of him, however, is far from pointing to a wasted effort. The great thing, whatever turn we take, is to find before us perspectives and to have a weight to throw; in accord-

ance with which wisdom the world he lived in received
for long no firmer nor more gallant and generous impress
than that of Charles Eliot Norton.

PART TWO

Other Voices

*

MR. WALT WHITMAN [1]

IT HAS BEEN a melancholy task to read this book; and
it is a still more melancholy one to write about it. Perhaps since the day of Mr. Tupper's *Philosophy* there has
been no more difficult reading of the poetic sort. It exhibits the effort of an essentially prosaic mind to lift itself,
by a prolonged muscular strain, into poetry. Like hundreds
of other good patriots, during the last four years, Mr.
Walt Whitman has imagined that a certain amount of
violent sympathy with the great deeds and sufferings of
our soldiers, and of admiration for our national energy,
together with a ready command of picturesque language,
are sufficient inspiration for a poet. If this were the case,

[1] This review of Walt Whitman's *Drum-Taps* appeared unsigned in the *Nation* of November 16, 1865, when James was
twenty-two. In 1903, a friend and former editor of the
New York *World*, Manton Marble, wrote him: "Not yet have
I perused that early paper of yours on Walt Whitman, but
the hope to see you blush inspires my pursuit." This evoked
the following reply from James on October 10, 1903: "I can
. . . bring out a thank you for your intimation in respect to
the little atrocity I mentioned remembering to have perpe-
trated (on W. W.) in the gross impudence of youth—yes,
even a thank-you-very-much-indeed. But nothing would induce
me to reveal the whereabouts of my disgrace, which I only
recollect as deep and damning. The place I dimly remember,
but the year is utterly vague to me—I only know that I haven't
seen the accursed thing for more than thirty years, and that
if it were to cross my path nothing would induce me to look
at it. I am so far from 'keeping' the abominations of my early
innocence that I destroy them wherever I spy them—which,
thank goodness, occurs rarely." (Unpublished letter in the
Houghton Library, Harvard University.)

we had been a nation of poets. The constant developments
of the war moved us continually to strong feeling and to
strong expression of it. But in those cases in which these
expressions were written out and printed with all due
regard to prosody, they failed to make poetry, as anyone
may see by consulting now in cold blood the back volumes of the "Rebellion Record." *Of course* the city of
Manhattan, as Mr. Whitman delights to call it, when
regiments poured through it in the first months of the
war, and its own sole god, to borrow the words of a real
poet, ceased for a while to be the millionaire, was a noble
spectacle, and a poetical statement to this effect is possible. *Of course* the tumult of a battle is grand, the results
of a battle tragic, and the untimely deaths of young men
a theme for elegies. But he is not a poet who merely re-
iterates these plain facts *ore rotundo*. He only sings them
worthily who views them from a height. Every tragic
event collects about it a number of persons who delight
to dwell upon its superficial points—of minds which are
bullied by the *accidents* of the affair. The temper of such
minds seems to us to be the reverse of the poetic temper;
for the poet, although he incidentally masters, grasps,
and uses the superficial traits of his theme, is really a poet
only in so far as he extracts its latent meaning and holds
it up to common eyes. And yet from such minds most of
our war-verses have come, and Mr. Whitman's utterances,
much as the assertion may surprise his friends, are in this
respect no exception to general fashion. They are an exception, however, in that they openly pretend to be
something better; and this it is that makes them melancholy reading. Mr. Whitman is very fond of blowing his
own trumpet, and he has made very explicit claims for
his book. "Shut not your doors," he exclaims at the outset—

"Shut not your doors to me, proud libraries,
   For that which was lacking among you all, yet needed
      most, I bring;

A book I have made for your dear sake, O soldiers,
And for you, O soul of man, and you, love of comrades;
The words of my book nothing, the life of it everything;
A book separate, not link'd with the rest, nor felt by the
    intellect;
But you will feel every word, O Libertad! arm'd Liber-
    tad!
It shall pass by the intellect to swim the sea, the air,
With joy with you, O soul of man."

These are great pretensions, but it seems to us that the
following are even greater:

"From Paumanok starting, I fly like a bird,
Around and around to soar, to sing the idea of all;
To the north betaking myself, to sing there arctic songs,
To Kanada, 'till I absorb Kanada in myself—to Michigan
    then,
To Wisconsin, Iowa, Minnesota, to sing their songs (they
    are inimitable);
Then to Ohio and Indiana, to sing theirs—to Missouri
    and Kansas and Arkansas to sing theirs,
To Tennessee and Kentucky—to the Carolinas and
    Georgia, to sing theirs,
To Texas, and so along up toward California, to roam
    accepted everywhere;
To sing first (to the tap of the war-drum, if need be)
The idea of all—of the western world, one and insepa-
    rable,
And then the song of each member of these States."

Mr. Whitman's primary purpose is to celebrate the
greatness of our armies; his secondary purpose is to celebrate the greatness of the city of New York. He pursues
these objects through a hundred pages of matter which
remind us irresistibly of the story of the college professor who, on a venturesome youth's bringing him a theme
done in blank verse, reminded him that it was not cus-

tomary in writing prose to begin each line with a capital. The frequent capitals are the only marks of verse in Mr. Whitman's writing. There is, fortunately, but one attempt at rhyme. We say fortunately, for if the inequality of Mr. Whitman's lines were self-registering, as it would be in the case of an anticipated syllable at their close, the effect would be painful in the extreme. As the case stands, each line starts off by itself, in resolute independence of its companions, without a visible goal. But if Mr. Whitman does not write verse, he does not write ordinary prose. The reader has seen that liberty is "libertad." In like manner, comrade is "camerado"; Americans are "Americanos"; a pavement is a "trottoir," and Mr. Whitman himself is a "chansonnier." If there is one thing that Mr. Whitman is not, it is this, for Béranger was a *chansonnier*. To appreciate the force of our conjunction, the reader should compare his military lyrics with Mr. Whitman's declamations. Our author's novelty, however, is not in his words, but in the form of his writing. As we have said, it begins for all the world like verse and turns out to be arrant prose. It is more like Mr. Tupper's proverbs than anything we have met. But what if, in form, it *is* prose? it may be asked. Very good poetry has come out of prose before this. To this we would reply that it must first have gone into it. Prose, in order to be good poetry, must first be good prose. As a general principle, we know of no circumstance more likely to impugn a writer's earnestness than the adoption of an anomalous style. He must have something very original to say if none of the old vehicles will carry his thoughts. Of course he *may* be surprisingly original. Still, presumption is against him. If on examination the matter of his discourse proves very valuable, it justifies, or at any rate excuses, his literary innovation.

But if, on the other hand, it is of a common quality, with nothing new about it but its manners, the public will judge the writer harshly. The most that can be said of Mr. Whitman's vaticinations is, that, cast in a fluent and familiar manner, the average substance of them might escape unchallenged. But we have seen that Mr. Whitman prides himself especially on the substance—the life—of his poetry. It may be rough, it may be grim, it may be clumsy—such we take to be the author's argument—but it is sincere, it is sublime, it appeals to the soul of man, it is the voice of a people. He tells us, in the lines quoted, that the words of his book are nothing. To our perception they are everything, and very little at that. A great deal of verse that is nothing but words has, during the war, been sympathetically sighed over and cut out of newspaper corners, because it has possessed a certain simple melody. But Mr. Whitman's verse, we are confident, would have failed even of this triumph, for the simple reason that no triumph, however small, is won but through the exercise of art, and that this volume is an offense against art. It is not enough to be grim and rough and careless; common sense is also necessary, for it is by common sense that we are judged. There exists in even the commonest minds, in literary matters, a certain precise instinct of conservatism, which is very shrewd in detecting wanton eccentricities. To this instinct Mr. Whitman's attitude seems monstrous. It is monstrous because it pretends to persuade the soul while it slights the intellect; because it pretends to gratify the feelings while it outrages the taste. The point is that it does this *on theory*, wilfully, consciously, arrogantly. It is the little nursery game of "open your mouth and shut your eyes." Our hearts are often touched through a compromise with the artistic sense, but never in direct violation of it. Mr. Whitman sits down at the outset and counts out the intelligence. This were indeed a wise precaution on his part if the intelligence were only submissive! But when she is deliberately insulted, she takes her revenge by simply standing erect and open-eyed. This is assuredly the best she can do. And if she could find a voice she would probably address Mr. Whitman as follows: "You came to woo my sister, the human soul. Instead of giving me a kick as you approach, you should either greet me courteously, or, at least, steal in unobserved. But now you have me on your hands. Your chances are poor. What the human heart desires above all is sincerity, and you do not appear to me sincere. For a lover you talk entirely too much about yourself. In one place you threaten to absorb Kanada. In another you call upon the city of New York to incarnate you, as you have incarnated it. In another you inform us that neither youth pertains to you nor "delicatesse," that you are awkward in the parlor, that you do not dance, and that you have neither bearing, beauty, knowledge, nor fortune. In another place, by an allusion to your "little songs," you seem to identify yourself with the third person of the Trinity. For a poet who claims to sing "the idea of all," this is tolerably egotistical. We look in vain, however, through your book for a single idea. We find nothing but flashy imitations of ideas. We find a medley of extravagances and commonplaces. We find art, measure, grace, sense sneered at on every page, and nothing positive given us in their stead. To be positive one must have something to say; to be positive requires reason, labor, and art; and art requires, above all things, a suppression of one's self, a subordination of one's self to an idea. This will never do for you, whose plan is to adapt the scheme of the universe to your own limitations. You cannot entertain and exhibit ideas; but, as we have seen, you are prepared to incarnate them. It is for this reason, doubtless, that when once you have planted yourself squarely before the public, and in view of the great service you have done to the ideal, have become, as you say, "accepted everywhere," you can afford to deal exclusively in words. What would be bald nonsense and dreary platitudes in anyone else becomes sublimity in you. But all this is a mistake. To become adopted as a national poet, it is not enough to discard everything in particular and to accept everything in general, to amass crudity

upon crudity, to discharge the undigested contents of
your blotting-book into the lap of the public. You must
respect the public which you address; for it has taste,
if you have not. It delights in the grand, the heroic,
and the masculine; but it delights to see these conceptions
cast into worthy form. It is indifferent to brute sublimity.
It will never do for you to thrust your hands into your
pockets and cry out that, as the research of form is an
intolerable bore, the shortest and most economical way
for the public to embrace its idols—for the nation to
realize its genius—is in your own person. This democratic, liberty-loving, American populace, this stern and
war-tried people, is a great civilizer. It is devoted to refinement. If it has sustained a monstrous war, and practiced human nature's best in so many ways for the last
five years, it is not to put up with spurious poetry afterwards. To sing aright our battles and our glories it is not
enough to have served in a hospital (however praise-
worthy the task in itself), to be aggressively careless, in-
elegant, and ignorant, and to be constantly preoccupied
with yourself. It is not enough to be rude, lugubrious, and
grim. You must also be serious. You must forget yourself
in your ideas. Your personal qualities—the vigor of your
temperament, the manly independence of your nature, the
tenderness of your heart—these facts are impertinent.
You must be *possessed*, and you must strive to possess
your possession. If in your striving you break into divine
eloquence, then you are a poet. If the idea which possesses
you is the idea of your country's greatness, then you are
a national poet; and not otherwise."

FRANCIS PARKMAN

THE OLD RÉGIME IN CANADA[1]

CANADA, though it is a large corner of the world, is a small
corner of history; but such as it is, Mr. Parkman has made
it his own province. He has just added another volume to
the series of deeply interesting chronicles in which he has
been tracing, for the last ten years, the more distinctively
heroic element in American history. Looking at the matter
superficially, we need to make a certain effort to interest
ourselves in the Canadian past. It is hard not to imagine its
records to be as bleak and arid and provincial as the
aspects of nature and of society in this frigid colony, and
we instinctively transpose the climate into a moral key,
and think of human emotion there as having been always
rather numb and unproductive. Canadian history is, moreover, meager in quantity; it deals with small enterprises,
small numbers, small names, names at least which have not
become household words nearly as often as they deserved
to do. And then it swarms with savages, and the Iroquois

---

[1] *The Old Régime in Canada*, by Francis Parkman (Boston:
Little, Brown & Co.; 1874). This review appeared unsigned in
the *Nation*, October 15, 1874.

and the Mohawk are essentially monotonous and unhis-
torical. But to Mr. Parkman belongs the credit of having
perceived the capacities of all this unpromising material,
and felt that if his work must be a slender chronicle of
events separated from the main current of modern civilization, in the quality of its interest, at least, it would be
second to none. It is the history of an heroic undertaking,
and the heroism pervades the most obscure details. The
men and women by whose help the settlement of Canada
was effected offer an exhibition of conduct which needed
nothing but a stage placed a little more in the foreground
of human affairs to have become a familiar lesson in
morals. It is hard to see in what element of grandeur such
an incident as the resistance of Adam Daulac, with his
seventeen Frenchmen and his forty Hurons, related by
Mr. Parkman in his present volume, is inferior to the
struggle of Leonidas and his Greeks at Thermopylæ. And
yet while all the world, for two thousand years, has heard
of Leonidas, who until now had heard of Adam Daulac?
He made a stand for a week against a thousand Iroquois
whom he had gone forth with sublime temerity to chas-
tise, and died fighting hard and hacked to pieces, with
history to close about him as duskily as the Northern
forests that witnessed his struggle. Of course Greece de-
pended on Leonidas, and only Quebec on poor Daulac,
but we cannot but feel nevertheless that fame in this world
is rather capriciously apportioned. In the same chapter
which narrates Daulac's crusade, Mr. Parkman prints a
short letter of the time, which seems to us worth quoting.
It was written by a lad of eighteen, François Hertel by
name, who had been captured by the Mohawks:

"MY MOST DEAR AND HONORED MOTHER: I know very
well that my capture must have distressed you very
much. I ask you to forgive my disobedience. It is my
sins that have placed me where I am. I owe my life
to your prayers and those of M. de Saint-Quentin and

of my sisters. I hope to see you again before winter. I
pray you to tell the good brethren of Notre Dame to
pray to God and the Holy Virgin for me, my dear
mother, and for you and all my sisters.—Your poor
                                        FANCHON."

With this had been sent another letter to a friend, to
whom he confides that his right hand has been burned,
and the thumb of the other one chopped off by the
Mohawks. He begs, however, his mother may not hear
of it. Poor Fanchon's sad little note seems therefore an
epitome of the early Canadian character at its best. Stout
endurance and orthodox Catholicism form the simple
sum of it, and the note of devout manliness, as this young
adventurer strikes it, is heard as distinctly through two
centuries as if it had been sounded but yesterday.
Whether François Hertel kept his devotion to the end
we are unable to say, but he never lost his pluck. Thirty
years afterwards he led a raid into New England, and
indeed it is probable that the writer of the foregoing lines
hated the Massachusetts colonists no less heartily as her-
etics than as rivals. Rugged courage, active and passive
alike, is the constant savor of Mr. Parkman's subject, and
it has at last very much the effect of giving his work the
air (minus the dryness) of a stoical treatise on morals.
It is as wholesome as Epictetus, and, as a proof of what
may be achieved by the rigid human will, it is extremely
inspiring. Such works make one think better of mankind,
and we can imagine, in this age of cultivated sensibility,
no better reading for generous boys and girls. Mr. Parkman has been himself inspired by his theme—as during
much of his labor, amid the interruptions of failing
eyesight and ill health, he has well needed to be. He
treats his subject as one who knows it in a personal as
well as in a literary way, and is evidently no less at
home among the Northern woods and lakes than among
the archives of the French Marine. His descriptive touches

are never vague and rhetorical (except once, perhaps,
where he speaks of the "gorgeous euthanasia of the dying
season"); they make definite, characteristic pictures. His
Jesuits and trappers are excellent, but his Indians are even
better, and he has plainly ventured to look at the squalid
savage *de près* and for himself. His style is a capital
narrative style, and though abundantly vivid, resists the
modern temptation to be picturesque at any cost. Material
for his task is indeed apparently so plentiful that he is
spared the necessity for that familiarly conjectural discourse on the unknown and unknowable which marks the
latest school of historians. He is, moreover, a very sufficient philosopher, and competent at all points to read
the political lesson of his story. We have been especially
struck with his fairness. He is an incorruptible Protestant,
dealing with an intensely Catholic theme, but he appears
wholly free from any disposition to serve his personages'
narrow measure, or bear more heavily on their foibles
than his facts exactly warrant. He can hardly expect
to have fully pleased Catholic readers, but he must have
displeased them singularly little. Never, it must be added,
was there a case in which Catholicism could so easily
afford to be judged on its own strict merits as in this
early history of Canada.

With his present volume Mr. Parkman has brought
his narrative well on towards its climax, and in no portion
of it has the need to read the political lesson been more
urgent. We have here related the fortunes of the infant
colony from the time Louis XIV took it paternally by the
hand until his decline and death left it again to do battle
unaided with its native wilderness. They form a very
curious and, in some aspects, an almost comical history.
It would be difficult to find a more pregnant and convenient example of the vicious side of the great French
virtue—the passion for administration. The example is the
more striking, as Mr. Parkman forcibly points out, that we
see it contrasted with an equally eminent embodiment

of the great English virtue—the faculty of shifting for one's self. How extremely artifical a creation was French Canada, how it was nursed and coddled and bribed and caressed; by what innumerable devices it was enticed and encouraged into a certain prosperity, and propped and legislated into a certain stability; how everything came to it from without, and as time went on, and security was established, and the need for the more acutely heroic virtues declined, nothing from within; how it was a fancy of Colbert's and a hobby of the King's, and how it languished when they passed away—all this is unfolded by Mr. Parkman with superabundance of illustration. It was a sort of luxury of the King's conscience, and one of the trappings of his grandeur, and it offers the oddest combination of the Versailles view of things and the hard reality of things themselves. It has become the fashion to smile a good deal at the so-called greatness of Louis XIV, and there is no doubt that, when tapped by the impudent knuckle of modern criticism, much of it rings very hollow. French Canada was hollow enough, and yet it bears in a manner the stamp of a brilliant period. There was greatness in the idea of establishing a purely religious colony for the glory of God and the most Christian King —a disinterested focus of conversion for hordes of thankless savages. The way chosen was sadly erratic, but the error was of a splendid kind. The King's generosity was boundless, and Mr. Parkman says that no application for money was ever refused. Applications were incessant; the colonists never dreamed of doing anything without a premium from the home Government. Mr. Parkman gives us a minute and entertaining picture of Canadian manners and morals while the royal bounty was at its height. The most general impression we derive from it is that human nature under the old régime was made of stouter stuff than now. French society, at Quebec and Montreal, adapted itself to its new circumstances with a pliancy for which we should now look in vain, and exhibited, for a time at least, a talent for emigration which has quite passed out of its character. Life, for the poorer sort, was hard enough at home, but they could make easier terms with it than with the Canadian cold and the Indians. The poverty was horrible, and even the colonial gentry, which became extremely numerous, lived in almost abject destitution. Existence was a hand-to-hand fight with the wilderness, with the climate, with the Iroquois, and with native jealousies and treacheries. Ships arrived from France but once a year, and were usually laden with disease. They brought the King's instructions, and the primitive little machine was wound up again, and set running for another twelvemonth. There was only one industry—the traffic in beaver skins —and, as everyone followed it, the market was glutted, and the furriers, who were compelled by the Government to buy the skins whether or no, became bankrupt. Over all this hovered the rigid rule of the priests, enforcing, in intention, as grim a Puritanism as that which prevailed in Massachusetts. The Jesuits were the guiding spirits of early Canadian civilization, and they had no disposition to be dislodged from the field. We noticed in these pages the really thrilling volume in which a few years since Mr. Parkman commemorated their early explorations and sufferings, and it must be confessed that they had a certain right to an authority which they had purchased with their heroism and their blood. But they governed as priests govern, irritatingly and meddlingly, and, as if ice and Indians between them might not have been trusted to impart a wholesome severity to life, they urged war against such meager forms of luxury as had straggled across the sea, and prohibited all consolations but those of religion. The natural result was that the hardier spirits of the colony broke loose from their rule, rambled away to the woods, and, finding tipsy Indians more congenial company than super-sober Jesuits, founded the picturesque tradition of the Canadian *coureur de bois*. One of the priestly rulers of Quebec, the Vicar-General Laval, forms in Mr. Parkman's pages an impressive and interesting figure. He was an ascetic of the rigorous mediæval pattern, but, with all his personal sanctity, he relished vastly having his own way, and he held his power against all intruders. The author gives a copious account of his squabbles with the bishops (of Quebec) on one side, and the King's governors and intendants on the other. It is a report, for all who are curious, of the current politics of Quebec. Mr. Parkman justly remarks that it is singular that none of the Canadian worthies, male or female, should have been deemed worthy of canonization. There were plenty of thoroughgoing saints among them, and the Sisters of Charity were not less devoted and courageous than the Jesuit brothers. There was a certain Jeanne Le Ber, in especial, who as a picturesque anchorite of questionable sanity leaves nothing to be desired. She lived for twenty years in a narrow cell behind the altar of a church at Quebec, in such an odor of sanctity that, during a time of apprehension of an attack from the English, a storm which overtook and destroyed their ships was attributed to the virtue of her prayers. That such a name as this, and as many another among the missionary brothers who braved the scalping-knife and the death-torture, should be wanting on the Romish calendar of saints, is a sort of crushing proof of the predestined provincialism of Canada—of its being out of the great world, out of the current. Nearer headquarters, in bright, warm Italy, people were canonized on easier terms. In this frigid atmosphere, however, where virtue was to miss even that ultimate reward with the thought of which it consoles itself for present hardship, men and women not only assembled in numbers, but increased and multiplied and prospered and grew strong. It was a capital illustration of the law of the survival of the fittest. The weaklings perished, but the stronger grew magnificently tough. The climate, strange to say, was especially friendly to women, and the mothers of Canada had enormous families. The King set every imaginable premium upon breeding, and the most curious pages in Mr. Parkman's volume describe his ingenious attempts to stimulate it. Not only were early marriages generously rewarded, but bachelors were made thoroughly uncomfortable, and had finally either to marry in self-defense or to buy themselves off from persecution. Marriageable young women were shipped in even excessive numbers from France, and stepped off the vessel into the arms of a husband. They appreciated their market, and their alacrity had to be checked. "Not quite so many demoiselles," the governor wrote to the emigration agent at home. "Instead of the four I asked you for last year, you sent me fifteen." This odd combination of celibate priests and nuns and excessively prolific citizens gives us a rough measure of the something artificial and anomalous in the history of New France. Mr. Parkman is to trace his subject further, and although his concluding volume will lack the interest peculiar to his *Jesuits* and to the early chapters of the present one, it will deal, in the collapse of the French power, with an abundantly dramatic episode, and, in Wolfe and Montcalm, with figures as heroic as any he has sketched.

WILLIAM DEAN HOWELLS [1]

As THE EXISTENCE of a man of letters (so far as the public is concerned with it) may be said to begin with his first appearance in literature, that of Mr. Howells, who was born at Martinsville, Ohio, in 1837, and spent his entire youth in his native State, dates properly from the publication of his delightful volume on *Venetian Life*—than which he has produced nothing since of a literary quality more pure—which he put forth in 1865, after his return from the consular post in the city of St. Mark which he had filled for four years. He had, indeed, before going to live in Venice, and during the autumn of 1860, published, in conjunction with his friend Mr. Piatt, a so-called "campaign" biography of Abraham Lincoln; but as this composition, which I have never seen, emanated probably more from a good Republican than from a suitor of the Muse, I mention it simply for the sake of exactitude, adding, however, that I have never heard of the Muse having taken it ill. When a man is a born artist, everything that happens to him confirms his perverse

[1] This essay appeared in *Harper's Weekly*, June 19, 1886, and was never reprinted by James.

tendency; and it may be considered that the happiest
thing that could have been invented on Mr. Howells's
behalf was his residence in Venice at the most sensitive
and responsive period of life; for Venice, bewritten and
bepainted as she has ever been, does nothing to you
unless to persuade you that you also can paint, that you
also can write. Her only fault is that she sometimes too
flatteringly—for she is shameless in the exercise of such
arts—addresses the remark to those who cannot. Mr.
Howells could, fortunately, for his writing was painting
as well in those days. The papers on Venice prove it,
equally with the artistic whimsical chapters of the *Italian
Journeys*, made up in 1867 from his notes and memories
(the latter as tender as most glances shot eastward in
working hours across the Atlantic) of the holidays and
excursions which carried him occasionally away from
his consulate.

The mingled freshness and irony of these things gave
them an originality which has not been superseded, to
my knowledge, by any impressions of European life from
an American standpoint. At Venice Mr. Howells married
a lady of artistic accomplishment and association, passed
through the sharp alternations of anxiety and hope to
which those who spent the long years of the Civil War
in foreign lands were inevitably condemned, and of
which the effect was not rendered less wearing by the
perusal of the London *Times* and the conversation of the
British tourist. The irritation, so far as it proceeded from
the latter source, may even yet be perceived in Mr.
Howells's pages. He wrote poetry at Venice, as he had
done of old in Ohio, and his poems were subsequently
collected into two thin volumes, the fruit, evidently, of
a rigorous selection. They have left more traces in the
mind of many persons who read and enjoyed them than
they appear to have done in the author's own. It is not
nowadays as a cultivator of rhythmic periods that Mr.
Howells most willingly presents himself. Everything in

the evolution, as we must all learn to call it today, of a
talent of this order is interesting, but one of the things
that are most so is the separation that has taken place, in
Mr. Howells's case, between its early and its later manner.
There is nothing in *Silas Lapham*, or in *Doctor Breen's
Practice*, or in *A Modern Instance*, or in *The Undiscovered Country*, to suggest that its author had at one
time either wooed the lyric Muse or surrendered himself
to those Italian initiations without which we of other
countries remain always, after all, more or less barbarians.
It is often a good, as it is sometimes an evil, that one
cannot disestablish one's past, and Mr. Howells cannot
help having rhymed and romanced in deluded hours,
nor would he, no doubt, if he could. The repudiation of
the weakness which leads to such aberrations is more
apparent than real, and the spirit which made him care
a little for the poor factitious Old World and the
superstition of "form" is only latent in pages which express a marked preference for the novelties of civilization
and a perceptible mistrust of the purist. I hasten to add
that Mr. Howells has had moments of reappreciation of
Italy in later years, and has even taken the trouble to
write a book (the magnificent volume on *Tuscan Cities*)
to show it. Moreover, the exquisite tale *A Foregone Conclusion*, and many touches in the recent novel of *Indian
Summer* (both this and the *Cities* the fruit of a second
visit to Italy), sound the note of a charming inconsist-
ency.

On his return from Venice he settled in the vicinity of
Boston, and began to edit the *Atlantic Monthly*, accommodating himself to this grave complication with infinite
tact and industry. He conferred further distinction upon
the magazine; he wrote the fine series of "Suburban
Sketches," one of the least known of his productions, but
one of the most perfect, and on Sunday afternoons he
took a suburban walk—perfect also, no doubt, in its
way. I know not exactly how long this phase of his career

lasted, but I imagine that if he were asked, he would reply: "Oh, a hundred years." He was meant for better things than this—things better, I mean, than superintending the private life of even the most eminent periodical —but I am not sure that I would speak of this experience as a series of wasted years. They were years rather of economized talent, of observation and accumulation. They laid the foundation of what is most remarkable, or most, at least, the peculiar sign, in his effort as a novelist—his unerring sentiment of the American character. Mr. Howells knows more about it than anyone, and it was during this period of what we may suppose to have been rather perfunctory administration that he must have gathered many of his impressions of it. An editor is in the nature of the case much exposed, so exposed as not to be protected even by the seclusion (the security to a superficial eye so complete) of a Boston suburb. His manner of contact with the world is almost violent, and whatever bruises he may confer, those he receives are the most telling, inasmuch as the former are distributed among many, and the latter all to be endured by one. Mr. Howells's accessibilities and sufferings were destined to fructify. Other persons have considered and discoursed upon American life, but no one, surely, has *felt* it so completely as he. I will not say that Mr. Howells feels it all equally, for are we not perpetually conscious how vast and deep it is?—but he is an authority upon many of those parts of it which are most representative.

He was still under the shadow of his editorship when, in the intervals of his letter-writing and reviewing, he made his first cautious attempts in the walk of fiction. I say cautious, for in looking back nothing is more clear than that he had determined to advance only step by step. In his first story, *Their Wedding Journey*, there are only two persons, and in his next, *A Chance Acquaintance*, which contains one of his very happiest studies of a girl's character, the number is not lavishly increased.

In *A Foregone Conclusion,* where the girl again is admirable, as well as the young Italian priest, also a kind of maidenly figure, the actors are but four. Today Mr. Howells doesn't count, and confers life with a generous and unerring hand. If the profusion of forms in which it presents itself to him is remarkable, this is perhaps partly because he had the good fortune of not approaching the novel until he had lived considerably, until his inclination for it had ripened. His attitude was as little as possible that of the gifted young person who, at twenty, puts forth a work of imagination of which the merit is mainly in its establishing the presumption that the next one will be better. It is my impression that long after he was twenty he still cultivated the belief that the faculty of the novelist was not in him, and was even capable of producing certain unfinished chapters (in the candor of his good faith he would sometimes communicate them to a listener) in triumphant support of this contention. He believed, in particular, that he could not make people talk, and such have been the revenges of time that a cynical critic might almost say of him today that he cannot make them keep silent. It was life itself that finally dissipated his doubts, life that reasoned with him and persuaded him. The feeling of life is strong in all his tales, and any one of them has this rare (always rarer) and indispensable sign of a happy origin, that it is an impression at first hand. Mr. Howells is literary, on certain sides exquisitely so, though with a singular and not unamiable perversity he sometimes endeavors not to be; but his vision of the human scene is never a literary reminiscence, a reflection of books and pictures, of tradition and fashion and hearsay. I know of no English novelist of our hour whose work is so exclusively a matter of painting what he sees, and who is so sure of what he sees. People are always wanting a writer of Mr. Howells's temperament to see certain things that he doesn't (that he doesn't sometimes even want to), but I must content myself with congratulating the author of *A Modern Instance* and *Silas Lapham* on the admirable quality of his vision. The American life which he for the most part depicts is certainly neither very rich nor very fair, but it is tremendously positive, and as his manner of presenting it is as little as possible conventional, the reader can have no doubt about it. This is an immense luxury; the ingenuous character of the witness (I can give it no higher praise) deepens the value of the report.

Mr. Howells has gone from one success to another, has taken possession of the field, and has become copious without detriment to his freshness. I need not enumerate his works in their order, for, both in America and in England (where it is a marked feature of the growing curiosity felt about American life that they are constantly referred to for information and verification), they have long been in everybody's hands. Quietly and steadily they have become better and better; one may like some of them more than others, but it is noticeable that from effort to effort the author has constantly enlarged his scope. His work is of a kind of which it is good that there should be much today—work of observation, of patient and definite notation. Neither in theory nor in practice is Mr. Howells a romancer; but the romancers can spare him; there will always be plenty of people to do their work. He has definite and downright convictions on the subject of the work that calls out to be done in opposition to theirs, and this fact is a source of much of the interest that he excites.

It is a singular circumstance that to know what one wishes to do should be, in the field of art, a rare distinction; but it is incontestable that, as one looks about in our English and American fiction, one does not perceive any very striking examples of a vivifying faith. There is no discussion of the great question of how best to write, no exchange of ideas, no vivacity nor variety of experiment. A vivifying faith Mr. Howells may distinctly

be said to possess, and he conceals it so little as to afford
every facility to those people who are anxious to prove
that it is the wrong one. He is animated by a love of the
common, the immediate, the familiar and vulgar elements
of life, and holds that in proportion as we move into the
rare and strange we become vague and arbitrary; that
truth of representation, in a word, can be achieved only
so long as it is in our power to test and measure it. He
thinks scarcely anything too paltry to be interesting, that
the small and the vulgar have been terribly neglected,
and would rather see an exact account of a sentiment or
a character he stumbles against every day than a brilliant
evocation of a passion or a type he has never seen and
does not even particularly believe in. He adores the real,
the natural, the colloquial, the moderate, the optimistic,
the domestic, and the democratic; looking askance at
exceptions and perversities and superiorities, at surprising
and incongruous phenomena in general. One must have
seen a great deal before one concludes; the world is
very large, and life is a mixture of many things; she by
no means eschews the strange, and often risks combinations and effects that make one rub one's eyes. Nevertheless, Mr. Howells's standpoint is an excellent one for
seeing a large part of the truth, and even if it were less
advantageous, there would be a great deal to admire in the
firmness with which he has planted himself. He hates a
"story," and (this private feat is not impossible) has probably made up his mind very definitely as to what the
pestilent thing consists of. In this respect he is more logical
than M. Émile Zola, who partakes of the same aversion,
but has greater lapses as well as greater audacities. Mr.
Howells hates an artificial fable and a *dénouement* that is
pressed into the service; he likes things to occur as they
occur in life, where the manner of a great many of
them is not to occur at all. (He has observed that heroic
emotion and brilliant opportunity are not particularly
interwoven with our days, and indeed, in the way of

omission, he *has* often practiced in his pages a very considerable boldness. It has not, however, made what we find there any less interesting and less human.)

The picture of American life on Mr. Howells's canvas is not of a dazzling brightness, and many readers have probably wondered why it is that (among a sensitive people) he has so successfully escaped the imputation of a want of patriotism. The manners he describes—the desolation of the whole social prospect in *A Modern Instance* is perhaps the strongest expression of those influences—are eminently of a nature to discourage the intending visitor, and yet the westward pilgrim continues to arrive, in spite of the Bartley Hubbards and the Laphams, and the terrible practices at the country hotel in *Doctor Breen,* and at the Boston boarding-house in *A Woman's Reason.* This tolerance of depressing revelations is explained partly, no doubt, by the fact that Mr. Howells's truthfulness imposes itself—the representation is so vivid that the reader accepts it as he accepts, in his own affairs, the mystery of fate—and partly by a very different consideration, which is simply that if many of his characters are disagreeable, almost all of them are extraordinarily good, and with a goodness which is a ground for national complacency. If American life is on the whole, as I make no doubt whatever, more innocent than that of any other country, nowhere is the fact more patent than in Mr. Howells's novels, which exhibit so constant a study of the actual and so small a perception of evil. His women, in particular, are of the best—except, indeed, in the sense of being the best to live with. Purity of life, fineness of conscience, benevolence of motive, decency of speech, good nature, kindness, charity, tolerance (though, indeed, there is little but each other's manners for the people to tolerate), govern all the scene; the only immoralities are aberrations of thought, like that of Silas Lapham, or excesses of beer, like that of Bartley Hubbard. In the gallery of Mr. Howells's portraits there are none more living than the admirable, humorous images of those two ineffectual sinners. Lapham, in particular, is magnificent, understood down to the ground, inside and out—a creation which does Mr. Howells the highest honor. I do not say that the figure of his wife is as good as his own, only because I wish to say that it is as good as that of the minister's wife in the history of *Lemuel Barker*, which is unfolding itself from month to month at the moment I write. These two ladies are exhaustive renderings of the type of virtue that worries. But everything in *Silas Lapham* is superior —nothing more so than the whole picture of casual female youth and contemporaneous "engaging" one's self, in the daughters of the proprietor of the mineral paint.

This production had struck me as the author's high-water mark, until I opened the monthly sheets of *Lemuel Barker*, in which the art of imparting a palpitating interest to common things and unheroic lives is pursued (or is destined, apparently, to be pursued) to an even higher point. The four (or is it eight?) repeated "good-mornings" between the liberated Lemuel and the shopgirl who has crudely been the cause of his being locked up by the police all night are a poem, an idyl, a trait of genius, and a compendium of American good nature. The whole episode is inimitable, and I know fellow novelists of Mr. Howells's who would have given their eyes to produce that interchange of salutations, which only an American reader, I think, can understand. Indeed, the only limitation, in general, to his extreme truthfulness is, I will not say his constant sense of the comedy of life, for that is irresistible, but the verbal drollery of many of his people. It is extreme and perpetual, but I fear the reader will find it a venial sin. Theodore Colville, in *Indian Summer*, is so irrepressibly and happily facetious as to make one wonder whether the author is not prompting him a little, and whether he could be quite so amusing without help from outside. This criticism, however, is the only one I find it urgent to make, and Mr. Howells doubtless will not suffer from my saying that, being a humorist himself, he is strong in the representation of humorists. There are other reflections that I might indulge in if I had more space. I should like, for instance, to allude in passing, for purposes of respectful remonstrance, to a phrase that he suffered the other day to fall from his pen (in a periodical, but not in a novel), to the effect that the style of a work of fiction is a thing that matters less and less all the while. Why less and less? It seems to me as great a mistake to say so as it would be to say that it matters more and more. It is difficult to see how it can matter either less or more. The style of a novel is a part of the execution of a work of art; the execution of a work of art is a part of its very essence, and that, it seems to me, must have mattered in all ages in exactly the same degree, and be destined always to do so. I can conceive of no state of civilization in which it shall not be deemed important, though of course there are states in which executants are clumsy. I should also venture to express a certain regret that Mr. Howells (whose style, in practice, after all, as I have intimated, treats itself to felicities which his theory perhaps would condemn) should appear increasingly to hold composition too cheap—by which I mean, should neglect the effect that comes from alternation, distribution, relief. He has an increasing tendency to tell his story altogether in conversations, so that a critical reader sometimes wishes, not that the dialogue might be suppressed (it is too good for that), but that it might be distributed, interspaced with narrative and pictorial matter. The author forgets sometimes to paint, to evoke the conditions and appearances, to build in the subject. He is doubtless afraid of doing these things in excess, having seen in other hands what disastrous effects that error may have; but all the same I cannot help thinking that the divinest thing in a valid novel is the compendious, descriptive, pictorial touch, *à la Daudet*.

It would be absurd to speak of Mr. Howells today in the encouraging tone that one would apply to a young writer who had given fine pledges, and one feels half guilty of that mistake if one makes a cheerful remark about his future. And yet we cannot pretend not to take a still more lively intereest in his future than we have done in his past. It is hard to see how it can help being more and more fruitful, for his face is turned in the right direction, and his work is fed from sources which play us no tricks.

LETTER TO WILLIAM DEAN HOWELLS

ON HIS SEVENTY-FIFTH BIRTHDAY

London, February 19, 1912

My dear Howells,[1]

It is made known to me that they are soon to feast in New York the newest and freshest of the splendid birth-

[1] The letter was written to be read at a dinner in New York in celebration of Howells's seventy-fifth birthday. It was published in the *North American Review*, April 1912. From THE LETTERS OF HENRY JAMES, Selected and Edited by Percy Lubbock, Volume II; copyright 1920 by Charles Scribner's Sons, 1948 by William James and Margaret James Porter. Reprinted by permission of the publishers.

days to which you keep treating us, and that your many friends will meet round you to rejoice in it and reaffirm their allegiance. I shall not be there, to my sorrow, and though this is inevitable I yet want to be missed, peculiarly and monstrously missed; so that these words shall be a public apology for my absence: read by you, if you like and can stand it, but better still read *to* you and in fact straight *at* you, by whoever will be so kind and so loud and so distinct. For I doubt, you see, whether any of your toasters and acclaimers have anything like my ground and title for being with you at such an hour. There can scarce be one, I think, today, who has known you from so far back, who has kept so close to you for so long, and who has such fine old reasons—so old, yet so well preserved—to feel your virtue and sound your praise. My debt to you began well-nigh half a century ago, in the most personal way possible, and then kept growing with your own admirable growth—but always rooted in the early intimate benefit. This benefit was that you held out your open editorial hand to me at the time I began to write—and I allude especially to the summer of 1866 —with a frankness and sweetness of hospitality that was really the making of me, the making of the confidence that required help and sympathy and that I should other- wise, I think, have strayed and stumbled about a long time without acquiring. You showed me the way and opened me the door; you wrote to me, and confessed yourself struck with me—I have never forgotten the beautiful thrill of *that*. You published me at once—and paid me, above all, with a dazzling promptitude; magnificently, I felt, and so that nothing since has ever quite come up to it. More than this even, you cheered me on with a sympathy that was in itself an inspiration. I mean that you talked to me and listened to me—ever so patiently and genially and suggestively conversed and consorted with me. This won me to you irresistibly and made you the most interesting person I knew—lost as I was in the

charming sense that my best friend was an editor, and
an almost insatiable editor, and that such a delicious
being as that was a kind of property of my own. Yet
how didn't that interest still quicken and spread when I
became aware that—with such attention as you could
spare from us, for I recognized my fellow beneficiaries—
you had started to cultivate *your* great garden as well;
the tract of virgin soil that, beginning as a cluster of
bright, fresh, sunny, and savory patches, close about
the house, as it were, was to become that vast woodly
pleasaunce of art and observation, of appreciation and
creation, in which you have labored, without a break or
a lapse, to this day, and in which you have grown so
grand a show of—well, really of everything. Your liberal
visits to *my* plot, and your free-handed purchases there,
were still greater events when I began to see you handle,
yourself, with such ease the key to our rich and inexhaustible mystery. Then the question of what you
would make of your own powers began to be even
more interesting than the question of what you would
make of mine—all the more, I confess, as you had ended
by settling this one so happily. My confidence in myself,
which you had so helped me to, gave way to a fasci-
nated impression of your own spread and growth; for you
broke out so insistently and variously that it was a charm
to watch and an excitement to follow you. The only
drawback that I remember suffering from was that *I*,
your original debtor, couldn't print or publish or pay you
—which would have been a sort of ideal *re*payment and
of enhanced credit; you could take care of yourself so
beautifully, and I could (unless by some occasional happy
chance or rare favor) scarce so much as glance at your
proofs or have a glimpse of your "endings." I could only
read you, full-blown and finished—and see, with the rest
of the world, how you were doing it again and again.

That then was what I had with time to settle down to
—the common attitude of seeing you do it again and

again; keep on doing it, with your heroic consistency and your noble, genial abundance, during all the years that have seen so many apparitions come and go, so many vain flourishes attempted and achieved, so many little fortunes made and unmade, so many weaker inspirations betrayed and spent. Having myself to practice meaner economies, I have admired, from period to period, your so ample and liberal flow; wondered at your secret for doing positively a little—what do I say, a little? I mean a magnificent deal!—of Everything. I seem to myself to have faltered and languished, to have missed more occasions than I have grasped, while you have piled up your monument just by remaining at your post. For you have had the advantage, after all, of breathing an air that has suited and nourished you; of sitting up to your neck, as I may say—or at least up to your waist—amid the sources of your inspiration. There and so you were at your post; there and so the spell could ever work for you, there and so your relation to all your material grow closer and stronger, your perception penetrate, your authority accumulate. They make a great array, a literature in themselves, your studies of American life, so acute, so direct, so disinterested, so preoccupied but with the fine truth of the case; and the more attaching to me, always, for their referring themselves to a time and an order when we knew together what American life *was* —or thought we did, deluded though we may have been! I don't pretend to measure the effect, or to sound the depths, if they be not the shallows, of the huge wholesale importations and so-called assimilations of this later time; I can only feel and speak for those conditions in which, as "quiet observers," as careful painters, as sincere artists, we could still, in our native, our human and social element, know more or less where we were and feel more or less what we had hold of. You knew and felt these things better than I; you had learnt them earlier and more intimately, and it was impossible, I think, to be in more

instinctive and more informed possession of the general
truth of your subject than you happily found yourself.
The *real* affair of the American case and character, as
it met your view and brushed your sensibility, that was
what inspired and attached you, and, heedless of foolish
flurries from other quarters, of all wild or weak slashings
of the air and wavings in the void, you gave yourself
to it with an incorruptible faith. You saw your field
with a rare lucidity; you saw all it had to give in the
way of the romance of the real and the interest and the
thrill and the charm of the common, as one may put it;
the character and the comedy, the point, the pathos, the
tragedy, the particular home-grown humanity under
your eyes and your hand and with which the life all
about you was closely interknitted. Your hand reached
out to these things with a fondness that was in itself a
literary gift, and played with them as the artist only and
always can play: freely, quaintly, incalculably, with all
the assurance of his fancy and his irony, and yet with
that fine taste for the truth and the pity and the meaning
of the matter which keeps the temper of observation both
sharp and sweet. To observe, by such an instinct and by
such reflection, is to find work to one's hand and a
challenge in every bush; and as the familiar American
scene thus bristled about you, so, year by year, your
vision more and more justly responded and swarmed.
You put forth *A Modern Instance*, and *The Rise of Silas
Lapham*, and *A Hazard of New Fortunes*, and *The Land-
lord at Lion's Head*, and *The Kentons* (that perfectly
classic illustration of your spirit and your form), after
having put forth in perhaps lighter-fingered prelude *A
Foregone Conclusion*, and *The Undiscovered Country*,
and *The Lady of the Aroostook*, and *The Minister's
Charge*—to make of a long list too short a one; with the
effect, again and again, of a feeling for the human relation, as the social climate of our country qualifies,
intensifies, generally conditions and colors it, which,

married in perfect felicity to the expression you found for its service, constituted the originality that we want to fasten upon you, as with silver nails, tonight. Stroke by stroke and book by book your work was to become, for this exquisite notation of our whole democratic light and shade and give and take, in the highest degree *documentary;* so that none other, through all your fine long season, could approach it in value and amplitude. None, let me say too, was to approach it in essential distinction; for you had grown master, by insidious practices best known to yourself, of a method so easy and so natural, so marked with the personal element of your humor and the play, not less personal, of your sympathy, that the critic kept coming on its secret connection with the grace of letters much as Fenimore Cooper's Leatherstocking—so knowing to be able to do it!—comes, in the forest, on the subtle tracks of Indian braves. However, these things take us far, and what I wished mainly to put on record is my sense of that unfailing, testifying truth in you which will keep you from ever being neglected. The critical intelligence—if any such fitful and discredited light may still be conceived as within our sphere—has not at all begun to render you its tribute. The more inquiringly and perceivingly it shall still be projected upon the American life we used to know, the more it shall be moved by the analytic and historic spirit, the more indispensable, the more a vessel of light, will you be found. It's a great thing to have used one's genius and done one's work with such quiet and robust consistency that they fall by their own weight into that happy service. You may remember perhaps, and I like to recall, how the great and admirable Taine, in one of the fine excursions of his French curiosity, greeted you as a precious painter and a sovereign witness. But his appreciation, I want you to believe with me, will yet be carried much further, and then—though you may have argued yourself happy, in your generous way and with your incurable optimism, even while noting yourself not understood—your really beautiful time will come. Nothing so much as feeling that he may himself perhaps help a little to bring it on can give pleasure to yours all faithfully,

Henry James

MISS WOOLSON [1]

FLOODED as we have been in these latter days with copious discussion as to the admission of women to various offices, colleges, functions, and privileges, singularly little attention has been paid, by themselves at least, to the fact that in one highly important department of human affairs their cause is already gained—gained in such a way as to deprive them largely of their ground, formerly so substantial, for complaining of the intolerance of man. In America, in England, today, it is no longer a question of their admission into the world of literature: they are there in force; they have been admitted, with all the

---

[1] James's essay on Miss Woolson first appeared in *Harper's Weekly*, February 12, 1887, and was reprinted by him in *Partial Portraits* the following year. Constance Fenimore Woolson (1840–94), a grand-niece of James Fenimore Cooper, wrote a series of novels and sketches largely regional in character, and was widely read in her time.

honors, on a perfectly equal footing. In America, at least, one feels tempted at moments to exclaim that they are in themselves the world of literature. In Germany and in France, in this line of production, their presence is less to be perceived. To speak only of the latter country, France has brought forth in the persons of Mme de Sévigné, Mme de Staël, and Mme Sand, three female writers of the first rank, without counting a hundred ladies to whom we owe charming memoirs and volumes of reminiscence; but in the table of contents of the *Revue des Deux Mondes*, that epitome of the literary movement (as regards everything, at least, but the famous doctrine, in fiction, of "naturalism"), it is rare to encounter the name of a female contributor. The covers of American and English periodicals tell a different story; in these monthly joints of the ladder of fame the ladies stand as thick as on the staircase at a crowded evening party.

There are, of course, two points of view from which this free possession of the public ear may be considered—as regards its effect upon the life of women, and as regards its effect upon literature. I hasten to add that I do not propose to consider either, and I touch on the general fact simply because the writer whose name I have placed at the head of these remarks happens to be a striking illustration of it. The work of Miss Constance Fenimore Woolson is an excellent example of the way the door stands open between the personal life of American women and the immeasurable world of print, and what makes it so is the particular quality that this work happens to possess. It breathes a spirit singularly and essentially conservative—the sort of spirit which, but for a special indication pointing the other way, would in advance seem most to oppose itself to the introduction into the feminine lot of new and complicating elements. Miss Woolson evidently thinks that lot sufficiently complicated, with the sensibilities which even in primitive ages women were acknowledged to possess; fenced in by the old disabilities and prejudices, they seem to her to have been by their very nature only too much exposed, and it would never occur to her to lend her voice to the plea for further exposure—for a revolution which should place her sex in the thick of the struggle for power. She sees it in preference surrounded certainly by plenty of doors and windows (she has not, I take it, a love of bolts and Oriental shutters), but distinctly on the private side of that somewhat evasive and exceedingly shifting line which divides human affairs into the profane and the sacred. Such is the turn of mind of the author of *Rodman the Keeper* and *East Angels*, and if it has not prevented her from writing books, from competing for the literary laurel, this is a proof of the strength of the current which today carries both sexes alike to that mode of expression.

Miss Woolson's first productions were two collections of short tales, published in 1875 and 1880, and entitled respectively *Castle Nowhere* and *Rodman the Keeper*. I may not profess an acquaintance with the former of these volumes, but the latter is full of interesting artistic work. Miss Woolson has done nothing better than the best pages in this succession of careful, strenuous studies of certain aspects of life, after the war, in Florida, Georgia, and the Carolinas. As the fruit of a remarkable minuteness of observation and tenderness of feeling on the part of one who evidently did not glance and pass, but lingered and analyzed, they have a high value, especially when regarded in the light of the *voicelessness* of the conquered and reconstructed South. Miss Woolson strikes the reader as having a compassionate sense of this pathetic dumbness—having perceived that no social revolution of equal magnitude had ever reflected itself so little in literature, remained so unrecorded, so unpainted and unsung. She has attempted to give an impression of this circumstance, among others, and a sympathy altogether feminine has guided her pen. She loves the whole region, and no daughter of the land could

have handled its peculiarities more indulgently, or communicated to us more of the sense of close observation
and intimate knowledge. Nevertheless it must be confessed that the picture, on the whole, is a picture of
dreariness—of impressions that may have been gathered
in the course of lonely afternoon walks at the end of hot
days, when the sunset was wan, on the edge of rice-fields,
dismal swamps, and other brackish inlets. The author is
to be congratulated in so far as such expeditions may
have been the source of her singularly exact familiarity
with the "natural objects" of the region, including the
Negro of reality. She knows every plant and flower,
every vague odor and sound, the song and flight of every
bird, every tint of the sky and murmur of the forest,
and she has noted scientifically the dialect of the freed-
men. It is not too much to say that the Negroes in *Rodman the Keeper* and in *East Angels* are a careful philo-
logical study, and that if Miss Woolson preceded Uncle
Remus by a considerable interval, she may have the credit
of the initiative—of having been the first to take their
words straight from their lips.

No doubt that if in *East Angels*, as well as in the volume of tales, the sadness of Miss Woolson's South is more
striking than its high spirits, this is owing somewhat to
the author's taste in the way of subject and situation, and
especially to her predilection for cases of heroic sacrifice
—sacrifice sometimes unsuspected and always unappreci-
ated. She is fond of irretrievable personal failures, of people who have had to give up even the memory of happiness, who love and suffer in silence, and minister in secret
to the happiness of those who look over their heads. She
is interested in general in secret histories, in the "inner
life" of the weak, the superfluous, the disappointed, the
bereaved, the unmarried. She believes in personal renunciation, in its frequency as well as its beauty. It plays a
prominent part in each of her novels, especially in the last
two, and the interest of *East Angels* at least is largely

owing to her success in having made an extreme case of the virtue in question credible to the reader. It is because this element is weaker in *Anne*, which was published in 1882, that *Anne* strikes me as the least happily composed of the author's works? The early chapters are charming and full of promise, but the story wanders away from them, and the pledge is not taken up. The reader has built great hopes upon Tita, but Tita vanishes into the vague, after putting him out of countenance by an infant marriage —an accident in regard to which, on the whole, throughout her stories, Miss Woolson shows perhaps an excessive indulgence. She likes the unmarried, as I have mentioned, but she likes marriages even better, and also sometimes hurries them forward in advance of the reader's exaction. The only complaint it would occur to me to make of *East Angels* is that Garda Thorne, whom we cannot think of as anything but a little girl, discounts the projects we have formed for her by marrying twice; and somehow the case is not bettered by the fact that nothing is more natural than that she should marry twice, unless it be that she should marry three times. We have perceived her, after all, from the first, to be peculiarly adapted to a succession of pretty widowhoods.

For the Major has an idea, a little fantastic perhaps, but eminently definite. This idea is the secret effort of an elderly woman to appear really as young to her husband as (owing to peculiar circumstances) he believed her to be when he married her. Nature helps her (she happens to preserve, late in life, the look of comparative youth), and art helps nature, and her husband's illusions, fostered by failing health and a weakened brain, help them both, so that she is able to keep on the mask till his death, when she pulls it off with a passionate cry of relief—ventures at last, gives herself the luxury, to be old. The sacrifice in this case has been the sacrifice of the maternal instinct, she having had a son, now a man grown, by a former marriage, who reappears after unsuccessful wanderings

in far lands, and whom she may not permit herself openly
to recognize. The sacrificial attitude is indeed repeated
on the part of her stepdaughter, who, being at last taken
into Madam Carroll's confidence, suffers the young man—
a shabby, compromising, inglorious acquaintance—to pass
for her lover, thereby discrediting herself almost fatally
(till the situation is straightened out), with the Rev.
Frederick Owen, who has really been marked out by
Providence for the character, and who cannot explain on
any comfortable hypothesis her relations with the mysterious Bohemian. Miss Woolson's women in general are
capable of these refinements of devotion and exaltations
of conscience, and she has a singular talent for making
our sympathies go with them. The conception of Madam
Carroll is highly ingenious and original, and the small
stippled portrait has a real fascination. It is the first time
that a woman has been represented as painting her face,
dyeing her hair, and "dressing young," out of tenderness
for another: the effort usually has its source in tenderness
for herself. But Miss Woolson has done nothing of a
neater execution than this fanciful figure of the little
ringleted, white-frocked, falsely juvenile lady, who has the
toilet-table of an actress and the conscience of a Puritan.

The author likes a glamour, and by minute touches and
gentle, conciliatory arts, she usually succeeds in producing
a valid one. If I had more space I should like to count
over these cumulative strokes, in which a delicate manipu-
lation of the real is mingled with an occasionally frank
appeal to the romantic muse. But I can only mention two
of the most obvious: one the frequency of her reference
to the Episcopal church as an institution giving a tone to
American life (the sort of tone which it is usually assumed
that we must seek in civilizations more permeated with
ecclesiasticism); the other her fondness for family histories—for the idea of perpetuation of race, especially in
the backward direction. I hasten to add that there is
nothing of the crudity of sectarianism in the former of

these manifestations, or of the dreariness of the purely genealogical passion in the latter; but none the less is it clear that Miss Woolson likes little country churches that are dedicated to saints not vulgarized by too much notoriety, that are dressed with greenery (and would be with holly if there were any), at Christmas and Easter; that have "rectors," well connected, who are properly garmented, and organists, slightly deformed if possible, and addicted to playing Gregorian chants in the twilight, who are adequately artistic; likes also generations that have a pleasant consciousness of a few warm generations behind them, screening them in from too bleak a past, from vulgar drafts in the rear. I know not whether for the most part we are either so Anglican or so long-descended as in Miss Woolson's pages we strike ourselves as being, but it is certain that as we read we protest but little against the soft impeachment. She represents us at least as we should like to be, and she does so with such discretion and taste that we have no fear of incurring ridicule by assent. She has a high sense of the picturesque; she cannot get on without a social atmosphere. Once, I think, she has looked for these things in the wrong place—at the country boarding-house denominated Caryl's, in *Anne*, where there must have been flies and grease in the dining-room, and the ladies must have been overdressed; but as a general thing her quest is remarkably happy. She stays at home, and yet gives us a sense of being "abroad"; she has a remarkable faculty of making the New World seem ancient. She succeeds in representing Far Edgerly, the mountain village in *For the Major*, as bathed in the precious medium I speak of. Where is it meant to be, and where was the place that gave her the pattern of it? We gather vaguely, though there are no Negroes, that it is in the South; but this, after all, is a tolerably indefinite part of the United States. It is somewhere in the midst of forests, and yet it has as many idiosyncrasies as Mrs. Gaskell's *Cranford*, with

added possibilities of the pathetic and the tragic. What
new town is so composite? What composite town is so
new? Miss Woolson anticipates these questions; that is,
she prevents us from asking them: we swallow Far
Edgerly whole, or say at most, with a sigh, that if it
couldn't have been like that it certainly ought to have
been.

It is, however, in *East Angels* that she has been most
successful in this feat of evoking a local tone, and this is
a part of the general superiority of that very interesting
work, which to my mind represents a long stride of her
talent, and has more than the value of all else she has
done. In *East Angels* the attempt to create an atmosphere
has had, to a considerable degree, the benefit of the actual
quality of things in the warm, rank peninsula which she
has studied so exhaustively and loves so well. Miss
Woolson found a tone in the air of Florida, but it is not
too much to say that she has left it still more agreeably
rich—converted it into a fine golden haze. Wonderful
is the tact with which she has pressed it into the service
of her story, draped the bare spots of the scene with it,
and hung it there half as a curtain and half as a background. *East Angels* is a performance which does Miss
Woolson the highest honor, and if her talent is capable,
in another novel, of making an advance equal to that
represented by this work in relation to its predecessors,
she will have made a substantial contribution to our new
literature of fiction. Long, comprehensive, copious, still
more elaborate than her other elaborations, *East Angels*
presents the interest of a large and well-founded scheme.
The result is not flawless at every point, but the undertaking is of a fine, high kind, and, for the most part, the
effect produced is thoroughly worthy of it. The author
has, in other words, proposed to give us the complete
natural history, as it were, of a group of persons collected,
in a complicated relationship, in a little winter city on a
Southern shore, and she has expended on her subject stores

of just observation and an infinite deal of the true historical spirit. How much of this spirit and of artistic feeling there is in the book, only an attentive perusal will reveal. The central situation is a very interesting one, and is triumphantly treated, but I confess that what is most substantial to me in the book is the writer's general conception of her task, her general attitude of watching life, waiting upon it, and trying to catch it in the fact. I know not what theories she may hold in relation to all this business, to what camp or league she may belong; my impression indeed would be that she is perfectly free—that she considers that though camps and leagues may be useful organizations for looking for the truth, it is not in their own bosom that it is usually to be found. However this, may be, it is striking that, artistically, she has had a fruitful instinct in seeing the novel as a picture of the actual, of the characteristic—a study of human types and passions, of the evolution of personal relations. In *East Angels* she has gone much farther in this direction than in either of her other novels.

The book has, to my sense, two defects, which I may as well mention at once—two which are perhaps, however, but different faces of the same. One is that the group on which she has bent her lens strikes us as too detached, too isolated, too much on a desert island. Its different members go to and fro a good deal, to New York and to Europe, but they have a certain shipwrecked air, as of extreme dependence on each other, though surrounded with every convenience. The other fault is that the famous "tender sentiment" usurps among them a place even greater perhaps than that which it holds in life, great as the latter very admittedly is. I spoke just now of their complicated relationships, but the complications are almost exclusively the complications of love. Our impression is of sky and sand—the sky of azure, the sand of silver—and between them, conspicuous, immense, against the low horizon, the question of engagement and

marriage. I must add that I do not mean to imply that
this question is not, in the very nature of things, at any
time and in any place, immense, or that in a novel it
should be expected to lose its magnitude. I take it indeed
that on such as simple shore as Miss Woolson has described, love (with the passions that flow from it), is
almost inevitably the subject, and that the perspective is
not really false. It is not that the people are represented
as hanging together by that cord to an abnormal degree,
but that, there being few accessories and circumstances,
there is no tangle and overgrowth to disguise the effect.
It is a question of effect, but it is characteristic of the
feminine, as distinguished from the masculine hand, that
in any portrait of a corner of human affairs the particular
effect produced in *East Angels,* that of what we used to
call the love-story, will be the dominant one. The love-
story is a composition in which the elements are distributed in a particular proportion, and every tale which
contains a great deal of love has not necessarily a title to
the name. That title depends not upon how much love
there may be, but upon how little of other things. In
novels by men other things are there to a greater or less
degree, and I therefore doubt whether a man may be said
ever to have produced a work exactly belonging to the
class in question. In men's novels, even of the simplest
strain, there are still other references and other explanations; in women's, when they are of the category to
which I allude, there are none but that one. And there
is certainly much to be said for it.

In *East Angels* the sacrifice, as all Miss Woolson's
readers know, is the great sacrifice of Margaret Harold,
who immolates herself—there is no other word—deliberately, completely, and repeatedly, to a husband whose
behavior may as distinctly be held to have absolved her.
The problem was a very interesting one, and worthy to
challenge a superior talent—that of making real and
natural a transcendent, exceptional act, representing a case

in which the sense of duty is raised to exaltation. What makes Margaret Harold's behavior exceptional and transcendent is that, in order to render the barrier between herself and the man who loves her, and whom she loves, absolutely insurmountable, she does her best to bring about his marriage, endeavors to put another woman into the frame of mind to respond to him in the event (possible, as she is a woman whom he has once appeared to love) of his attempting to console himself for a bitter failure. The care, the ingenuity, the precautions the author has exhibited, to make us accept Mrs. Harold in her integrity, are perceptible on every page, and they leave us finally no alternative but to accept her; she remains exalted, but she remains at the same time thoroughly sound. For it is not a simple question of cleverness of detail, but a question of the larger sort of imagination, and Margaret Harold would have halted considerably if her creator had not taken the supreme precaution of all, and conceived her from the germ as capable of a certain heroism—of clinging at the cost of a grave personal loss to an idea which she believes to be a high one, and taking such a fancy to it that she endeavors to paint it, by a refinement of magnanimity, with still richer hues. She is a picture, not of a woman indulging in a great spasmodic flight or moral *tour de force*, but of a nature bent upon looking at life from a high point of view, an attitude in which there is nothing abnormal, and which the author illustrates, as it were, by a test case. She has drawn Margaret with so close and firm and living a line that she seems to put us in the quandary, if we repudiate her, of denying that a woman *may* look at life from a high point of view. She seems to say to us: "Are there distinguished natures, or are there not? Very well, if there are, that's what they can do—they can try and provide for the happiness of others (when they adore them) even to their own injury." And we feel that we wish to be the first to agree that there *are* distinguished natures.

Garda Thorne is the next best thing in the book to Margaret, and she is indeed equally good in this, that she is conceived with an equal clearness. But Margaret produces her impression upon us by moving before us and doing certain things, whereas Garda is more explained, or rather she explains herself more, tells us more about herself. She says somewhere, or someone says of her, that she doesn't narrate, but in fact she does narrate a good deal, for the purpose of making the reader understand her. This the reader does, very constantly, and Garda is a brilliant success. I must not, however, touch upon the different parts of *East Angels,* because in a work of so much patience and conscience a single example carries us too far. I will only add that in three places in especial the author has been so well inspired as to give a definite pledge of high accomplishment in the future. One of these salient passages is the description of the closing days of Mrs. Thorne, the little starved yet ardent daughter of the Puritans, who has been condemned to spend her life in the land of the relaxed, and who, before she dies, pours out her accumulations of bitterness—relieves herself in a passionate confession of everything she has suffered and missed, of how she has hated the very skies and fragrances of Florida, even when, as a consistent Christian, thankful for every mercy, she has pretended most to appreciate them. Mrs. Thorne is the pathetic, tragic form of the type of which Mrs. Stowe's Miss Ophelia was the comic. In almost all of Miss Woolson's stories the New England woman is represented as regretting the wholesome austerities of the region of her birth. She reverts to them, in solemn hours, even when, like Mrs. Thorne, she may appear for a time to have been converted to mild winters. Remarkably fine is the account of the expedition undertaken by Margaret Harold and Evert Winthrop to look for Lanse in the forest, when they believe him, or his wife thinks there may be reason to believe him, to have been lost and overtaken by a storm. The picture of their paddling the boat by torchlight into the reaches of the river, more or less smothered in the pestilent jungle, with the personal drama, in the unnatural place, reaching an acute stage between them—this whole episode is in a high degree vivid, strange, and powerful. Lastly, Miss Woolson has risen altogether to the occasion in the scene in which Margaret "has it out," as it were, with Evert Winthrop, parts from him and, leaving him baffled and unsurpassably sore, gives him the measure of her determination to accept the necessity of her fate. These three episodes are not alike, yet they have, in the high finish of Miss Woolson's treatment of them, a family resemblance. Moreover, they all have the stamp which I spoke of at first—the stamp of the author's conservative feeling, the implication that for her the life of a woman is essentially an affair of private relations.

✳

WOLCOTT BALESTIER[1]

THEY HAVE A PLACE apart in the record of the dead, the
young names which represent less for the big indifferent
public than for a knot of friends who remember and
regret, and yet on behalf of which we discreetly plead
for some attenuation, in the general memory, of the
common fate. So far as they *are* spared by oblivion they
form a ghostly but enviable little band—the company of
those who were estimated early and rescued early, who
created expectations and cherished hopes, and for whom
there remains no question of disappointment or of failure.
We can think of them as it most pleases us to think,
allude to them with unchallengeable faith, and give our
imagination the luxury of filling out the vague disk of the
possible. Charles Wolcott Balestier, who died in Dresden

[1] Charles Wolcott Balestier (1861–91) wrote novels and
short stories but is remembered best for his collaboration with
Rudyard Kipling, his brother-in-law, on *The Naulahka*
(1892), a novel about a California speculator in India, the
American chapters of which were written by Balestier. James's
tribute to him first appeared in *Cosmopolitan Magazine*, May
1892, and served as introduction to Balestier's posthumous
volume *The Average Woman* (New York and London, 1892).

on December 6, 1891, just before he had reached his thirtieth year, participates in this dim distinction and becomes one of the mute appealers to whom we are indulgent in proportion as we recognize that what there is to "show" for them accounts but imperfectly for our plea. We make the plea for the plea's sake, and because that is fairer than not to make it. He had not had time, though he had so many of the other conditions, and this particular use of a little of the time that we ourselves feel half-ashamed to have gained—as if we had gained it at his expense—presents itself as an act of common generosity.

Wolcott Balestier loved literature better than anything but his friends, and he had found opportunity to testify to this in a career as eagerly active as it was short. He left behind him a youthful unpublished novel, which is, conspicuously, to see the light; three very short tales, and the vivid mark of his collaboration with Mr. Rudyard Kipling in *The Naulahka*. His memory, therefore, may take its stand on a certain quantity of performance; but I confess that it is not mainly under the impression of this little sum of literary achievement that I find myself moved to speak of him. What he wrote, what he would have published, will be largely and sympathetically scrutinized, but there are persons for whom it will remain both only the smaller part of what he did and the pledge of a talent smothered at the very moment it had begun to expand. He was conscious that he had only begun, and it would be an unkindness to his memory to represent that, in spite of the extreme vividness of "Reffey," and of "Captain, my Captain!" his slender relics were very sacred in his own eyes. They are interesting, and in glimpses original, but their greatest merit is perhaps that by making him for the hour an actuality they give us a pretext for attempting to preserve some little record of his beneficence. He was a man of business of altogether peculiar genius, and it was in this light that he figured, with singular intensity, to a large number of charmed, befriended people during the part of his brief life in which I judge that he had lived more than in all its preceding time, the three crowded London years that began in December 1888. This was the period of my acquaintance with him; my personal relations with him became close, and I speak of him, of course, essentially as I had the good fortune to know him. I freely confess that I should not add my voice to the commemorative hum if it were a question of taking any less affectionate a point of view.

I speak of his having "figured," in London, because he was from the first, in his bright young ingenuity, his suggestion of immediate capacity, an apparition essentially salient. This was what he remained to the end, unmistakably an influence exotic and curious, dropped down from without, not thrown up from within. He made London, on the ground on which he dealt with it, so extraordinarily his own that the contrast between the spirit and the matter, the agent and the medium, could only grow more striking and, if I may frankly say so, more amusing. Nothing feeds more actively some of our reflections than the sight of that animated symbol, the "cultured American," entangled for the first time in the dense meshes of the great London net. The manner in which his native faculty deals with them is often an instructive spectacle. We see it, however, for the most part, exercised in a merely contemplative or "sight-seeing" way, in the interest of leisure and shopping, or at the most of patriotism and consolation. But Wolcott Balestier, at twenty-seven, with a very complicated and characteristic American past already behind him—born at Rochester, N.Y., in 1861, he had haunted colleges, administered libraries, started "businesses," explored territories, conducted theatricals, edited periodicals, and published "works"—this penetrating representative of a peculiarly transatlantic interest in books alighted in the formidable city, in the dusky void of Christmas week, on no merely passive errand. He had a specific mission, business to transact for an American publishing firm, but I trust I do no injustice to the perfection with which he transacted it if I say that such things could, in the nature of the case, give him only his pretext and his introduction. What he had really come for, as it turned out, was to find a field large enough for his admirable spirit. The field was largest in London because London was an extension without being a substitution. It "took in," as it were, the great agglomerations he had left beyond the sea and added others to them. It had, in a word—it always has—the advantage of being the biggest box at the theater, the highest seat of observation of the English-speaking multitude as a whole—with nothing less than which was Wolcott Balestier prompted to concern himself.

I met him, accidentally, soon after his arrival, and was struck with his happy perceptions and with his acute appreciation of London. Young and fresh as he was, he rejoiced in the dim vastness of the great city; this was a quality which he found altogether inspiring. He delighted in space and number, and dealt with the latter element in particular in a way which, at his age, was already masterly. He never was so happy as when he had too many things to do, and he could view the infinite multiplication of detail with pure exhilaration. This is partly what I mean by his admirable spirit, which was his love of handling large things, of handling everything in a large way. In the poor little three years to which the best of his activity was restricted he of course had established but imperfectly his independence; but they were sufficient to give the measure of his capacity. It was those who knew him best who "chaffed" him most about his Napoleonic propensities—his complete incompacity to recognize difficulties, his immediate adoption of his own or, in other words, of an original solution. It never could have occurred to him that there not a way round an obstacle so long as a way was inventable, and the invented

way, which in almost all cases was the one he embraced—
he suspected stupidity, with which he had no patience,
in the ready-made—always proved in fact the most
amusing. This was a high recommendation to him, for
observant and genial as he was, he liked to enjoy trans-
actions for themselves, as one is happy in the exercise of
any implanted faculty, quite apart from purpose and
profit. The Copyright bill had not yet been passed, and
it appeared to him that there might be much to be done
in helping the English author in America to a temporary
modus vivendi. This was an idea at the service of which
he put all his ingenuity—an ingenuity sharpened by his
detestation of the ignoble state of the law. This acute and
sympathetic interest in the fruits of literary labor, as they
concern the laborer, generalized and systematized itself
with extraordinary rapidity, and became, by the time he
had been six months in London, a very remarkable and
singularly interesting passion, a passion which, for those
who had the advantage of seeing it in exercise, quickly
assumed all the authority of genius.

It was a faculty altogether individual, and one of the
most original I have ever known. It consisted, in its
simplest expression, of an extraordinary agility in putting
himself in the place of the man, and quite as easily, when
the need was, of the woman, of letters; and it sprang from
an intense and curious appreciation of the literary character, and an odd, charmed, amused acceptance of the
dominion of the book. Nothing could be quite ultimate
for a spirit so humorous, but Wolcott Balestier found in
the importunity of the book the elements of a kind of
cheerful fatalism, a state of mind that went hand in hand,
in a whimsical way, with the critical instinct. To see the
book through—almost even through the press—was a perpetual pastime to him, and one that varied of course according to what the book might be. It was far greater in
some cases than in others; but in the free play of his ingenuity he could *faire un sort,* prepare a kind of respect-

able future, for almost anything newly printed and published, take a peep from any point of view that passed muster as literary. In this way, in our scribbling hour, he multiplied immensely his relations with the pen-driving class, even in the persons of some of its most pathetic representatives, of whom he became, in the shortest space of time, the clever providence and kindly adviser. Signs were not wanting from many of these after his death, signs of their mourning for him as the most trusted of friends. And all this, on the young man's part, in a spirit so disinterested and so sincerely sympathetic that one hardly knew what name to give to the genius of the market when the genius of the market appeared in a form so human.

He had the greatest appetite for success, and had begun to be a man of business of the very largest conceptions, but I have never seen this characteristic combined with so visible an indifference to the usual lures and ideals of commerce. As the faithful representative of others he could only be jealous of their interests, but a high and imaginative talent for affairs could not well have been associated with less reverence for mere acquisition. He had, in fact, none at all—he seemed to me to care nothing for money. What he cared for was the drama of business—the various human game. To make money, up to a certain point, would have been convenient to him, and if he proposed to do so it was simply because this meant freedom, freedom to make a very different use of his time when (at no very distant day, as he hoped) the hour should strike. Much as he was absorbed in the literary affairs of other people, he was excusable for keeping a commodious chamber of his brain open to his own; and he had the most definite purpose of hammering away at the modern, the very modern, novel, as soon as he should get out of the glare of the market-place and be able to command the conditions. He had already given pledges in this direction—had published two boyish fictions before coming to England, and in the intervals of his busy first year in London had put together a long story of much maturer, of really confident, promise. An intimate personal alliance with Mr. Rudyard Kipling had led to his working in concert with that extraordinary genius, a lesson precious, doubtless, and wasted, like so many of his irrepressible young experiments—wasted, I mean, in the sense of its being a morning without a morrow.

Wolcott Balestier's death came too soon, in my judgment, to permit of a just calculation of what he might have done; we must recognize the limits of the evidence that his talent was real and remarkably capable of growth —evidence confirmed, on the part of those who knew him, by the sense of his acuteness and his ambition. He was all for the novel of observation, the undiscourageable study of the actual; he professed an intense relish for the works of Mr. Howells, and there is little reason to doubt that if he had lived to give what was in him, the followers of some of the ancient ways would have had many a bone to pick with him. The prospect of picking such bones was, for himself, a thing to add zest to the existence he was not destined to enjoy. His imagination, so far as he had given a hint of it, was all American, and a long stay in the Far West, a familiarity with mining-camps and infant cities, had given it, for the time at least, the turn of the new convention. He was prejudiced in favor of American humor—it was his only prejudice that I can remember; fortunately it is not one that is fatal to intellectual growth. He liked little, raw, new places only one degree less than he liked London, where he had established himself, in the heart of Westminster, under the Abbey towers, just within the old archway of that Dean's Yard which makes a kind of provincial backwater, like the corner of a cathedral close, in a roaring "imperial" neighborhood. But when once it had begun to go, his talent would probably have had many moods and seasons. I remember thinking (on first observing what dreams he had of becoming a literary artist) that as the presumption is always against the duplication of a special gift, it was not particularly probable that the subtle secret of creation had been vouchsafed to a man who, in his natural mastery of affairs, might already account himself fortunately equipped. What community was there, in the same mind, between the noisy world of affairs and the hushed little chamber of literary art? That question was eventually answered—there could be none unless such a mind should be a rare exception. This was indeed the fact with Wolcott Balestier, and it made him, in my experience, unique.

I have known literary folk who were full, for themselves, of the commercial spirit, but I have in no other case known a commercial connection with literature to have had a twinship with an artistic one. Wolcott Balestier, however, was commercial, as I may say, for others; it was for himself that he cherished the hope of achieving some painted picture of life. Moreover, the technical term seems invidious as applied to a part played so easily and gracefully, with such friendly personal perceptions. This function cost him nothing intellectually— it was too instinctive, and, incidentally, as I have said, too suggestive. It had advantages from the point of view of what he intended when a better day should have begun; it meant perpetual contact with the world of men and women, and innumerable opportunities for observation. In this he ironically exulted, and indeed it made him enviable. He had a particular aptitude for the personal part of affairs, for arranging things in talk and face to face. He had instincts and ideals of rapidity, and a talent for dispensing with the matter of course (which seemed to him flat and prosaic), calculated often to bewilder the children of a postponing habit. And it was given to him moreover to encounter the human, not to say the supposedly literary spirit, bared of factitious graces, in the simple severity of some of its appetites. He saw many

realities, and had already learned not to blink many
uglinesses. Young as he was he had perceived what was of
the essence. He was a well of discretion, and it was
charming and interesting in him that even when he was
most humorously communicative, his talk was traversed
by little wandering airs of the unsaid; nevertheless he
was not without nameless anecdotes and illustrations of
this same tenacity of grasp—all the more striking that
in general no man could be less prejudiced in favor of the
publishing interest. Such an incident as the quick foundation of the "English Library"—an association for the
larger diffusion on the Continent of English and American books—not only was a remarkable example of his
fertility of resource (his idea always became a fact as
soon as he could personally represent it and act for it),
but brought with it an extension of experience of the
sort which was really most remunerative to him, and as
to which he could be independently and delightfully
descriptive. It was partly on business connected with this
happy undertaking, and partly exactly to do nothing at
all—to rest from a torment of detail and a strain of responsibility—that he made, sadly unwell when he started,
in November 1891, that excursion to Germany from
which he was not to return. He had only once or twice
in his life been gravely ill, but those who were fond of
him were never persuaded by his gallantry of optimism
about himself, reinforced as it was by a thoroughly consistent and characteristic ingenuity in neglecting dull
precautions, to think of his slender structure as really
adequate to the service—the formidable service—of his
generously restless spirit. It was not, in fact, and the
disparity made him touching—makes his present image so
in memory, though he doubtless would have carried on
the brave deception much longer had it not been for the
miserable typhoidal infection, from an undiscoverable
source, that he bore with him from London, and to which,
in happy unconsciousness, he succumbed.

It is vain to attempt to exclude the egotistical note from a memorial like the present, and the better course is frankly to enjoy the benefit of it. I may therefore mention that, during the last year of his life in particular, I saw him so often and so closely that, as I write, my page is overscored with importunate reminiscence and picture. These things are the possession of the private eye, but one would fain reflect something of their clearness in one's words. A wet winter night in a windy Lancashire town, for instance—a formidable "first night" at a troubled provincial theater to which he had made a long and loyal pilgrimage for purposes of "support" at a grotesquely nervous hour—such an occasion comes back to me, vividly, with the very quality of the support afforded, lavish and eager and shrewd; with the pleasantness of the little commemorative inn-supper, half histrionic and wholly confident, and with the dragged-out drollery of the sequel next day, our sociable, amused participation in a collective theatrical flitting, effected in pottering Sunday trains, besprinkled with refreshment-room impressions and terminating that night, at an all but inaccessible Birmingham, in independent repose and relaxed criticism. He had taken, the summer before his death, a house on the Isle of Wight—on the south shore, well on the way to the Freshwater end—and I cannot withhold the emphasis of an allusion to a couple of August days spent there with him. One of them had a rare perfection and made the purest medium for the high finish—as if it were a leaf out of an old-fashioned drawing-book—of the little penciled island. It was given all to a long drive to Freshwater, much of the way over the firm grass of the great downs, and a lunch there and a rambling lazy lounge on the high cliffs, with the full sense of summer, for once, in a summerless year, and a still lazier return in the golden afternoon, amid all sorts of delicacies of effect of sea and land. He loved the little temporary home he had made on the edge of the sea and even the great wind-storms of the early autumn, and no season of his life, probably, in spite of haunting illness, had given him more contented hours. Now he lies in the last place he could have dreamed of, the bristling alien cemetery, contracted and charmless, of the foreign city to which he had made his feverish way only to die. There was something in him so actively modern, so open to new reciprocities and assimilations, that it is not fanciful to say that he would have worked originally, in his degree, for civilization. He had the real cosmopolitan spirit, the easy imagination of differences and hindrances surmounted. He struck me as a bright young forerunner of some higher common conveniences, some greater international transfusions. He had just had time to begin, and that is exactly what makes the exceeding pity of his early end.

THE STORY-TELLER AT LARGE:
MR. HENRY HARLAND [1]

WE RECEIVE now and then an impression that seems to hint at the advent of a time for looking more closely into the old notion that, to have a quality of his own, a writer must needs draw his sap from the soil of his origin. The great writers of the world have, as a general thing, struck us so as fed by their native air and furnished forth with things near and dear to them that an author without a country would have come long ago—had anyone ever presumed to imagine him—to be a figure as formless as an author without a pen, a publisher, or a subject. Such would have been especially, to the inner vision, and for the very best reasons, the deep incongruity of the novelist at large. We are ridden by the influence of types established, and as the novelist is essentially a painter we assign him to his climate and circumstances as confidently

[1] This essay appeared in the *Fortnightly Review*, April 1898, and was never reprinted by James. Henry Harland (1861–1905) was born in Russia of American parents, educated in Europe and at Harvard, and wrote a series of novels under the pseudonym of Sidney Luska. In 1890 he discarded the pseudonym and became the original editor of the *Yellow Book* in London.

as we assign Velasquez and Gainsborough to their schools. Does he not paint the things he knows? and are not the things he knows—knows best, of course—just the things for which he has the warrant of the local, the national consciousness? We settle the question easily—have settled it, that is, once for all; nothing being easier than to appeal for proof, with a fond and loyal glance, to Dickens, to Scott, to Balzac, to Hawthorne, respectively so English, so Scotch, so French, so American, particularly in the matter of subject, to which part of the business an analysis not prone to sin by excess of penetration has mainly found itself confined.

But if our analysis limps along as it may, the elements of the matter and the field of criticism so change and so extend themselves that an increase of refreshment will practically perhaps not be denied us even by the pace obtained. If it was perfectly true earlier in the century and in a larger world—I speak of the globe itself—that he was apt to paint best who painted nearest home, the case may well be, according to some symptoms, in course of modification. Who shall say, at the rate things are going, what is to be "near" home in the future and what is to be far from it? London, in the time of Fenimore Cooper, was fearfully—or perhaps only fortunately—far from Chicago, and Paris stood to London in a relation almost equally awkward for an Easter run, though singularly favorable, on either side, for concentration. The forces that are changing all this need scarce be mentioned at a moment when each day's breakfast-table—if the morning paper be part of its furniture—fairly bristles with revelations of them. The globe is fast shrinking, for the imagination, to the size of an orange that can be played with; the hurry to and fro over its surface is that of ants when you turn up a stone, and there are times when we feel as if, as regards his habitat—and especially as regards *hers*, for women wander as they have never wandered—almost everyone must have changed place, and changed language, with everyone else. The ancient local concentration that was so involuntary in Dickens and Balzac is less and less a matter of course; and the period is calculably near when successfully to emulate it will figure to the critical eye as a rare and possibly beautiful *tour de force*.

The prospect, surely, therefore, is already interesting, and while it widens and the marks of it multiply we may watch the omens and wonder if they have a lesson for us. I find myself much prompted to some such speculation by Mr. Henry Harland's new volume of *Comedies and Errors;* though I confess that in reading into the influences behind it the idea of dispatriation I take a liberty for which, on its face, it opens no door. To speak of a writer as detached, one must at least know what he is detached from, and in this collection of curiously ingenious prose pieces there is not a single clear sound of the fundamental, the native note, not the tip of a finger held out indeed to any easy classifying. This very fact in itself perhaps constitutes the main scrap of evidence on behalf of a postulate of that particular set of circumstances—those of the transatlantic setting—that lends itself to being most unceremoniously, as it were, escaped from. There is not a single direct glance at American life in these pages, and only two or three implied; but the very oddity of the case is in our gradual impression, as we read, that conclusive proof resides most of all in what is absent, in the very quality that has dropped out. This quality, when it is present, is that of the bird in the cage or the branch on the tree—the fact of being confined, attached, continuous. Mr. Harland is at the worst in a cage of wires remarkably interspaced, and not on the tree save so far as we may suppose it to put forth branches of fantastic length. He is the branch broken off and converted to other useful and agreeable purposes—even in portions to that of giving out, in a state of combustion, charming red and blue flame.

To put it less indirectly, I have found half the interest

of *Comedies and Errors* to be the peculiar intensity of that
mark of the imagination that may best be described as the
acute sense of the "Europe"—synthetic symbol!—of the
American mind, and that therefore, until Asia and Africa
shall pour in their contingent of observers, we are reduced
to regarding as almost the sharpest American characteristic. If it be not quite always the liveliest of all, it is
certainly the liveliest on the showing of such work as I
here consider, the author's maturest—work which probably gives quite the best occasion the critic in quest of an
adventure can find today for sounding, by way of a
change, the mystery of what nutrition may eventually be
offered to those artistic spirits for whom the "countries"
are committed to the process, that I have glanced at, of
overlapping and getting mixed. A special instance is illuminating, and Mr. Harland is a distinguished one. He is
the more of one that he has clearly thought out a form—
of great interest and promise, a form that tempers the
obscurity of our question by eliminating one danger. If
we are to watch the "cosmopolitan" painter on trial, it
will always be so much to the good for him that he has
mastered a method and learned how to paint. *Then* we
may, with all due exhilaration, set down all his shipwrecks
to his unanchored state.

Mr. Harland's method is that of the "short story,"
which has of late become an object of such almost extravagant dissertation. If it has awaked to consciousness,
however, it has doubtless only done what most things are
doing in an age of organized talk. It took itself, in the
comparatively silent years, less seriously, and there was
perhaps a more general feeling that you both wrote and
read your short story best when you did so in peace
and patience. To turn it out, at any rate, as well as
possible, by private, and almost diffident, instinct and
reflection, was a part of the general virtue of the individual, the kind of virtue that shunned the high light
of the public square. The public square is now the

whole city, and taking us all in, has acoustic properties so remarkable that thoughts barely whispered in a corner are heard all over the place. Therefore each of us already knows what every other of us thinks of the short story, though he knows perhaps at the same time that not every other can write it. Anything we may say about it is at best but a compendium of the current wisdom. It is a form delightful and difficult, and with one of these qualities—as, for that matter, one of them almost everywhere is—the direct reason of the other. It is an easy thing, no doubt, to do a little with, but the interest quickens at a high rate on an approximation to that liberal *more* of which we speedily learn it to be capable. The charm I find in Mr. Harland's tales is that he is always trying for the more, for the extension of the picture, the full and vivid summary, and trying with an art of ingenuity, an art of a reflective order, all alive with felicities and delicacies.

Are there not two quite distinct effects to be produced by this rigor of brevity—the two that best make up for the many left unachieved as requiring a larger canvas? The one with which we are most familiar is that of the detached incident, single and sharp, as clear as a pistol-shot; the other, of rarer performance, is that of the impression, comparatively generalized—simplified, fore-shortened, reduced to a particular perspective—of a complexity or a continuity. The former is an adventure comparatively safe, in which you have, for the most part, but to put one foot after the other. It is just the risks of the latter, on the contrary, that make the best of the sport. These are naturally—given the general reduced scale—immense, for nothing is less intelligible than bad foreshortening, which, if it fails to mean everything intended, means less than nothing. It is to Mr. Harland's honor that he always "goes in" for the risks. *The Friend of Man,* for instance, is an attempt as far removed as possible from the snap of the pistol-shot; it is an excellent

example of the large in a small dose, the smaller form
put on its mettle and trying to do—by sharp selection,
composition, presentation and the sacrifice of verbiage—
what the longer alone is mostly supposed capable of. It
is the picture of a particular figure—eccentric, comic,
pathetic, tragic—disengaged from old remembrances, encounters, accidents, exhibitions, and exposures, and re-
solving these glimpses and patches into the unity of air
and feeling that makes up a character. It is all a matter of
odds and ends recovered and interpreted. The "story" is
nothing, the subject everything, and the manner in which
the whole thing becomes expressive strikes me as an excellent specimen of what can be done on the minor scale
when art comes in. There are, of course, particular effects
that insist on space, and the thing, above all, that the short
story has to renounce is the actual *pursuit* of a character.
Temperaments and mixtures, the development of a nature,
are shown us perforce in a tale, as they are shown us in
life, only by illustration more or less copious and frequent; and the drawback is that when the tale is short
the figure, before we have had time to catch up with it,
gets beyond and away, dips below the horizon made by
the little square of space that we have accepted.

Yet, in the actual and prospective flood of fiction, the
greatest of all, the streams that empty into the sea of
the verbose, the relief may still be immense that comes
even from escapes for which we pay by incidental losses.
We are often tempted to wonder if almost any escape
is not better than mere submersion. *Petit-Bleu*, in this
volume, *Cousin Rosalys*, *Tirala-Tirala*, *Rooms*, all show
the same love of evocation for evocation's sake, if need
be; the successful suggestion of conditions, states, circumstances, aspects; the suggestion of the feeling of things
in youth, of the remembrance of this feeling in age; the
suggestion, above all, of that most difficult of all things
for the novelist to render, the duration of time, the drag
and friction of its passage, the fact that things have not

taken place, as the fashionable fables of our day, with their terrific abuse of dialogue and absence of composition, seem to have embraced the mission of representing, just in the hour or two it may take to estimate the manner of the book. The feeling of things—in especial of the particular place, of the lost and regretted period and chance, always, to fond fancy, supremely charming and queer and exquisite—is, in fact, Mr. Harland's general subject and most frequent inspiration. And what I find characteristic and curious in this is that the feeling is, in the most candid way in the world, but with new infatuations and refinements, the feeling of the American for his famous Europe.

It is a very wonderful thing, this Europe of the American in general and of the author of *Comedies and Errors* in particular—in particular, I say, because Mr. Harland tends, in a degree quite his own, to give in the romantic and tender voice, the voice of fancy pure and simple, without the disturbance of other elements, such as comparison and reaction, either violent or merciful. He is not even "international," which it, after all, but another way, perhaps, of being a slave to the "countries," possibly twice or even three times a jingo. It is a complete surrender of that province of the mind with which registration and subscription have to do. Thus is presented a disencumbered, sensitive surface for the wonderful Europe to play on. The question for the critic is that of the value of what this surface, so liberally, so artfully prepared, may give back. What strikes me as making the author of the volume before me a case to watch, as I have said, is that fact that he has a form so compact and an execution so light and firm. He is just yet, I think, a little too much everywhere, a trifle astray, as regards his inspiration, in the very wealth of his memories and the excess, even, of his wit—specimens of which I might gather, had I space, from the charming *Invisible Prince*, from *The Queen's Pleasure*, from *Flower o' the Clove*,

from each indeed, I have noted as I read, of these compositions.

He is lost in the vision, all whimsical and picturesque,
of palace secrets, rulers and pretenders and ministers of
bewilderingly light comedy, in undiscoverable Balkan
States, Bohemias of the seaboard, where the queens have
platonic friendships with professional English, though
not American, humorists; in the heavy, many-voiced
air of the old Roman streets and of the high Roman
saloons where cardinals are part of the furniture; in the
hum of prodigious Paris, heard in corners of old cafés;
in the sense of the deep English background as much as
that of any of these; in a general facility of reference; in
short, to the composite spectacle and the polyglot doom.
Most of his situations are treated in the first person, and
as they skip across frontiers and pop up in parks and
palaces they give us the impression that, all suffused
with youth as the whole thing seems, it is the play of
a memory that has had half a dozen lives. Nothing is
more charming in it than the reverberation of the old
delicate, sociable France that the author loves most of
all to conjure up and that fills the exquisite little picture
of *Rooms* with an odor of faint lavender in wonderful
bowls and a rustle of ancient silk on polished floors. But
these, I dare say, are mere exuberances of curiosity and
levities of independence. He has, as I have sufficiently
hinted, the sense of subject and the sense of shape, and
it is when, under the coercion of these things, he really
stops and begins to dig that the critic will more attentively
look out for him. Then we shall come back to the
question of soil—the question with which I started—and
of the possible ups and downs, as an artist, of the citizen
of the world.

PART THREE

American Letters
1898

*

AMERICAN LETTERS

THE QUESTION OF THE OPPORTUNITIES

ANY FRESH start of speech today on American literature seems to me so inevitably a more direct and even a slightly affrighted look at the mere numbers of the huge, homogeneous, and fast-growing population from which the flood of books issues and to which it returns that this particular impression admonishes the observer to pause long enough on the threshold to be sure he takes it well in. Whatever the "literature" already is, whatever it may be destined yet to be, the public to which it addresses itself is of proportions that no other single public has approached, least of all those of the periods and societies to which we owe the comparatively small library of books that we rank as the most precious thing in our heritage. This question of numbers is brought home to us again and again with force by the amazing fortune apparently open now, any year, to the individual book—usually the lucky novel—that happens to please; by the extraordinary career, for instance, yesterday, of Trilby, or, today (as I hear it reported) of an historical fiction translated from the Polish and entitled *Quo Vadis?* It is clear enough that such a public must be, for the observer,

[1] During the spring and summer of 1898 Henry James wrote a series of "American Letters" for the English magazine *Literature*, of which H. D. Traill was editor. The large folio Saturday journal was devoted essentially to belles-lettres, and James wrote, in all, eleven letters. Most of them are reprinted here for the first time.

an immense part of the whole question of the concatenation and quality of books, must present it in conditions
hitherto almost unobserved and of a nature probably to
give an interest of a kind so new as to suggest for the
critic—even the critic least sure of where the chase will
bring him out—a delicious rest from the oppressive *a
priori*. There can be no real sport for him—if I may use
the term that fits best the critical energy—save in proportion as he gets rid of *that;* and he can hardly fail to
get rid of it just in the degree in which the conditions
are vivid to his mind. They are, of course, largely those
of other publics as well, in an age in which, everywhere,
more people than ever before buy and sell, and read and
write, and run about; but their scale, in the great com-
mon-schooled and newspapered democracy, is the largest
and their pressure the greatest we see; their characteristics
are magnified and multiplied. From these characteristics
no intelligent forecast of the part played in the community in question by the printed and circulated page
will suffer its attention too widely to wander.

Homogeneous I call the huge American public, with a
due sense of the variety of races and idioms that are
more and more under contribution to build it up, for
it is precisely in the great mill of the language, our
predominant and triumphant English, taking so much,
suffering perhaps even so much, in the process, but
giving so much more, on the whole, than it has to "put
up" with, that the elements are ground into unity. Into
its vast motherly lap the supreme speech manages somehow or other—with a robust indifference to trifles and
shades—to see these elements poured; and just in this
unique situation of the tongue itself we may surely find,
if we attend, the interest of the drama and the excitement
of the question. It is a situation that strikes me as presenting to the critic some of the strain and stress—those
of suspense, of life, movement, change, the multiplication of possibilities, surprises, disappointments (emotions,

whatever they may be, of the truth-hunter)—that the
critic likes most to encounter. What may be, from point
to point, noted as charming, or even as alarming, consequences? What forms, what colors, what sounds may the
language take on or throw off in accommodating itself
to such a growth of experience; what life may it—and
most of all may the literature that shall so copiously
testify for it—reflect and embody? The answer to these
inquiries is simply the march of the critic's drama and
the bliss, when not the misery, of that spectator; but
while the endless play goes on the spectator may at
least so far anticipate deferred conclusions as to find a
savor in the very fact that it has been reserved not
for French, not for German, not for Italian to meet fate
on such a scale. That consciousness is an emotion in
itself and, for large views, which are the only amusing
ones, a great portent; so that we can surely say to ourselves that we shall not have been called upon to supply
the biggest public for nothing.

To overflow with the same confidence to others is
indeed perhaps to expose ourselves to hearing it declared
improbable that we have been called upon to supply it,
at any rate, for literature—the moral mainly latent in
literature for the million, or rather for the fast-arriving
billion, finding here inevitably a tempting application.
But is not our instant rejoinder to that, as inevitably,
that such an application is precipitate and premature?
Whether, in the conditions we consider, the supply shall
achieve sufficient vitality and distinction really to be
sure of itself as literature, and to communicate the certi-
tude, is the very thing we watch and wait to discover.
If the retort to that remark be in turn that all this depends
on what we may take it into our heads to *call* literature,
we work round to a ground of easy assent. It truly does
much depend on that. But that, in its order, depends on
new light—on the new light struck out by the material
itself, the distinguishable symptoms of which are the

justification for what I have called the critic's happy release from the cramped posture of foregone conclusions and narrow rules. There will be no real amusement if we are positively prepared to be stupid. It is assuredly true that literature for the billion will not be literature as we have hitherto known it at its best. But if the billion give the pitch of production and circulation, they do something else besides; they hang before us a wide picture of opportunities—opportunities that would be opportunities still even if, reduced to the *minimum*, they should be only those offered by the vastness of the implied habitat and the complexity of the implied history. It is impossible not to entertain with patience and curiosity the presumption that life so colossal must break into expression at points of proportionate frequency. These places, these moments will be the chances.

The first chance that, in the longer run, expression avails herself of may, of course, very well be that of breaking up into pieces and showing thereby that—as has been hitherto and in other parts of the world but imperfectly indicated—the public we somewhat loosely talk of as for literature or for anything else is really as subdivided as a chessboard, with each little square confessing only to its own *kind* of accessibility. The comparison too much sharpens and equalizes; but there are certainly, as on a map of countries, divisions and boundaries; and if these varieties become, to assist individual genius or save individual life, accentuated in American letters, we shall immediately to that tune be rewarded for our faith. It is, in other words, just from the very force of the conditions making for reaction in spots and phases that the liveliest appeal of future American production may spring—reaction, I mean, against the grossness of any view, any taste or tone, in danger of becoming so extravagantly general as to efface the really interesting thing, the traceability of the individual. Then, for all we know, we may get individual publics positively more sifted and evolved than anywhere else, shoals of fish rising to more delicate bait. That is a possibility that makes meanwhile for good humor, though I must hasten to add that it by no means exhausts the favorable list. We know what the list actually shows or what, in the past, it has mainly shown—New England quite predominantly, almost exclusively, the literary voice and dealing with little else than material supplied by herself. I have just been reading two new books that mark strikingly how the Puritan culture both used and exhausted its opportunity, how its place knows it no longer with any approach to the same intensity. Mrs. Fields's *Life and Letters of Harriet Beecher Stowe* and Mr. John Jay Chapman's acute and admirable *Emerson and Other Essays* (the most penetrating study, as regards his main subject, to my sense, of which that subject has been made the occasion) appear to refer to a past already left long behind, and are each, moreover, on this ground and on others, well worth returning to. The American world of today is a world of combinations and proportions different from those amid which Emerson and Mrs. Stowe could reach right and left far enough to fill it.

The note of the difference—at least of some of it— is sharply enough struck in an equally recent volume from which I have gathered many suggestions and that exhibits a talent distinctly to come back to—Mr. Owen Wister's *Lin McLean* (episodes in the career of a young "cattle-puncher"), in which the manners of the remoter West are worked into the general context, the American air at large, by a hand of a singularly trained and modern lightness. I but glance in passing, not to lose my thread, at these things; but Mr. Owen Wister's tales (an earlier strong cluster of which, *Red Men and White*, I a year or two ago also much appreciated) give me a pretext for saying that, not inexplicably perhaps, a novelist interested in the general outlook of his trade may find the sharpest appeal of all in the idea of the chances in reserve for

the work of the imagination in particular—the vision
of the distinguishable poetry of things, whether expressed in such verse or (rarer phenomenon) in such
prose as really does arrive at expression. I cannot but
think that the American novel has in a special, far-
reaching direction to sail much closer to the wind.
"Business" plays a part in the United States that other
interests dispute much less showily than they sometimes
dispute it in the life of European countries; in conse-
quence of which the typical American figure is above
all that "business man" whom the novelist and the dramatist have scarce yet seriously touched, whose song
has still to be sung and his picture still to be painted.
He is often an obscure, but not less often an epic, hero,
seamed all over with the wounds of the market and the
dangers of the field, launched into action and passion
by the immensity and complexity of the general struggle,
a boundless ferocity of battle—driven above all by the
extraordinary, the unique relation in which he for the
most part stands to the life of his lawful, his immitigable
womankind, the wives and daughters who float, who
splash on the surface and ride the waves, his terrific link
with civilization, his social substitutes and representatives,
while, like a diver for shipwrecked treasure, he gasps in
the depths and breathes through an air-tube.

This relation, even taken alone, contains elements
that strike me as only yearning for their interpreter—
elements, moreover, that would present the further merit
of melting into the huge neighboring province of the
special situation of women in an order of things where
to be a woman at all—certainly to be a young one—
constitutes in itself a social position. The difficulty,
doubtless, is that the world of affairs, as affairs are understood in the panting cities, though around us all the
while, before us, behind us, beside us, and under our
feet, is as special and occult a one to the outsider as
the world, say, of Arctic exploration—as impenetrable

save as a result of special training. Those who know it
are not the men to paint it; those who might attempt
it are not the men who know it. The most energetic
attempt at portrayal that we have anywhere had—
L'Argent, of Émile Zola—is precisely a warning of the
difference between false and true initiation. The subject
there, though so richly imagined, is all too mechanically,
if prodigiously, "got up." Meanwhile, accordingly, the
American "business man" remains, thanks to the length
and strength of the wires that move him, *the* magnificent
theme *en disponibilité*. The romance of fact, indeed, has
touched him in a way that quite puts to shame the
romance of fiction. It gives his measure for purposes of
art that it was he, essentially, who embarked in the great
war of 1861–4, and who, carrying it on in the North
to a triumphant conclusion, went back, since business was
his standpoint, to his very "own" with an undimmed
capacity to mind it. When, in imagination, you give the
type, as it exists today, the benefit of its great double
luster—that of these recorded antecedents and that of its
preoccupied, systematic, and magnanimous abasement
before the other sex—you will easily feel your sense
of what may be done with its overflow.

To glance at that is, at the point to which the English-
speaking world has brought the matter, to remember by
the same stroke that if there be no virtue in any forecast
of the prospect of letters, any sounding of their deeps
and shallows that fails to take account of the almost
predominant hand now exercised about them by women,
the precaution is doubly needful in respect to the American situation. Whether the extraordinary dimensions of
the public be a promise or a threat, nothing is more unmistakable than the sex of some of the largest masses.
The longest lines are feminine—feminine, it may almost
be said, the principal front. Both as readers and as writers
on the other side of the Atlantic women have, in fine,
"arrived" in numbers not equaled even in England, and

they have succeeded in giving the pitch and marking the limits more completely than elsewhere. The public taste, as our fathers used to say, has become so largely *their* taste, their tone, their experiment, that nothing is at last more apparent than that the public cares little for anything that they cannot do. And what, after all, may the very finest opportunity of American literature be but just to show that they can do what the peoples will have ended by regarding as everything? The settlement of such a question, the ups and downs of such a process surely more than justify that sense of sport, in this direction, that I have spoken of as the privilege of the vigilant critic.

—March 26, 1898

THE AMERICAN NOVEL

It was not unknown to the irresponsible critic—by which I mean, not the critic who overflowed, but him who sought the refuge of the other extreme—that in the United States, as in England, in France, in Germany, the flood of fiction is a rising tide; the truth was not to come fully home, however, till he perceived the effect of the exhibition of his notebook, the gleam of a single poor page of which reminded him, in the way of instant action on the ranks of romance, of the convergence of the ducks in a pond on the production of a biscuit. He can only therefore be quick to reflect on the early need of some principle of selection; though he may indeed, with scarce less promptitude, discover that no simplification in the matter is really easy. It is very well to say that the things of merit are the only ones that signify; that leaves on his hands the very question itself—the mystery, the delicacy of merit. With the quality, in any very thrilling form, the air may not always strike him as intensely charged; it may, moreover, as he feels it, so often be absent from

works that have formed the delight of thousands that
he is thrown back on his inner consciousness and on a
queer secret code. He must at any rate arrive at some
sort of working measure, have in his list signs enough to
make, as it were, alternatives, so that if he do not
recognize a book under one of them he shall under
another.

I grasp, for instance, with Mrs. Gertrude Atherton,
at the eminent fact that she is "international," finding
this at least an interesting symptom and a mark, moreover, of something that we shall probably all, not long
hence, be talking of as a "movement." As the novel in
America multiplies, it will seek more room, I seem to
foresee, by coming for inspiration to Europe; reversing
in this manner, on another plane, oddly enough, a great
historical fact. Just exactly for room these three centuries
Europe has been crossing the ocean westward. We
may yet therefore find it sufficiently curious to see the
Western imagination, so planted, come back. This
imagination will find for a long time, to my sense—
it will find doubtless always—its most interesting business
in staying where it has grown; but if there is to be a
great deal of it, it must obviously follow the fashion of
other matters, seek all adventures, and take all chances.
Fiction as yet in the United States strikes me, none the
less, as most curious when most confined and most local;
this is so much the case that when it is even abjectly
passive to surrounding conditions I find it capable of
yielding an interest that almost makes me dread undue
enlargement. There are moments when we are tempted
to say that there is nothing like saturation—to pronounce
it a safer thing than talent. I find myself rejoicing, for
example, in Mr. Hamlin Garland, a case of saturation
so precious as to have almost the value of genius.
There are moods in which we seem to see that the
painter, of whatever sort, is most for us when he is
most, so to speak, the soaked sponge of his air and

time; and of Mr. Hamlin Garland—as to whom I hasten
to parenthesize that there are many other things to
remember, things for which I almost impatiently await
the first occasion—I express his price, to my own taste,
with all honor if I call him the soaked sponge of
Wisconsin. Saturation and talent are, of course, compatible, talent being really but one's own sense and use
of one's saturation; but we must come round again to
that. The point I for the moment make is simply that
in the American air I am nervous, in general, lest talent
should wish to "sail for Europe." Let me now, indeed,
recognize that it by no means inveterately does. Even
so great and active a faculty as that of the author of
The Rise of Silas Lapham has suffered him to remain,
after all, very prosperously at home. On the day Miss
Mary Wilkins should "sail" I would positively have
detectives versed in the practice of extradition posted
at Liverpool.

Mrs. Atherton, however, *has* sailed, and we must make
the best of it—by which I mean give her the benefit of
what she has come in search of. She strikes me at first, I
confess—in *American Wives and English Husbands*—as
looking for a situation rather than as finding one. I am not
guilty, I think, of that last ineptitude of the helpless com-
mentator—a quarrel with the artist's subject, so always
his affair, and not, thank goodness, the critic's—when I
say that she has passed beside her chance. A man of the
trade may perhaps be excused for the habit, in reading a
novel, of thinking of what, in the conditions, *he* would
have done. I hold, indeed, that there is, without some such
attitude, no real acceptance on the critic's part of the
author's ground and standpoint. It is no such dishonor,
after all, for an artist's problem to be rehandled mentally
by a brother. I promised myself at the outset of Mrs.
Atherton's volume the liveliest moments, foresaw the
drama of the confrontation, in all original good faith, of
incompatibles—the habit on the part of the Californian

girl of the Californian view of the "relation of the sexes"
and the habit on the part of the young Englishman foredoomed to political life, a peerage, and a hundred other
grand things, of a different attitude altogether. The relation of the sexes is, to the Californian mind, especially
when tinged, as in the case of Mrs. Atherton's heroine,
with a Southern influence, that the husband—for we are
mainly reduced to husbands—shall button his wife's boots
and kiss her instep, these tributes being in fact but the
byplay of his general prostration. The early promise in
American Wives and English Husbands is the greater that
the author gives the gleam of something like detached
spectatorship, of really seeing the situation she appears to
desire to evoke. But, in fact, as it strikes me, she not only
fails to see it, but leaves us wondering what she has supposed herself to see instead. The conflict of character, of
tradition, in which the reader has expected the drama to
reside, is reduced to proportions so insignificant that we
never catch it in the act. It consists wholly in the momentary and quite unpresented feeling, on the part of the
American wife, domiciled, in much splendor, in England,
that she would like to see California again, followed almost
immediately by the conviction that after all she would
not. She has a young Californian kinsman who is fond of
her and who, coming to stay with her in her grandeur,
wants her to go back with him; but the intervention of
this personage—into which the reader immediately begins
to drop the psychological plummet—promptly fails of
interest through want, as the playwrights say, of preparation. Nothing has been given us to see him work on,
none of the dramatic essence of the matter, the opposition,
from husband to wife and vice versa, of the famous relation. The relation, after all, seems, in the case, simple—
as, I hasten to add, it may in general veritably become, I
think, to a degree eventually disconcerting perhaps to
international fiction. On that day the story-teller will
frankly find his liveliest effect in showing not how much,

but how little, the "American wife" has to get rid of for remote adjustments. There, possibly, is the real psychological well.

—April 9, 1898

GRANT'S LETTERS; WHITMAN'S *Calamus*

I HAVE on my table three volumes of letters, and I lay the first hand on those of the greatest name. Here, in one of the extraordinarily pretty little books of which American taste and typography show themselves more and more capable, is a fragment, to be swallowed at a sitting, of the correspondence of General Grant; as to which I am not sure if it may bring home to us anything quite so much as the almost unfair advantage enjoyed in literature by the man who has played a great part out of it. If this part, to the reader's imagination, does not make the literary element, it may terribly often make something under the impression of which the want of that element enjoys a discouraging impunity. Such, at least, may easily be the despair of an observer accustomed to holding that there are no short cuts, yet reduced to recognizing here and there a presence that has certainly not got in by the regular way. General Grant is a case for us—I mean, of course, if we be at all open to a hint—of the absolute privilege of having got in by fame. It is easy, of course, to deny that he *is* "in," and assuredly no man ever pretended less to write. But somehow he expresses his own figure, and, for the rest, association helps.

It is doubtless association that *makes* his element—the ground on which, on the printed page, we meet him; it simply crowds the other questions out. It is a matter about which I may very well be superstitious; but I should perhaps be ashamed if I were not, and I admit that the sentiment that has enabled me to enjoy these scant pages—as hard and dry as sandpaper—is one in support of which I can scarcely give chapter and verse. Great is the name—that is all one can say—when so great a bareness practically blooms. These few bald little letters have a ray of the hard limpidity of the writer's strong and simple Autobiography—they have nothing more; yet for those of a particular generation—not the latest—they can still transport, even if merely by reminding us not so much of what is required as of what is left out to make a man of action. As addressed to one of his most intimate friends, Mr. E. B. Washburne, at one time his Secretary of State, at another his Minister to France—whose name, oddly enough, Grant always curtailed of what he appeared to think the nonsense of its final "e"—they breathe an austerity in attachment that helps, with various other singular signs, to make them seem scarcely of our time. The old American note sounds in them, the sense of the "hard" life and the plain speech. "Some men are only made by their staff appointments . . . while others give respectability to the position." "Friends must not think hard of me for holding on to Galena as my home." He always held on, as to expression, to Galena. There is scarcely a "shall" or a "should" in the whole little volume. The later letters are written during his great tour of the nations after he had ceased to be President. "The fact is, however, that I have seen nothing to make me regret that I am an American." "As Mr. Young, who is travelling with me, gives accurate and detailed accounts of every place we visit . . . nothing of this sort is necessary from me." Nothing of this sort could encumber, in any direction, his correspondence; but the tone has something of the quality that, when we meet its equivalent in an old, dry portrait or even an old angular piece of furniture, affects the historic, not to say the æsthetic, sense.

What sense shall I speak of as affected by the series of letters published, under the title of *Calamus*, by Dr. R. M. Bucke, one of the literary executors of Walt Whitman? The democratic would be doubtless a prompt and simple answer, and as an illustration of democratic social conditions their interest is lively. The person to whom, from 1868 to 1880, they were addressed was a young laboring man, employed in rough railway work, whom Whitman met by accident—the account of the meeting, in his correspondent's own words, is the most charming passage in the volume—and constituted for the rest of life a subject of a friendship of the regular "eternal," the legendary sort. The little book appeals, I dare say, mainly to the Whitmanite already made, but I should be surprised if it has actually failed of power to make a few more. I mean by the Whitmanite those for whom the author of *Leaves of Grass* is, with all his rags and tatters, an upright figure, a *successful* original. It has in a singular way something of the same relation to poetry that may be made out in the luckiest—few, but fine—of the writer's other pages; I call the way singular because it squeezes through the narrowest, humblest gate of prose.

There is not even by accident a line with a hint of style —it is all flat, familiar, affectionate, illiterate colloquy. If the absolute natural be, when the writer is interesting, the supreme merit of letters, these, accordingly, should stand high on the list. (I am taking for granted, of course, the interest of Whitman.) The beauty of the natural is, here, the beauty of the particular nature, the man's own overflow in the deadly dry setting, the personal passion, the love of life plucked like a flower in a desert of innocent, unconscious ugliness. To call the whole thing vividly American is to challenge, doubtless, plenty of dissent—on the ground, presumably, that the figure in evidence was no less queer a feature of Camden, New Jersey, than it would have been of South Kensington. That may perfectly be; but a thousand images of patient, homely, American life, else undistinguishable, are what its queerness—however startling—happened to express. In this little book is an audible New Jersey voice, charged thick with such impressions, and the reader will miss a chance who does not find in it many odd and pleasant human harmonies. Whitman wrote to his friend of what they both saw and touched, enormities of the common, sordid occupations, dreary amusements, undesirable food; and the record remains, by a mysterious marvel, a thing positively delightful. If we ever find out why, it must be another time. The riddle meanwhile is a neat one for the sphinx of democracy to offer.

Mr. Harding Davis's letters have neither the austerity of Grant's nor the intimacy of Whitman's, but I am not sure that I have not equally found in them their moral—found it, where the moral of so many present signs and portents seems to lurk, in the quarter of the possibly fatal extravagance of our growing world-hunger. The author is one of the fresh, ubiquitous young spirits who make me sometimes fear we may eat up our orange too fast. *A Year from a Correspondent's Note-Book* owes, of course, nothing of its origin to the indulgence of the private ear; it is the last word of alert, familiar journalism, the world-hunger made easy, made, for the time, irresistible, placed in everyone's reach. It gobbles up with the grace of a sword-swallower the showiest events of a remarkably showy year—from the coronation of the Russian Emperor to the Jubilee of the British Queen, taking by the way the inauguration of a President, the Hungarian Banderium, the insurrection of the Cubans, and the defeat of the Greeks. It speaks of the initiation of the billion, and the span seems, for some reason, greatest when it starts from New York. Budapest "has the best club in the world, the Park Club"—that has the air, on the surface, of a harmless phrase enough; but I seem to recognize in it a freedom of consumption that may soon throw one back on all one's instincts of thrift. I am more uneasy still over the young Hungarian gentlemen who were medieval at home, but who, "when I met some of them later in London," were in varnished boots and frock coats. There are depths, for the nervous mind, in the inevitability of Mr. Harding

Davis's meetings. But he consumes with joy, with grace—
magnificently. The Victorian Jubilee can scarcely have
been better than his account of it.

—April 16, 1898

DEMOCRACY AND THEODORE ROOSEVELT

MR. THEODORE ROOSEVELT appears to propose—in *American Ideals and Other Essays Social and Political*—to
tighten the screws of the national consciousness as they
have never been tightened before. The national consciousness for Mr. Theodore Roosevelt is, moreover, at the best
a very fierce affair. He may be said neither to wear it
easily nor to enjoin any such wearing on anyone else.
Particularly interesting is the spirit of his plea at a time
when the infatuated peoples in general, under the pressure
of nearer and nearer neighborhood, show a tendency to
relinquish the mere theory of patriotism in favor of—as
on the whole more convenient—the mere practice. It is
not the practice, but the theory that is violent, or that, at
any rate, may easily carry that air in an age when so
much of the ingenuity of the world goes to multiplying
contact and communication, to reducing separation and
distance, to promoting, in short, an inter-penetration that
would have been the wonder of our fathers, as the comparative inefficiency of our devices will probably be the
wonder of our sons. We may have been great fools to
develop the post office, to invent the newspaper and the
railway; but the harm is done—it will be our children
who will see it; we have created a Frankenstein monster
at whom our simplicity can only gape. Mr. Roosevelt
leaves us gaping—deserts us as an adviser when we most
need him. The best he can do for us is to turn us out, for
our course, with a pair of smart, patent blinders.

It is "purely as an American," he constantly reminds
us, that each of us must live and breathe. Breathing, in-

deed, is a trifle; it is purely as Americans that we must
think, and all that is wanting to the author's demonstration is that he shall give us a receipt for the process. He
labors, however, on the whole question, under the drollest
confusion of mind. To say that a man thinks as an
American is to say that he expresses his thought, in whatever field, as one. That may be vividly—it may be su-
perbly—to describe him after the fact; but to describe
the way an American thought *shall* be expressed is surely
a formidable feat, one that at any rate requires resources
not brought by Mr. Roosevelt to the question. His American subject has only to happen to be encumbered with a
mind to put him out altogether. Mr. Roosevelt, I surmise,
deprecates the recognition of the encumbrance—would at
least have the danger kept well under. He seems, that is,
but just barely to allow for it, as when, for instance, mentioning that he would not deny, in the public sphere,
the utility of criticism. "The politician who cheats or
swindles, or the newspaper man who lies in any form,
should be made to feel that he is an object of scorn for
all honest men." That is luminous; but, none the less, "an
educated man must not go into politics as such; he must
go in simply as an American . . . or he will be upset by
some other American with no education at all. . . ."
A better way perhaps than to barbarize the upset—already, surely, sufficiently unfortunate—would be to civi-
lize the upsetter.

Mr. Roosevelt makes very free with the "American"
name, but it is after all not a symbol revealed once for
all in some book of Mormon dug up under a tree. Just
as it is not criticism that makes critics, but critics who
make criticism, so the national type is the result, not of
what we take from it, but of what we give to it, not of
our impoverishment, but of our enrichment of it. We are
all making it, in truth, as hard as we can, and few of us
will subscribe to any invitation to forgo the privilege—in
the exercise of which stupidity is really the great danger

to avoid. The author has a happier touch when he ceases to deal with doctrine. Excellent are those chapters in his volume—the papers on "machine" politics in New York, on the work of the Civil Service Reform Commission, on the reorganization of the New York police force—that are in each case a record of experience and participation. These pages give an impression of high competence—of Mr. Roosevelt's being a very useful force for example. But his value is impaired for intelligible precept by the puerility of his simplifications.

It scarcely takes that impression, however, to make me find a high lucidity in the admirable *Essays on the Civil War and Reconstruction* of Professor W. A. Dunning, of Columbia University—a volume I commend, I hasten to add, with scant special competence and only in recognition of the roundabout and sentimental interest I have extracted from it. Professor Dunning's essays are not a picture—they had no concern whatever to be and every concern not to; yet I have found it irresistible to read into them, page by page, some nearer vision of the immense social revolution of which they trace the complicated legal steps and which, of all dramas equally vast— if many such indeed there have been—remains, save in the legal record, the least commemorated, the most unsung. The Civil War had to adjust itself to a thousand hard conditions, and that history has been voluminously told. Professor Dunning's business is the history of some of the conditions—the constitutional, legal, doctrinal—that had, with no less asperity, to adjust themselves to the war. It was waged on a basis of law, which, however, had to be supplied step by step as the whole great field grew greater, and in which the various "bulwarks of our liberties" went, as was inevitable, through extraordinary adventures.

These adventures, as here unfolded, are so remarkable that I have found myself, even in Professor Dunning's

mere dry light, sometimes holding my breath. As the great
war recedes the whole drama more and more rounds and
composes itself, with its huge complexities falling into
place and perspective; but one element, more than ever,
in the business—and especially under the impression of
such a volume as this—occupies the foreground of the
scene. I mean, of course, the full front-face of the question at issue—the fond old figment of the Sovereign State.
This romantic idea becomes for us a living, conscious
figure, the protagonist of the epic. Their "rights" had
been, in their time, from State to State, among the proud
things of earth, but here we have chapter and verse for
each stage of their abasement. These rights—at least as to
what they were most prized for—utterly perished in the
fray, not only trampled in the dust of battle, but stamped
to death in angry senates; so that there can never be again,
for the individual civic mind, the particular deluded glory
of a Virginian or a Carolinian, or even of a son of Massachusetts or of Ohio. The sound doctrine, I suppose, is that
we find consolation for that in the total gain of honor.

I have before me an assortment of the newest fiction,
which I must mainly postpone, but as to which I meanwhile escape from a discrimination so marked as to be
invidious by remembering in time that the most edifying
volume of the group—*The Workers* of Mr. Walter
Wyckoff—is as little as possible a novel. It is, however, a
picture—of a subject highly interesting—and, as a picture,
leaves an opening for the question of art. Let me say at
once that the book has held me as under a spell, so as the
sooner to meet and dispose of the difficulty, of the hu-
miliation indeed, of my having succumbed to the *minimum* of magic. The *maximum* of magic is style, and of
style Mr. Wyckoff has not a solitary ray. He is only one
of those happy adventurers—always to be so rebuked in
advance and so rewarded afterwards—who have it in
them to scramble through simply by hanging on. Nine

out of ten of them perish miserably by the way—all the more honor, therefore, to the tenth who arrives. What Mr. Wyckoff had to hang on to was a capital chance.

—April 23, 1898

WINSTON CHURCHILL; BRET HARTE

THE QUESTION of groups and directions in American fiction would take more observation than I have as yet been able to give it—I mean with the closeness looked for in a regular record. *Are* there groups, directions, schools, as French criticism, for instance, deals with such matters? Are there influences—definable, namable—either already established or in process of formation? That is precisely what it concerns us to ascertain, even though much obscurity should, at the outset, cluster about the inquiry and much ambiguity should, as is not impossible, finally, crown it. Nothing venture, nothing have: it will take some attentive experiment to assure us either of our poverty or of our wealth. It would certainly be difficult enough in England today—so much should be remembered—to put one's finger on the *chefs d'école*. Is Miss Marie Corelli, is Mr. Hall Caine, is Miss Braddon to be so denominated? Is Mr. George Meredith, is Mr. Rudyard Kipling, is Mrs. Humphry Ward? The question would probably require a great clearing up, and might even end by suggesting to us the failure of application to our conditions of most terms of criticism borrowed from across the Channel.

The great difference—to speak broadly—between the French reading public and the English is that "literary success" is for the one the success of the author and for the other the success of the book. The book has often, for the English public, the air of a result of some impersonal, some mechanical process, in which, on the part of the producing mind, a particular quality or identity, a recognizable character and cast, are not involved. It is as if the production, like the babies whose advent is summarily explained to children, had been found in the heart of a cabbage. This explains why one of a writer's volumes may circulate largely and the next not at all. There is no vision of a connection. In France, on the contrary, the book has a human parentage, and this humanity remains a conspicuous part of the matter. Is the parentage, in the United States, taken in the same degree into account, or does the cabbage-origin, as I may for convenience call it, also there predominate? We must travel a few stages more for evidence on this point, and in the meantime must stay our curiosity with such aids as we happen to meet. Grouping them is, yet awhile, not easy; grouping them, at least, in relation to each other.

This may indeed, in some cases, prove difficult in any light. There are many eminent specimens of the satirical novel, and Mr. Winston Churchill is, in *The Celebrity*, beyond all doubt satirical. The intention at least is there —everything is there but the subject of satire. Mr. Churchill strikes the note of scathing irony on the first page of his book and keeps it up to the last; yet between the first and the last he never really puts us into possession of the object of his attentions. This object we gather to be an individual—not a class; a ridiculous personal instance—not, as in Thackeray, for example, and in minor masters, a social condition or a set of such. "The Celebrity" is a young man—so much we piece together— who has made a great reputation by writing fiction of a character that, in spite of several lively digs and thrusts, the author quite fails to enable the reader to grasp; and that practically remains to the end the total of our knowledge of him. The action moves in an air, meanwhile, in which everyone, and most of all Mr. Churchill, is so desperately sly, so bewilderingly crushing, and so unfathomably clever at his expense that we are reduced to saying we should doubtless enjoy the joke if we only knew what it is about.

The book strikes me as an extraordinarily unconscious and effective object-lesson. Satire, sarcasm, irony may be, as a hundred triumphs have taught us, vivid and comforting enough when two precautions have been taken; the first in regard to the reality, the second in regard to the folly, the criminality, or whatever it may be, of the thing satirized. Mr. Churchill, as I make out, has, with magnificent high spirits, neglected all precautions; his elaborate exposure of something or of somebody strikes us, therefore, as mere slashing at the wall. The movements are all in the air, and blood is never drawn. There could be no better illustration than his first short chapter of his reversal of the secure method. It is both allusive and scathing, but so much more scathing than constructive that we feel this not to be the way to build up the victim. The victim must be erect and solid—must be set upon his feet before he can be knocked down. The Celebrity is down from the first—we look straight over him. He has been exposed too young and never recovers.

I grasp provisionally, perhaps, at some shadow of classification in saying that in *His Fortunate Grace* Mrs. Gertrude Atherton, of whose *American Wives and English Husbands* I lately spoke, is also, I surmise, sharply satiric. Her intention is apparently to give us a picture of the conditions making for success, on the part of "wealthy" New York ladies, in any conspiracy against the *paterfamilias*. These conditions Mrs. Atherton represents, I gather, as diffused and striking, resident in the general "upper hand" of the women; so much so that it would perhaps have been, artistically, in her interest not to complicate the particular case she offers by throwing in—into the defeat of Mr. Forbes—an agency not quite of the essence. The case is that of a managing mother who brings to pass, in the teeth of a protesting father, that her

daughter shall marry an extremely dilapidated English
duke. The situation is antique and the freshness to be
looked for, doubtless, in the details and the local color, the
latter of which the author applies with a bold big brush.
The difficulty is that we are too often at a loss with her,
too uncertain as to the degree of intelligence and intention
with which she presents these wonderful persons as so
uncannily terrible.

Do I come late in the day to invoke from Mr. Bret
Harte such aid as may be gathered—in the field in which
he has mainly worked—toward the supposition of a
"school"? Is not Mr. Bret Harte perhaps, after all, just
one of the chiefs I am in search of? No one probably
meets more the conditions. I seem, with a little ingenuity,
to make out his pupils—to trace, in his descendants, a
lineage. If I take little time, however, to insist on this,
it is because, in speaking of Mr. Bret Harte, a livelier
speculation still arises and causes my thought to deflect.
This is not the wonder of what others may have learned
from him, but the question of what he has learned from
himself. He has been his own school and his own pupil
—that, in short, simplifies the question. Since his literary
fortune, nearly thirty years ago, with *The Luck of Roaring Camp*, sprang into being full-armed and full-blown,
he has accepted it as that moment made it and bent his
back to it with a docility that is, to my sense, one of
the most touching things in all American literary annals.
Removed, early in his career, from all sound, all refreshing and fertilizing plash, of the original fount of
inspiration, he has, nevertheless, continued to draw
water there and to fill his pitcher to the brim. He has
stretched a long arm across seas and continents; there
was never a more striking image—one could almost
pencil it—of the act of keeping "in touch."

He has dealt in the wild West and in the wild West
alone; but to say as much as this, I immediately feel, is
to meet, in regard to the total feat, more questions than

I shall find place or answer for. The essence of them is, after all—in the presence of such a volume as *Tales of Trail and Town*—the mere curiosity of the critic. It is, none the less, just the sense of such encounters that makes, I think, the critic. Is Mr. Bret Harte's supply of the demand—in an alien air, I mean, and across the still wider gulf of time—an extraordinary case of intellectual discipline, as it were, or only an extraordinary case of intellectual sympathy, sympathy keeping alive in spite of deterrent things? Has he continued to distill and dilute the wild West because the public would only take him as wild and Western, or has he achieved the feat, at whatever cost, out of the necessity of his conscience? But I go too far: the problem would have been a subject for Browning, who would, I imagine, have found in it a "psychological" monologue and all sorts of other interesting things.

—April 30, 1898

WHITMAN'S *The Wound Dresser*

THE SUDDEN STATE of war confounds larger calculations than those I am here concerned with; I need, therefore, I suppose, not be ashamed to show my small scheme as instantly affected. Whether or no there be a prospect of a commensurate outburst—after time given—of war literature, it is interesting to recognize today on the printed page the impulse felt during the long pressure of the early sixties, especially in a case of which the echo reaches us for the first time. I had been meaning to keep for some congruous association my allusion to the small volume of letters addressed between the end of '62 and the summer of '64 by Walt Whitman to his mother, and lately published by Dr. R. M. Bucke, to whom the writer's reputation has already been happily indebted. But I yield on the spot to the occasion—this interesting and touching collection is so relevant to the sound of cannon. It is at the same time—thus resembling, or rather, for the finer air of truth, exceeding, *La Débâcle* of Zola— not such a document as the recruiting-officer, at the beginning of a campaign, would rejoice to see in many hands.

Walt Whitman, then occupying at Washington an obscure administrative post, became, under strong, simple pressure of personal charity, a constant, a permitted and encouraged familiar of the great hospitals rapidly instituted, profusely, and in some cases erratically, extemporized, as the whole scale of ministration widened, and the pages published by Dr. Bucke give out to such readers as can bear it the very breath of the terrible conditions. I know not what is most vivid, the dreadful back of the tapestry, the price paid on the spot, the immediate heritage of woe, or Whitman's own admirable, original gift of sympathy, his homely, racy, yet extraordinarily delicate personal devotion, exercised wholly at his own cost and risk. He affects us all the more that these pages, quite woefully, almost abjectly familiar and undressed, contain not a single bid for publicity. His correspondent, his obscure, laborious mother, was indeed, it is easy to see, a bountiful, worthy recipient, but the letters were meant for humble hands, hands quite unconscious of the light thus thrown, as it happened, on the interesting question of the heredity of strong originals. It had plainly taken a solid stock, a family circle, to produce Walt Whitman, and *The Wound Dresser*, "documentary" in so many ways, is—like *Calamus*, of which I lately spoke—particularly so on the general democratic head. It holds up, for us, today, its jagged morsel of spotted looking-glass to the innumerable nameless of the troublous years, the poor and obscure, the suffering and sacrifice of the American people. The good Walt, without unhappy verbiage or luckless barbarism here, sounds a note of native feeling, pity and horror and helplessness, that is like the wail of a mother for her mangled young; and in so far the little volume may doubtless take its place on the much-mixed shelf of the literature of patriotism. But let it, none the less, not be too much presumed upon to fire the blood; it will live its life not unworthily, too, in failing to assume that extreme responsibility.

I find myself turning instinctively to what may smell of gunpowder, and, in the presence of that element, have done my best to read a certain intensity into the *Southern Soldier Stories* of Mr. George Cary Eggleston, who fought through the Civil War on the side of Secession, and who has here collected, in very brief form for each episode, some of his reminiscences and observations, keeping them wholly anecdotical, sticking altogether to the "story." This is a kind of volume, I feel, as to which a critic who is a man of peace finds himself hesitate and perhaps even slightly stammer—aware as he is that he may appear, if at all restrictive, to cheapen a considerable quantity of heroic matter. The man of military memories can always retort that he would like to see *him* do half so well. But such a critic has, of course, only to do with Mr. Eggleston's book, which, indeed, causes him to groan exactly by reason of the high privilege of the writer's experience. It is just the writer's own inadequate sense of this privilege that strikes the serious reader. It passes the comprehension of an unfortunate shut out from such generous matters that Mr. Eggleston, rich in the possession of them, should have cared to do so little with them. He was more than welcome to his brevity; it was a question of eyes and senses. To what particular passive public of all the patient publics were these anecedotes supposedly addressed? Is it another case of the dreadful "boys' story"?—the product of our time, in these walks, that has probably done most to minimize frankness of treatment. It seems the baleful gift of the "boys" to put, for compositions directly addressed to them, a high

premium upon almost every unreality. Here is Mr. Eggleston, all grimed and scarred, coated with blood and dust,
and yet contenting himself with a series of small *ber-
quinades* that make the grimmest things rosy and vague
—make them seem to reach us at third and fourth hand.
· But if I muse, much mystified, upon Mr. Eggleston's
particular public, what shall I say of the special audience
to which, as I learn from a note prefixed to *The Honorable Peter Stirling*, Mr. Paul Leicester Ford so successfully
appeals? It must also be a fraction of the mass, and yet
the moment is here recorded at which it numbered readers
represented by a circulation of thirty thousand copies.
Something of the fascination of the abyss solicits the
mind in fixing this fact. That the much-bought novel
may, on a turning of the pages, cause the speculative
faculty wildly to wander is probably, for many a reader,
no new discovery—nor even that there are two directions
in which any reader may pensively lose himself.

There are great and ever-remembered days when we
find the public so touched and penetrated by some writer
dear to our heart that we give ourselves up to the
fancy of the charming persons who must compose it. But
most often, I fear, the rush, the reverberation, is, in the
given case, out of all proportion to our individual measure
of the magic; and then this incongruity itself, to the ex-
clusion of all power really to speak of the book, ends by
placing us under a spell. When fully conscious of the
spell, indeed, we positively surrender to it as to a refuge
from a painful duty. We try not to be invidious—try
to make the public and not the book responsible. It is like
turning one's back to an object and fixing the reflection
in the mirror. I am afraid that, for today, I must take
that method with Mr. Leicester Ford's long novel—a
work so disconnected, to my view, from almost any consideration with which an artistic product is at any point
concerned, any effect of presentation, any prescription
of form, composition, proportion, taste, art, that I am

reduced merely to noting, for curiosity, the circumstance that it so remarkably triumphs. Then comes in the riddle, the critic's inevitable desire to touch bottom somewhere—to sound the gulf. But I must try this some other time.

—May 7, 1898

LOCAL HISTORY; AMERICAN CRITICISM

THE RECORD, for the moment, is almost negative, and I might devote some enumeration to the absence, in each quarter successively, of events interesting to the curious critic. "American literature" has, for the most part, taken refuge in the newspapers—to find itself improved by the sojourn to a degree that there may be some future occasion to measure. There is one department, however, the local history—local in the sense of being of the country, town, and village—that involves ventures, we recognize, less likely than others to be disappointed at not doing, on any particular occasion, any better than usual. It is the type, here, at best, that flourishes, rather than the individual.

The special product, let me hasten to add, in the case of Mr. Sanford H. Cobb's *Story of the Palatines: An Episode in Colonial History*, profits by a happy sacrifice of rigor in relation to the district commemorated. This district, the valley of Schoharie, in the State of New York, between Albany and Cooperstown, is the central image in Mr. Cobb's interesting recital, precisely, indeed, because his story is that of a pursuit eluded, a development nipped in the bud. His book deals with the immensely numerous German immigration to New York and Pennsylvania in the early years of the last century —the avalanche, as it afterwards proved, first loosened by Louis XIV from the Palatinate of the Rhine. The first company of unfortunates driven westward from that desolation made, on their way, a remarkable halt in England, on the occasion of which, and as a means of speeding them further, they received from the English goverment certain vague and magnificent assurances in respect to the land of possible plenty, the special blessed spot, that awaited them. Mr. Cobb, who holds that the subjects of his melancholy epic have received scant justice from history, has to narrate, in such detail as is now accessible, the dismal frustration of these hopes, and to present with lucidity the substantial, squalid facts, into which I have no space to follow him.

This German invasion of 1710 was an invasion of the extremest misery, to which the misery that beset it all round added such abundance of rigor that the melting down of numbers was on the scale of a great pestilence; yet it had moved, from the first, under the attraction of a localy habitation and a name, and the mere speck in the vastness—still charming when seen—which now bears that name has probably no other association so interesting as that of having contributed in this degree to something like a world-migration. For though Schoharie proved a deep delusion, the floodgates had been opened, and the incident was the beginning of a succession of waves through which Pennsylvania—New York, in the sequel, being rigidly boycotted—profited to the extent of barely escaping complete Germanization. That particular circumstance suggests, I think, the main interest of the *Story of the Palatines,* which, otherwise, in spite of the charm of the author's singularly unsophisticated manner, almost limits itself to the usual woeful reminder of all the dreary conditions, the obscure, undiscriminated, multitudinous life and death it takes to make even the smallest quantity of rather dull presentable history. So many miserable Teutons, so many brave generations, and so many ugly names—very interesting Mr. Cobb's few notes on the Americanization of certain of these last —only that the curious reader of the next century,

with his wanton daily need of "impressions," shall feel
that he scarcely detaches any; any, at least, save the
great and general one, the fabulous capacity for absorption and assimilation on the part of the primal English
stock. It is the same old story—that we are a little
prouder of the stock in question, I think, on each fresh
occasion of seeing, in this way, that, taking so much—and
there was a fearful numerosity in this contingent—it
could yet, wherever it took, give so much more. It
began to take the "Palatines"—marvelous fact—near two
hundred years ago, and has been taking them regularly
ever since, but only to grind them and their type and
their tongue, their Zollicoffers and Dochstaters and Hart-
ranfts, in its great inexorable mill.

This is more or less, I surmise, the sort of fact that
prompts Mr. Charles F. Dole to the touching refinement
of optimism exhibted in the little volume of exhortation
and prophecy to which he gives the name of *The Coming
People*. The coming people, for Mr. Dole, as I make out,
are people who will, in every circumstance, behave with
the highest propriety, and will be aided thereto—I cannot
express otherwise my impression of Mr. Dole's outlook,
and indeed his philosophy—by an absence, within them,
of anything that shall prevent. There will be no more
badness in the world, assuredly, when everyone is good,
and I gather from these pages that there are persons so
happily constituted as to be struck with the manner in
which, practically, everyone is becoming so. The interest
of ingenuous volumes proves not always the exact interest
they may have proposed to excite; and so it is that the
point I seem here chiefly to see established is that an
extreme earnestness is not necessarily the guarantee of
a firm sense of the real. Mr. Dole's earnestness, indeed,
is compatible, like that of many other sermonizers, with
an undue love, both for retreat and for advance, of the
figure and the metaphor; but the displacement of a
certain amount of moral vulgarity is, no doubt, involved

and, if we could measure such things, effected by the very temper of his plea. Only, the temper seems too much of the sort that is too frightened by the passions and perversities of men really to look them in the face. There are one or two of these that the author would seem even to have a scruple about mentioning. Can there be any effectual disposing of them as Mr. Dole sees them disposed of without our becoming a little clearer as to what they are? Meanwhile, alas—before the "coming people" have come—we make the most of the leisure left us to rejoice, with the aid of the newspapers, at riddled and burning ships that go gloriously down "with every soul on board." Mr. Dole's exhortations address themselves really to those already so good that they scarce need to be better.

I can speak but for myself, but nothing, in the United States, appeals so to the attention at any moment as the symptom, in any quarter of the world of letters, of the possible growth of a real influence in criticism. That alertness causes me to lay a prompt hand upon the *Literary Statesmen and Others* of Mr. Norman Hapgood, and to feel, toward him, as toward one not unconscious of opportunity, a considerable warming of the heart. This is not, indeed, so much because I seem to see his own hand often upon the right place as because, in a state of things in which we are reduced to prayerful hope and desire, we try to extract promise from almost any stir of the air. The opportunity for a critic of authority in the field I speak of strikes me as, at the present hour, on the whole, so much one of the most dazzling in the world that there is no precaution in favor of his advent that it is not positively criminal to neglect. The signs of his presence are as yet so incommensurate with the need of him that the spectacle is, among the peoples, almost a thing by itself. And let no one, looking at our literature with an interrogative eye, say that his work is not cut out for him: if it be a question of subject he has surely the largest he need desire. Such a public is in itself a subject—the greatest mass of consumers, I conjecture, that, since the beginning of time, have been left, in their consumption, so gregariously, as it were, alone. Mr. Hapgood may have the stuff of a shepherd; his interests—Lord Rosebery, Mr. John Morley, Mr. Arthur Balfour, Stendhal, the American art critics, the American cosmopolites—are various and honorable; he is serious, moreover—too serious—and informed and urbane; but he strikes me, as yet, rather as feeling for his perceptions—hunting for his intelligence. But he is doubtless on the way to find these things, and there are gleams in his predominant confusion which suggest that they may prove excellent.

—May 21, 1898

MILITARY NOVELS

Such fiction as I am, for the hour, most definitely aware of has, at any rate, the merit of pertinence—it appeals to me, to begin with, in the shape of three military novels. These are delicate matters, I again remind myself, for, whatever else such books may be, they may be very good soldiering. The critic falls back, at the same time, perforce, on one or two principles early grasped and cherished, as to which he seems fondly to remember that they have seen him safely through still deeper waters. The "military" work of art, of any sort, is in no degree a critical term, and we never really get near a book save on the question of its being good or bad, of its really treating, that is, or not treating, its subject. That is a classification that covers everything—covers even the marvels and mysteries, for instance, offered us in Mr. Robert W. Chambers's *Lorraine, a Romance*, a work as to which I must promptly make the grateful acknowledgment that it has set me a-thinking. Yet I scarce know how to express my thoughts without appearing to travel far from Mr. Chambers. By what odd arrangement of the mind does it come to pass that a writer may have such remarkable energy and yet so little artistic sincerity?—that is the desert of speculation into which the author of Lorraine drives me forth to wander. How can he have cared enough for an epic theme—or call it even a mere brave, bustling business—to plunge into it up to his neck and with a grand air of gallantry and waving of banners, and yet not have cared enough to see it in some other light than limelight, stage-light, and blue and red fire? He writes about the outbreak of the Franco-Prussian War, the events culminating at Sedan, with the liveliest rattling assurance, a mastery of military detail, and a pleasant, showy, general all-knowingness for which I have nothing but admiration. But his puppets and his incidents, their movements and concussions, their adventures, complications, emotions, solutions, belong wholly to the realm of elaborately "produced" operetta, the world of wonders in which we are supposed to take it kindly that a war correspondent of a New York newspaper, a brother-in-arms of the famous "Archibald Grahame"—operating before our eyes, with all his signs and symptoms, in the interest of another journal—shall lead a fantastic war-dance round the remarkable person of a daughter of Napoleon III (himself amazingly introduced to us), "Princess Imperial" by a first marriage, who becomes, on the last page, his bonny bride, and sits beside him with "fathomless blue eyes dreaming in the sunlight . . . of her Province of Lorraine, of the Honour of France, of the Justice of God." It is one of Mr. Chambers's happy touches that this young lady, costumed as for a music-hall and appropriated and brought up in secret by an irreconcilable Legitimist nobleman, has received, to make confusion worse confounded, the same name as the land of tribulation in which he, for the most part, sets up his footlights. All this is, doubtless, of an inexpensiveness past praying for; and yet, in spite of it, there is a question that haunts the critic's mind. Whence, in the depths of things, does it proceed that so much real initiation as, to a profane sense, the writer's swinging pace and descriptive ease seem to imply, *can* have failed to impose on him some happier pitch of truth, some neater piecing together of parts? Why in the world operetta— operetta, at best, with guns? The mystery seems to point to dark and far-reaching things—the fatal observation of other impunities, the baleful effect of mistaken examples.

I am afraid we are again brought round to these things by *A Soldier of Manhattan;* we are, at all events, at the outset, moved to muse afresh upon the deep difficulty, often so misrepresented, of casting a fictitious recital into the tone of another age. This difficulty, so particular, so extreme, has been braved, unblinkingly, by Mr. J. A. Altsheler, and without, so far as I can see, a single precaution against the dangers with which it bristles. They have proved, I think, much too many for him; I cannot pretend to see him emerge with any remnant of life from the superincumbent mass. Such a volume as Mr. Altsheler's gives us the measure of all that the "historical" novel, with which we are drenched in these days, has to answer for— in a direction, especially, which leads straight to the silliest falsity from the moment it does not lead more or less directly to tolerable truth. Ministering, as a fashion, to the pleasant delusion that the old-time speech and the old-time view are easy things to catch and still easier ones to keep, it conducts its unhappy victims into drear desolation. The knowledge and the imagination, the saturation, perception, vigilance, taste, tact, required to achieve even a passable historic pastiche are surely a small enough order when we consider the feat involved —the feat of completely putting off one consciousness before beginning to take on another.

Success depends, above all, on the "modernity" we get rid of, and the amount of this in solution in the air

under the reign of the newspaper is inevitably huge. A
single false note is a sufficient betrayal—by which I do
not mean to imply, on the other hand, that the avoidance
of many is at all possible. Mr. Altsheler, frankly, strikes
me as all false notes; we strain our ear, through his
volume, for the ring of a true one. So I can only gather
from it that, like Mr. Chambers, he is a young man of
honorable ambition misled by false lights. The grievous
wrong they have done him has been simply in putting
him off his guard. If he be, as would seem possible, a
New Yorker of today still at the sensitive age, let him
take to heart that to get into the skin of a New Yorker, at
any age, of the middle of the last century, the primary
need is to get out of his own. In his own, alas! I fear
Mr. Altsheler is destined, intellectually, to abide. I ask
myself, moreover, by what more general test, at all, the
reader is helped to find himself in effective relation with
such attempts as *A Soldier of Manhattan* and *Lorraine*.
Any attempt whatever, in such an order, has for its
primary intelligibility its treatment of a subject. But what
"subject," what discoverable obedience to any idea illustrated, any determinant motive, may I even dimly
suppose the productions before me to profit by? One
wants but little, in the way of an idea—nor does one
always want that little "long"; but it must at least be
susceptible of identification. When it is not, the mere
arbitrary seems to reign; and the mere arbitrary, in a
work of imagination, is apt to be a very woful thing.
An imagination of great power will sometimes carry
it off, but who are we that we should have a right to
look every day for a *Trois Mousquetaires* or a *St. Ives?*
Captain Charles King is much more sustaining, and
yet it would be a mistake to say that, as a picture of
manners or of passions, his novel of *The General's Double*
is particularly nutritive. He writes, as it strikes me, from
positive excess of knowledge—knowledge of the be-
wildering record of the army of the Potomac during

the earlier passages of the Civil War; which knowledge, moreover, if it proceed from old experience, is remarkable for freshness, and if it be founded on research, is remarkable for the air of truth. I am at a loss, none the less, completely to account for the lively sympathy with which many parts of *The General's Double* have inspired me, and that mystification, after all, is not, as from reader to book, a bad relation to have accepted. Captain King has almost let his specific, dramatic subject go altogether; we see it smothered in his sense, and his overflowing expression, of the general military medley of the time, so that his presentation of it remains decidely confused and confusing. He has even, it would appear, never quite made up his mind as to what his specific, dramatic subject exactly is. It might have been, we seem to see, the concatenation of discomfitures for the North of which, before the general tide turned at Gettysburg, the country of the Potomac and the Shenandoah was so constantly the scene —but this, even, only on condition of its having got itself embodied in some personal, concrete case or group of cases. These cases, under the author's hand, never really come to light—they lose themselves in the general hurly-burly, the clash of arms and the smoke of battle. He has a romantic hero and a distracted heroine whom we never really get intelligently near; the more so that he sadly compromises the former, to our imagination, by speaking of him not only as "natty," but—deeper depth! —as "brainy." These are dark spots, and yet the book is a brave book, with maturity, manliness and vividness even in its want of art, and with passages—like the long story of Stuart's wonderful cavalry raid into Pennsylvania in the summer of 1862, and the few pages given to the Battle of Gettysburg—that readers who, in the American phrase, go back will find full of the stirring and the touching.

—May 28, 1898

AMERICAN MAGAZINES;
JOHN JAY CHAPMAN

THERE IS no month in the year, I suppose, in which, in
any view of actual aspects, the magazines, in the United
States, may not with a certain assurance be called upon
to speak for literature—that is, for literature as it is, for
the most part, at present understood in countries of
English speech. They may be taken at any moment and
not be found wanting to their pledge; they are committed
to an immense energy, and move at an altitude at which
things are not "kept back" for any trifle of war or
other agitation—for any supposed state, in short, of the
public mind. They are themselves, doubtless, to their
own view—as they may very well also be to ours—the
public mind; and in a sense other, and certainly higher,
than the newspapers; which is exactly what makes them
particularly interesting. There would be much to be said,
I seem to discern, on the marked superiority, in America,
of the magazines to the newspapers; but this is a scent
the critic might be drawn on to follow too far, to
follow even to the point where the idea would almost
certainly present itself—thereby becoming less agreeable
to treat—as that of the inferiority, not only marked,
but extravagant, of the newspapers to the magazines.
With this latter phenomenon I fortunately feel myself
not concerned; save in so far as to observe that if most
Americans capable of the act of comparison would
rather suffer much extremity than admit that the manners
of many of the "great dailies"—and even of the small—
offer a correspondence with the private and personal
manners of the nation, so, on the other hand, few of them
would probably not be glad to recognize that the tone

of life and the state of taste are largely and faithfully reflected in the periodicals based upon selection.

The intelligence and liberality with which a great number of these are conducted, and the remarkable extent of their diffusion, make them so representative of the conditions in which they circulate that they strike me as speaking for their native public—comparing other publics and other circulations—with a responsibility quite their own. There are more monthly and quarterly periodicals in England—I forbear to go into the numerical relation, but they are certainly read by fewer persons and take fewer pains to be read at all; and there is in France a fortnightly publication—venerable, magnificent, comprehensive—the mere view of the rich resources and honorable life of which endears it, throughout the world, to the mind of the man of letters. But there is distinctly something more usual and mutual in the established American patronage of *Harper, Scribner,* the *Century,* the *Cosmopolitan,* than in any English patronage of anything of the monthly order or even than in any patronage anywhere of the august *Revue des Deux Mondes.* Therefore, on any occasion—whether books abound or, more beneficently, hang back—the magazines testify, punctually, for ideas and interests. The books moreover, at best or worst, never swamp them; they have the art of remaining thoroughly in view. But the most suggestive consideration of them, I hasten to add, strikes me not as a matter of reporting upon their contents at a given moment; it involves rather a glance at their general attempt and their general deviation.

These two things are intimately bound up and represent both the prize and the penalty. That the magazines are, above all, copiously "illustrated," expressess portentously, for better or worse, their character and situation; the fact, by itself, speaks volumes on the whole subject— their success, their limits, their standards, their concessions, the temper of the public, and the state of letters.

The history of illustration in the United States is moreover a very long story and one as to which a mature
observer might easily drop into an excess of reminiscence.
Such a critic goes back irrepressibly and fondly to the
charming time—charming, I mean for infatuated authors
—before the confirmed reign of the picture. This golden
age of familiar letters doubtless puts on, to his imagination,
something of the happy haze of fable. Yet, perhaps, had
he time and space, he might be ready with chapter and
verse for anything he should attempt to say. There was
never, within my recollection, a time when the article
was not, now and then, to some extent, the pictures; but
there was certainly a time when it was, at the worst,
very much less the pictures than today. The pictures, in
that mild age, besides being scant, were, blissfully, too
bad to do harm—harm, I mean, of course, to the general
or particular air of literary authority, as in the case of the
great galleons now weighed down by them. I miss a
few links perhaps if I absolutely assume that the feeble-
ness of the illustrations made the strength of the text;
but I make no mistake as to its having been, with innocent
intensity, essentially a question of the text. Did the
charming *Putnam* of far-away years—the early fifties—
already then, guilelessly, lay its slim white neck upon the
wood-block? Nothing would induce me really to inquire
or to spoil a faint memory of very young pleasure in prose
that was not *all* prose only when it was all poetry—
the prose, as mild and easy as an Indian summer in the
woods, of Herman Melville, of George William Curtis
and "Ik Marvel."

The magazines that have not succumbed to the wood-
engraver—notably the *North American Review* and the
Atlantic Monthly—have retained by that fact a distinction
that many an American reader is beguiled by mere contrast almost into feeling to be positive. The truth is,
however, that if literary studies, literary curiosity, and the
play of criticism, are the element most absent from the

American magazines, it is not in every case the added absence of illustration that makes the loss least sensible. The *North American Review*, as it has been carried on for years past, deals almost wholly with subjects political, commercial, economical, scientific, offering in this manner a marked contrast to its earlier annals. The *Forum*, though of a similar color, occasionally publishes a critical study, but one of the striking notes, in general, of the American, as of the English, contribution is an extreme of brevity that excludes everything but the rapid business-statement. This particular form of bribe to the public patience is doubtless one of the ways in which the magazine without the attraction of the picture attempts to cope with the magazine in which the attraction of the picture has so immitigably led to the reduction of the text. In the distribution of space it is the text that has come off worst, and the sacrifice of mere prose, from being a relative charm, has finally become an absolute one. It is still in the *Atlantic Monthly* that the banner of that frail interest is most honorably borne. The *Atlantic* remains, with a distinction of its own, practically the single refuge of the essay and the literary portrait. The great picture-books occasionally admit these things—opening the door, however, but, as children say, on a crack. In the *Atlantic* the book-lover, the student, the painter standing on his own feet continue to have room to turn round.

But there are a hundred notes in all this matter, and I can pretend to strike but few of them; the most interesting, moreover, are those to be made on the character of the public at which the great galleons, as I have called them, are directed. Vast indeed is the variety of interest and curiosity to which they minister, and nothing more curious than the arranged and adjusted nature of the ground on which the demand and the supply thus meet. The whole spectacle becomes, for observation on this scale, admirable. The magazines are—taking the huge nation as a whole—richly educative, and if the huge nation as a whole is considerably restrictive, that only makes a process of ingenuity, of step by step advance and retreat, in which one's sympathies must be with the side destined in the long run to be the most insidious. If the periodicals are not overwhelmingly literary, they are at any rate just enough for easy working more literary than the people, and the end is yet far off. They mostly love dialect, but they make for civilization. The extraordinary extension they have given to the art of illustration is, of course, an absolute boon, and only a fanatic, probably, here and there, holding that good prose is itself full dress, will resent the amount of costume they tend to superimpose.

The charming volume in which Mr. Hugh L. Willoughby commemorates his ingenious trip *Across the Everglades* falls into its somewhat overshadowed place among the influences that draw the much-mixed attention of the hour to Florida. Before Mr. Willoughby's fortunate adventure no white explorer had made his way through the mysterious watery wilderness of the southernmost part of the peninsula—a supposedly pathless, dismal swamp—and 1892 saw the discomfiture of an elaborate expedition. I have no space to enumerate the various qualifications that, as a man of science and of patience, an inquirer and a sportsman, the author appears to have brought to his task; the suggestion of them forms, assuredly, a part of the attaching quality of the book, which carries the imagination into a region of strange animated solitude and monotonous, yet, as Mr. Willoughby's sobriety of touch seems still to enable us to gather, delicate and melancholy beauty. I fear that, as a reader of this kind of record, I have a habit that qualifies me but scantly for reporting lucidly upon definite results —a habit under the influence of which nothing in books of travel is to interesting as the amount of "psychology" they may suffer to be read into them—to say nothing of the amount of personal impression and visible picture.

There is, to my sense, a fascination in almost any veracious notes of exploration that afford a clutch to this especial fond dependence. The game played with nature alone—above all when played with pluck and modesty and gaiety as well as with all sorts of dedicated tools—may become a drama as intense as any other; and the consecration of romance will, to the end of time, or, at the least, to the end of the complete suburbanization of the globe, rest on any pair of adventurers, master and man if need be, who go forth in loyal comradeship, with no matter how much apparatus from the Strand or Broadway, for even a week in the positive unknown. Mr. Willoughby's unknown, moreover—on the evidence of this happy issue from it—was, with its beautiful name and its so peculiar composition, as uncanny, yet in as good taste, as some subtle invention of Edgar Poe. The book contributes to the irresistible appeal resident, for the American reader especially, in the very letters of the name of the Floridian peninsula; bringing vividly home, at this time of day, the rich anomaly, in a "health-resort" State, of a region as untrodden, if not, in spite of its extent, as vast, as the heart of Africa. There is something of the contemporary "boys' book"—or say of the spirit of Mr. Rider Haggard, who would find a title, "The Secret of the Seminoles," ready to his hand—in the great lonely, freshwater lagoons, the baffling channels, the maddening circuits, the supposed Great Snakes, and the clothed and contracted Indians. Mr. Willoughby fairly discovered the "secret" of these last—for a revelation of which, however, I must refer to his pages.

Colonel T. W. Higginson has published, under the name of *Cheerful Yesterdays,* an interesting volume in which the virtue expressed by the title covers a great deal of ground: from that of the impressions of childhood in the Cambridge (Massachusetts) of old time to the Abolitionist "rescues" in Northern cities under the now so incredible Fugitive Slave Law; from the organization and conduct of Negro troops in the turmoil of the early sixties to the feast-days of literary Boston and the crown of labor, at the end of years, among the hospitalities of London and Paris. The volume is the abbreviated record of a very full life, in which action and art have been unusually mingled, with the final result of much serenity and charity, various good stories and the purest possible echo of a Boston of a past fashion. A conspicuous figure in almost all the many New England reforms and radicalisms, Colonel Higginson has lived long enough to see not a few "movements," temporary exaltations and intensities, foreshortened and relaxed, and, looking about him on changed conditions, is able to marshal his ghosts with a friendliness, a familiarity, that are documentary for the historian or the critic. *Cheerful Yesterdays* is indeed, in spite of its cheer, a book of ghosts, a roll of names, some still vivid, but many faded, redolent of a New England in general and a Boston in particular that will always be interesting to the moralist. This small corner of the land had, in relation to the whole, the consciousness of a great part to play—a consciousness from which, doubtless, much of the intensity has dropped. But the part was played, none the less, with unshrinking consistency, and the story is full of curious chapters. Colonel Higginson has the interesting quality of having reflected almost everything that was in the New England air, of vibrating with it all round. I can scarce perhaps express discreetly how the pleasantest ring of Boston is in his tone—of the Boston that involved a Harvard not as the Harvard of today, involved the birth-time of the *Atlantic*, the storm and stress of the war, the agitations on behalf of everything, almost, but especially of the Negroes and the ladies. Of a completely enlarged citizenship for women the author has been an eminent advocate, as well, I gather, as one of the depositaries of the belief in their full adaptation to public uses—the universality of their endowment. These, however, are details; the value of the record lies, for readers old enough to be reminiscent of connections, in a general accent that is unmistakable. One would know it anywhere.

I had occasion to allude some weeks ago to the *Emerson and Other Essays* of Mr. John Jay Chapman—a volume in which what was most distinguished in the near New England past reverberates in a manner so different as to give it a relation of contrast to such a retrospect as Colonel Higginson's. Very much the most striking thing in Mr. Chapman's book is his long study of Emerson, and particularly striking in this study is the detachment of the younger critic, the product of another air and a new generation. Mr. Chapman's is a voice of young New York, and his subject one with which young New York clearly feels that it may take its intellectual ease. The detachment, for that matter, was presumably wanted, and the subject, I hasten to add, by no means, on the whole, a loser by it. This essay is the most effective critical attempt made in the United States, or I should suppose anywhere, really to get near the philosopher of Concord. The earnestness of the new generation can permit itself no such freedom in respect to the earnestness of the old without, in its day, being accused of "patronage." That is a trifle—we are all patronized in our turn when we are not simply neglected. I cannot deal with Mr. Chapman's discriminations further than to say that many of them strike me both as going straight and as going deep. The New England spirit in prose and verse was, on a certain side, wanting in life—and this is one of the sides that Mr. Chapman has happily expressed. His study, none the less, is the result of a really critical process—a literary portrait out of which the subject shines with the rare beauty and originality that belong to it. Does Mr. Chapman, on this showing, however, contain the adumbration of the literary critic for whom I a short time since spoke of the country as yearning even to its core—quite as with the apprehension that without

him it may literally totter to its fall? I should perhaps
be rather more prepared with an answer had I found the
author, throughout the remaining essays in his volume
—those on Walt Whitman, Browning, R. L. Stevenson,
Michelangelo's sonnets—equally firm on his feet. But he
is liable to extreme acuteness, is indeed highly refreshing in "A Study of Romeo," and cannot, in general,
be too pressingly urged to proceed.

—June 11, 1898

AMERICAN DEMOCRACY AND
AMERICAN EDUCATION

No MORE interesting volume has lately been published
than Mr. E. L. Godkin's *Unforeseen Tendencies of
Democracy*, which is interesting not only by reason of
the general situation or predicament in which we are
all more or less conscious of being steeped, but also as
a result of the author's singular mastery of his subject,
the impression he is able to give us, on that score, of
extreme, of intense saturation. Conducting, these thirty-
five years, the journal which, in all the American press,
may certainly be said to have been—and independently of
its other attributes—the most systematically and acutely
observant, he treats today, with an accumulation of
authority, of the more general public conditions in which
this long activity has been carried on. The present series
of papers is the sequel to a volume—on the same democratic mystery—put forth a year ago, a sequel devoted
mainly to anomalous aspects which have, before anything
else can be done with them, to be made clear. Mr. Godkin
makes them, these anomalies, vividly, strikingly, in some
cases almost luridly so; no such distinct, detailed, yet
patient and positively appreciative statement of most of
the American political facts that make for perplexity has,
I judge, anywhere been put forth. The author takes

without blinking the measure of all these things and threshes out with the steadiest hand, on behalf of the whole case, that most interesting part of it—as we are apt almost always to find—which embodies its weakness. Yet it is not immediately, with him, a question either of weakness or of strength, so little is his inquiry conducted on the assumption of any early arrival at the last word.

I cannot pretend, on a question of this order, to speak save as one of the most casual of observers, and much of the suggestiveness I have found in Mr. Godkin's book, and in the spectacle it reflects, springs exactly from the immense and inspiring extension given to the problem by his fundamental reservation of judgment. The time required for development and correction, for further exposure of dangers and further betrayal of signs, is the very moral of his pages. He would give, I take it, a general application to what he says of the vices of the actual nominating system. "Is the situation then hopeless? Are we tied up inexorably simply to a choice of evils? I think not. It seems to me that the nomination of candidates is another of the problems of democracy which are never seriously attacked without prolonged perception and discussion of their importance. One of these was the formation of the federal government; another was the abolition of slavery; another was the reform of the civil service. Every one of them looked hopeless in the beginning; but the solution came, in each case, through the popular determination to find some better way." What indeed may well give the book a positive fascination for almost any American who feels how much he owes it to his country that he is what he may happen to be is the way in which the enumeration of strange accidents—and some of the accidents described by Mr. Godkin are of the strangest—modifies in no degree a final acceptance of the huge democratic fact. That provides, for such a reader, an element of air and

space that amounts almost to a sense of æsthetic conditions, gives him firm ground for not being obliged to
feel mistaken, on the whole, on the general question of
American life. One feels it to be a pity that, in such a
survey, the reference to the social conditions as well
should not somehow be interwoven: at so many points
are they—whether for contradiction, confirmation, attenuation, or aggravation—but another aspect of the
political.

Such interweavings would result, however, in the volu-
minous, and the writer has had to eschew them; yet his
picture, none the less, becomes suggestive in proportion
as we read into it some adequate vision of the manners,
compensatory or not, with which the different political
phenomena he lays bare—the vicious Nominating System,
the Decline of Legislatures, the irregularities in Municipal
Government, the incalculabilities of Public Opinion—are
intermixed. For the reader to be able at all reflectively to
do this is to do justice to the point of view which both
takes the democratic era unreservedly for granted and yet
declines to take for granted that it has shown the whole,
or anything like the whole, of its hand. Its inexorability
and its great scale are thus converted into a more exciting
element to reckon with—for the student of manners at
least—than anything actually less absolute that might be
put in its place. If, in other words, we are imprisoned in
it, the prison is probably so vast that we need not even
meditate plans of escape: it will be enough to relieve ourselves with dreams of such wider circulation as the
premises themselves may afford. If it were not for these
dreams there might be a grim despair in Mr. Godkin's
quite mercilessly lucid and quite imperturbably good-
humored register of present bewilderments. I am unable
to dip into such a multitude of showings, but what most
comes to the surface is surely the comparative personal
indifference with which, in the United States, questions
of the mere public order are visited. The public order is

at once so vast and so light that the private beguiles, absorbs, exhausts. The author gives a hundred illustrations of this, tracing it into many singular extremes, which take, mostly, their rank among the "unforeseen." It was unforeseen, to begin with—and this is the standing surprise—that so unqualified a democracy should prove, in proportion to its size, the society in the world least disposed to "meddle" in politics. The thing that Mr. Godkin's examples bring out is, above all, that circumstance—the marked singularity of which an inexpert judge may perhaps be excused for saying that he finds still more striking than almost any of its special forms of objectionableness. This oddity would doubtless be still more salient if the great alternative interest were, for some reason, in our social scene, mysterious: then the wondering observer might cudgel his brain and work on our suspense for the particular pursuit actually felt by so vast a number of freemen revelling in their freedom as more attaching. The particular pursuit, as it happens, however, is not, in the most money-making country in the world, far to seek; and it is what leaves the ground clear for a presentation of the reverse of the tapestry.

That side of the matter has been simply the evolution of the "boss," and the figure of the boss—I had almost said his portrait—is the most striking thing in Mr. Godkin's pages. If he is not absolutely portrayed, this is partly the effect of their non-social side and partly the result of the fact that, as the author well points out, he is, after all, singularly obscure and featureless. He is known almost wholly by negatives. He is silent, and he prescribes silence; he is too much in earnest even for speech. His arduous political career is unattended with discoverable views, opinions, judgments, with any sort of public physiognomy or attitude; it resides entirely—dumbly and darkly—in his work, and his work abides only in his nominations of candidates and appointments to offices. He is probably the most important person in the world of whom it may be said that he is simply what he is, and nothing else. A boss is a boss, and so his fellow citizens leave him, getting on in the most marvelous way, as it were, both without him and with him. He has indeed, as helping all this, an odd, indefinable shade of modesty. "He hardly ever," our author says, "pleads merits of his own." I might gather from Mr. Godkin's pages innumerable lights on his so effaced, but so universal political rôle— such, for example, as the glimpse of the personal control of the situation given him by the fact of the insignificance of most of the State capitals, in which he may, remote from a developed civilization, be alone, as it were, with his nominees and the more undisturbedly put them through their paces.

But I must not attempt to take up the writer at particular points—they follow each other too closely and are all too significant. His most interesting chapter is perhaps that of "The Decline of Legislatures," which he regards as scarcely less marked in other countries and as largely, in the United States at least, the result of something that may most simply be put as the failure of attraction in them for the candidate. In the immense activity of American life the ambitious young man finds, without supreme difficulty, positions that repay ambition better than the obscurity and monotony even of Congressional work, composed mainly of secret service on committees and deprived of opportunities for speech and for distinction. The "good time" that, of old, could be had in parliaments in such plenitude and that was for so long had in such perfection in the English, appears to be passing away everywhere, and has certainly passed away in America. The delegation to the boss, accordingly, of the care of recruiting these in some degree discredited assemblies is probably, even in America, not a finality; it is seemingly a step in the complex process of discovery that the solution may lie in the direction rather of a smaller than of a greater quantity of government. This solution was never supposed to be the one that the democracy was, as it would perhaps itself say, "after"; but the signs and symptoms are, in the United States, considerable. We were counted upon rather to overdo public affairs, and it turns out that, on the whole, we do not even like them. Dimly, as yet, but discernibly, it begins to appear to us that they may perhaps easily *be* overdone. Mr. Godkin notes by no means wholly as a morbid sign the very limited eagerness felt among us at almost any time for the convocation of almost any legislature. A thousand doubts and ambiguities, a thousand speculations and reserves are permitted the American who, in his own country, has seen how much energy in some directions is compatible with how much abdication in others. This, possibly—or certainly, rather, when premature—is a vicious state of mind to cultivate; and it is at all events unmistakable that Mr. Godkin has, on behalf of some of the conditions that produce it, stated the case with a maturity of knowledge and a simplicity of effect that make his four principal chapters a work of art.

It is a direct effect of any meditation provoked by such a book as Mr. Godkin's that we promptly, perhaps too promptly, revert to certain reminders, among our multitudinous aspects, that nothing here is grimly ultimate or, yet awhile—as may, even at the risk of the air of flippancy, be said for convenience—fatal; become aware that the correctives to doubt, the omens and promises of health and happiness, are on the scale of all the rest and at least as frequent as the tokens before which the face of the bold observer has its hours of elongation. If there were nothing else to hold on to—which I hasten to add I am far from implying—it may well come home to the reader of so admirable, so deeply interesting a volume as *The Meaning of Education*, by Mr. Nicholas Murray Butler, Professor of Philosophy and Education in Columbia University, that the vast array of "the colleges" in the United States is, with every qualification to the prospect that a near view

may suggest, nothing else, so far as it goes, than the pledge
of a possibly magnificent national life. The value of Mr.
Butler's testimony to such a possibility resides precisely
in its being the result of a near view and of the most
acute and enlightened criticism. The seven papers of
which his book is composed are critical in the distinguished sense of being in a high degree constructive, as
reflecting not only a knowledge of his subject, but a view
of the particular complex relations in which the subject
presents itself. They begin with an inquiry into "The
Meaning of Education," put the questions of "What
Knowledge is of Most Worth?" and "Is There a New
Education?" proceed then to a study on "Democracy and
Education," and wind up with examinations of "The
American College and the American University" and of
"The Function of the Secondary School." These addresses
and articles handle in detail a hundred considerations that
are matter for the specialist and as to which I am not in
a position to weigh the author's authority: I can only
admire the great elevation of his conception of such machinery for the pursuit of knowledge as is involved in any
real attainment by a numerous people of a high future,
and the general clearness and beauty that he gives to
statement and argument.

To read him under the influence of these things is to
feel in an extraordinary degree—as may so often be felt
in other American connections—that the question of education takes from some of the primary circumstances of
the nation that particular character of vastness, of the
great scale, that mainly constitutes the idea of the
splendid chance. Mr. Butler so beguiles and evokes—and
this by mere force of logic—that, not knowing what
things in America may be limited, I have, in turning his
pages, surrendered myself almost romantically to the
impression that nothing of this especial sort at least need
ever be. Where will the great institutions of learning, the
great fountains of civilization, so evidently, at this rate,

yet to grow up there, find, in the path, anyone or anything to say to them "Only so far"? And I say nothing
of the small institutions, though into these, in a singularly
interesting way, the author also abundantly enters. He
speaks in the name of a higher synthesis of cultivation
altogether, and when he asks if there be a "new education"
leads us by all sorts of admirable reasons to answer in the
affirmative. He is most suggestive on the subject of the
secondary period, as to which he lights a lamp that shows
us in what darkness we have, in this country, for the most
part, walked; and he has, in respect of its connection with
what may follow it, some lucid remarks that I am tempted
to quote.

"Instead of forcing the course of study to suit the
necessities of some preconceived system of educational
organization, it should determine and control that organization absolutely. Were this done, the troubles of the
secondary school, the Cinderella of our educational system, would disappear. Just at present it is jammed into
the space left between the elementary school and the
college, without any rational and ordered relation to
either. The ever-present problem of college entrance is
purely artificial, and has no business to exist at all. We
have ingeniously created it, and are much less ingeniously
trying to solve it. . . . The idea that there is a great
gulf fixed between the sixteenth and seventeenth years, or
between the seventeenth and eighteenth, that nothing but
a college entrance examination can bridge, is a mere
superstition that not even age can make respectable. It
ought to be as easy and natural for the student to pass
from the secondary school to the college as it is for him
to pass from one class to another in the school or in the
college. In like fashion the work and methods of the one
ought to lead easily and gradually to those of the other.
That they do not do so in the educational systems of
France and Germany is one of the main defects of those
systems. . . . Happily, there are in the United States no

artificial obstacles interposed between the college and the
university; we make it very easy to pass from the one to
the other; the custom is to accept any college degree for
just what it means. We make it equally easy to pass from
one grade or class to another and from elementary school
to secondary school. . . . The barrier between secondary
school and college is the only one we insist upon re-
taining. The intending collegian alone is required to run
the gauntlet of college professors and tutors, who, in
utter ignorance of his character, training, and acquire-
ments, bruise him for hours with such knotty questions as
their fancy may suggest. In the interest of an increased
college attendance, not to mention that of a sounder educational theory, this practice ought to be stopped and the
formal tests at entrance reduced to a minimum."

I may not pretend, however, to follow him far, but
content myself with speaking of his book as a singularly
luminous plea for the great social unity, as it may be
called, of education and life. "The difficulties of democracy," he excellently says, "are the opportunities of education"; and if we are to solidify at present rates, what
almost seems clearest is that our collective response to
these opportunities cannot, on the whole and at last, be
unworthy. In the light of what "culture" is getting to
mean, this response will, at the worst, be multiform; and
I confess that such a reflection contributes, to my ear, in
the whole concert, the deepest of all the voices that bid
the observer wait. There will be much to wait for. The
prospect, for a man of letters, certainly for a man of
imagination, can scarce fail to come back to the most constant of his secret passions, the idea of the great things
that, from quarters so interspaced, may more and more
find themselves gathered together under the wide wings
of the language. This fond fancy may borrow further
force from three interesting articles on education in the
Atlantic Monthly for June. Though the first of these,
Mr. C. Hanford Henderson's "New Programme," is the

most general, the least technical, I cannot pronounce it, oddly enough, the one I best understand—partly perhaps from a failure on the part of the writer to get into close quarters with his terminology. Let me add, however, that the spirit of his plea—a plea for "life" rather than for learning—has at least the interest of making the reader uneasy, afresh, about one of the most frequent notes of the age, the singular stupidity of countenance revealed in those photographic, those "process" groups of congregations of athletes and game-players with which the pictorial press and the shop windows of town and country more and more abound. There would seem in general to be too great a disposition to accept what such faces represent as a representation of "life." But there is a vision of life of another sort in the two other excellent *Atlantic* articles, that of Mr. Frederic Burk on Normal Schools—which is not destitute of curious anecdote—and that of Mr. D. S. Sanford on "High School Extension." "Extension" is, in short, as we look about, more and more the inspiring dream.

—June 25, 1898

THE NOVEL OF DIALECT; W. D. HOWELLS

WHATEVER books may be, at the present hour, "kept back," the flood of fiction shows—so far as volume is concerned—few signs, as yet, of running thin. It is doubtless capable, at the same time, of flowing a little clearer, and would do so but for the temporary check of some of its tributary streams. Meanwhile there would be many things to say about *The Juggler*, the latest production of the lady writing under the name of Charles Egbert Craddock—so many that I feel perhaps a little guilty of evading a duty in finding myself, since the question is one of selection, disposed not to say those things that spring most directly from a perusal of the work. This is because of the superior interest—so I frankly confess the matter strikes me—of some of its more circuitous suggestions. The author deals unstintingly with dialect and has so dealt from the first, and thereby, more forcibly perhaps than other workers of the same wondrous vein, confronts us with some of the particular consequences, artistically speaking, of the worship of that divinity. "Mr. Craddock" is the most serious case, as being, I judge, the most reflective and most deliberate. I have also just been reading—and with the liveliest interest—a short and formless fiction by Miss Sarah Barnwell Elliott, which reinforces many of the impressions derived from *The Juggler;* but in *The Durket Sperret*—the troubled tide of dialect here rising into the title itself—an artless spontaneity, an instinct, on the author's part, at times, I hasten to add, remarkably happy, has the matter wholly in charge. Both of these ladies have made a study of the life and speech of the mountaineers of Tennessee, and what is most their own appears, on the showing, to be their close notation of the language in particular. The reproduction of the latter would seem, in each book, so far as the inexpert may judge, extraordinarily close and vivid, but with the palm for humor, for a certain audible ring of nature and of the homelier, the homeliest truth, probably to be awarded to Miss Barnwell Elliott. *The Durket Sperret* shows at some points so much sincerity of observation that the critic would be reduced—were he not, in the literary work of women especially, familiar with the sad phenomenon—wearily to wonder at the inconsequent drop, on other sides, of this and of other merits. Half the critic's business is in learning to adjust his expectations, and it would be a dreadful trade if there were not sometimes some return for the lonely heroism of this effort. The return is still a return perhaps even when he has, as I may say, to call for it in person and carry it home.

There are pages of Miss Barnwell Elliott's novel in which, through the ignoble jargon of the population she depicts, the vibration of life—the life, such as it is, this population appears to lead—comes to us as straight as if talent had set it moving, pages, in short, for which I should be sorry not to express my admiration. Talent, accordingly, seems for the moment concerned; but suddenly there are lapses and surrenders before which we rub our eyes and wonder if we have only dreamt. The author's subject, so far as the candid reader would see his way to state it, is the predicament of a young woman of "mountain" origin, and thereby a child of nature, independent and unafraid, besides being by race, on her mother's side, still more upliftedly a Durket, who is reduced by domestic stress to taking a situation as "waitress" in the family of a professor at a neighboring "University," and who, in that office, is so grievously compromised by the attentions of an undergraduate that the Tennessee hills and valleys fairly ring with the scandal. If there was anything clearly enjoined by this *donnée* it would surely be some presentation of the relations between the parties; the effect serving only to bewilder us so long as we vainly look for the cause. Was the cause, by chance, one of those appearances of extreme intimacy which, even when only appearances, a large body of the American public would seem to deny to those aspiring to represent its manners the privilege of so much as intelligibly alluding to? We grope in darkness—that airless gloom of false delicacy in which the light of life quite goes out. But that is an old inconvenience and, at any rate, a different matter from my concern at this moment. My point is the question of what may be implied as a training for the painter of manners even by such a quest of dialectical treasure as may yield a hatful of queer pieces. Miss Elliott gives us in the hideous figure of her old passionate, pipe-smoking crone—"Mrs. John Warren," a domestic despot instinct with pride of race—an admirable success, but she gives us nothing else. There is no picture, no evocation of anything for any sense but the lacerated ear, no expression of space or time or aspect or motion. Fainter than faint are the "University" shadows and curiously suggestive of how little the cultivation of the truth of vulgar linguistics is a guarantee of the cultivation of any other truth.

That, I am afraid, is the moral, not less, of the impressions suggested by "Mr. Craddock," whose work presents to my puzzled sense the oddest association of incongruous things. The "Covites," the uncouth valley-people of the middle Southwest, are again—and as in the case of Miss Elliott—her theme, but the general air of the picture loses itself in the strange overgrowth of expression into which the writer appears to feel the need of extravagantly rebounding from the simplicities about which I cannot but think it rather a perversion of her conscience to be insistently literal. The author sits down by herself, as it were, whenever she can, to a perfect treat of "modernity," of contemporary newspaperese. The flower of an English often stranger still than the mountain variety blooms bright in this soil, and that brings me precisely to what is really interesting in the general exhibition—the question of the possible bearing, on the art of the representation of manners, of the predominance more and more enjoyed by the representation of those particular manners with which dialect is intimately allied. It is not a question, doubtless, on which we are pressed to conclude, and that indeed is not the least of its attractions. We can conclude only in the light of a good deal of evidence, and the evidence, at present rates, promises to be still more abundant and various. A part of the value of the two writers I have just glanced at is that they liberally contribute to it. More and more, as we go through it, taking it as occasion serves, certain lessons will scarcely fail to disengage themselves, and there will, at the worst, have been a great deal of entertainment by the way. Nothing is more striking, in fact, than the invasive part played by the element of dialect in the subject-matter of the American fiction of the day. Nothing like it, probably—nothing like any such predominance—exists in English, in French, in German work of the same order; the difference, therefore, clearly has its reasons and suggests its reflections. I am struck, right and left, with the fact that most of the "cleverness" goes to the study of the conditions—conditions primitive often to the limit of extreme barbarism—in which colloquial speech arrives at complete debasement; if present signs are made good it would seem destined, in the United States, to be, for a period, more active and fruitful than any corresponding appreciation of the phenomena of the civilized soul. It is a part, in its way, to all appearance, of the great general wave of curiosity on the subject of the soul aboundingly *not* civilized that has lately begun to roll over the Anglo-Saxon globe and that has borne Mr. Rudyard Kipling, say, so supremely high on its crest.

Critically, then, the needful thing is first to make sure of it, observe and follow it; it may still have unsuspected pearls—for it occasionally deals in these trophies—to cast at our feet. What, above all, makes the distinction in the literatures I have just mentioned is that, whether or no the portrayal of the simpler folk flourishes or fails, there always goes on beside it a tradition of portrayal (assuming this to be in cases effective) of those who are the product of circumstances more complex. England just now shows us Mr. Kipling, but shows us also Mrs. Humphry Ward. France has a handful of close observers of special rustic manners, but has also M. Paul Bourget. France, indeed, has even yet a good deal of everything. We possess in America Mr. Howells; but Mr. Howells's imagination, though remarkably comprehensive, does itself most justice, I think, in those relations in which it can commune most persuasively with the democratic passion that is really the prompter's voice—the voice that may at mo-

ments almost reach an ear or two even above the bustle
of the play—of his whole performance as a novelist.
Leaving out Hawthorne and beginning after him, I can
think of no such neat hands as the hands dealing with the
orders that in other countries are spoken of as the
"lower." The American novel that has made most noise in
the world—Mrs. Beecher Stowe's famous tale—is a picture of the life of Negro slaves. I have before me a considerable group of "stories," long and short, in which
rigorously hard conditions and a fashion of English—
or call it of American—more or less abnormal are a
general sign of the types represented. In *Chimmie Fadden,*
by Mr. Edward Townsend, the very riot of the abnormal—the dialect of the New York newsboy and boot-
black—is itself the text of the volume of two hundred
pages. And these are the great successes; the great successes are not the studies of the human plant under
cultivation. The answer to the Why? of it all would
probably take us far, land us even perhaps in the lap of
an inquiry as to what cultivation the human plant, in the
country at large, *is* under.

But I must not, after all, take up the inquiry just now.
Mr. W. D. Howells's *Story of a Play* and the *Silence* of
the admirable Miss Mary Wilkins suddenly rise before me
with an air of dissuasion. Mr. Howells's short and charming novel, which perhaps might more fitly have been
named *The Story of a Wife,* moves in a medium at which
we are at the opposite end of the scale from the illustrations prompting the foregoing remarks—in a world of
wit, perception, intellectual curiosity which have at their
service an expression highly developed. The book—admirably light, and dealing, for the most part, only with the
comedy of the particular relation depicted—is an interesting contribution to the history of one of the liveliest and
most diffused necessities of the contemporary man—and
perhaps even more of the contemporary woman—of letters, the necessity of passing a longer or a shorter time in

the valley of the shadow of the theater. The recital of this spasmodic connection on the part of almost anyone who has known it and is capable of treating it can never fail to be rich alike in movement and in lessons, and the only restriction Mr. Howells's volume has suggested to me is that he has not cut into the subject quite so deep as the intensity of the experience—for I assume his experience— might have made possible. It is a chapter of bewilderments, but they are for the most part cleared up, and the writer's fundamental optimism appears to have, on the whole matter, the last word. There can surely be no stronger proof of it. He has perhaps indeed even purposely approached his subject at an angle that compelled him to graze rather than to penetrate—I mean in opening the door only upon such a part of the traffic as might come within the ken of the lady who here figures as the partner of the hero's discipline. The latter's experiment is hardly more than a glimpse of the business so long as it includes, as it were, the collaboration of this lady; his initiation is imperfect so long as hers gives the pace at which it proceeds. In short I think the general opportunity a great one, and am brought back, by the limits of the particular impression Mr. Howells has been content to give of it, to that final sense of the predestined beauty of behavior on the part of everyone concerned—kindness, patience, submission to boredom, and general innocent humanity—which is what most remains with me from almost any picture he produces. It is sure to be, at the worst, a world all lubricated with good nature and the tone of pleasantry. Life, in his pages, is never too hard, too ugly, passions and perversities never too sharp, not to allow, on the part of his people, of such an exercise of friendly wit about each other as may well, when one considers it, minimize shocks and strains. So it muffles and softens, all round, the edges of *The Story of a Play*. The mutual indulgences of the whole thing fairly bathe the prospect in something like a suffusion of that "ro-

mantic" to which the author's theory of the novel offers
so little hospitality. And that, for the moment, is an odd
consummation.

Miss Wilkins, in *Silence*—a collection of six short tales
—has "gone in" for the romantic with visible relish; the
remark here is at least true of half her volume. The
critic's promptest attitude toward it—that is if the critic
happen to have cherished for her earlier productions the
enthusiastic admiration to which I am glad to commit
myself—can only be an uplifting of the heart at the sight
of her return, safe and sound again, from the dangerous
desert of the "long" story. It is in pieces on the minor
scale that her instinct of presentation most happily serves
her, and that instinct, in the things before me, suffers only
a partial eclipse. If I say this instead of saying that it
suffers none at all, that is simply because of my recognizing the opportunity to make a point that would be
spoiled by my not insisting on my reserve. The actual, the
immediate, the whole sound and sense of the dry realities
of rustic New England are what, for comedy and elegy,
she has touched with the firmest hand. In her new book,
however, she invokes in a manner the muse of history,
summons to her aid with much earnestness the predominant picturesqueness—as we are all so oddly committed to
consider it—of the past. I cannot help thinking that, in
spite of her good will, the past withholds from her that
natural note which she extracts so happily from the present. The natural note is the touching, the stirring one;
and thus it befalls that she really plays the trick, the trick
the romancer tries for, much more effectually with the
common objects about her than with the objects preserved, and sufficiently faded and dusty, in the cracked
glass case of the rococo.

—July 9, 1898

PART FOUR

American Memories

*

MR. AND MRS. FIELDS [1]

IF AT SUCH a time as this a man of my generation finds himself on occasion revert to our ancient peace in some soreness of confusion between envy and pity, I know well how best to clear up the matter for myself at least and to recover a workable relation with the blessing in eclipse. I recover it in some degree with pity, as I say, by reason of the deep illusions and fallacies in which the great glare of the present seems to show us as then steeped; there being always, we can scarce not feel, something pathetic in the recoil from fond fatuities. When these are general enough, however, they make their own law and impose their own scheme; they go on, with their fine earnestness, to their utmost limit, and the best of course are those that go on longest. When I think that the innocent confidence cultivated over a considerable part of the earth, over all the parts most offered to my own view, was to last well-nigh my whole lifetime, I cannot deny myself a large respect for it, cannot but see that if our illusion was complete we were at least insidiously and artfully beguiled. What we had taken so actively to believing in was to bring us out at the brink of the abyss, yet as I look back I see nothing but our excuses; I cherish at any rate the image of their bright plausibility. We really, we nobly, we insanely (as it can only now strike us) held ourselves comfortably clear of the worst horror that in the past had attended the life of nations, and to the grounds of this conviction we could

[1] This essay was published in England in the *Cornhill Magazine* and in America in the *Atlantic Monthly*, July 1915 and is here reprinted for the first time.

point with lively assurance. They all come back, one now recognizes, to a single supporting proposition, to the question of when in the world peace had so prodigiously flourished. It had been broken, and was again briefly broken, within our view, but only as if to show with what force and authority it could freshly assert itself; whereby it grew to look too increasingly big, positively too massive even in its blandness, for interruptions not to be afraid of it.

It is in the light of this memory, I confess, that I bend fondly over the age—so prolonged, I have noted, as to yield ample space for the exercise—in which any challenge to our faith fell below the sweet serenity of it. I see that by any measure I might personally have applied, the American, or at least the Northern, state of mind and of life that began to develop just after the Civil War formed the headspring of our assumption. Odd enough might it have indeed appeared that this conception should need four years of free carnage to launch it; yet what did that mean, after all, in New York and Boston, into which places remembrance reads the complacency soon to be the most established—what did that mean unless that we had exactly *shed* the bad possibilities, were publicly purged of the dreadful disease which had come within an inch of being fatal to us, and were by that token warranted sound forever, superlatively safe?—as we could see that during the previous existence of the country we had been but comparatively so. The breathless campaign of Sadowa, which occurred but a year after our own sublime conclusion had been sealed by Lee's surrender, enlarged the prospect much rather than ruffled it, and though we had to confess that the siege of Paris, four years later, was a false note, it was drowned in the solidification of Germany, so true, so resounding, and for all we then suspected to the contrary so portentously pacific a one. How could peace not flourish, moreover, when wars either took only seven weeks or lasted but a

summer and scarce more than a long-drawn autumn?—
the siege of Paris dragging out, to our pitying sense, at
the time, but raised before all the rest of us, preparing
food-succor, could well turn round, and with the splendid
recovery of France to follow so close on her amputation
that violence fairly struck us as moving away confounded.
So it was that our faith was confirmed—violence sitting
down again with averted face, and the conquests we felt
the truly golden ones spreading and spreading behind its
back.

It was not perhaps in the purest gold of the matter that
we pretended to deal in the New York and the Boston to
which I have referred, but if I wish to catch again the
silver tinkle at least, straining my ear for it through the
sounds of today, I have but to recall the dawn of those associations that seemed then to promise everything, and the
last declining ray of which rests, just long enough to be
caught, on the benign figure of Mrs. Fields, of the latter
city, recently deceased and leaving behind her much of
the material out of which legend obligingly grows. She
herself had the good fortune to assist, during all her
later years, at an excellent case of such growth, for which
nature not less than circumstance had perfectly fitted her
—she was so intrinsically charming a link with the past
and abounded so in the pleasure of reference and the
grace of fidelity. She helped the present, that of her own
actuality, to think well of her producing conditions, to
think better of them than of many of those that open for
our wonderment today: what a note of distinction *they*
were able to contribute, she moved us to remark, what a
quality of refinement they appeared to have encouraged,
what a minor form of the monstrous modern noise they
seemed to have been consistent with! The truth was of
course very decidedly that the seed I speak of, the seed
that has flowered into legend, and with the thick growth
of which her domestic scene was quite embowered, had

been sown in soil peculiarly grateful and favored by pleasing accidents. The personal beauty of her younger years, long retained and not even at the end of such a stretch of life quite lost; the exquisite native tone and mode of appeal, which anciently we perhaps thought a little "precious," but from which the distinctive and the preservative were in time to be snatched, a greater extravagance supervening; the signal sweetness of temper and lightness of tact, in fine, were things that prepared together the easy and infallible exercise of what I have called her references. It adds greatly to one's own measure of the accumulated years to have seen her reach the age at which she could appear to the younger world about her to "go back" wonderfully far, to be almost the only person extant who did, and to owe much of her value to this delicate aroma of antiquity. My title for thus speaking of her is that of being myself still extant enough to have known by ocular and other observational evidence what it was she went back to and why the connection should consecrate her. Every society that amounts, as we say, to anything has its own annals, and luckless any to which this cultivation of the sense of a golden age that has left a precious deposit happens to be closed. A local present of proper pretensions has in fact to invent a set of antecedents, something in the nature of an epoch either of giants or of fairies, when literal history may in this respect have failed it, in order to look other temporal claims of a like complexion in the face. Boston, all letterless and unashamed as she verily seems today, needs luckily, for recovery of self-respect, no resort to such make-believes— to legend, that is, before the fact; all her legend is well after it, absolutely upon it, the large, firm fact, and to the point of covering, and covering yet again, every discernible inch of it. I felt myself during the half-dozen years of my younger time spent thereabouts just a little late for history perhaps, though well before, or at least well abreast of, poetry; whereas now it all densely fore-

shortens, it positively all melts beautifully together, and
I square mysef in the state of mind of an authority not
to be questioned. In other words, my impression of the
golden age was a first-hand one, not a second nor a third,
and since those with whom I shared it have dropped off
one by one—I can think of but two or three of the distinguished, the intelligent and participant, that is, as left
—I fear there is no arrogance of authority that I am not
capable of taking on.

James T. Fields must have had about him when I first
knew him much of the freshness of the season, but I remember thinking him invested with a stately past; this
as an effect of the spell cast from an early, or at least
from *my* early, time by the "Ticknor, Reed and Fields"
at the bottom of every title-page of the period that con-
veyed, however shyly, one of the finer presumptions. I
look back with wonder to what would seem a preco-
cious interest in title-pages, and above all into the mysterious or behind-the-scenes world suggested by publishers'
names—which, in their various collocations, had a color
and a character beyond even those of authors, even those
of books themselves; an anomaly that I seek not now to
fathom, but which the brilliant Mr. Fields, as I aspiringly
saw him, had the full benefit of, not less when I first
came to know him than before. Mr. Reed, Mr. Ticknor,
were never at all to materialize for me; the former was
soon to forfeit any pertinence, and the latter, so far as I
was concerned, never so much as peeped round the titular
screen. Mr. Fields on the other hand planted himself well
before that expanse; not only had he shone betimes with
the reflected light of Longfellow and Lowell, of Emerson
and Hawthorne and Whittier, but to meet him was, for
an ingenuous young mind, to find that he was understood to return with interest any borrowed glory and to
keep the social, or I should perhaps rather say the sentimental, account straight with each of his stars. What he
truly shed back of course was a prompt sympathy and

conversability; it was in this social and personal color that he emerged from the mere imprint, and was alone, I gather, among the American publishers of the time in emerging. He had a conception of possibilities of relation with his authors and contributors that I judge no other member of his body in all the land to have had, and one easily makes out for that matter that his firm was all but alone in improving, to this effect of amenity, on the crude relation—crude I mean on the part of the author. Few were our native authors, and the friendly Boston house had gathered them in almost all: the other, the New York and Philadelphia houses (practically all we had), were friendly, I make out at this distance of time, to the public in particular, whose appetite they met to abundance with cheap reprints of the products of the London press, but were doomed to represent in a lower, sometimes indeed in the very lowest, degree the element of consideration for the British original. The British original had during that age been reduced to the solatium of publicity pure and simple; knowing, or at least presuming, that he was read in America by the fact of his being appropriated, he could himself appropriate but the complacency of this consciousness.

To the Boston constellation then almost exclusively belonged the higher complacency, as one may surely call it, of being able to measure with some closeness the good purpose to which they glittered. The Fieldses could imagine so much happier a scene that the fond fancy they brought to it seems to flush it all, as I look back, with the richest tints. I so describe the sweet influence because by the time I found myself taking more direct notice, the singularly graceful young wife had become, so to speak, a highly noticeable feature; her beautiful head and hair and smile and voice (we wonder if a social circle worth naming was ever ruled by a voice without charm of quality) were so many happy items in a general array. Childless, what is vulgarly called unencumbered, addicted

to every hospitality and every benevolence, addicted to
the cultivation of talk and wit and to the ingenious
multiplication of such ties as could link the upper half of
the title-page with the lower, their vivacity, their curiosity, their mobility, the felicity of their instinct for any
manner of gathered relic, remnant or tribute, conspired to
their helping the "literary world" roundabout to a self-
consciousness more fluttered, no doubt, yet also more
romantically resolute. To turn attention from any present
hour to a past that has become distant is always to have
to look through overgrowths and reckon with perversions;
but even so the domestic, the waterside museum of the
Fieldses hangs there clear to me; their salon positively, so
far as salons were in the old Puritan city dreamt of—by
which I mean allowing for a couple of exceptions not
here to be lingered on. We knew in those days little of
collectors; the name of the class, however, already much
impressed us, and in that long and narrow drawing-room
of odd dimensions—unfortunately somewhat sacrificed,
I frankly confess, as American drawing-rooms are apt to
be, to its main aperture or command of outward resonance
—one learned for the first time how vivid a collection
might be. Nothing would reconcile me at this hour to
any attempt to resolve back into its elements the brave
effect of the exhibition, in which the inclusive range of
"old" portrait and letter, of old pictorial and literal auto-
graph and other material gage or illustration, of old
original edition or still more authentically consecrated
current copy, disposed itself over against the cool sea-
presence of the innermost great basin of Boston's port.
Most does it come to me, I think, that the enviable pair
went abroad with freedom and frequency, and that the
inscribed and figured walls were a record of delightful
adventure, a display as of votive objects attached by re-
stored and grateful mariners to the nearest shrine. To go
abroad, to *be* abroad (for the return thence was to the
advantage, after all, only of those who couldn't so pro-

ceed) represented success in life, and our couple were
immensely successful. Dickens at that time went a great
way with us, the best of him falling after this fashion well
within the compass of our life; and Thackeray, for my
own circle, went, I think, a greater way still, even if
already, at the season I recall, to a more ghostly effect and
as a presence definitely immortalized. The register of his
two American visits was piously, though without the least
solemnity, kept in Charles Street; which assisted, however,
at Dickens's second coming to the States and a comparatively profane contemporaneity. I was not to see him
there; I was, save for a brief moment elsewhere, but to
hear him and to wonder at his strange histrionic force in
public; nevertheless the waterside museum never ceased to
retain, for my earnest recognition, certain fine vibrations
and dying echoes of all that episode. I liked to think of
the house, I couldn't do without thinking of it, as the
great man's safest harborage through the tremendous gale
of those even more leave-taking appearances, as fate was
to appoint, than we then understood; and this was a fact
about it, to my taste, which made all sorts of other, much
more prolonged and reiterated, facts comparatively subordinate and flat. The single drawback was that the
intimacies and privileges it witnessed for in that most
precious connection seemed scarce credible; the inimitable
presence was anecdotically enough attested, but I somehow rather missed the evidential sample, "a feather, an
eagle's feather," as Browning says, which I should, ideally
speaking, have picked up on the stairs.

I doubtless meanwhile found it the most salient of all
the circumstances that the *Atlantic Monthly* had at no
ancient date virtually come into being under the fostering
roof, and that a charm, or at least a felt soft weight, attached to one's thinking of its full-flushed earlier form as
very much edited from there. There its contributors, or
many of them, dined and supped and went to tea, and

there above all, in many a case, was almost gloriously revealed to them the possible relation between such amenities and hospitalities and the due degree of inspiration. It would take me too far to say how I dispose of J. R. Lowell in this reconstruction, the very first editor as he was, if I mistake not, of the supremely sympathetic light miscellany that I figure; but though I have here to pick woefully among my reminiscences I must spare a word or two for another presence too intimately associated with the scene and too constantly predominant there to be overlooked. The *Atlantic* was for years practically the sole organ of that admirable writer and wit, that master of almost every form of observational, of meditational and of humorous ingenuity, the author of *The Autocrat of the Breakfast Table* and of *Elsie Venner*. Dr. Oliver Wendell Holmes had been from the first the great "card" of the new *recueil*, and this with due deference to the fact that Emerson and Longfellow and Whittier, that Lowell himself and Hawthorne and Francis Parkman, were prone to figure in no other periodical (speaking thus of course but of the worthies originally drawn upon). Mr. Longfellow was frequent and remarkably even, neither rising above nor falling below a level ruled as straight as a line for a copybook; Emerson on the other hand was rare, but, to make up for it, sometimes surprising; and when I ask myself what best distinction the magazine owed to our remaining hands I of course at once remember that it put forth the whole later array of *The Biglow Papers* and that the impressions and reminiscences of England gathered up by Hawthorne into *Our Old Home* had enjoyed their first bloom of publicity from month to month under Fields's protection. These things drew themselves out in delightful progression, to say nothing of other cognate felicities—everything that either Lowell or Hawthorne published in those days making its first appearance, inveterately, in the *Atlantic* pages. Lowell's serious as well as his hilarious, that is his broadly satiric, verse was pressed into their service; though of his literary criticism, I recall, the magazine was less avid —little indeed, at the same time, as it could emulate in advance its American-born fellows of today in apparent dread of that insidious appeal to attention. Which remarks, as I make them, but throw into relief for me the admirable vivacity and liberality of Dr. Holmes's *Atlantic* career, quite warranting, as they again flicker and glow, no matter what easy talk about a golden age. *The Autocrat of the Breakfast Table*, the American contribution to literature, that I can recall, most nearly meeting the conditions and enjoying the fortune of a classic, quite sufficiently accounts, I think, for our sense not only at the time, but during a long stretch of the subsequent, that we had there the most precious of the metals in the very finest fusion. Such perhaps was not entirely the air in which we saw *Elsie Venner* bathed— since if this too was a case of the shining substance of the author's mind, so extraordinarily agile within its own circle of content, the application of the admirable engine was yet not perhaps so happy; in spite of all of which nothing would induce me now to lower our then claim for this fiction as the charmingest of the "old" American group, the romances of Hawthorne of course always excepted.

The new American novel—for that was preparing— had at the season I refer to scarce glimmered into view; but its first seeds were to be sown very exactly in *Atlantic* soil, where my super-excellent friend and confrère W. D. Howells soon began editorially to cultivate them. I should find myself crossing in this reference the edge of a later period were I moved here at all to stiff discriminations; which I am so far from being that I absolutely *like* to remember, pressing out elated irony in it, that the magazine seemed pleased to profit by Howells, whether as wise editor or delightful writer, only up to the verge of his broadening out into mastership. He broadened gradually, and far-away back numbers exhibit the tentative light footprints that were to become such firm and confident steps; but affectionate appreciation quite consciously assisted at a process in which it could mark and measure each stage—up to the time, that is, when the process quite outgrew, as who should say, the walls of the drill-ground itself. By this time many things, as was inevitable—things not of the earlier tradition—had come to pass; not the least of these being that J. T. Fields, faithfully fathering man, had fallen for always out of the circle. What was to follow his death made for itself other connections, many of which indeed had already begun; but what I think of in particular, as his beguiled loose chronicler straightening out a little—though I wouldn't for the world overmuch—the confusion of old and doubtless in some cases rather shrunken importances, what I especially run to earth is that there were forms of increase which the "original" organ might have seemed to grow rather weak in the knees for carrying. I pin my remembrance, however, only to the Fieldses—that is, above all, to *his* active relation to the affair, and to the image left with me of guiding and nursing pleasure shown always as the intensity of personal pleasure. No confident proprietor can ever have drawn more happiness from a cherished and computed value than he drew from Dr. Holmes's success, which likewise provided so blest a medium for the "Autocrat's" own expansive spirit that I see the whole commerce and inspiration in the cheerful waterside light. I find myself couple together the two Charles Street houses, though even with most weight of consideration for that where *The Autocrat, The Professor, Elsie Venner*, and the long and bright succession of the unsurpassed Boston *pièces de circonstance* in verse, to say nothing of all the eagerest and easiest and funniest, all the most winged and kept-up, most illustrational and suggestional table-talk that ever was sprang smiling to life. Ineffaceably present to me is all *that* atmosphere, though I enjoyed it of course at the time but as the most wonderstruck and most indulged of extreme juniors; and in the mere ghostly breath of it old unspeakable vibrations revive. I find innumerable such for instance between the faded leaves of *Sounding from the* Atlantic, and in one of the papers there reprinted, "My Hunt for the Captain" in especial, the recital of the author's search among the Virginia battlefields for his gallant wounded son; which, with its companions, evokes for me also at this end of time, and mere fond memory aiding, a greater group of sacred images than I may begin to name, as well as the charm and community of that overlooking of the wide inlet which so corrected the towniness. The "Autocrat's" insuperable instinct for the double sense of words, when the drollery of the collocation was pointed enough, has its note in the title of the volume I have just mentioned (where innumerable other neglected notes would respond again, I imagine, to the ear a bit earnestly applied); but the clue that has lengthened out so far is primarily attached, no doubt, to the eloquence of the final passage of the paper in which the rejoicing father, back from his anxious quest, sees Boston bristle again on his lifelong horizon, the immemorial signs multiply, the great dome of the State House rise not a whit less high than before, and the Bunker Hill obelisk point as sharply as ever its beveled capstone against the sky.

The charm I thus rake out of the period, and the aspect of the Fieldses as bathed in that soft medium—*so* soft after the long internecine harshness—gloss over to my present view every troubled face of my young relation with the *Atlantic;* the poor pathetic faces, as they now pass before me, being troubled for more reasons than I can recall, but above all, I think, because from the first I found "writing for the magazines" an art still more difficult than delightful. Yet I doubt whether I wince at this hour any more than I winced on the spot at hearing it quoted from this proprietor of the first of those with which I effected an understanding that such a strain of pessimism in the would-be picture of life had an odd, had even a ridiculous, air on the part of an author with his mother's milk scarce yet dry on his lips. It was to my amused W. D. H. that I owed this communication, as I was to owe him ever such numberless invitations to partake of his amusement; and I trace back to that with interest the first note of the warning against not "ending happily" that was for the rest of my literary life to be sounded in my ear with a good faith of which the very terms failed to reach me intelligibly enough to correct my apparent perversity. I labored always under the conviction that to terminate a fond æsthetic effort in felicity had to be as much one's obeyed law as to begin it and carry it on in the same; whereby how could one be anything less than bewildered at the nonrecognition of one's inveterately plotted climax of expression and intensity? One went so far as literally to claim that in a decent production— such as one at least hoped any particular specimen of one's art to show for—the terminal virtue, driven by the whole momentum gathered on the way, *had* to be most expressional of one's subject, and thereby more fortunately pointed than whatever should have gone before. I remember clinging to that measure of the point really made even in the tender dawn of the bewilderment I glance at and which I associate with the general precarious element in those first *Atlantic* efforts. It really won me to an anxious kindness for Mr. Fields that though finding me precociously dismal he yet indulgently suffered me— and this not the less for my always feeling that Howells, during a season his sub-editor, must more or less have intervened with a good result.

The great, the reconciling thing, however, was the easy medium, the generally teeming Fields atmosphere, out of which possibilities that ravished me increasingly sprang; though doubtless these may speak in the modern light quite preponderantly of the young observer's and devourer's irrepressible need to appreciate—as compared, I mean, with his need to *be* appreciated, and a due admixture of that recognized. I preserve doubtless imperfectly the old order of these successions, the thrill sometimes but blandly transmitted, sometimes directly snatched, the presented occasion and the rather ruefully missed, the apprehension that in such a circle—with center and circumference, in Charles Street, coming well together despite the crowded, the verily crammed, space between them—the brush of æsthetic, of social, of cultural suggestion worked, when most lively, at the end of a long handle that had stretched all the way over from Europe. How it struck me as working, I remember well, on a certain afternoon when the great Swedish singer Christine Nilsson, then young and beautiful and glorious, was received among us—that is, when she stood between a pair of the windows of the Fields museum, to which she was for the moment the most actual recruit, and accepted the homage of extremely presented and fluttered persons, not one of whom could fail to be dazzled by her extraordinary combination of different kinds of luster. Then there was the period of Charles Fechter, who had come over from London, whither he had originally come from Paris, to establish a theater in Boston, where he was to establish it to no great purpose, alas! and who during the early brightness of his legend seemed to create for us on the same spot an absolute community of interests with the tremendously knowing dilettanti to whom he referred. He referred most of course to Dickens, who had directed him straight upon Charles Street under a benediction that was at first to do much for him, launch him violently and to admiration, even if he was before long, no doubt, to presume overmuch on its virtue. Highly effective too in this connection, while the first portents lasted, was the bustling virtue of the Fieldses—on that ground and on various others indeed directly communicated from Dickens's own, and infinitely promoting the delightful roused state under which we grasped at the æsthetic freshness of Fechter's Hamlet in particular. Didn't we react with the finest collective and perceptive intensity against the manner of our great and up to that time unquestioned exponent of the part, Edwin Booth?—who, however he might come into his own again after the Fechter flurry, never recovered real credit, it was interesting to note, for the tradition of his "head," his facial and physiognomic make-up, of a sudden quite luridly revealed as provincial, as formed even to suggest the powerful support rendered the Ophelia of Pendennis's Miss Fotheringay. I remember, in fine, thinking that the emissary of Dickens and the fondling of the Fieldses, to express it freely, seemed to play over our classic, our livid ringleted image a sort of Scandinavian smoky torch, out of the lurid flicker of which it never fully emerged.

These are trivial and perhaps a bit tawdry illustrations; but there were plenty of finer accidents: projected assurances and encountered figures and snatched impressions, such as naturally make at present but a faded show and yet not one of which has lost its distinctness for my own infatuated piety. I see now what an overcharged glory could attach to the fact that Anthony Trollope, in his habit as he lived, was at a given moment literally dining in Charles Street. I can do justice to the rich notability of my partaking of Sunday supper there in company with Mrs. Beecher Stowe and making out to my satisfaction that if she had, of intensely local New England type as she struck me as being, not a little of the nonchalance of real renown, she "took in" circumjacent objects and more agitated presences with the true economy of genius. I even invest with the color of romance, or I did at the time, the bestowal on me, for temporary use, of the precursory pages of Matthew

Arnold's *Essays in Criticism*, honorably smirched by the American compositor's fingers, from which the Boston edition of that volume, with the classicism of its future awaiting it, had just been set up. I can still recover the rapture with which, then suffering under the effects of a bad accident, I lay all day on a sofa in Ashburton Place and was somehow transported, as in a shining silvery dream, to London, to Oxford, to the French Academy, to Languedoc, to Brittany, to ancient Greece; all under the fingered spell of the little loose smutty London sheets. And I somehow even felt in my face the soft sidewind of that "arranging" for punctualities of production of the great George Eliot, with whom our friends literally conversed, to the last credibility, every time they went to London, and thanks to whose intimate confidence in them doesn't it seem to me that I enjoyed the fragrant foretaste of *Middlemarch?*—roundabout which I patch together certain confused reminiscences of a weekly periodical, a younger and plainer sister of the *Atlantic*, its title now lost to me and the activity of which was all derivative, consisting as it did of bang-on-the-hour English first-fruits, "advance" felicities of the London press. This must all have meant an elated season during which, in the still prolonged absence of an international copyright law, the favor of early copy, the alertness of postal transmission, in consideration of the benefit of the quickened fee, was to make international harmony prevail. I retain but an inferential sense of it all, yet gilded again to memory by perusals of Trollope, of Wilkie Collins, of Charles Reade, of others of the then distinguished, quite beneath their immediate rejoicing eye and with double the amount of quality we had up to that time extracted oozing gratefully through their pores.

Mrs. Fields was to survive her husband for many years and was to flourish as a copious second volume—the connection licenses the free figure—of the work anciently issued. She had a further and further, a very long life,

all of infinite goodness and grace, and, while ever insidiously referring to the past, could not help meeting
the future at least halfway. And all her implications
were gay, since no one so finely sentimental could be
noted as so humorous; just as no feminine humor was
perhaps ever so unmistakingly directed, and no state of
amusement, amid quantities of reminiscence, perhaps ever
so merciful. It was not that she could think no ill, but
that she couldn't see others thinking it, much less doing
it; which was quite compatible too with her being as
little trapped by any presumptuous form of it as if she
had had its measure to the last fineness. It became a case
of great felicity; she was all the gentle referee and
servant, the literary and social executor, so to speak, of
a hundred ghosts, but the scroll of her vivid commission
had never been rolled up, so that it hung there open to
whatever more names and pleas might softly inscribe
themselves. She kept her whole connection insistently
modern, in the sense that all new recruits to it found
themselves in concert with the charming old tone, and,
only wanting to benefit by its authority, were much
more affected by it than it was perhaps fortunately in
certain cases affected by them. Beautiful the instance of
an exquisite person for whom the mere grace of unim-
pared duration, drawing out and out the grace implanted,
established an importance that she never lifted so much
as a finger to claim, and the manner of which was that,
while people surrounded her, admiringly and tenderly,
only to do in their own interest all the reminding, she
was herself ever as little as possible caught in the more
or less invidious act. It was they who preferred her
possibilities of allusion to any aspect of the current
jostle, and her sweetness under their pressure made her
consentingly modern even while the very sound of the
consent was as the voice of a time so much less strident.

My sense of all this later phase was able on occasion
to renew itself, but perhaps never did so in happier

fashion than when Mrs. Fields, revisiting England, as
she continued to embrace every opportunity of doing,
kindly traveled down to see me in the country, bringing
with her a young friend of great talent whose prevailing
presence in her life had come little by little to give it
something like a new center. To speak in a mere paren-
thesis of Miss Jewett, mistress of an art of fiction all her
own, even though of a minor compass, and surpassed only
by Hawthorne as producer of the most finished and
penetrating of the numerous "short stories" that have
the domestic life of New England for their general and
their doubtless somewhat lean subject, is to do myself,
I feel, the violence of suppressing a chapter of appreciation that I should long since somewhere have found space
for. Her admirable gift, that artistic sensibility in her
which rivaled the rare personal, that sense for the finest
kind of truthful rendering, the sober and tender note,
the temperately touched, whether in the ironic or the
pathetic, would have deserved some more pointed commemoration than I judge her beautiful little quantum of
achievement, her free and high, yet all so generously
subdued character, a sort of elegance of humility or
fine flame of modesty, with her remarkably distinguished
outward stamp, to have called forth before the premature
and overdarkened close of her young course of production. She had come to Mrs. Fields as an adoptive daughter,
both a sharer and a sustainer, and nothing could more
have warmed the ancient faith of their confessingly a
bit disoriented countryman than the association of the
elder and the younger lady in such an emphasized
susceptibility. Their reach together was of the firmest
and easiest, and I verily remember being struck with
the stretch of wing that the spirit of Charles Street
could bring off on finding them all fragrant of a recent
immersion in the country life of France, where admiring
friends had opened to them iridescent vistas that made
it by comparison a charity they should show the least

dazzle from my so much ruder display. I preserve at any
rate the memory of a dazzle corresponding, or in other
words of my gratitude for their ready apprehension of the
greatness of big "composed" Sussex, which we explored
together almost to extravagance—the lesson to my own
sense all remaining that of how far the pure, the peculiarly pure, old Boston spirit, old even in these women
of whom one was miraculously and the other familiarly
young, could travel without a scrap of loss of its ancient
immunity to set against its gain of vivacity.

There was vivacity of a new sort somehow in the
fact that the elder of my visitors, the elder in mere
calculable years, had come fairly to cultivate, as it struck
me, a personal resemblance to the great George Eliot—
and this but through the quite lawful art of causing a
black lace mantilla to descend from her head and happily
consort with a droop of abundant hair, a formation of
brow and a general fine benignity: things that at once
markedly recalled the countenance of Sir Frederick
Burton's admirable portrait of the author of *Romola*
and made it a charming anomaly that such remains of
beauty should match at all a plainness not to be blinked
even under the play of Sir Frederick's harmonizing
crayon. Other amplified aspects of the whole legend, as
I have called it, I was afterwards to see presented on its
native scene—whereby it comes back to me that Sarah
Jewett's brave ghost would resent my too roughly
Bostonizing her: there hangs before me such a picture
of her right setting, the antique dignity (as antiquity
counts thereabouts) of a clear colonial house well over
the Maine border [sic] of Massachusetts, and a day spent
amid the very richest local revelations. These things
were not so much of like as of equally flushed complexion
with two or three occasions of view, at the same memorable time, of Mrs. Fields's happy alternative home on the
shining Massachusetts shore, where I seem to catch in
latest afternoon light the quite final form of all the

pleasant evidence. To say which, however, is still considerably to foreshorten; since there supervenes for me with force as the very last word, or the one conclusive for myself at least, a haunted little feast as of ghosts, if not of skeletons, at the banquet, with the image of that immemorial and inextinguishable lady Mrs. Julia Ward Howe, the most evidential and most eminent presence of them all, as she rises in her place, under the extremity of appeal, to declaim a little quaveringly, but ever so gallantly, that "Battle-hymn of the Republic" which she had caused to be chanted half a century before and still could accompany with a real breadth of gesture, her great clap of hands and indication of the complementary step, on the triumphant line "Be swift my hands to welcome him, be jubilant my feet!" The geniality of this performance swept into our collective breast again the whole matter of my record, which I thus commend to safe spirtual keeping.

NOTES FOR AN ESSAY ON
MR. AND MRS. FIELDS[1]

The draft typescript of the foregoing essay on Mr. and Mrs. J. T. Fields in the Houghton Library at Harvard contains two passages in which Henry James, who used to dictate directly to the typewriter, lapsed into a discussion of how he would handle certain of his memories of the old time—the time of his youth in Boston. These brief passages of self-communion are similar to the notes dictated aloud for his unfinished novels and certain of his soliloquies in his Notebooks. *The novelist dictated the following note after the*

[1] Copyright 1956 by the President and Fellows of Harvard College.

*passage in which he recalled the second visit of
Charles Dickens to the United States, and had begun
his discussion of the* Atlantic Monthly.

WHAT WAS to follow made for itself other connections,
many of which indeed had already begun; but what I
think of in particular as a veracious historian, or at any
rate as a beguiled memorizer, or say memorialist, straightening out a little, though not for the world overmuch,
the confusion of old and doubtless in some cases rather
faded importances, what I especially think of is how there
were forms of increase that the "original" magazine grew,
it might have seemed, rather weak in the knee for carrying. I pin my reference however only to the Fieldses,
discriminating for *him* and getting back to the something more I wanted to say about O[liver] W[endell]
H[olmes] and working in the vision of *his* waterside
windows too, with some pleasant little justice to his
beautiful abundance in the way of occasional bursts, and
how that was essentially one of the *Atlantic* assets. Round
off some decent little image of him. Catch with this
connection of Mrs. Beecher Stowe and her mixture in it
all, with reminiscence of my meeting her that time at the
Holmeses' and taking her for a great celebrity, as well as
noting her extraordinary little vaguely observant, slightly
wool-gathering, letting her eyes wander all over the place
kind of little way. Pin on to the Fieldses the various other
associations of memory, Hawthorne in fact and Hawthorne or his story or two about him—about going down
to Salem the winter day and seeing him, in his poor abode,
sitting by the stove with his head bound up for a tooth-
ache, or something of the sort and sadly and shyly producing the *Scarlet Letter* for Fields to take back home
and see if it would do. Fields's account of reading it that
night, and how I thought this more wonderful than
words, etc. What there may be about Fields—with

mention of his hospitality to my first things—Howells
too aiding; and what he said to H. about my infant pessimism—"his mother's milk scarce dry upon his lips," etc.
Then what may be, if anything about Aldrich, but this
very questionable; and a get back to Mrs. Fields, who
really will serve a little more than I thought; with a
stretch to the later time, Julia Ward Howe, Miss Jewett
and her early things, I mean her so very charming things,
something very nice about *her*, and their visit to me at
L. H. quite in the later time. Don't drop out of the Fields
himself part the something or other about George Eliot;
and don't drop above all the Matthew Arnold reference,
and how he gave me the English pages of *Essays in
Criticism*, then just out, and these having served for his
compositors, to read in Ashburton Place, and with what
intense emotion I read 'em. There is plenty, only too
much, to straighten out and compress, doing it well over,
and giving to it for title perhaps just "Mr. and Mrs.
Fields."

*James then dictated a further section of the essay,
and again lapsed into brief self-communion after the
passage dealing with Fechter, as follows:*

This right enough to develop but with getting on to
Christine Nilsson, Trollope, the note of the returns from
England again, with the waft of George Eliot; etc. and
some such foreshortened image of the mixture as will
fetch in the bit about M. Arnold already noted. Don't
leave out Leslie Stephen's having been there, and my
first sight of him so, first moment of what was to be
such a relation; and the lugging in possibly of Aldrich, in
the *Atlantic* connection, or the other thing, the weekly
publication connection, of which I have forgotten the
very name, but in which one read first some of the
Trollopes, and it seems to come back to me that certainly
Middlemarch. Apropos of which if there could be a word

about the Fields effort at *arrangement* with these two
or three English authors; arrangement with Browning,
arrangement with M[atthew] A[rnold] etc. etc. just
touched. Then when I have gouged out of all that the
modicum that will more than suffice to my purpose, get
on to Mrs. F. again for climax, up to the very "end," with
Mrs. Howe and the Battle Hymn, her reciting it, for
titivation, and for very last the note of the much later
Mrs. F., with Sarah Jewett and a good word about *her*
for the very last of all.

THE FOUNDING OF
THE NATION[1]

RECOLLECTIONS OF THE "FAIRIES"
THAT ATTENDED ITS BIRTH

MY RECOLLECTIONS of the very early life of the *Nation*
should fall by their slight intrinsic weight into a clear
enough form and make a straight and simple story, and
yet to take them up in the portentous light of our

[1] Written by Henry James for the fiftieth anniversary of the
Nation and published in the July 8, 1915 commemorative issue
of that journal.

present public conditions is to become aware at once
of a danger which ought perhaps to stay my hand.
That danger, I feel, is the exhibition of a complacency
out of all proportion to the modest little facts themselves,
such light matters of history as they must assuredly
appear. My difficulty comes from the sense that to turn
from our distracted world of today to the world of the
questions surrounding, even with their then so great
bustle of responsibility, the cradle of the most promising
scion of the newspaper stock as that stock had rooted
itself in American soil, is to sink into a social lap of such
soft, sweet material as to suggest comparatively a general
beatific state.

The whole scene and the whole time flushed to my
actual view with a felicity and a unity that make them
rather a page of romance than a picture of that degree of
the real, that potentially so terrible truth of the life of
man, which has now learnt to paint itself with so different
a brush. They *were*, they flourished, they temporarily
triumphed, that scene, that time, those conditions; they
are not a dream that we drug ourselves to enjoy, but a
chapter, and the most copious, of experience, experience
attested by documents that would fill the vastest of
treasure-houses. These things compose the record of the
general life of civilization for almost the whole period
during which men of my generation were to know it;
an immense good fortune to us, since if the backward
vision feeds upon bliss by the simple fact of not being
the immediate, the importunate, or the too precariously
forward, this bliss naturally grows with the extent of the
pasture. I measure the spread as that of half a century—
only with the air turning more and more to the golden
as space recedes, turning to the clearness of all the
sovereign exemptions, the serenity of all the fond assurances, that were to keep on and on, seeing themselves
not only so little menaced but so admirably crowned.
This we now perceive to have been so much their mistake

that as other periods of history have incurred, to our convenience, some distinctive and descriptive name, so it can only rest with us to write down the fifty years I speak of, in the very largest letters, as the Age of the Mistake.

That title might, of course, be blighting to retrospect if one chose to take it so; it might present the whole time as too tragically stupid, too deplorably wasted, to be lived over again critically without sickness and shame. There is, however, another way of taking it, which is to live it over personally and sentimentally, exactly to the sought confusion and reprobation of the forces now preying upon us, exactly to the effect of saving it at least for the imagination if we may not save it for the reconciling reason. To look at it in the light of its good faith is to measure the depth of its delusion, not to say the height of its fatuity, but the good faith may nevertheless figure for us, it figures at least for the author of these remarks, thanks to its vast proportions, the inattackable sphere of romance, all at one with itself—and this, too, while remembering that the romantic condition does involve certain dangers and doubts, if only for the thrill of tilting at them and knocking them quite over. We had that thrill in ample measure, and our difficulties went down before us. To think of all this is to cultivate the complacency into which such a trival fact as that I contributed, in my young innocence, an "important" article to the first number of the enterprise is capable of beguiling me; the fact tastes so, to memory, of our innocence; our innocence tastes so of our confidence, and our confidence of the appearances that crowded gracefully about it. These might have been the very fairies themselves, the invoked and approving godmothers who surround in any proper legend the earliest pillow of the new born great, a group with no interfering "bad" fairy in this case, or none worth speaking of now. I might recall an influence that would serve indeed, a hand stretched out to rock the cradle, by the apprehension of most of the company, quite with the wrong violence, and in that manner gain credit as one of the very few witnesses now left so to testify; but I prefer to retrace the fashion after which I seemed to see the very first and greatest blessing possible flutter down upon the infant scene.

This was in the course of a visit to Shady Hill, at Cambridge, where my admirable friend the late Charles Eliot Norton, spoke to me of his having just returned from New York, whither he had gone, as he smilingly said, on affairs of the *Nation*—the freshness of the joke was, of course, fleeting. The light that was so to spread and brighten then first broke upon me, as I had also never heard before pronounced the name of E. L. Godkin, with whom I was soon to begin to cherish a relation, one of the best of my life, which lasted for long years. He "sounded" at that hour, I remember, most unusual and interesting, his antecedents being not in the least commonplace, as antecedents went with us then; and memory next jumps for me to the occasion of a visit from him in Ashburton Place (I then had a Boston domicile); where, prodigious to consider, he looked me up, in the course of a busy rush from New York, for the purpose of proposing to me to contribute to the weekly journal, for which every preparation—save, as it were, that of his actual instance!—had been made, to all appearance, most auspiciously, and of which he had undertaken the editorship. The verb to contribute took on at once to my ears a weird beauty of its own, and I applied it during that early time with my best frequency and zeal; which doesn't, however, now prevent my asking myself, and with no grain of mock humility, little indeed as humility of any sort costs at my age, what price could have seemed to attach to antecedents of mine, that I should have been so fondly selected. I was very young and very willing, but only as literary and as critical as I knew how to be—by which I mean, of course, as I had been able to learn of myself. Round *my* cradle, in the connection, the favoring fairies, and this time with never a wicked one at all, must have absurdly elbowed each other. That winter of Ashburton Place, the winter following the early summer-birth of the confident sheet, fairly reeks for me, as I carry myself back to it, with the romantic bustle of getting my reviews of books off.

I got them off, bustle as I would, inveterately too late, it seemed, for the return of a proof from New York; which is why there also lives on with me from those so well-meant years the direst memory of a certain blindly inveterate defacement of what I was pleased to suppose my style, a misrepresentation as ingenious as if it had been intended, though this it was never in the smallest degree, and only owing its fatal action to its being so little self-confessed. I was never "cut" that I can remember, never corrected nor disapproved, postponed, nor omitted; but just sweetly and profusely and plausibly misprinted, so as to make a sense which was a dreadful sense—though one for which I dare say my awkwardness of hand gave large occasion. The happy, if imperfect, relation went on, but I see it as much rectified during the winter and spring of 1875, which I spent in New York, on a return from three or four years of Europe; to the effect of my being for the first time able to provide against accidents. These were small things, and the occasions of them small things, but the sense of those months is almost in a prime degree the sense of the luxury of proof. The great thing really, of course, was that my personal relation with Godkin had become in itself a blest element.

I should like to light a taper at the shrine of his memory here, but the altar is necessarily scant, and I forgo the rite. I should like also, I confess, to treat myself to some expression of my sense of those aspects of my native city to which I then offered their last free chance to play in upon me; but though such a hint of my having on the occasion had to conclude against them does but scant justice to the beautiful theme—I really should be able, I think, to draw both smiles and tears from it—I find myself again smothered. I had contributed, on one opportunity and another, during my stretches of absence in Europe, just as I had done so during '67 and '68, the years preceding my more or less settled resumption of the European habit, and just as I was not definitely to break till this habit had learnt to know the adverse pressure that '76, '77, and '78, in Paris and in London, were to apply to it. I had ceased to be able to "notice books" —that faculty seemed to diminish for me, perversely, as my acquaintance with books grew; and though I suppose I should have liked regularly to correspond from London, nothing came of that but three or four pious efforts which broke down under the appearance that people liked most to hear of what I could least, of what in fact nothing would have induced me to, write about. What I could write about they seemed, on the other hand, to view askance; on any complete lapse of which tendency in them I must not now, however, too much presume.

*

INDEX